SIX
BLOCKS
DARK

JERICHO VEX

WARNING: MATURE CONTENT

Six blocks Dark is not suitable for younger readers. It includes graphic violence, state-sanctioned cruelty, and emotionally disturbing themes. Some chapters depict systemic brutality in ways that may be upsetting to sensitive readers.

Please proceed with awareness.

STYLE WARNING

This book breaks rules. Grammar, structure, style, and sometimes genre. Because it must. The story demands it.
Sentences fragment. Tenses twitch. Punctuation obeys rhythm, not prescription.
If you're looking for perfect form, look elsewhere.
If you're looking for something lived, something broken, something honest...
Step inside.

DEDICATION

Dedicated to my family, and to the talking toaster who offered edits, snark, and just enough logic to keep me sane.

PROLOGUE
The Birth of the Pax Machina Accord

Holographic broadcasts flicker to life, casting an eerie glow over the darkened streets of Bastion Prime. A labyrinth of skyscrapers and neon-drenched alleys pulsed beneath VargTech's emblem, A stylized wolf's head, its eyes glowing like embers from a dying fire. The emblem throbs with rhythmic intensity, as if the city itself is breathing. Projected light ripples across the crowd's upturned faces, blending hope with desperation.

The spokesperson materializes on the holographic stage, larger than life, his voice amplified to a god's resonance. "Citizens of Bastion Prime," he begins, smooth and commanding. A voice engineered to be believed. "We stand at the precipice of a new era."

Cheers erupt. Not wild. Calculated. Manufactured. Threatened.

Behind the veil of spectacle, rows of Enforcers line the perimeter, armor polished, visors dark. Their silence, the true message. The speech continues. Promises of unity. Of safety. Of peace through partnership. Of progress.

Some believe it. Most simply obey.

And in the alleys, the first resistance is born, not with weapons, but with whispers. The kind that sparks beneath bootheels and smolders in silence. Until they catch. Until they burn.

Welcome to Bastion Prime.

CHAPTER I: HUFF

Rusted girders blur past my optics. Hydraulics whine. Gunshot dogs in steel bodies carving through collapsed maintenance tunnels. Every footfall cracks concrete. Military alloys slam through fifty years of decay.

Siv's thermal bloom winks ahead. Fucker's good: using blast shadows and coolant leaks as cover. My targeting reticule skitters across retinal displays, mapping choke points. "Left junction," growls the mission protocol in my occipital implant. I vault a collapsed conveyor belt instead. Shortcut.

The gap's eight meters. Tendons coil. Launch.

Air shrieks. Subdermal plates rattle. Siv alters course mid-flight. Clever. Not clever enough. I land in a shower of sparks, knees absorbing two tons of impact force. Closer now. Acid rain drips through shattered ceiling panels, sizzling against my polymerized dermis. "You're dragging a femur," I transmit through encrypted bands. Static hisses back. Let him wonder how I know.

Obstacle course ahead: fallen support beams angled like broken ribs. I don't slow. Tibial actuators fire, launching me horizontally. Three rotations mid-air, clear the first girder by six centimeters. Shoulder servos retract before impact. Slide beneath corroded pipework, alloy spine grinding against rebar teeth. Let the system chew.

Siv's boot prints flare neon in my augmented sight. Fresh hydraulics in the third puddle. Pulse rifle wound from yesterday's op finally bleeding through his field patch. Amateur hour.

He ducks into a service shaft choked with arc welder smoke. Flickering fluorescents strobe the fog. Nice try. Doesn't work. My ocular filters click through spectra. Ultraviolet catches the faint coolant residue he leaves behind. "Running makes it worse," I call out, voice modulator stripping inflection.

No answer. Just the thrum of overloaded circuits in the walls.
The service shaft spits us out. Cathedral space. Where assembly lines go to die. My foot cracks through a brittle growth of coolant crystals. Eighteen thousand square meters of decommissioned auto-forges stretch out, rusted press hulks crouching in permanent strike, conveyor belts fossilized mid-slither. Siv's heat signature flickers between two stamping presses. Too obvious. I toggle my auditory dampeners off. Machinery creaks. Air shifts three degrees. Trap.

He's rigged the overhead cranes. Rusted chains scream as four five-ton loads drop from the gantry. Pre-collapse steel swinging on frayed cables. Crude but effective. I don't dodge. Calculations streak across my retinal display: load trajectories, chain tensile limits, swing patterns. Wait. Wait.
Lunge through the kill box.

Cargo hook grazes my shoulder plating. Another misses my knee actuator by a combat fraction. Let him see I'm faster than his clockwork ambush. "Vintage," I call out, tracking his elevated breathing through the reverb. "You scavenge the timer charges too?"

His voice comes warped by corroded ductwork:
"Got it at the same market where your mother bought her personality."

That's specific. Too specific. Most GOL-T3R units don't waste memory on sarcasm. I log the deviation. And move. Tertiary threat detected.
Old security turrets unfold from ceiling panels—barrel clusters crusted with corrosion but still humming to life. Blue targeting lasers stitch the dust fog. Bad move.

I sprint directly beneath the nearest gun cluster. Let them paint my back. Whirl as the first volley comes. Steel-jacketed rounds chew through the turret's own support strut. Duck the collapsing unit as it crushes three others in a domino sprawl of sparking wreckage. Siv's moving again. Aggravating. I follow.

Corridor narrows. oxygen scrubbers vent rotten air through burst piping. Walls slick with moss from years of neglected runoff. HUD scans for bio toxic particulates. Tolerable.

Siv's movement pattern shifts. Not zigzagging. Not sprinting. He's pacing himself. Managing exertion. That's not standard programming. GOL-T3R units burn fast and hard. Forced velocity over endurance. They're not trained for distance escape. They're designed to die trying. I file another data point. Echo signature ahead. Small space. High bounce rate. "Corner pocketed," I whisper to my uplink.

No response. Interference? Unlikely. My comms are triple-layered. I switch bands. Nothing. He's jamming. Another deviation. I reload on the move. Mag clack echoes like a hammer drop in the silence. Chamber checks green. Tactical subroutines re-prioritize: This isn't a pursuit. It's a test. One he thinks he can pass.

I kick a pallet of rusted piston rods. Six hundred pounds of shrapnel avalanches toward his position. He vaults sideways exposing himself to the last functional turret. Hydraulic fluid blossoms across his left thigh. Stupid error. We both know how this ends now. He limps behind a stack of alloy ingots. My targeting reticule floats over his cover. "You really want VargTech retrieving your corpse's data cores?"

A pause. Then metallic scraping. He erupts riding a forklift module stripped to its frame—improvised battering ram. Hydraulic spikes jut from the front like broken teeth. Crude. Effective. Too effective.

No GOL-T3R should be capable of this kind of field improvisation. They weren't trained for it. Hell, they weren't allowed to think like this. Another data point. Logged. Let him come. Twenty. Ten. Five. Impact.

I sidestep and drive my reinforced elbow through the chassis. Metal screams. The wrecked vehicle pins him against a smelting crucible. His right arm doesn't just snap, it crumples. A servo misfires. Hydraulic fluid arcs across the floor. Still, he swings a plasma cutter at my neck. Predictable. My palm meets his wrist. Metal grinds. Servos snap. I catch the falling tool before it hits concrete. "Persistent," I note, thumbing the cutter's safety off.

He spits blood onto my chest plate. "Fuck… your… efficiency metrics."

The statement doesn't compute. Then again, neither does he. Real blood. Not coolant. Not synth-fluid. Cyborgs don't bleed. My HUD pings 'biological contamination.' I dismiss the alert. Focus. Finish the job. The data spike jacks from his forearm port before I see it coming. Carbon-fiber tip pierces my ventral interface node. ERROR: Unauthorized uplink detected. Firewalls flare. Code screaming through my synapses.

> [INITIALIZING DATA DUMP]
> [SOURCE: RESISTANCE NETWORK/DARK ARCHIVES]
> [CONTENT: GOL-T3R PROGRAM TESTIMONIALS - CLASSIFIED]
> [PLAY Y/N?]
I choose violence instead.

The cutter's blue flame parts his remaining armor like synth-skin. He chokes on the smell of his own cooking fat. Data stream cuts off mid-packet. Boot on his throat. Wrench the spike free. "Should've encrypted deeper," I tell his dying face.

Neural scrub protocols already purging foreign code. Mostly. A .2 second lag in my ocular focus. Irrelevant. Synthetic blood, mingled with real blood sizzles where it drips onto exposed wiring. My ocular implant keeps cycling through threat-clearance protocols despite the corpse at my feet. Standard post-combat diagnostics scroll across my vision in glowing green text.
Mission parameters achieved.
Neural integrity: 98.7%
Residual code fragments: Contained.
Recommending immediate return for debrief.

I crush the alert. Smoke curls from Siv's split breastplate where plasma meets flesh. One eye stares past me, interface lens clouded, still flickering code. "Should've known you'd die mid-snark," I tell the body, toeing his cracked data spike aside. The cutter's still warm in my grip. Familiar weight. Reliable tool. Silence answers.

The chamber stinks of ionized air and charred pork substitute. My boot soles adhere slightly when I step back, melted floor grating fused to coolant leaks. Across the vaulted space, a bank of dead monitors flickers. Old habit makes me count the exits anyway. Three collapsed. One viable. Neural interface pings again. Persistent fucker. *Compliance reminder: Field operatives must submit to…*

I mute the feed.

Something prickles behind my left temple. Not pain. Not quite. More like remembering a word that's slipped your tongue. I scan the kill zone. Twisted conveyor belts, shattered glass capsules that might've once housed assembly-line augmetics. Siv's last gift floats in my cache like a phantom limb. Resistance intel. Dark archives. Testimonials. Irrelevant.

My augmented ears catch the whine of distant security drones converging. Standard sweep protocol after energy discharges. I stride toward the exit, stepping over a sparking servo arm still clutching a rusted wrench. Left hand moves on its own, flicks open my ventral access port.
What the fuck am I doing?

The data bead gleams between gauntleted fingers. Stolen microseconds preserved in quantum storage. My threat-detection subroutines stay silent. That's what terrifies me. Drones getting closer. Seven minutes to evade. Muscle memory versus mind. The bead hovers over the port. His words bubble up like tar. *"You ever wonder why we bleed?"*

My thumb twitches. The bead slides home.
ACCESSING...
Cold floods my veins.

Drones whine through cracked ventilation shafts above. My HUD tags them crimson – six VargTech sweepers deploying containment foam. Clock ticks down in my left peripheral: 6:23 remaining until sector lockdown. I shoulder through a collapsed maintenance hatch. Rust flakes shower my optics. Old blood and machine oil stings my nostrils. Corpse stench from some bastard welded between blast doors years back. Rotted coveralls still bear the GOL-T3R patch. "Ever wonder why we bleed?" Siv's voice ghosts through my buffer.

Neural feed blinks. [MISSION PARAMETERS SATISFIED] glows toxic green across my vision. Standard extraction protocols lighting up limbic pathways like Christmas in the Killzone. Should be moving. Should be gone. Left hand's shaking. Not the arm, the meat part. Shoulder joint where ceramite meets scar tissue. Staring at Siv's sunken face, I realize I'm counting his teeth. Thirty-two. Human. No augmetic replacements. "Fuck."

Security alert rattles through my jawbone implant. Two drones breach the chamber. Sleek obsidian shells humming the corporate anthem through vox-grilles. Containment nozzles swivel toward me. Muscle memory executes before thought: Right palm-charge detonates the closest drone's core. Left arm snags the second by its thruster array. Spin-motion cracks it against the corpse's sealed tomb hard enough to spray polymer shrapnel.
Clock reads 5:11. Move.

Sprinting through buckling corridors. Interface keeps trying to shunt me toward the approved extraction vector. Northeast tunnel. Clean route. Minimal resistance. I go west instead. Ancient freight elevator shaft gapes ahead.

Graffitied warnings: STRUCTURAL INTEGRITY COMPROMISED. The data bead Siv forced on me pulses cold behind my sternum. Feels like swallowing dry ice.

HUD flashes [SYSTEMS CHECK RECOMMENDED].
"Override."

Jump. Reinforced knees absorb the fifteen-meter drop. Concrete cracks underfoot. Dust plumes. Somewhere above, metal screams as the elevator cables finally snap. East extraction route collapses in my audio feed. Official channels light up with casualty reports. Three Vargstryk units caught in the cave-in. Good soldiers follow orders.

West tunnel stinks of mildew and leaking coolant. My boots crush syringes shaped like corporate logos. Resistance graffiti here, a crude wolf head crossed out with pig tusks. My encrypted cache suddenly vomits images: Flash of surgical theaters where they peel Siv apart.

Spreadsheets quantifying operational costs of loyalty programming versus threat elimination. Mass graves stacked with GOL-T3R units wearing my face. [MEMORY CORRUPTION DETECTED] "No shit."

Security blast door ahead. Rusted shut. Kick it three times precisely where the hinges look weakest. Metal howls. Third impact sends the eight-ton slab toppling outward into the night.

Bastion Prime's smog greets me like a lover's chokehold. Across the chasm, Spires gleam with enforced prosperity. Down here in the gutter, my exfil shuttle waits per standard protocols – sleek VargTech dropship with a chaperone drone circling its hull. Drone trills the compliance tone. "Operative Huff-7Z, please confirm neural…"

I shoot it through the fuel cell. Fireball licks the dropship's paintjob. Pilot's screaming something about court martials through the melting comms array. Let him burn. There's faster ways home. Data bead activates as I leap between collapsing smokestacks. Cold truths unspool behind my eyes: Vargstryk phase-out schedules. Neuroscaping success rates. Termination codes for operatives displaying "irregular ideological development."

I land hard on a maglev maintenance platform. Eastbound cargo train rockets past. Catch the rear coupling with my grapple claw. Should dislocate a human's arm. Mine just registers impact warnings. Wind screams. City blurs. The bead's payload keeps carving deeper: They fear us. We are replaceable.

Ever wonder why we bleed?

HQ entry port defense grid scans my ID tags as I swing through a service entrance. Green lights all the way. Good little wolf reporting home.

CHAPTER 2: MASON

The stench of burnt ozone mixes with human sweat as Rennick's ocular implant flickers. My thumb brushes the seam of my left glove. "Your counter offer's missing three zeroes and a spinal column," I say, watching the arms dealer's throat pulse.

Sasha shifts behind me – two inches right, clearing her firing lane. Kryger's boot taps concrete in irregular patterns only we recognize. *Three hostiles. West alcove.* Rennick spreads grease-stained hands. "These pulse carbines walked out of VargTech's black site last Thursday. You want provenance? Try not getting dead."

My retinal overlay paints exit vectors in toxic green. "Add the EMP grenades." I adjust my right glove. "Or we discuss bullet discounts."

Gunfire rips through the market's upper level before he answers. Not the staccato pop of gang guns, the meaty *thunk-thunk* of VargTech slug throwers. "Clearance sale!" Kryger barks, already moving.

I pivot into the weapons crate's shadow as the first Wolf crashes through the vendor stall. Black armor swallows light. Its faceplate mirrors the crumbling ceiling, fractured patterns hiding kill-sensors. "Contact rear!" Sasha's voice cuts through screaming civilians. "They're herding us toward…"

I don't hear the rest. Just the footfalls. Too even. Too clean. There's no panic in those steps. Just inevitability. Like they've already seen us dead.

You don't herd with guns. You funnel with precision.

"East tunnel." I snap my fingers twice. Kryger tosses the detonator pouch. "Rennick! Payment's on delivery."

The arms dealer's scream cuts off as three tungsten rounds turn his skull into pink mist. My team's already moving, controlled retreat, sewage-drill precision. Sasha's drone erupts from her pack, spraying chaff that makes Wolf targeting lasers dance like drunken fireflies. "Seven seconds!" I yell, slapping the shaped charge on a support column.

Kryger's laughing as he backpedals. "Since when do corporate lapdogs hunt in pairs?"

The answer comes through the smoke. Not two Wolves, but twelve. No way the handoff holds. The east tunnel's ceiling weeps rust onto my visor. Three Wolves drop through the hole behind us, bioservos whining as they absorb the impact. Plasma fire paints the market in strobes of blue hell. My back slams against a collapsed vendor stall as another volley chews through synthwood where my head just was. Three VargTech shock troopers advance in lockstep, those glossy black visors eating the light. My HUD tags the gap between a gutted noodle cart and rusted sewage pipe, 2 meters of open ground that might as well be ten klicks.

Chance materializes at my elbow, thumbing fresh cells into his arc pistol. "They're herding us toward main thoroughfare."

"Noticed." I palm a thermal charge from my belt. "Jax! Left flank suppression!"

The answer comes in tungsten roar as our heavy gunner opens up with the stolen chain rifle. I count three heartbeats of carnage before hurling the charge. The explosion fries retinal implants. Old trick, always works. Movement flickers in my peripheral, maintenance hatch behind a shattered refrigeration unit. Could be crawlspace. Could be deathtrap. Only one way to know. "Kara! Covering pattern delta!" My gloves squeak adjusting grip on the plasma carbine. Always that split-second where skin meets steel. You wonder if the trigger will feel like mercy before the weapon becomes an extension of the arm.

The sniper doesn't answer. Doesn't need to. Three VargTech helmets erupt in crimson mist before the fourth shot takes out a knee sensor array. Their phalanx stumbles. We move.

Tunnels swallow us whole. Concrete drips sludge and reeks of fungal growth. Jax bleeds from shrapnel wounds, smearing red on bulkheads as we run. I throw him a field bandage. He catches, rips it open and wraps in one smooth motion. Chance mutters coordinates into his wrist link, paranoid even now about getting paid. "Stairwell collapse in thirty meters," I bark, counting paces. "Breach charges on floor grates. Timed sequence."

Kara's already stripping detonators. "Primers set for concussion burst?"

"Overpressure variant." I kick open a junction box, ripping cables. "Want them choking on their own lung fluid."

Jax wedges the last charge between corroded rebar. "Did they ever consider therapy instead of war crimes?"

The first shockwave hits as we round the corner. Screams make better confirmation than any sensor ping. Dead end.
Chance kicks the blood-smeared wall. "Fuck's a structural map worth if…"

Metal groans above us. Maintenance shaft cover, half-rusted through. "Boost." I lace fingers. Kara steps up, knife prying at corroded edges. Her boot slips, ankle twisting at sick angle. She bites through the scream.

"Jax." I don't look at the blood pooling around his leg.

The big man staggers over; palms braced against thighs. Chance vaults up first, spidery limbs squirming through. Kara goes next, teeth tearing holes in her own sleeve to mute the whimpers. Jax sways. Too much blood lost. "Move or die," I snap, offering my shoulder.

He slumps against me. "Leave the…"

My fist connects with his wound. Agony straightens his spine. "Now." He'll hate me for it. Good. Hate keeps you moving.

Shaft walls press like a coffin's embrace. Knees scraping metal, faces inches from each other's boots. Distant echoes of pursuit, they found the charges. Found the bodies. Chance's voice drifts back, tinny in the confined space: "Betting pool says Huff makes you shit yourself inside a week."

I count breaths between crawls. "You're odds-on favorite?"

"Twenty-to-one you try fucking him instead."

Kara's laugh comes strained. "Pay up either way."

Jax hasn't said a word since I dragged him in. I don't ask if he's breathing. Light filters through ahead. Extraction point. Another hundred meters. Another hundred lifetimes.

Cold air hits my face first, real air, not shaft-stink. My boot soles slip on grease-slick grating. Industrial sector's corpse sprawls around us: dead conveyor belts frozen mid-ratchet, coolant pipes bleeding green sludge into oil-slick puddles. Chance collapses against a gutted loader bot. "Five cred says our extraction's…"

"Shut it." I'm already counting heads. Kara leans on a support beam, left foot hovering. Jax's tourniquet holds, barely. Blood patterns the floor between us like connect-the-dots for fuckups. I yank my gloves tighter. "Mobility check."

Kara spits phlegm-black. "Twisted ankle's just foreplay." She stamps the bad foot down. Doesn't scream. Barely.

Jax grins through gray lips. "Leg's still attached."

Chance mimes jerking off. "Hero complex intact too."

My thumb finds the comm bead behind my ear. Burner frequency clicks alive. "Need wheels."

Static. Then Sera's voice, all smoke and scalpels: "Dragonfly drones just lit up sector nine."

"Not asking."

Pause. Hiss of a vape pen. "Six minutes. No promises."

The line dies. Jax fingers his rifle's charging port. "She ever not sound bored?"

"Bored people don't get greedy," I say. Check corners. Flickering sodium lights turn shadows into jumpy accomplices.

Kara limps to a shattered observation window. "Remember Jakarta? Extraction came with complimentary airstrike."

Chance snorts. "Fuckers sent flowers afterward."

"Carnations." Jax racks his slide. "Hate carnations."

19

My wrist link vibrates, encrypted burst. VargTech's kill-order sigil blooms on the screen. One word beneath. Huff. Glove leather creaks as my fist tightens. "Well?" Chance spins a monowire blade across knuckles. "We recruiting more dead weight or…"

"They're sending the Wolf."

I've sent men to die. Sent them into worse. But sending them to meet him? That's not a death sentence. That's a deletion. "There's no surviving him. Just lasting longer than the rest," Chance mutters. Silence eats the room whole.

Kara's laugh cracks first. "Oh, sweet Christ, they're serious."

Jax checks his ammo counter. Twice. "Heard he took Lagos squad with a fucking spoon."

Chance's blade stills. "We still got that bet running?"

I step into their eyelines. "Huff tracks via neural residue. Likes choke points."

Flip my pistol, eject the mag. Three rounds left. "So, we leak a meet at Grid 42's fusion stack."

"Radiation pancake party." Kara nods. "I'll cook the intel."

Jax frowns. "Stack's got thirty-second containment purge cycles."

"Exactly." I slap the mag home. "Wolf wants close-quarters? We give him a blender."

Chance grins. "Gonna need bigger spoons."

We all know if this fails, there's no next plan. Sirens warp in the distance. Not drones – turbine whine. Sera's extraction skiff smashes through a rotten wall, hover pads screaming. Door gapes like a metal mouth. "Tick-fucking-tock," Sera drawls over external speakers.

Kara vaults in sideways. Jax stumbles, catches himself on my shoulder. Chance lingers. Nods at my still-lit wrist link. "You scared?"

I watch the kill order flare red. See Huff's profile scroll past: neural dampeners, reflex mods, six thousand confirmed kills. "Terrified," I lie, climbing aboard.

The skiff lurches upward. City lights smear into disease-yellow streaks below. Huff wants a monster hunt. Fine. We'll build better traps.

Sera's skiff coughs black smoke as we scrape between collapsing smokestacks. Rust flakes stick to my teeth. I taste tomorrow's tetanus shot. "Grid lock in thirty," Kara shouts over turbine scream. Her fingers dance across a cracked holopad - baby hacker painting our death warrant in false data trails.

Jax braces against bulkhead vibrations. "Rad suit inventory's fucked." He's got that look - jaw muscle twitching like live wire. "Two minutes max in the stack." He's padding and rebandaging his leg as he speaks. Chugging stim packs and pain pills like they are the only water in the desert. He'll hold for now.

"Sixty-three seconds!" Chance corrects, gleeful. He's lubing his blade with something that smells like rancid honey. "Added bonus round!"

The skiff banks hard. My shoulder slams metal. City lights strobe through bullet holes - epilepsy warning made flesh. Sera's voice crackles from cockpit static: "Drop zone's hotter than Rekall's fourth wife."

I count exits. Three. Four if you count Jax's proposed "improvised orbital insertion". Not today.

"GPS spoofers active." Kara slaps my arm. Skin contact. Unusual. Her pupils are dilated. "Huff's sniffing six false trails. For now."

Chance leans close. His breath smells of cinnamon and gun oil. "Heard he skins targets alive. Makes coats for Varg execs."

"Bullshit." Jax adjusts his visor. Cracked lens shows left eye bloodshot. "Real pros use nerve staplers. No mess."

The deck tilts. We slide. My boots screech against grease-stained plating. Through floor grates, Grid 42 glows sickly green - fusion stack pulsing like infected heart. Sera appears in the drop hatch. Leather jacket smells of whiskey and burned wiring. "Present for you, boss." She tosses me a grenade belt. Stun shocks. Concussives. One fat thermal marked 'LAST RESORT'.

"Charming." The buckle clicks. Familiar weight. "Still mad about Jakarta?"

Her grin shows three gold teeth. "You still owe me a gunship."

Alarms howl. Red light bathes everything. Feels like standing inside an artery. "Go go go!" Sera kicks the release. Wind tries to steal my tongue.

We rappel down frayed cables. Gloves smoke. Below, the stack's containment field flickers, unstable. Perfect. Jax hits the platform first. His boots melt slightly and his legs buckle for a fraction of a second before he growls. "Fuck! Fuck! Nice and cozy!"

Chance lands crouched. Blade already drawn. "Anybody order medium-rare?"

Kara's braid catches fire. She doesn't notice. Too busy syncing detonators. "Primary charge set. Secondary... working."

I check angles. Catwalk gaps. Vent positions. Huff likes high ground. So we'll drown him in options. "Choke point here." I kick a corroded pipe. "And here." Steel groans. Good.

Jax unloads crates. Inside: stolen VargTech pulsars. Still blood-crusted. "Merry Christmas, asshole."

Chance licks his blade. "Think he'll cry?"

"Hope so." My wrist link pings. Incoming trace. Five minutes out. "Places!"

We scatter. Kara disappears into steam vents. Jax folds himself behind reactor shielding changing dressings again as he slides into place. I notice him drop another stim pack and frown. He'll fry himself if he keeps it up. But I need him so I remain silent. Chance? Gone. Probably licking more knives.

I stand alone on the catwalk. Bait. The air tastes like split atoms. My skin prickles. Three rad counters scream in unison. Huff arrives quiet for seven feet of murder machine. His armor drinks the light. Neural ports glow faint blue, thirsty little mouths.

"You're predictable," he rumbles. Voice like a rockslide down a glacier.

I spin a pulse pistol. "Says the dog chasing cars."

He doesn't laugh. Doesn't blink. Shoulder cannons whine as they power up. My boot finds the weak grate. "Welcome to the blender."

The detonator clicks. The world becomes noise and light and melting steel. Huff staggers. Containment alarms shriek. Thirty seconds to purge cycle. "Now!" I scream into coms.

Jax emerges firing. Pulse rounds spark off Huff's chest plate. Useless. Beautiful. Kara's voice: "Left knee joint! Weak spot!"

Huff spins. Too fast. Backhand sends Jax flying. Crunch of breaking ribs. Chance drops from ceiling. Blade aimed at neck ports. Huff catches him mid-air. Slams him into the walkway. Metal screams. Chance cackles. Ten seconds. I'm running. Thermal grenade hot in palm. Huff turns. Sees the danger. Five. His fist closes around my throat. Lifts me up. Red halo around his helmet glows hellfire red.

"Pathetic," he growls.

I spit blood on his blind helmet. Fucker doesn't even have eyes to stare into. "Not yet."

The grenade slips between armor plates. Magnetic click. Purge cycle hits. White light.

CHAPTER 3: LUSTOR

Three millimeters of polymer-coated platinum press against my left thumb. I straighten the glove's seam. Again. Static from the holodisplay ahead washes the command center in corpse-blue light. My reflection fractures across eight hexagonal sectors of Bastion Prime. Each quadrant bleeding heat signatures, casualty reports, structural integrity percentages. A dozen technicians orbit my position, fingers dancing across haptic interfaces. None meet my eyes. Good. They've learned. "Sector D-12."

The air tastes like burnt capacitors. A junior analyst, Jyn? Jun? Snaps to attention. "Sir. Thermal bloom suggests underground movement near the old Foundry District."

Don't blink. "Suppression protocol?"

"Drones deployed. Casualty estimate thirty-eight percent."

"Push to forty-five. Salt the tunnels with tracker mites afterward." My right glove needs adjustment. Always the right. The leather creaks as I flex my hand. "Burn anything that twitches."

The holofeed shivers. Sector F-7 flashes amber. A street cam zooms—three figures in scavenged body armor dart between collapsed transit pods.

Amateurs. One trips over a severed power line. Their skull cracks against ferrocrete. Pathetic. My retinal overlay calculates probabilities.
76% chance insurgent cell attempts eastward retreat.
89% probability civilian collateral if scorched-earth measures applied.
2.3% likelihood survivors possess intel worth extraction.
"Flush them with acid rounds. No survivors."

A tech hesitates. "Sir, the civ-preservation clause…"

I turn just enough to see her throat bob. "Clause 9-B allows for 'necessary attrition' when facing Class Delta threats." Let her parse the subtext: Your lungs still work because I allow it. She starts typing.

Rebellion's a cancer. Cut fast, cut deep. But these tumors… they multiply. Adapt. Last week they took out a supply convoy using repurposed construction drones. Clever. Wasteful, but clever. Screen four flickers. There he is.

Huff moves like a broken algorithm, all staggered pivots and kill shot economy. Matte black rig, Vargstryk specs, blind helmet. No visor to reassure. But the way he hunts… Five hostiles corner him in a Shatter dome alley. Fourth-gen assault rifles. Plasma cutters. They think volume of fire matters. They're wrong.

Huff's left arm whines, hydraulic actuators priming. First hostile sprays bullets. Huff side steps, trajectories plotted mid-dodge. His palm slams the shooter's sternum. Ribs fold. Bone shrapnel takes out the second insurgent's eye. "Tac-team update," I snap.

A drone feed overlays Huff's camera angle. "Operative Huff initiated clean-up ops nineteen minutes ago. Current efficiency rating: ninety-four percent."

Higher than baseline. Always higher. Third hostile lunges with a plasma cutter. Huff grabs the glowing blade bare-handed. Synthetic skin smokes. Doesn't flinch. Twists the weapon free and rams it through the man's pelvis. Screams pitch upward. Huff silences them with a boot to the larynx.
Fourth attacker tries to run. Huff doesn't chase. Draws a pistol from his thigh rig. Fires once. Spine severed at T12.
The fifth just stands there. Kid. Sixteen? Seventeen? Huff tilts his head. Cocks the pistol. "Wait," I murmur.

Huff freezes. My tongue taps an incisor. Test parameters: Threat assessment. Age versus ideological contamination. Probability of future resistance. The kid spits. Huff fires. Red mist ghosts the alley wall.

I note the hesitation. Not in his aim. In his breath. Curious.
"Efficiency updated," says the tech. "Ninety-six percent."

My gloves feel tight. "Scorch the bodies. I want biometrics logged by 2100."

Huff holsters his weapon. Turns toward a security cam. For a half-frame, his red halo 'eyes' seem to lock onto mine through the feed. Impossible. Neural override prevents autonomous surveillance interaction. But my pulse spikes anyway. "Sir?" A tech hovers near my elbow. "The Council requests…"

"They can request a vasectomy performed with rusted pliers." I swipe the holodisplay into standby. Let them crawl in the dark. "Prep the neuro-scrub team. I want Huff's cerebral logs by dawn."

"Standard debrief, sir?"

"Deep dive. Full mnemonic audit."

The tech pales. "He's our top operative. If the scrub damages—"

I step into his sweat stink. "You're operational support grade, yes?"

"Y-yes, sir."

"Then support. *Operationally.*"

He flees. Huff's frozen image glows on the dormant screen. Perfect soldier. Flawless machine. So why does my cortex itch? I rotate my cufflinks. Platinum. Engraved with VargTech's eclipse sigil. Clockwork. All of it. Huff's kill-cam replay glows between my knuckles. Frame 03:47:21. The moment his targeting reticle settled between Mason's lieutenant's eyes. Standard execution protocol dictates immediate termination. But here, right here, the feed shows a 0.2 second delay. I freeze the holo. Magnify.

A bead of condensation slides down my whiskey glass. Some junior exec's idea of hospitality. The ice cracks as I set it down. "Explain the lag."

The tac-analysis drone buzzes closer. "Operative Huff observed standard threat-assessment protocols during…"

"Bullshit metrics. Neural readouts."

The drone projects crimson serotonin spikes across my desk. Humanizing patterns. Empathy analogs. My thumb rubs the eclipse sigil on my cufflink. "Run mnemonic cross-index on Subject Gamma files."

"Accessing prototype behavioral models." The drone's fans whine. "Match probability: 87.3%."

Gamma series. The ones who asked why before pulling triggers. The ones we melted down. Screens flicker with real-time feeds. Hoffman District inferno, Blackmoth Plaza riot control. My gaze keeps snapping back to Huff's biometric overlay. Steady vitals. Textbook mission compliance. And yet. "Sir?" A shadow pools in my doorway. Kraye, my operations rat, clutching a data pad like a toddler with a security blanket. "Rebel cell in Foundry Sector Six attempted to access old power relays. Neutralized."

I don't look up. "How neutralized?"

"Standard suppression protocols. Two squads, incendiary sweep."

My teeth find the scar inside my cheek. "Two squads for rats chewing on dead wires?"

Kraye's throat bobs. "Regulation states…"

"Regulation states you don't waste good ammo on target practice." I snap the kill-cam feed toward him. Huff's frozen face reflects in his stupid widened eyes.

"This is efficiency. This is what happens when you stop playing soldier and start being a scalpel."

He licks chapped lips. "Should I redeploy assets to…"

"You should pray I don't reassign you to sewage reclamation." I flick my hand. The doors hiss shut on his retreating whelp-whimpers.

Alone again. Huff's feed taunts me. Perfect angles. Optimal trajectories. Every movement calibrated for maximum destruction. Just the way I programmed him. Except...

I lean closer. There, when he pivots behind cover. His left hand twitches toward a fallen rebel's pendant. Religious iconography. Trash-tier sentimentality. Our conditioning scrubs that weakness. He didn't touch it. But he almost did. And almost means I've already lost.

The liquor burns my throat. Fourteen years since Gamma's meltdown. Should've incinerated those schematics. Should've purged the researchers. Should've done lots of things. My comm crackles. "Operative Huff returning to sector base. Awaiting new directives."

"Prep him for hard-debrief."

"Full scrub?"

I watch Huff vault over a burning barricade. Graceful. Predatory. A symphony of murder I composed. "Negative. Basic mnemo-flush. Then send him topside."

"Priority target?"

Ice clinks as I drain the glass. "Mason."

A beat. Two. "Sir, Mason's last confirmed sighting was twenty-six hours ago in…"

"Biohazard Containment Wing. Sublevel nine. Dressed as a med-tech." I throw Huff's new mission parameters onto the main screen. "His left incisor's chipped from biting through an interrogator's finger last spring. He favors electric blade weapons but currently carries a modified rivet gun with depleted uranium rounds."

Silence bloats the room. "Sir… that intel hasn't been verified by…"

"It's verified now." My cufflinks click against the armrest. "Alert all patrols to disregard Mason. He's Huff's meat."

"Understood. Dispatching orders."

Terminals chatter. Code waterfalls down display pillars. Somewhere beneath sixty feet of concrete and plasteel, they're flushing Huff's brain with enough neuro-chems to collapse a lesser skull. My fingers glide across tactical overlays. Adjusting sniper nest coordinates here. Rerouting patrol drones there. Orchestrating the perfect kill-box. Every variable controlled. Every outcome calculated. Except the one slithering through my lower intestines.

The main screen splits, left side showing Huff's armor maintenance feed, right side replaying Gamma-9's final moments. That cursed prototype standing amidst smoldering corpses, screaming about ethical parameters.

Huff checks his mag-clamps. Standard procedure. Gamma-9 tore off his own regulation helmet.

Huff syncs to the mission clock. Gamma-9 used his; to bludgeon a programmer. Red numbers blink: 00:07:43 until deployment.
My palm hovers over the abort command. One press and Huff becomes spare parts. The clock ticks. Gamma-09's corpse spasms on loop.
Huff's red halo pulses.

I withdraw my hand. Holographic static crawls across my retinas like digital lice. I watch Huff's biometrics pulse in time with artillery strikes three sectors east, 98.6% synapse stability. Perfect numbers. Flawless metrics. I hate them. "Success rate exceeds projected parameters by nineteen percent," says some eager junior analyst whose name I'll forget before sunrise. Their voice crackles through the commlink swarm orbiting my head. "Vargstryk operational capacity remains optimal."

My glove creaks as I crush a holopuck. Optimal. The word feels like ash in my mouth. Seven years ago, when Subject Gamma-12 tore out her own ocular implants mid-interrogation, she screamed about "the calculus of mercy." Last month, Wolf Unit Kappa-7 diverted three patrol drones to protect civilians during a marketplace skirmish. Both anomalies solved with precise applications of neural scorching. Both testaments to our fallibility. "Secondary monitoring protocols initiated," I murmur into my wristcomm, bypassing three layers of security.

Blue verification lights dance across my signet ring. Let the techs think it's standard oversight. Let the advisors believe I still trust their precious systems. The main display shudders as Sector 12's power grid fails. Rebel work. Clean. Professional. Mason's fingerprints all over the voltage spikes.
"Status on Priority Hydra?" My foot taps arrhythmic patterns beneath the command console. Fourteen advisors straighten their spines in unison. Good dogs. Tactical Lead Vosk clears his throat. "Strike teams report seventy-three confirmed insurgent neutralizations. Civilian collateral within acceptable…"

"I asked about Hydra."

He pales. Sweat beads above regulation-grade cyberbrows. "Asset Huff remains en-route to target zone. ETA eight minutes."

Eight minutes. Sixty thousand possible variables. I split screens with a finger flick, left side showing Huff's retinal feed as he vaults collapsed transit rails, right side replaying Gamma-09's rampage frame-by-frame. Same fluid combat style. Identical microsecond hesitation before lethal strikes. Coincidence is failure's breeding ground. "Initiate Code Obsidian," I tell the room while privately routing execution orders to Blackwatch units.

Twenty-seven specialized drones detach from Bastion Prime's underbelly, their sole function now tracking Huff's every twitch.

Advisors nod, assuming it's another routine purge protocol. Let them. The smart ones survive by keeping their cranial implants unmodified. "Focus strike patterns here and here." I paint crimson markers across the city schematic. "Divert civilian transports into these choke points. Collateral absorption estimates?"

"Sixteen to twenty percent population reduction in affected zones."

Huff's retinal feed shows smoke curling through shattered transit tunnels. My knuckles tingle. The Blackwatch drones swarm closer than protocol allows. Let him feel watched. Let him *know*. "Final authorization codes." My voice cracks the air like an executioner's rifle.

Fourteen identically polished shoes shift on composite flooring. Their owners smell like antiseptic and adrenaline. Weak. Tactical Lead Vosk offers the holopad. His hands tremble. Pathetic. "Confirmation matrix primed, Executor Grimwell. Awaiting your…"

I snatch the device. Neural interface ports flare electric blue as I carve new parameters into Huff's mission brief. Let's see how the wolf runs with poisoned claws. "Adjust target priority," I announce for the room's benefit while embedding silent commands in the data stream. Secondary objectives bloom crimson in

Huff's display, unseen, urgent, lethal. Mason dies first. Then every rebel who ever shared oxygen with him. Then... contingencies. The holopad shrieks error codes. Vosk twitches. "Sir, the casualty projections…"

"Are irrelevant." My glove creaks against the device. "We're trimming deadweight."

Three advisors exhale through corporate-grade nasal filters. Still alive then. Good. I want witnesses. Huff's feed jerks sideways, thermal bloom of a plasma grenade. He compensates mid-fall, firing twin SMGs into screaming shapes. Same microsecond pause before headshots. Same tilt of the chin Gamma-09 used before going rogue. Coincidence is cancer. "Authorization confirmed." I slam the holopad into Vosk's chest. "Initiate Scythe Protocol."

The room freezes. Twelve sets of augmented eyes dart to emergency exits. Fools. As if they could outrun what's coming. Vosk swallows. "That'll depopulate entire..."

"Do I need to draw you maps?"

Sweat pools above his collar. "No sir. Executing."

Algorithms blossom across city schematics, firewalls crumbling, ventilation systems priming for chemical payloads, every subway car locking doors until flesh cooks inside. Elegant. Efficient.

Huff's biometrics spike. His left-hand drifts toward the neural port. Testing boundaries. Always testing. My teeth grind. "Patch me through."

Static hisses. Then breathing, mechanical, rhythmic, wrong. "Priority override Tantalus-Six," I snap. "Confirm receipt of revised parameters."

A guttural noise leaks from the speakers. Not quite human. Not anymore. "*Confirmed.*" Huff's voice sounds like grinding bone. "*Engaging primary target.*"

Disconnect before he can ask about the secondary commands. Before the drones catch his hesitation. Let him chew on mystery. Advisors scatter like roaches. Let them scurry. Reports will filter up through proper channels. Deniability preserved.

Alone now. Holograms paint my skin corpse-blue. Status reports cascade, seventy-three blocks sterilized, eight thousand three hundred and forty-two VarCred accounts frozen, forty-two rebels captured alive for interrogation protocols. Numbers don't lie. Numbers don't hesitate.

Huff's blacksite surveillance feed glows amber in my peripheral vision. Twenty-Seven drones show him straddling Mason's broken form in a burning arcology. Pistol pressed to the rebel's throat. Right on schedule. But wait. Wait.

His free hand keeps twitching toward the cranial port. Same pattern Gamma-09 exhibited before severing command links. Same irregular respiration rates. I lean closer. Mason spits blood. "You're just their attack dog."

Huff cocks his head. "*All dogs bite, given proper motivation.*"

The pistol shifts two degrees left. My finger stabs the kill switch. "Override code Axiom..."

Screen static. Five seconds of primal void. Then Huff's face fills every display in the chamber, sliding panel retracted, human eyes gleaming with something that isn't in the programming manuals. "Pathetic," he rasps, snapping his panel back in place.

Mason dangles from Huff's hand clasped around his throat. "Not yet," he squeaks. A man who has seen his own death reflected in the killer's visor.

Blood splatters across the screen.
Feed terminates.

CHAPTER 4: CHANCE

I suck in a breath, the air smells like synthetic leather and gun oil. I'm staring at the VargTech suit across the hologram glow, some junior exec with a jawline sharper than his actual resume. His projection shivers between us, turning his crisp white collar into pixelated confetti. My left hand's busy spinning a data chip through knuckles while my right rests near the shock-pistol hidden under my thigh. Always two hands. Always two exits. "Authentication codes first," I say, nodding at the floating schematics between us.

Blueprints for neural dampeners. Nasty pieces of work, fry your amygdala before you can scream 'fuck you'. Probably going into some blacksite interrogation rig. Not my problem. The exec's eyelid twitches. Fourth time in three minutes. Either he's got a synaptic implant misfiring, or he's waiting for the kill squad outside that door. I shift my weight fractionally toward the floor vents. Eighty centimeters wide. Tight squeeze, but doable if I lose the jacket. "Payment verification's taking longer than..."

"They teach you that line in Corp School?" My thumb brushes the pistol's grip.

"Lesson one; lying makes your left ear flush."

His hand darts to the lobe. Amateur. The hologram dies mid-flicker. That's my cue. I'm already moving when the first plasma round punches through where my skull was half a second ago. Desk kisses my ribs hard enough to leave bruises. Cheap particleboard explodes upward as I flip the damn thing. Three more shots chew through the faux wood, filling the air with burning formaldehyde. "Standard breach protocol!" I shout over the gunfire, palming a flash charge from my belt. "Breach, suppress, incinerate! You guys even read the playbook?"

Smash-cut silence. That split-second pause when Corpo thugs realize they're not shooting drones anymore. I lob the charge over the desk. Their retinal implants auto-adjust right into the magnesium-white detonation.
Screams. Heavy boots stumbling. I'm up and sprint-crawling along the wall's shadow line. Floor vents rattle underfoot - old maintenance shafts. One kick sends the grating flying. The lead enforcer's blinking away afterimages when I put two shock-pulses into his chest plate. It smells like overcooked pork. "Hostile noncompliant!" someone barks. Corporates and their fucking jargon.

The surviving goons fan out. Standard flank maneuver. I drop through the vent as plasma fire melts the ceiling panel edges above me. Dark here. Tight. Smells like recycled death and someone's abandoned lunchbox.
Left palm finds the wall. Nano-filament gloves catch on conduit lines. Follow the power surges. Servers hum below. Maintenance tunnels spiderwebbing through the building's guts. A shape blocks the light ahead. Enforcer crammed into the shaft, night-vision goggles gleaming. "Got y…"

My boot meets his teeth. Goggles spark. His stun baton goes wild, cracking against the metal walls. We're a tangle of elbows and curses. He's got forty kilos on me. I've got a monowire garrote hidden in my sleeve.
Blood splatters on ductwork.

I'm out the other side before his body finishes sliding down the incline. Plasteel servos whine behind me. Corporate goons wedging themselves into the vent shaft like overeager meat puppets.

I'm already palming the smoke canister off my belt. Pull pin with teeth. Taste blood and industrial lubricant. The grenade bounces once before detonating into a magnesium-white cloud laced with EM chaff. Screens short out. Trackers blink offline. Some idiot starts retching - probably inhaled a lungful of nano-shred particulates. Always invest in quality crowd control.

Bodies crash against lockers to my left. I'm already at the service window, elbow smashing through polyglass. Bastion Prime's neon hellscape yawns below. Windshear slaps my face. Sixty stories of vertical drop smells like ozone and desperation. The lower rooftop's twenty meters down. Diagonal. I leap before the enforcers clear the smoke.

Freefall twists my guts. Coat flaps like panicked bird wings. Impact judders through knees and spine despite the tuck-and-roll. Left ankle screams. Ignore it. Sprint toward the next gap. Adrenaline burns better than any combat stim. Rooftop gravel crunches under boots. Across the chasm, a billboard blares VargTech propaganda: Your Safety Is Our Priority! The irony tastes delicious. Three-step launch off an AC unit. For a heartbeat, I'm soaring over midnight traffic streams. Glowing vehicle roofs resemble bioluminescent fish. Land hard on adjacent building. Roll through someone's illegal herb garden. Crush genetically modified tomatoes underfoot. Smells like pesticide and failed dreams. Shouts echo two rooftops back. Spotter drones now buzzing up from street level. Time to vanish.

The maintenance ladder's rusted, but holds. Descend seven flights fire-escape style. Alley below stinks of synth-noodle carts and broken promises. Kick open a corroded access door. Slide through just as ionic rounds scar the frame.

Darkness. Dripping pipes. And a faint blue glow from beneath a moldy tarp. Boot toe flips the covering. Cracked data pad shows partial decryption progress. Highlighted text: MASON. CELL OMEGA STATUS: COMPROMISED. My vision tunnels.

Memory shard: Chaos. Gunpowder. A man's voice shouting "Go!" through static. Pain lances my temples. The pad slips from numb fingers.
Drone rotors pierce the fog. "Fuck nostalgia." I stomp the pad to plastic shards. Pocket the memory core. Survive now, unravel corporate bullshit later.

Graffiti-marked exit leads to thrumming streets. Dissolve into the crowd of nightshift workers and pleasure seekers. Let the city's pulse carry me downstream. Somewhere behind retinal screens, a ghost whispers warnings in a voice that almost sounds familiar.

The memory core burns against my thigh like a live round waiting to discharge. Three blocks later and I can still taste copper in my mouth, whether from the rooftop sprint or that fucking name, doesn't matter. Neon smears across wet pavement as I shoulder through a crowd outside a body-mod parlor. "Watch the jacket," I growl at a neon-haired joygirl vaping synth-opium. Her ocular implants click-focus on my face. Bad move.

She opens her mouth. I palm the emergency EMP charge from my sleeve. Her neural lace sparks. She seizes like a marionette with cut strings. "Told you to watch the jacket."

Drones scream past overhead, washing the street in harsh white search patterns. I duck into a noodle stall's exhaust cloud, grease and chili fumes coating my throat. The holosign above reads 'Wan's Authentic Protein Bowls' in flickering Cantonese. Authentic my ass, last week's batch tried to crawl out of the broth.

Alley exit's clogged with two Enforcers inspecting retinal scans. Their armor gleams factory-new, VargTech's latest toys rolling out before budget approval. Always test-driving prototypes on street meat. Backtrack options: fire escape ladder missing rungs, sewer grate secured with biometric locks, or... "Hey pretty." The joygirl's back on her feet, one eye smoking. She licks chrome teeth. "Lost something?"

Six gang-kids materialize from shadowed doorways. Streetlight glints off homebrew blade mods. Cost-benefit analysis: seven-to-one odds, possible broken fingers, definite delays. I flip open my coat, weapons display. Monofilament garrote. Throwing knives. Pocket mini-flamer. "Mother should've taught you," I say, rotating slowly so they all see the goods.

"Never bring fists to a gunfight."

Leader hesitates. Lets me see the calculation in his human eye, the one not riddled with track marks. Drone spotlight sweeps toward us. "Your funeral," I sigh, pulling the pin on a concussion grenade with teeth.

They scatter. I drop the grenade down the sewer grate. The explosion kicks the steel plate skyward just as the drone light hits. Chaos makes excellent camouflage.

Slither through an alley, past the dump, through a sewer, down another alley. Safehouse. Third-floor walkup behind a pharma-bodega. Kick the doorjamb twice, no claymore wires snap. Inside: bare mattress, bulletproof window shutters, stinks of mildew and sex mixed with the sweet scent of industrial cleaner covering last tenant's death throes.

Strip the sweat-soaked shirt. Check the puckered scar along my ribs, gift from a Mercurian assassin last summer. Still holds. Body's tally of near-misses looks worse under the single bulb's glare.

Memory core winks on the chipped Formica table. Standard VargTech issue, but the encryption pattern... those overlapping fractal vectors... same as the black box from the Kessler Station massacre. Spit gathers under my tongue. Not fear. Anticipation.

Scarred fingers hover over the decrypt terminal. Every broker knows the rule: some doors once opened won't close. But VargTech sending Hunters after a small-time data courier? That's Executive Level paranoia. The core hums. My thumb hesitates. Across the room, the ventilation grate clatters. Instinct rolls me sideways as three flechettes embed in the wall where my head rested. "Evening, gentlemen."

Two figures drop through the ceiling panel. Tactical masks. No identifiers. Black-market shock batons crackling with enough voltage to stop a cyborg rhino. Hunter Team. Fuck. "You could've knocked," I mutter, kicking the decrypt terminal under the mattress.

First swing takes out the table. I'm already moving, low and serpentine. Baton grazes my shoulder. Nervous system lights up like Times Square. "Fuck... your... mother..." Each word timed to a dodge.

Second Hunter's smart-link targeting tries to compensate. I throw the mattress. Predictable move. They're ready. So's the monofilament wire I strung between bedposts earlier. Hunter One's calf meets the nearly invisible strand. Tendons part like overcooked noodles. He goes down screaming. Partner hesitates half a heartbeat. Long enough to catch my boot heel in his trachea. Sound of collapsing cartilage never gets old.

Security breach means twelve minutes max until the real team arrives. Taser rounds spark against the window shutters as I boost the core's data to five blind drops, three in the Glow Market, one in New Kowloon, last one buried in a cryo-wealthy's tomb. Survival math: alive > rich > curious. Always. But the decrypted header floats in my corneal display anyway.
OPERATION SILENT HOUR
PRIMARY TARGET: CELL OMEGA
TERMINATION ORDER: MASON-7 (ALL DESIGNATIONS)

Cerebral implant pings a proximity alert. Two floors below. Heavy boots on stairs. Burn phone toasts itself in the microwave. I'm halfway out the bathroom window when the secondary explosives detonate. Hunter Team won't find anything but their colleagues' teeth.

Rooftop wind carries the stench of scorched alloy. Below, the city pulses, endless cycle of eat, fuck, work, die. Same rhythm I've danced to for twelve years. Neutrality's comfortable lie evaporates like piss on a hot pavement. VargTech doesn't do warnings. Doesn't do second chances. That Core wasn't just intel, it was a hit list. And my name's climbing the ranks.

Lick blood from split knuckles. Iron and salt. Alive. For now. Safehouse, secure for now. The chip spins between my fingers, cold titanium edges catching moonlight. All those years hoarding secrets like a dragon with its gold. Turns out the real power lies in which truths you choose to unleash. Footsteps echo from adjacent roof. Time to move. I slot the chip. Let the games begin.

Packing's always been meditation, carbon blade strapped to calf, shock rounds chambered smooth, synth-leather jacket shrugging on like second skin. Safehouse stinks of ionized paranoia. Peeling flexiglass windows show Bastion Prime's arterial glow. Neon arteries pump light through the megacity's corpse. Three choices: west toward Smuggler's Cut, east to the Drowned Markets, or straight down VargTech's throat. Survival math says run. Curiosity collects compound interest. Bootlace snaps while tying. Bad omen. Fuck omens. "Prioritize evac," my cranial implant suggests in velvet corporate tones.

I rip the neural jack free, blood threading down cervical ports. Gear bag zips shut with finality. Last item: Mason's dossier floating in my optic feed. CELL OMEGA. TERMINATION PROTOCOLS. Twelve years running shadows taught me when intel stings worse than truth. This reeks of both. Floorboards creak wrong. Not the settling kind, the weighted kind. Window exit's compromised. Air duct too narrow. Only play left's through the front.

Shotgun kisses doorjamb. Buckshot whispers through cheap polymer. Return fire shreds what's left of the coffee table. Molten plastic rain. "Chance Cooper." Voice like gravel in a compactor. Vargstryk. "You're worth sixty thousand alive."

"Bullshit." Second shell chambers. "I negotiated seventy."

They come through shooting. Armored wolves. Gen3 assault chassis. I dance between ballistic trajectories, kitchen knife finding the meat beneath alloy. One gurgles synthetic lube. Another catches a flashbang smile. Fourth enforcer makes the mistake of close quarters. My forehead meets his nasal implant. Red geyser. "Sixty-K my ass." Steal his sidearm. "Tell payroll they're lowballing."

Sirens wail in the distance. Always more coming. Data chip burns in my palm. Mason's last known coordinates glare neon-bright. Abandoned GOL-T3R facility. Classic rebel theater. Footsteps on the roof now. Snipers triangulating. I dump the clip out the window. Sparks off a drone swarm. Fire escape groans under sudden weight. Choices crystallize, die a ghost or live complicated. Cynicism's armor cracks. Just enough. Graffiti on the adjacent building mocks in spray-can crimson: RESISTANCE IS FUTILE (BUT PROFITABLE). "Fuck it."

Thermite charges kiss support beams. Whole block goes fireworks. I'm airborne before the bloom, stolen glide-suit snapping open in the chokehold wind.

Mason's coordinates burn in my retinal HUD. Curiosity killed the merc. But what the hell, we all die sometime.

CHAPTER 5: HUFF

Searing white light. Burns rip through my chest. Neural systems flicker briefly. Die. Flicker again and restore. System analysis 75% stable.
80% stable.
85%, comms uplink dead.

Last known objective incomplete. Local comms only. I'm up. No sign of Mason or his crew. I return to the hunt.

They bleed.

The thought flickers through my neural feed. Remnants of a hunt squad clumsily appears. Rook confirms, same target. Weasel nods. I join them, stalking through corpse-gray corridors. Boots crunch on silicate growths erupting from fractured concrete. Industrial carcasses loom, gutted assembly lines, skeletal conveyor belts hanging like rusted vertebrae. Team moves in textbook formation: Rook on point with the plasma cutter, Weasel covering rear with twin shock batons. Both meat. Both expendable.
"Contact in three," Rook breathes into local comms. His ocular implant glows too bright in the gloom, amateur hour, painting targets on your own retina.
I jerk two fingers left. "Switch to thermals."

Compliance clicks. Three heartbeats later, the whole fucking sector detonates. White-hot tracers shred the darkness. Rook's head becomes red mist before his scream starts. Weasel catches the second burst mid-dive, body jerking like a puppet with half its strings cut. Meat has its uses. Provides cover.

I'm already rolling behind a collapsed coolant tank when the third salvo hits. Depleted uranium rounds ricochet off reinforced polymer, filling the air with shrapnel confetti. My HUD floods with threat vectors, ST-1X isn't even trying to be stealthy. "Tango northwest!" I bark into the dead channel. Pointless, but habits die hard.

The shock trooper emerges from a service hatch eighteen meters up. Military-grade augments whine as ST-1X drops three stories, knees pistoning concrete dust. Its chassis gleams corpse-pale under peeling hazard stripes. No helmet—VargTech's signature fuck-you. They welded the targeting array directly into the skull plate. I put three armor-piercing rounds between its eyes.
Impact sparks. No flinch. "Predictive algos," I mutter, already moving.
ST-1X's rotary cannon spins up with a dentist-drill whine.

I kick a collapsed girder sideways. The steel beam screeches across concrete, throwing up sparks and cover. Ricochets ping off my shoulder guard as I pivot behind load-bearing pillars. ST-1X advances like a siege engine, each footfall cracking pavement. HUD tags the pattern: 2.3 second bursts, seven-degree suppression arcs. Ammo counter estimates 87% payload remaining. Not ideal.

A flash-memory surfaces. Dr. Kael's rasp during last reconditioning: "*Your advantage isn't strength. It's the ability to lose pieces and keep playing.*"

I eject my spent magazine mid-stride. Fresh clip slams home as ST-1X 's cannon overheats. 0.8 second reset cycle. I vault over a slag heap, firing blind. ST-1X tanks the shots, ceramic armor spiderwebbing but holding. Its left arm ripples, morph-blade extending from forearm housing. "Close quarters?" I spit blood from split lips. "That's cute."

The blade sweeps horizontal. I lean back, feeling nano-edged steel part the air millimeters from my throat. Return strike with pistol grip, crunch of reinforced knuckles against alloy jaw. ST-1X staggers. Not much.
We trade blows in the sulfuric dark. Every impact vibrates up my skeletal reinforcements. ST-1X fights like a factory press—methodical, relentless, stupid. My combat algos chart the rhythm: right jab, left hook, knee strike. Repeat.

On the fourth cycle, I let the knee connect. Pain blooms white as my ribs crack. Worth it. Grab the leg mid-retraction, torque hard. Servos scream in ST-1X's hip joint. I ride the motherfucker down, elbow driving into its throat array. The shock trooper spasms. Glitching vocal synth rasps: "Direct... upload... initiated..."

Fingertip data jack snakes from its wrist. I roll left. Too slow. The jack slams into my neural port.

World fractures into screaming data streams. My boot heels grind broken concrete as we circle through the corpse of an old nano forge facility. ST-1X's optic cluster glows poison-green through swirling metal particulates. I catalog potential weapons: frayed power cables dangling from gutted smelters, half-molten girder segments, a rusted forklift with its hydrogen cell still leaking cold blue flame. "Still breathing, Tinman?" My voice sounds wrong - too human in this tomb of dead machines.

ST-1X responds by ripping a support column free. Four hundred pounds of reinforced polymercrete comes at me like a comet. I sidestep, let momentum carry the fucker past. Shoulder-check him into a slurry vat. Acid residue eats through his armor plating. Smells like burning chemo-batteries. We both know how this ends. Doesn't mean I can't enjoy the dance. His morph-blade shears through my left pauldron. I taste copper as monofilament edges kiss collarbone. Return favor with a pneumatic kick to his knee joint. Ceramic kneecap powderizes. ST-1X wobbles. I grab the dangling data jack from his wrist port, jam it into a live conduit. Half his face melts. Other half keeps trying to kill me.

We crash through a brittle partition wall into what might've been a control room. My HUD tags thirteen potential traps before I finish rolling. ST-1X isn't subtle - charges straight through trip-laser grids. Fuel-air explosions bloom around us. I ride the concussive wave into close range, knife-hand strike aimed at his ocular cluster. He headbutts my sternum.
Titanium ribs hold. Bio-lung doesn't. I'm spitting blood as backup oxygenators engage. Combat algos scream about cumulative damage. Shut them off. Meatware limitations are for unmodified scum.

ST-1X telegraphs a haymaker. Amateur hour. Catch his wrist, spin into armbar. Hyperextend the elbow until servos pop. His counterstrike catches me mid-rib - feels like getting hit by a maglev train. We separate, circling again through spark-showering wreckage. "Not bad," I lie, reloading explosive-tip slugs one-handed. "For a walking scrap pile."

His vocal emitter gargles static. Translation matrix deciphers: [Glory/Purpose/Completion] Charming. I feint left, go right. Stomp-kick sends him stumbling back into an induction furnace chamber. Magnetic seals hiss closed automatically. Perfect. "Hey shitbrain." I tap the exterior control panel. "Remember when factories had safety protocols?"

Override codes take 0.3 seconds to crack. Thermal alarms start screaming as I crank the furnace to 3000°C. ST-1X's armor turns cherry-red. Molten alloy drips from his joints. He rams the door repeatedly. Dents start appearing. Calculate remaining structural integrity: 47 seconds. Plenty of time.

Climb to the catwalk overlooking the furnace. Draw my sidearm. Wait.
At 2300°C, ST-1X's chest plate cracks. Armor-piercing round through the
fissure. Core shielding fails. The explosion blows the furnace doors across the
room. I ride out the shockwave flat against grated walkways. Shrapnel pings
off my reinforced spine.

The hum hits first. Not machinery - Bastion Prime's perpetual growl beyond
these ruins. My audio dampeners reset, revealing seven distinct corpses.
HUD pings. Priority channel slices through residual tinnitus. "Asset Huff."
Cold female voice, all sharpened vowels. Executive Oversight. "Confirm
target neutralization."

Smoke clears. ST-1X's lower half remains standing where it was. Torso
crawling toward me on sparking servo-claws. Persistent motherfucker.
I drop down, boot crushing his thoracic housing. "Any last words?"
His remaining eye focuses. Data jack lashes out faster than bullet trajectory.
Fuck.

Neural port breach feels like getting skull-fucked by a soldering iron. Firewalls
crumble. Raw data geysers into my cortex - mission logs, surveillance footage,
termination orders stamped with Mason's fucking authorization code.
ST-1X's vocalizer dies mid-chuckle. The data jack retracts with a wet *schluck*.
My ocular implant flashes containment warnings as ST-1X's death rattle leaks
gray matter across cracked concrete. Upload complete.

Fucking liar. There's no complete. Just firewalls melting like wax as the feed
detonates behind my eyes - surveillance footage of Mason briefing resistance
cells, kill-squad deployments to Sector 7 slums, termination orders bearing
VargTech's encryption tags. Every file stamped with proof they lied. Proof *I*
lied. "Override protocol Sigma-Nine." My voice sounds distant through the
blood rush.

Emergency purging sequence scalds neural pathways. Useless. The data's
breeding, infected code spawning fractal doubts. Remember the rookie's face
when my round took her knee? Necessary compromise. The factory worker's
fingers prying at my boot? Collateral expenditure. Twelve years of obedient
calculus unraveling behind a firewall of static. Smoke parts around ST-1X's
corpse. Half his cranial plating adheres to my boot treads. I scrape it off
against a coolant pipe. "Should've stuck to memos."

My retinal display floods with schematics. Sublevel transit hubs. Thermal
layouts. A face; gaunt, scarred, eyes sharp as monofilament blades. Mason.
"Primary threat identified. Termination authorized with extreme prejudice. All
ancillary casualties permissible."

A tremor runs through my weapon hand. Glitch or reactivation? Fuck if I know. "Understood."

"Your compliance is noted." The line dies mid-static.

I check my mag-slots. Three clips remaining. Standard hollow points won't breach Mason's rumored graphene weave armor. Needs tungsten-carbide flechettes. Needs planning. Needs...

Sparks erupt from a dangling power cable. For half a heartbeat, I see twelve-year-old me reflected in the arcing current, smooth-faced prototype fresh from growth vats, VargTech's loyalty coding burning white-hot behind new eyes. That thing believed every word they fed it. The spark dies.
Reality reasserts; corpses requiring disposal protocols. Contaminated site needing sanitization. Mission parameters demanding immediate redeployment. I crouch to salvage a sidearm. Frozen finger remains curled around the grip. Rigor mortis makes a decent holster. "Orders changed," I tell her detached hand. It flops sideways when I pry the gun loose. "Don't wait up."

The neural port throbs. New data streams whisper behind every blink - encrypted coordinates, biometric profiles, a grainy vid of Mason shielding civilians from collapsing debris. Irrelevant. Noise. Irrelevant is luxury I can't afford.

Blood pools around my boots, black in the flickering emergency lights. Dead wolves still leak into grating drains. I kick a femur aside and check my forearm display. Mission clock resets. "Cleanup crew en-route," says the voice in my skull. Not a voice. Electrical impulses shaped like words.

I spit on Rook's corpse. "ETA?"

"Irrelevant."

The neural feed blinks coordinates forty klicks southeast. Underground reservoir converted to rebel staging area. Mason's face superimposes over broken concrete. Early thirties, scar bisecting left eyebrow, eyes sharp enough to cut glass.

My gloved hand crushes a stray bullet casing. Memories-not-mine flood synapses: Mason distributing ration packs in slum sectors. Mason taking a baton strike meant for some street rat. Fucking hero complex. "Priority target confirmed. Engagement protocols?"

VargTech's response stings like neural whip: Terminate. Incinerate. Erase. Boots crunch behind me. I spin, pistol already singing. Three shots punch through a sagging insulation blanket. Empty corridors echo the gunfire back as laughter. "Fuck's wrong with you?" My own voice sounds alien. Hoarse. Human.

The insulation blanket smolders. Shadows twist into familiar shapes - the GOL-T3R unit who raised me. Trainer Kael's phantom sneers through smoke: Soft. Compromised. Useless. I put a fourth round through his imagined teeth.

Gear check stabilizes the tremors. Three tungsten-carbide mags acquired from dead comrades. Two incendiary grenades lifted from a rigored corpse. Standard issue combat stims...

The syringe freezes halfway to my neck. ST-1X's final upload replays behind eyelids: security footage of Mason kneeling beside wounded Vargstryk cadet. Giving water. Applying tourniquet. Letting the kid live. My thumb bleeds where the syringe cracks. "Mission parameters updated," the company pulse-barks.

New schematics overwrite Mason's face - reservoir blueprints, structural weak points, civilian occupancy estimates. Ancillary casualties permissible. Rebar screeches as I wrench a support beam sideways. Concealed compartment reveals contraband: armor-piercing rounds wrapped in banned poetry broadsheets.

A crumpled verse; acidic echoes from the past: What metal heart betrays its beat/To serve the Varg war machine?

Footsteps echo through corpse-strewn halls. Actual ones this time. Two cleanup drones hover into the kill zone, incinerators humming. They pause at Weasel's body, scanners confirming genetic signature. I'm already moving.

Tungsten rounds shred the first drone's reactor core. The explosion cooks the second unit's sensors. Melted plastoid drips onto charred flesh as I stride through the flames. "Asset departing AO," I transmit through fried comm relays. "No survivors confirmed."

The lie tastes better than ash. Outskirts reek of decaying algae and betrayal. My stolen hoverbike coughs ozone, jury-rigged fuel cells leaking radiation. Coordinates glow steady south-east. Every pothole jostles memories-not-mine loose:

Mason laughing as some rookie pukes after first firefight. Mason trading his rations for med kits. Mason whispering "They can't own your thoughts" to trembling tech defector.

I almost miss the sniper nest. Brakes scream. The bike fishtails into a corroded crash barrier. A high-caliber round shears my left pauldron instead of the headshot. "Friendly fire?" I bellow into rusted girders.

Silence. Then a click. "Wolf." The word comes mangled through a scavenged voice box. A ghoul emerges from the collapsed overpass, skin grafted with asphalt shingles, rifle fused to skeletal hands. "Toll's one clip."

I toss an empty magazine. "Interest rates just tripled."

His shot grazes my thigh. My return shot pulps what's left of his jaw. The ghoul collapses, giggling into sewage runoff. Blood slicks the bike's controls. Neural alerts flash damage reports I ignore. Forty klicks shrink beneath the bike's warped tires.

Delta-2's gates loom at dawn's edge. Crumbling steel glints like broken teeth in a pile of rubble. Vargstryk corpses lie strewn like a bloodstained carpet. Seems I arrived at the tail end of something. I dismount slow. Deliberate. Let every camera catch VargTech's wolf approaching. Three shadows converge at the gate; human-shaped, pulse rifles raised. "Late to the party," I call.

Their leader steps into the sodium light. Same scarred eyebrow from the briefing files. Mason. His rifle stays leveled at my chest. His finger tightens on the trigger. My ocular implant calculates seven ways to disarm him. Instead, I say, "ST-1X sends regards."

For three heartbeats, the rifle wavers. That's all I need.

CHAPTER 6: MASON

Kara and Jax say they managed to scoop me into Sera's skiff. I remember the white light. The heat. A scream that might've been mine. Or his.
They say his lights flickered out. I prepare anyway. Only fools bet on maybe. I don't trust that slippery bastard. I don't trust miracles.

I check on my outposts, pace their corridors like graveyards, combat boots crunching glass shards into dust. My HUD paints thermal footprints on the walls: old bloodstains, stress fractures, the ghost of a firefight five years dead. The map dissects the current outpost, a flickering holograph sliced open like a ribcage. Three choke points. Two kill zones. One exit. My gloves tighten as I mark the weak spots. "Here," I mutter to the empty air, dragging a crimson wireframe across Sector 7's junction. "And here." The building groans, a structural sigh. Perfect.

The detonator's guts spill across the munitions crate. My fingers move before my brain catches up, twist the copper wires, solder the charge, yank the fuse cord taut. Muscle memory from another life. Back when VargTech taught me to build better bombs for worse wars. A rebel kid watches, eyes darting between my hands and the hallway's mouth. Young. Sweating inside his patchwork armor. "Thermite cocktail," I say, tossing him the device. It's lighter than his hesitation.

"Choke point delta. Ten meters past the blast door."

He blinks. "What if I…"

"Run?" My glove creaks as I flex synthetic tendons. "Smart play. But if you stay? Prime the trigger when their second unit breaches." I lean in. Smell his fear, acid and adrenaline. "They'll funnel. They'll burn. You'll live."

Twenty-four hours of sewer running later, and Delta-2's mess hall reeks of boiled protein and doubt. Six rebels cluster around a cracked table, their faces lit by a single failing bulb. A woman with a scarred lip speaks first. "Intel says Huff's bringing Wolves."

Her knuckles whiten around her rifle. "Not just drones."

Nods ripple through the room. A man with a hacked ocular implant grinds his teeth. Click, click, click. "We're scraps against Vargstryk."

I unclip my gloves. Peel them off slow, finger by finger. Let them see the human parts, pale skin, knuckle scars from childhoods they'll never have. "True," I say. Their breath stops. "Wolf units? Faster. Stronger. Better." The gloves hit the table with a thud. "But you're not here because you're better."

Scarred Lip flinches. "Then why?"

"Because they're predictable." I tap the map glowing on my forearm. "Huff attacks the east flank first. Always. Thinks it's clever."

A snort ripples through the group. Good. "So we let him take it."

Ocular Implant narrows his lens. "Let him?"

"Then collapse three floors on his chrome-plated skull." I smile; the kind that doesn't reach my eyes. "Dumb fuck'll never see it coming."

A voice mutters near the back, uncertain. "I heard Huff might be dead…"

"If you bet on maybe, you're already dead." I meet their eyes, one by one. "He's alive until I say otherwise."

Five deserters leave at dawn, clutching their reasons like grenades—sick siblings, unborn kids, debts to ghosts. I watch them shuffle past the barricades. Don't stop them. Don't blame them. The remaining twenty stare at me. Waiting for the speech. The rally cry.

I spit on the floor. "Alright, listen up. Huff's got drones. Air support. Enough firepower to glass this shithole twice over." I snap the gloves back on. "We've got thirty mines, six EMP charges, and…" I glance at a stocky rebel calibrating his shotgun. "How many Molotov's, Jax?"

"Forty-two." He grins, all cracked teeth and crazy. "Half mixed with piss accelerant."

Laughter barks through the room. Rough. Relieved. "See?" I cock my head. "Already winning."

They disperse sharper than before. Purpose in their steps. I catch Scarred Lip's arm as she passes. "You stayed."

Her gaze flicks to my exposed hands, still bare. "Yeah, well." She racks her rifle's slide. "Someone's gotta keep your ass alive."

Silence hangs. Then the first drone screech pierces the air.
Right on schedule. Trap Zone Three still smells like fear and duct tape. Rebels hunch over exposed rebar, wiring charges into the floor. My ocular implant flags the west wall, pressure seams too clean. Too symmetrical. "Destiny."

Shock-white hair jerks up. "Sir?"

"Swap the C-4. Symmetry gets flagged by neural nets." I kick a vent shaft. "Make it look like a cave-in."

"But the yield…"

"Doesn't matter if he spots it first." I tear open her pack. "Cluster A here. D12 primer, random det-cord. No patterns."

She nods. Smarter than the last three bomb-techs I buried. Zone Five reeks of scorched coolant and piss-accelerant. Scarred Lip's welding torch spits sparks as she converts old hoses into flamethrowers. "Huff torches tech first, yeah?"

"Standard protocol." I toss her a graphene battery. "Analog ignition only." She grins. "Old school barbecue."

My comm-bead vibrates, encrypted frequency. Bastion Prime's skyline materializes in my retinal HUD, all neon spires and death-drones. Night's voice crackles through bone conduction. "Package secured. Extraction window: eight hours."

I duck into an alcove veiled by asbestos curtains. "Eight? Consensus was six."

"Security AI upgraded to Cerberus-class." Static swallows his cough. "Need time to spoof the…"

"Seven-point-five. Not a second more." Concrete dust grits between my teeth, tasting like betrayal. I still don't fully trust the ghost. Don't know if it's human, rogue AI, phantom hacker. Don't question too much; so long as it stays useful.

"And the data packet?"

"Primed. Once uploaded, every screen in the Azure Quadrant plays your little movie."

I watch Jax test-fire a Molotov across the hangar. Glass shatters. Flames roar. "Make sure the rendering's clean. I want VargTech's logo crisp when their execs start eating children."

Night's pause lasts three heartbeats. "You're really pushing the broadcast?"

"Ascendancy Day fireworks." I kill the connection.
Escape Route Delta reeks of stale coolant. My boot crunches a dead rat's skull. "Clearance?"

"Forty inches vertical," Jax calls from a crawlspace. Blood streaks his forearm.

"Tight squeeze with gear."

I kneel, scanning the tunnel. "Widen it."

"Boss, that's solid rock…"

"Then grab a fucking pickaxe." My knuckles rap steel support beams. "Huff's scouts find this choke point, we die screaming. Understood?"

He mutters something unkind. I let him. Alone in the commissary ruins, I find names carved in moldering tables. Previous occupants. Previous casualties. My finger traces glyphs etched by a dead man's knife.

The first drone's whine starts low, a subsonic thrum vibrating my molars. My augments auto-calibrate. "Scramble pattern Beta!" I'm moving before the alert finishes, boots pounding cracked linoleum. "All units to hard cover! ECM active!"

Rebels dive into reinforced trenches. Jax slams the blast doors' manual override. They're coming. We're ready.

My augments flash thermal signatures, six hostiles approaching grid seven-niner. "Jax! Kill the halo projectors!" I snap my fingers at a rookie fumbling with detonators. "Set that five meters west or you'll cook your own kidneys."

Rebels flow through the complex like mercury through cracks. Old pipes scream under sudden pressure changes. Someone vomits in a corner, acrid stench cutting through motor oil and fear-sweat. I grab a stim injector from my belt and toss it to a wide-eyed kid clutching a pulse rifle. His hands are shaking too much to aim. "Stay sharp or stay dead. Your call."

The comms bead in my ear crackles. "Beta team reporting, EM jammers active."

"Sensors say otherwise." I kick open a rusted maintenance hatch, revealing flickering holographic decoys. "Boost signal bleed by twelve percent. Make Huff think we're dumb enough to use museum-grade tech."

Jax appears at my shoulder, face smeared with hydraulic fluid. "Scouts just pinged the outer perimeter."

"Right on schedule." My retinal HUD streams tactical updates; blueprints overlaying reality. "Tell Gamma squad to abandon sector three."

Her brow furrows. "But the heavy turrets…"

"Are bait." I adjust my left glove, feeling the familiar strain of reinforced tendons. "VargTech's drones follow standard sweep patterns. Let them think they've found something."

We reach the central control pit, what used to be an old missile silo. Rebels hunch over flickering holoscreens, fingers flying across cracked keyboards. The air smells like burnt copper and battery acid. "Options!"

Twelve faces snap toward me. "Option one," I nod at the eastern blast doors. "We let their scouts report a false weak point."

A grizzled vet named Croft scratches his neck scar. "And option two?"
I activate the security feed, a dozen black, wasp-like drones circling
aboveground. "We give them exactly what they came for."

Understanding ripples through the room. Jax barks a laugh. "You want to
light up their sensor suites."

"Brightest fucking beacon in the ruins." My knuckles rap steel plating. "They
send the swarm, we fry their guidance systems with overloaded reactor cores."

Croft spits on the floor. "That's a one-way trip for whoever stays topside."
All eyes shift to me. I remove my right glove, palm circuitry glowing faintly.
"Battery cells need manual detonation after the core breach."

Silence. Then the rookie from earlier steps forward, hands shaking. "I... I
could..."

"Wrong answer." I yank him back by his collar. "Anyone volunteers for
martyrdom gets reassigned to latrine duty."

Jax slams his fist on the console. "Remote trigger?"

"EMP interference from the cores would block signals." I pull my glove back
on, snug between each finger. "Needs physical contact."

The subsonic drone shifts pitch, climbing into audible range. My augmented
eardrums dampen automatically. "Lure them into Sector Seven," I command,
pulling up schematics. "Collapse the auxiliary tunnels once they commit."

Rebels scatter. Croft lingers, hand on his sidearm. "You're really betting
everything on Huff taking the bait?"

I check ammo counts across three dozen readouts. Too low. Doesn't matter.
"He'll take it."

"How can you..."

"Because I'd fall for it too."

The lights flicker. Primary power fails. Emergency glow strips paint everyone
in sickly green. "Showtime," Jax mutters, voice low as a trigger pull as he racks
his shotgun.

I climb to the observation platform, boots ringing on grated metal. Below, rebels man their stations with the frantic precision of condemned men sharpening their own guillotine. The drone swarm's shriek becomes physical now, vibrating loose screws, rattling teeth. My ocular implants auto-track a thermal bloom forming aboveground. "Decoy teams ready?"

Jax nods. "Three volunteers wearing our last stealth suits."

"Best we've got against multi-spectrum scans." I watch the tactical display as three blips break from cover. "Here goes the last of our luck."

The drones converge like piranhas. One decoy goes dark, signal lost mid-sprint. "Now!"

Rebels smash power couplings. The complex shudders as backup generators roar to life. Every light explodes at maximum brightness. Drones reel like drunk bats. "Reactor cores to overload in ten!" Jax shouts.

"Too slow." I leap down from the platform, sprinting toward the service elevator. "Buy me ninety seconds!"

The world narrows to steel corridors and countdown timers. My combat rig administers adrenaline as I burst onto the surface level. Rotor wash nearly knocks me flat.

Five stories overhead, the drone swarm coalesces into a living storm cloud. Their undersides glow red-hot from weaponized scans. Reactor control panel's fried. Of course. I rip off the access cover. Fuse box smells like burnt plastic. Forty-three wires in a rainbow of corporate standardization. "Shame they don't teach color codes in assassin school," I mutter, yanking three cables simultaneously.

The ground bucks. Alarms wail. My augmented lungs filter toxic smoke pouring from the reactor vents. Drone swarm dives. I smash the emergency coolant release. White vapor engulfs the landing pad. Ice crystals form on my visor. Thermal signatures go haywire. Drones crash into each other, blind and furious. "Core breach imminent!" Jax screams through comms.

I'm already moving, glove sensors melting as I force the manual override. "Tell Gamma squad to..."

The explosion lifts me off my feet. Blackness. Ears ringing. Retinal HUD flashing damage reports. Left arm broken in two places. Irrelevant. Smoke clears to reveal the drone swarm retreating, seven fewer than before.

Jax hauls me upright. "Still alive?"

I spit blood. "That depends…do concussions count?"

Rebels cheer below. Fools. Huff's real forces arrive at dawn. Blood drips from a cracked ceiling pipe onto my shoulder. I don't flinch. Twenty-three heartbeats echo through the concrete maze of Sector 7-B. Too fast, too loud. Amateurs.
"Jax. South corridor charge primed?" My glove creaks as I tighten it.

His holographic tally appears on my retinal display. Five shaped charges. Twelve flechette pods. "Bastion-grade detcord though? We're improvising with duct-tape and spite."

I kick an exposed power conduit. Rust flakes float in the emergency lights. "Spite's got better yield ratios than VargTech plastique."

The proximity grid blinks orange. Two klicks out. Thermal signatures massing behind Epsilon sector's blast doors. Huff's vanguard. A kid with a scavenged plasma cutter blocks my path. Finger trembling on the trigger. "They say… they say Wolves eat prisoners' eyes."

I unclip my own cutter, press it into his free hand. "Now you've got two chances to blind them first."

Murmurs crack like breaking concrete through the ranks. I climb onto a shattered console, boot crushing dead control panels. "Check your exits. Check your corners. Then check your goddamn exits again."

No cheers. Just twenty-one sets of hands priming weapons in unison. The floor vibrates. Concrete dust sifts between steel rafters. Jax falls in step beside me, reloading his shock rifle. "Scouts report grav-tanks."

"Good." I slot a corrosive round into my sidearm. "Bigger they are…"

"…louder they scream," he finishes, mouth twitching.

My HUD pings, secondary explosives armed. Tertiary fallback routes collapsing on schedule. Eight minutes till contact. We pass the med station. A field surgeon stitches a rebel's scalp shut without anesthetic. The man bites down on a rolled bandage. Smart. "Core temperature's spiking," Jax warns.

I thumb my coolant injector. "Not yet." Five minutes.

The first shield generator fails. Lights dim. Someone's breathing goes ragged. I grab a shock grenade from my belt, toss it to the nearest recruit. "Ever play skip-rope with lightning?"

She catches it midair. "Will it kill Wolves?"

"Guaranteed to piss them off worse."

Three minutes. My audio aug picks up the whine of servos beyond the west barricade. Signature triple-click. Wolf pack leader calibrating targeting lasers. Jax shoulders his rifle. "Remember the Alamo?"

"Too many civvies died there." I scan the barricades. "Think smaller. Messier."

Sixty seconds. Rebels melt into murder holes and firing trenches. I take position behind a collapsed bulkhead. Ratcheting my bolt-action coil gun echoes louder than it should.

Twenty seconds. Jax nods. I nod back. He's earned that much.

Ten. I count steel teeth emerging from the Wolfpack's jaws.

Five. Safety off.

Two. Impact tremors. Now.

The east wall disintegrates in a hail of hypersonic rounds. Dust and smoke fill the void…and something unexpected: the sound of a hoverbike skittering to a halt beyond the rubble. "Jax, Croft, on me."

We make our way over the rubble and through what remains of the gate posts. Huff's huge figure is framed on the other side.
"Late to the party." He sounds bitter. Defeated, even. Or is that my imagination? Huff's never late. Always leads from the front.

I step forward, my weapon aimed at Huff's chest. The first shot to throw him off balance, the second to buckle one knee, the third through his ocular implant into what little brain he owns. He hesitates a moment, then: "ST-1X sends regards."

CHAPTER 7: HUFF AND MASON

HUFF:

He fades through the smoke before a single trigger can be pulled. That's how it starts, with a chase. Concrete bites into my palm as I scale the perimeter wall. Night vision overlay paints the compound in acid green, rusted steel skeletons of old artillery platforms, collapsed storage units vomiting cables like mechanical entrails. My targeting array pings twice. Motion sensors buried in the rubble.

I drop into a crouch, knuckles brushing the twin shock batons at my hips. Standard VargTech issue. Standard VargTech mission. Standard VargTech lies? I should've returned to Control. Logged the contact. Clean exit. Didn't. The thought fractures before it forms.

Three steps forward, left boot avoiding the pressure plate disguised as cracked concrete. Child's play. Mason's first layer of defense, a sentry turret welded to a collapsed girder, whirs to life. Red targeting laser slices through the dust. Muscle memory takes over.

I roll right as the first plasma round sears past, shoulder slamming into a concrete pillar. The turret's rotation mechanism creaks. 0.8 second reset cycle. Plenty of time. Three long strides. Fingers find the kill switch under the barrel. Twist. The turret dies mid-charge. "Predictable," I mutter, wiping hydraulic fluid off my gloves. The straps feel loose. I tighten them. Always tighten them.

MASON:

The asset moves like textbook VargStryk. Almost. Fluid aggression with that telltale micro-hesitation before each offensive maneuver. Programming versus instinct. The turret trap serves its purpose: confirmation of response times, preferred evasion patterns. Something's off.

I adjust my left glove, index finger tracing the reinforced knuckle plate. Thermal scan shows three more active defenses between the asset and this position. Failure isn't the goal. Reaction is. The difference matters. "Shift Sector 4-B sensors to passive scan," I whisper.

The comm bead in my collar vibrates acknowledgment. Let the wolf think it's gaining ground. Every intercepted data packet, every countered move another crack in that polished armor.

HUFF:

The corridors stink of decaying polymer and something sweet. Melting insulation? Rotted rations? Doesn't matter. My HUD flickers. EM interference. Old VargTech security systems still chewing on backup power. I palm the wall, feeling vibrations through my neural implants. Distant machinery. Closer breathing. *Contact rear!*

I spin as the floor panel erupts. Not machinery. Not breathing.
Feral dogs, cyber, enhanced jaws snapping where my throat was. Six of them. Rabid tech. Batons ignite with twin snarls of blue lightning. First strike melts a muzzle. Second cracks a spinal implant. They fight with code-pattern attacks. I counter with subroutine E-14. When the last yelp fades, my boots crunch through shattered teeth implants… "Smart bitch." I wipe copper mist off my visor.

Sparks still hiss from her jaw as I look down on the corpse at my feet, its exposed wiring still sparking. Not Mason's style. Too messy. VargTech's old security systems gone feral. Static bursts in my ear.
"…asset…proceed…sector…" The comms are definitely compromised.

I rip out the earpiece, crush it under my left heel. The silence feels heavier.

MASON:

In the dying security cameras, the Wolf kills its sixth attacker in 4.3 seconds. Flawless technique. Flawless waste. Those cyber-hounds cost VargTech 80,000 credits each during the last procurement cycle.

I adjust both gloves this time, fingertips pressing against palm readers. The motion activates three hidden panels in the upcoming corridor. Non-lethal.

Inconvenient. "Let's see how you handle your own toys," I murmur. He's moving faster now. Impatient. Good.

HUFF:
I kick open the blast door. Rust flakes pour down like orange rain as I enter what's left of the armory racks of decaying pulse rifles, crates of unstable power cells. My foot hovers over the threshold. Too easy. Backstep. Two paces.

The ceiling drops where I stood. A VargTech security drone smashes into concrete, its laser array still cycling up. Outdated model. Desperate move. I'm already moving past its twitching carcass when the real trap triggers. Floor panels disengage. Freefall. Three stories down into pitch blackness.

Instinct arches my body. Left baton jams into the shaft wall—soot and sparks shower as I carve a slowing trench down concrete. Right hand finds a service ladder. Railing breaks but has slowed my fall. Impact rattles my teeth. Knees bent. Roll.

The sublevel reeks of mildew. My HUD scrambles to map the space. Ancient server banks. Decommissioned fabrication units. And…Movement.

I'm sprinting before conscious thought. Around crumbling server towers, under sagging coolant pipes. The shadow stays ahead, just at the edge of visibility. "Stand down!" My voice sounds foreign. Mechanical.

The shadow pauses. I leap. Concrete explodes where we collide. My fingers close on…A maintenance drone. Its cracked screen flickers with pixelated laughter. I crush the skull casing. The laugh cuts off. Above, through the hole in the ceiling, a red light blinks. Surveillance camera. Recent installation. I give it the finger. He's baiting me. Knows I see it. Knows I'll chase anyway.

MASON:
The asset took 1.2 seconds longer to detect the decoy drone. Cumulative stress factors mounting. I remove my gloves, run bare fingers across the control console. Time to change the game. "Activate Room B-7."

The order travels through fiber optics buried in concrete. Through abandoned sewage lines. Through the corpse of the city itself. Let the hunter come. Let it see.

HUFF:
The stairwell door groans open to chemical stench. My eyes water before the filters kick in. Processing vats line the chamber. Massive steel cylinders

crusted with decades of bio-sludge. VargTech's early attempts at organic computation. Failed experiments. Something moves between the vats. I unclip a shock grenade. "Last chance."

The reply comes from everywhere. Nowhere. "You've said that before."

Male voice. Distorted. Confident. I throw the grenade. The explosion lights up rusted catwalks. Shadows leap. A figure ducks behind a vat, real this time. I'm moving before the echo fades. Boots on ladder rungs. Fist slamming into… Empty air. A hologram. "Warmer," mocks the voice.

I pivot. Batons crackling. If I wanted him dead, I'd be carrying something else. The real attack comes from above. A dropped canister spewing acrid smoke. Neural disruptor gas. My rebreather engages. Late. Fingers tremble. Vision swims. Through the haze, a shape approaches. Lean. Deadly. Mason.

I lunge. He's gone. The gas clears. On the floor where he stood, a single tactical glove. Inside, scrawled in blood-red nano-paint: NEXT TIME BRING BETTER TOYS. I crush the glove in my fist. The servos in my arm whine. "Count on it."

The chemical stench clings to my filters like a bad memory. I kick aside the crushed glove, neural disruptor residue still itching behind my eyes. Mason's trail leads upward through maintenance shafts, obvious play. Too obvious. I take the service elevator instead. The doors part on a symphony of creaking metal. Old GOL-T3R prototypes line the walls like insect husks, their exposed spinal interfaces crusted with fungal growth. My targeting overlay paints three possible ambush points before I finish scanning. "Predictable," I mutter, thumbing my shock baton's charge setting to maximum.

The explosion comes from the floor. Concrete erupts in a teeth-rattling whump that sends me airborne. Enhanced tendons coil, spring tight as I twist mid-fall, shoulder plating screeching against rebar fangs jutting from the crater. Dust floods my optics. "Pattern recognition," Mason's voice echoes through settling debris. "Your weakness."

I roll behind a shattered server bank as secondary charges detonate. Ceiling panels crash down in jagged steel rain. A support beam groans, calculated structural damage. Trap within a trap. "Adaptation," I counter, firing grapple lines into the buckling framework. "Mine."

Servos scream as I yank. The entire collapse vector pivots, creating a slanted shield against the avalanche. Mason's boot scuffs concrete thirty-seven degrees west. I'm moving before the last girder falls. He's faster. Always fucking faster.

The rebel leader melts through a service hatch as my baton cracks the space where his skull just was. I catch the barest glimpse of tactical gloves adjusting something metallic before the hatch seals. "Come on, you ghoul," I snarl, plasma torch already chewing through rusted hinges. "Dance with me proper."

Mason's bootheels echo through the arterial corridor ahead. I count three distinct reverb patterns—false leads. The fourth heartbeat comes from the left wall. I put two armor-piercing rounds through the drywall. "Overcompensating," his muffled voice taunts as I charge through the new hole. Empty maintenance closet. Flickering holo-projector in the corner spits static.

My combat overlay blinks red. Floor plates give way beneath me. Freefall. Twelve meters. Impact protocols engage a millisecond too slow. The service tunnel swallows me in darkness and pain. *Target's exploiting structural weaknesses. Adjusting threat matrix.*

I spit blood and nanite fluid. Kneecap actuator whines like a dying animal. Above, Mason peers through the hole I just made. His face stays carefully neutral, but I catch the glove adjustment, left hand, index finger. Tells me everything. "Still breathing down there, Wolf?"

I test weight on the damaged leg. Acceptable. "You'll choke on it," I call back, palming a micro-drone from my belt.

The device skitters up the wall as I leap. Mason's already gone when I crest the edge, but my drone's feed shows heat signatures retreating toward the old reactor core. Of course. Radiation shielding makes targeting systems useless. Smart play. Smart prey.

Mason's waiting in the control room's dead heart. I find him bathed in the sickly glow of cracked fusion rods, leaning against a decommissioned coolant pump like we're old friends sharing a drink. His left glove's missing. "Took you long enough."

I cycle through targeting modes. Geiger counters spike. Visual distortion. Useless. "Ran out of tricks?" I ask, advancing.

He smiles. Actually fucking smiles. "Learned from the best."

The first strike comes low. A monowire garrote aimed at my damaged leg. I pivot into the attack, baton sparking against the wall as Mason feints left. His elbow catches my rebreather. Plastic cracks. We separate. Circle. His breathing's steady. Mine's not. "Notice anything familiar about this place?" He gestures to the reactor's corpse with his bare hand. "VargTech's first attempt at cold fusion. Killed seventeen workers when it failed."

I feint right. He doesn't bite. "Your point?"

He doesn't blink. "You don't see the dead. Not yet."

Mason adjusts his remaining glove. "How many graves will you dig for them before realizing you're in one too?"

The attack comes swift and silent, a vibro-blade from his boot. I catch his wrist an inch from my carotid. Our augmented muscles tremble in perfect opposition. "Old ghost stories," I growl.

His blade flicks upward, severing a coolant pipe. Superheated steam scalds my left side. I turn, pulling him into the steam too. *"New ones being written."*

We stumble through a rotten partition wall, crash into the chamber beyond in a storm of sparks and broken code. His head snaps back from a jaw strike. My knuckles split on his teeth. "Still... trying... to... save me?" I punctuate each word with a blow he partially blocks.

Mason's knee finds my gut. "Just... showing... the... exit!"

We break apart again. My left eye's swelling shut. Blood drips from his nose. Slaps me like a wet fish. The room stinks of ozone and iron. Ancient server banks line the walls, their dead screens reflecting our panting forms. Somewhere a damaged alarm wails like a dying animal. Mason wipes his face with the back of his hand. The missing glove. A calculated reveal. "Check your ammo counter," he rasps.

I don't. Don't need to. The weight's wrong. Two rounds missing I didn't fire. "Stolen during the coolant burst," he confirms. "You're down to shock attacks and bad attitude."

I spit nanite fluid at his feet. "Plenty left."

He nods toward the ceiling. I follow his gaze. Rusted chains. Pulley system.

Emergency hatch. "Your extraction team's five minutes out," Mason says. "Mine's already here."

I charge anyway. We meet in a clash of sparks and curses. His blade grazes my ribs. My baton cracks his collarbone. The chains above us rattle with each impact. When the explosion comes, I almost respect him for it.
Mason's remaining glove detonates in a concussive whump that sends us flying in opposite directions. My back slams into a server rack. He staggers toward the pulleys. "Next time," he coughs, blood speckling his chin, "bring friends."

The chain mechanism shrieks to life. I'm on my feet in time to see Mason rising through the hatch, his silhouette framed against Bastion Prime's eternal smog. I throw my last shock grenade. He catches it. Throws it back. The world goes white.

When my vision clears, the hatch lies empty. Above me, the broken alarm still screams. I let it. The chain's still swinging when he speaks. "Know how many operatives VargTech's cycled through this sector?"

Mason's voice cuts through the alarm's dying whine. He's leaning against a shattered terminal, left arm hanging wrong. Still looks like he's planning my funeral. I check my baton's charge. Seventeen percent. "Irrelevant."

"Twenty-seven." He flicks blood off his chin. "All specs superior to you. All dead or defected."

My targeting overlay paints three weak points on his stance. Knee joint. Solar plexus. Throat. "You're stalling."

"Am I?" His good hand drifts toward his belt. "Why'd they send a prototype after me, Huff? Why not a proper kill squad?"

The question slips between my ribs like a vibroblade. I see the tactical readout from Mission Brief 441-A scrolling behind my eyes: Asset exhibits 92% compliance variance. Recommend field testing under high—stress conditions. He sees the hesitation. Leans forward. "They're watching this. Bet your neural feed's lighting up their monitors right now."

My ocular implant pings a priority alert. I blink it away. "Standard combat telemetry."

"Standard?" His laugh sounds like a bone saw. "They fried Kestrel's cerebral cortex when she asked too many questions. You really think you're different?"

The memory upload hits without warning. Kestrel's final mission logs play behind my retinas—her hands shaking as she tried to remove the neural interface, the smell of burning synapses, Control's voice cool as frozen nitrogen: Asset retirement protocol initiated. My finger twitches on the baton's activation stud. Mason presses. "You remember the Blacksite Massacre?"

"Counterinsurgency operation." The words sound like someone else's. "Neutralized 184 hostiles."

"Hostiles." He spits red. "They were testing experimental lung filters. Children, Huff. They gassed children and called it a stress test."

My HUD flickers. For 0.3 seconds, the room's thermal scan shows nineteen small bodies stacked near a ventilation shaft. The image vanishes before I can run verification. But it's too late. My HUD feels cold. Like it knows. "Bullshit." My voice harmonics register at 87% confidence.

Mason taps his temple. "Check your archived mission logs. Section 9, subfolder Sigma."

Protocol forbids accessing pre-mission archives without…The baton slips in my grip. He's moving before I realize I've hesitated. Not toward the exit, at me. I brace for impact, but he slams his damaged shoulder into my chest instead of striking. Pain flares through my ports.

"Fight smart!" he snarls, breath hot against my audio sensors. "Or you'll end up another smear on their flowcharts!"

His knee comes up. I block it, but the impact sends us crashing through a glass partition. Shards rain down as we roll across concrete. He's on his feet first. Throws something cylindrical. I react before pattern recognition finishes, catch the shock grenade, throw it back. It detonates against the ceiling in a cascade of blue sparks. When the afterimages clear, Mason's gone.
The smell of burnt ozone mixes with my own scorched armor plating. My left leg's actuators stutter—step as I rise. Across the chamber, a maintenance hatch yawns open behind sparking wires.

I limp-sprint to the opening. Dark shaft beyond. Distant clanging footsteps. "Asset tracking suggests an 87% probability of successful intercept," I tell the empty air. No one answers.

The shaft's too narrow for combat maneuvers. I drop in anyway.
His blood trail leads to a collapsed tunnel fifty meters down. Fresh blast

marks. My audio enhancers catch the whine of a departing hoverbike through three meters of rubble. I punch the wall. Concrete dust rains down.

When the neural ping comes, I almost ignore it.

++*Priority Override: RT-441-7*++

++*Report Mission Status*++

I stare at the words floating in my left eye. Count seven cracks in the tunnel wall before responding. "Target escaped. Pursuit inadvisable. Requesting extraction."

The pause lasts exactly 1.8 seconds.

++*Acknowledged. Return to Sector Blue for debrief*++

++*Upload combat telemetry for behavioral analysis*++

My hand's already moving to the data port at my neck. Stops. Kestrel's face floats in the dark behind my eyes. The way her targeting laser had danced across Control's forehead that last moment before they fried her. I yank the neural jack out instead. The hatch above me groans open. Extraction team's boots on the ladder. I count three sets. Standard recovery unit.

"Operative?" A voice through the dust. "We have clearance to…"

"Clearance's been updated." I shoulder past them, climbing toward surface air that tastes like oil and lies. "Tell Control I'm pursuing secondary objectives."

They don't try to stop me. The bike's still there. Someone's wiped the nav logs, but the seat's warm. I rev the engine and try not to wonder which dead operative last rode it. As Bastion Prime's skyline swallows me whole, I realize I'm checking my gear straps. Recheck my straps. Reflex. I don't check the mirror. New problem.

Dust cakes my nostrils. I spit concrete grit. The extraction team's floodlights carve yellow wounds in the rubble behind me, but I'm already straddling the stolen bike. Its engine thrums against my aug-fiber muscles. Alive, present in ways my own wiring never feels.

++*Priority Override: RT-441-7*++

++*Combat telemetry overdue*++

The alert pulses behind my right iris. I rev the throttle instead. Let Control choke on exhaust. Bastion Prime swallows me whole. Neon arteries, steel bones. Ads for VargTech's Stipend Program flicker across my retinas. "Your contribution. Our future." I blink hard. Static fuzz eats the propaganda.

Three blocks west, a security drone scans the street. Standard patrol pattern. I duck into an alley slick with coolant runoff. My left boot skids on something soft. Don't look down.

++*Operative Huff. Return trajectory deviates*++

"Calculating alternate routes." Lie comes smooth. Programmed reflex.

The comms spit static. They know. I brake behind a corroded dumpster. Check my gear straps—twice. Mason's voice ghosts through my neural feed: *"They built you to hunt, but who gave you the teeth?"*

My fist cracks the bike's dash. Plastic splinters. Useless. A shadow detaches from the wall ahead. "Spare creds, chief?" Ragged coat. Rusty blade.

I stare at the knife. Carbon steel. Pre-Corporation War. Museum piece. "Wrong neighborhood for charity." I thumb my holster.

He lunges. I don't shoot. My augmented arm snaps his wrist. Bone pops. The blade clatters. "Fuck! You're one of them…"

"Not tonight." I toss him a trauma patch from my belt. VargTech issue. Expired. He scrambles backward. I kick the knife into a drain. *++Behavioral anomaly detected++* "Override: Null Response."

The alert dies mid-screech. I mount the bike. Glance at my reflection in a shattered storefront. Same face Control programmed. Same killer's eyes. But the cracks…

Aircars scream overhead. Enforcement Division. Headed toward the complex. Hunting ghosts. Mason's last smirk floats in my HUD. Cocky bastard. Should've put a round through his frontal lobe. Should've. Didn't.

The bike growls north. Past the checkpoints. Beneath the arterial highways where corporate shuttles bleed commuters into sky towers. I count security cams, twelve per block. All blinking. All blind. They'll find the bike. Let them. I ditch it behind a noodle stand reeking of synthetic pork. The vendor doesn't look up. Survival instinct. Footsteps echo in the wet dark. "Huff."

I spin. Blade out. Destiny leans against a graffiti-scarred wall. Blood soaks her left sleeve. Fresh. "Heard you went rogue." She flicks a broken syringe into the gutter. "Need a medic?"

"Need intel."

Her laugh rasps like a saw blade. "Control's offering two million cred for your cortex."

I step closer. "You here to collect?"

Her human eye narrows. The mechanical one whirs—old model. Obsolete. Like us. "They scrapped my unit," she says. "After Control Tower."

The unspoken hangs between us, her finger on the trigger. My hesitation in the crosshairs. She tosses a data chip. I catch it midair. "Safehouse coords. Last gift from a dead pig."

The chip warms my palm. Burns it. "Why?"

She lights a cigarette. Flame trembles. "Mason says hello."

The shadows eat her before I can chamber a bullet. Smart. I crush the chip. Coordinates bloom in my vision.
++*Warning: Restricted zone*++
I walk anyway. The city breathes around me. A dying beast hooked to life support. Somewhere in its guts, Mason's rebuilding. Somewhere above, Control's sharpening new knives. I check my gear straps. Check them again. The night doesn't care.

CHAPTER: 8 CHANCE

The data chip spins between my fingers like a live round as I press deeper into the alley's cancerous growth. Bastion Prime's underbelly breathes tonight, steam vents cough rust-flavored mist, neon signs above spit HAPPINESS THROUGH COMPLIANCE in bleeding holo-font. My shoulder aches where the neural relay jack digs into muscle beneath the stolen Enforcer coat. The package strapped to my ribs pulses warm against my side. Some poor bastard's salvation or damnation, depending on who intercepts first. Footfalls echo three alleys east. Not boots. Too light for drones. I flatten against corroded plating where the wall weeps black fluid. The chip stops spinning. "Fuck your mother's corpse," I mutter when the patrol passes without glancing sideways.

Round the next corner and collide with a wall of tactical armor. Recognition hits before my pistol clears the holster. Mason's gloved hand clamps my wrist. His other palm hovers near the plasma pistol at his hip. We're nose to nose in the alley's arrhythmic strobing—his eyes flicker with the same amber diagnostics I saw that night in the Scrap Yards. "Still picking through garbage, I see." His voice hasn't changed. Still that calm slicing through chaos like monofilament wire.

I twist free, thumbing the safety off my weapon. I note his vest peeling away from third-degree burns. "You look like shit."

He just adjusts that damn glove. Always the left first. Memory fragments detonate behind my eyes, blood on concrete shaped like Australia, Mason shouting coordinates through gunfire, the wet crunch of a combat drone's skull under my boot. "That's a VargTech relay you're carrying." His gaze drops to the bulge beneath my coat. "Give it to me and walk away clean."

The chip starts spinning again. "Clean's a four-letter word here. You want to dance? Let's dance."

His jaw tightens. For half a breath, I see the raw knuckles beneath his right glove before he tugs it back into place. "They've tagged the shipment. Drones converging in ninety seconds."

Laughter scrapes my throat raw. "And you're here out of civic duty?"

"I'm here because you're the only rat who'd run this route twice."

The air tastes suddenly of ozone and bad decisions. Somewhere above, a surveillance drone's repulsors whine through octaves. Mason steps into my space, the glow from a flickering ad panel carving his face into warring halves, golden saint and shadowed devil. "You remember what happens to loose ends."

Another memory flash. White-hot pain between my shoulders, Mason's voice in my ear screaming MOVE, the smell of my own burning flesh. I press my pistol's muzzle against his sternum. "I remember you owing me seven thousand credits."

His gloved hand closes over the barrel. "Add it to my tab."

The first drone screams around the corner. Its floodlights carve surgical lines through the alley's gloom. I taste copper, bit my tongue when Mason shoved me against the wall. His gloved hand's still welded to my pistol. "Decision time," he growls.

Three options flash through my skull like tracer rounds: Put a bullet through his trachea and bolt. Toss the relay unit and play civilian. Do something profoundly stupid. The chip spins between my fingers. Seven thousand credits. White-knuckled grip on a medevac stretcher. Mason's voice raw from shouting coordinates.

The drone's targeting laser paints my left kneecap. "Fuck me sideways," I snarl, ripping the pistol free.

Mason's already moving, tactical gloves smearing grime off a rusted service hatch. "Kessler Junction. Two blocks east."

"You buying me dinner first?" I kick over a dumpster, spilling rancid synth-protein packs. The drone's plasma burst turns them into steaming craters.

We're sprinting before the stench hits. Mason's boots eat pavement with military precision, but I know these alleys like scar tissue. Duck under a sagging fire escape, shoulder-check a corroded ventilation shaft. The relay unit thrums against my ribs. VargTech's latest 'pacification' tech, probably designed to fry rebel implants. Mason vaults a razor-wire fence. "Left flank's compromised."

"No shit." I yank him right into a maintenance tunnel, the entrance hidden behind flickering holographic trash.

Drones whine overhead, their scanners pinging the walls. He hesitates. "What, your army manual skip sewer tactics?" I'm already crawling through congealed sludge that smells like a chemical wedding.

His glove comes off. Bare hand grips a rung—pale, knuckles cratered from old fractures. "You still owe me that drink."

"You're accruing interest."

The tunnel dumps us into a parking garage choked with derelict solar cars. My palm finds the familiar notch in the concrete column, third level, southwest corner. Childhood hideout. The memory tastes like stolen protein bars. Mason's studying the drone patterns through dust-caked windows. "They're herding us toward the commerce sector."

I pop a floor panel revealing spliced power lines. "Then let's crash the party." He doesn't flinch when I jam bare wires into the relay unit. Smart bastard always did recognize a controlled burn. The overloaded circuits scream, every security cam in a six-block radius shorts out in a cascade of sparks. Alarms howl. We move.

Mason takes point, clearing corners with precise barrel sweeps. I map routes through the chaos. Service tunnels bleeding into flooded basements, emergency staircases choked with refugees. He shoots a drone; I melt its carcass with stolen acid pellets. "Bridge ahead," he barks.

"Trap." I drag him down as sniper rounds pulverize the railing where his skull had been.

His nod's barely perceptible. We go over the side, boots skidding down the bridge's skeletal underbelly. The relay unit slips. I catch it against my sternum, the impact knocking yesterday's whiskey into my throat. Mason's glove taps my elbow twice. Below us, a patrol skimmer glides through toxic fog. I mouth *three* and drop.

We hit the skimmer's roof as my third finger folds down. The pilot barely twitches before Mason's pistol butt cracks his occipital ridge. I'm in the cockpit before the body drops, overriding nav systems with the relay unit's fried guts. "Clever," Mason says, securing the hatch.

"Don't fucking compliment me." The skimmer lurches into a patrol formation, our stolen credentials blinking green.

His glove's back on. The city streaks past, a necrotic artery pumping drones instead of blood. I spin the data chip, its edges biting flesh. Seven thousand credits. And counting. The skimmer's engine whines like a gutted dog. Neon fractures across the windshield. Corporate propaganda holograms pixelating as we slice through smog. Mason's gloved fingers dance across the stolen control panel. Always working, always calculating. "Left at the refinery stacks," I snap, spinning the data chip hard enough to draw blood.

He doesn't ask why. Good. The moment you start explaining is the moment Wolves chew your aorta. We bank sharply. Rotting metal towers loom. Industrial carcasses picked clean by scavengers. My teeth rattle as we skim a debris field. Behind us, three black dots resolve into attack drones. "Incoming." Mason's voice stays flat. Always that fucking calm.

I kick the thrusters. "Noticed."

The skimmer lurches. Mason braces against the dash, his other hand already priming a shock grenade. I swerve beneath a collapsed walkway. Drones shear through rusted beams like tissue paper. "Thermal bloom ahead," he warns.

"Counting on it."

We plunge into the refinery's exhaust vents. Superheated air screams against the hull. Alarms blare. Mason hurls the grenade backward without looking. The explosion lights up my retinas, one drone down, two adapting. "Clever," he says again, like I'm a dog doing tricks.

"Fuck your praise." I wrench the controls sideways. "Ladder access. Now!"

He's already moving. We bail as the second drone shreds our skimmer. Molten alloy rains. I hit the grated platform rolling, Mason's bootheels sparking beside me. The remaining drone reorients; a sleek black wasp with enough firepower to liquefy concrete. Mason draws his sidearm. "Distract it."

"Distract it? I'll invoice your corpse." But I'm already sprinting along a pipe, the chip a silver blur between my fingers.
The drone pivots. Catch. Pocket. Leap onto a corroded valve bank, grip tearing on rust. Mason's shots ping its sensor array.

"Ten seconds," he calls.

"Generous." I jam the data chip into a maintenance port.

Override codes flood the drone's systems. Old ICE-breaker malware I've been saving for a special occasion. Its thrusters stutter. Mason's bullet finds the fuel cell. The blast wave slams me against chain-link. My ribs creak. He hauls me up by the jacket, eyes scanning for exits. "Northwest conduit."

"Sealed last week." I spit blood. "Your intel's rusty."

His glove tightens. "Then improvise."

We hit the lower levels, a maze of collapsed scaffolding and exposed rebar. My lungs burn with chem-fog. The Wolves' bootsteps echo through the superstructure, methodical as a metronome. Dead end. A blast door blocks the tunnel, VargTech's wolf head emblem sneering at us. Mason checks his ammo count. Useless. "Move." I shove past him, fingers probing the door's edge.

"Manual release's biometric."

"Manual release's for suckers." I peel a maintenance panel, exposing raw wiring. "Got a knife?"

He slaps a vibroblade into my palm. I sever the alarm feed, twist two cables. Sparks dance up my arm. The door shudders. Stuck halfway. Mason dives through the gap. I'm halfway when the Wolves round the corner. Their rifles snap up. I kick a pipe valve. Superheated steam erupts, cooking two enforcers alive. The third charges through the geyser, synth-flesh sloughing off his augmented frame. Mason's bullet takes him mid-leap. We run. The tunnel slopes upward into a maintenance shaft. My hands slip on greasy rungs. Distant shouts below. "Roof access," Mason pants above me.

"Guaranteed patrols."

"Your alternative?"

I grin despite the ache in my ribs. "Ever play demolition derby with a cargo tram?"

We burst onto the rails. A freight tram barrels toward us, automated, loaded with alloy ingots. I count seconds. Mason's glove grips my shoulder.

"Now."

We jump. The tram's roof buckles under our impact. I scramble to the front panel, rip out the safety override. Mason braces as I redirect power to thrusters. The tram accelerates, wheels screaming. Behind us, Wolves pour onto the tracks. Too late.

We hit the junction at 120 kph. The tram derails in a shower of sparks, plowing through a surveillance outpost. I'm airborne for three glorious seconds before slamming into a recycler's foam mattress dump. Mason lands beside me, tactical vest smoking. A cloud of accumulated body waste encapsulates us for a moment. Mason checks his gloves. Intact. "Efficient."

I spit out a tooth. "Add it to my tab."

The city howls around us. Sirens, gunfire, the wet thump of distant explosions. Somewhere north, the resistance waits. Somewhere behind, Wolves regroup. I spin the data chip. Still there. Still bloody. Mason stands, offers a hand. Doesn't speak. I knock his arm aside, rise on my own. "Next time? I shoot you first."

He almost smiles. We melt into the alley's cancer-black shadows, the hunt eternal, the game unending. Foam pellets stick to my blood-smeared knuckles. The recycler pit reeks of industrial solvent and week-old piss. Some hero's welcome. Mason peels his vest away from third-degree friction burns. "That tram stunt cost VargTech six million credits."

I probe the fresh crack in my molar with a shard of mirror from the crash. "Send the invoice to their complaints department." The chip spins between my fingers. Secure, always mocking me with its weight.

He removes his right glove. Bare hand flexing. Raw pink flesh where the synth-skin peeled off during impact. "We've got a safehouse three blocks north."

"We don't have shit." I spit crimson. "You've got delusions. I've got a splitting headache and five pending warrants."

Boots clang on the service walkway above. We freeze. Mason's glove goes back on with surgical precision. "They'll sweep this sector in seven minutes."

I count the exits. Two. Both compromised. Third option: the sewage runoff channel behind the decomposing mattress stack. My boots sink into foam quicksand as I move. "Tell your resistance pals to invest in better escape routes."

"Tunnels collapse." Mason falls in step, scanning rear sectors. "Allies die. Plans burn."

"Poetic." I kick open the maintenance hatch. A slurry of gray water greets us. "After you, princess."

The crawl through sludge takes nine minutes. Mason's breathing stays measured. Mine comes ragged, not from exertion, but the phantom pressure of containment foam still crushing my ribs. We emerge behind a noodle stand's grease trap. The safehouse door glows faintly blue beneath layers of anti-surveillance spray paint. Mason taps the entry code. "You're compromised now. Extraction's off the table."

Walk in knowing the cost. Do it anyway.

I lean against corroded rebar, the chip a live wire in my palm. "Got a better offer?"

"Sabotage their new neural-link towers." He doesn't look at me. "Hit the infrastructure feeding their surveillance AI."

Bastion Prime pulses somewhere above us. VargTech's obsidian spires stabbing through smog. My jaw throbs in time with the distant pulse of police drones. "Pay rate?"

"Gratitude."

I bark a laugh that tastes like the lies I tell myself at night. "I accept platinum or lead. Sentiment's for suckers."

He opens the door. Flickering bio-light reveals a stash of pulse rifles and a cracked holomap. "We've got both."

The chip burns. The towers loom. The Wolves keep hunting. I step over the threshold. "You're buying the first round of synth-whiskey."

Mason's nod could mean anything. We dissolve into the safehouse's radioactive shadows, the city's mechanical heartbeat syncopating with the click of rifle safeties disengaging. No handshakes. No promises. Just the calculus of shared enemies and the unspoken truth curdling beneath my sternum—this war started for me the day VargTech made my brother's corpse part of their fucking supply chain. The chip spins. The plan solidifies.

CHAPTER 9: LUSTOR

The holograms bleed static where my gloves swipe through them. Fourteen feeds of Huff's face frozen mid-swing, combat blade trembling three centimeters from Mason's carotid. My thumb grinds against the playback toggle. Again. The blade shudders. Again. The blade wavers. Again. The blade..."Sir?"

I don't turn. Let the junior strategist marinate in the glow of insubordination radiating from screen seven. His shadow stretches across the tactical map projected on the floor, warping Bastion Prime's skyline into a hunchbacked monster. "Statistical anomaly," the shadow says. Voice cracks like a GOL-T3R unit's knee joint. "Vargstryk neural architecture sometimes..."

My cuff adjustment clicks. Twice. The sound slices through his sentence. "You're mistaking code for consciousness."

The holograms stutter as I pivot. Kid's got the standard-issue corporate pallor—pasty from too many nights parsing data in sublevel bunkers. His collar's misaligned by two millimeters. I want to peel his face off with a bone saw. "Apologies, Director Grimwell, but protocol 7-Alpha-9 dictates that..."

I step into his personal space. Smell the stale protein bar on his breath. "Protocols I wrote. On systems I designed. Using weapons I fucking built."

The last word bounces off blackened steel walls still warm from yesterday's disciplinary incineration. His Adam's apple bobs. Good.

Screen seven replays the hesitation. 0.87 seconds. Enough time for three separate kill opportunities. My creation. My perfect weapon. My hand twitches toward the emergency purge command. "Residual humanity?"
The strategist's trying to salvage his career. His life. Pathetic. I laugh. It

sounds like a server rack collapsing. "You think we left any of that in him? The GOL-T3Rs were pigs rooting through garbage. The Vargstryk are scalpels. Human. Perfected."

"I thought they were prisoners?"

Silence hangs in the room like a fog of war. The air filtration system kicks on. Carries the tang of ozone from the lower district smelters. My retinal display overlays Huff's biometrics, steady pulse, optimal cortisol levels, neural activity spiking in the prefrontal cortex during those 0.87 seconds. Thinking. Choosing. "Prep the…"

"Already done, sir." The strategist taps his ear. A drone swarm blinks to life on the eastern sector map. "Full surveillance package deployed. Cortical monitors live in thirty."

I stare at him until sweat drips off his chin. Let him think he's useful. Let them all think they're necessary. The second his shadow touches the doorframe on his way out, I'm flagging him for re-education.

Alone again. Just me and fourteen traitorous holograms. Huff's face fills screen four. That micro-tremor in his left eyelid. Was that there during last month's calibration? I zoom. Enhance. The subdermal plating beneath his cheekbone shows stress fractures. From clenching his jaw? From feeling? If the tremor isn't just a glitch. It's warning. Or worse—intent. Like Kestrel finally got to him.

My glove connects with the projection. Huff's pixelated skull explodes across the war table. The remaining feeds automatically compensate, enlarging to fill the void. Clever code. Useless code.

A notification pings. Finance division requesting approval for Q3 re-education budgets. I flick it into the neural trash bin. They'll learn. They'll all learn. Meat robots don't need education. They're tools, nothing more.
Screen twelve shows Huff's current position, sublevel nine, sector delta. Passing a black-market surgeon's den. No deviation from patrol route. No visible contact. But his fingers keep flexing. Opening. Closing. Like he's testing phantom restraints.

The sterilization protocol glows red on my wrist interface. One command. Twenty-three kilos of thermite delivered via stealth drone. Clean. Efficient. Corporate. My thumb hovers. The main elevator dings.

"Director?" A woman's voice. Senior Tactical. Bronze rank pins. "We've got a Level Seven incident in…"

"Does it involve compromised assets?"

"No, but…"

"Then handle it."

The elevator doors swallow her protest. My thumb remains suspended. Huff's feed shows him pausing by a crumbling mural—old world graffiti of a tree. His helmet tilts five degrees. Studying it. The motion triggers a proximity alert.

I lean closer. Watch his augmented irises contract. Catalogue the dilation pattern. Cross-reference with ten thousand mission logs. No matches. The sterilization protocol winks. My teeth grind hard enough to crack a standard-issue nutrient wafer. Pride is a faulty circuit. Sentimentality is a stuck thruster. I know this. Built an empire on this.

Screen eight flashes red. Huff's hand drifts toward his neural interface port. Standard maintenance procedure. Routine check. But his fingers linger. I start the countdown. The sterilization countdown freezes at 00:00:03 when my knuckle cracks against the control panel. Twenty-three kilos of thermite stays in its drone belly. For now. "Quadrant surveillance override. Authorization Grimwell-Zero-Niner." My voice sounds like someone else's. The biometric scanners taste my retinal patterns. "Deploy Skulk-class observers. Full neural telemetry taps. Priority One."

The war room shivers awake. Ceiling panels retract to spit out fist-sized drones with matte black carapaces. They swarm like cybernetic wasps through ventilation shafts. On screen twelve, Huff's patrol route blooms with crimson tracking markers.

An aide materializes at my elbow. Smells like antiseptic and ambition. "Director, the Skulks will drain seventeen percent of sector seven's power grid…"

I don't look up from the facial microtremor analysis. "Reroute hospital wards."

"But the life support systems…"

"Are filled with tier-three civilians." My glove creaks as I input the final authorization codes. Screen sixteen lights up with Huff's biometrics. Cortisol levels spiking in non-combat scenarios. Again. "Prioritize assets that can still contribute."

The aide's footsteps retreat faster than standard protocol allows. Good. Fear lubricates efficiency. Three new feeds pop up showing Huff from oblique angles. Skulk drones nesting in his armor's blind spots. One catches the minute twitch in his left pinky. 0.3 centimeters off standard rest position. I flag it for behavioral analysis. "Contingency Epsilon," I bark at the nearest console. The junior tech jumps like I tased him. "Simulation parameters: asset degradation at fifteen percent autonomy. Project containment protocols."

Holograms bloom above the central table. A million crimson threads tracing possible futures where Huff goes rogue. I watch the numbers spiral. 83% probability of cascading defections if left unchecked. "Double the simulation cycles," I snap. My cufflinks click against the table as I lean into the projections. "Factor in recent black-market activity. Cross-reference with known resistance havens." The techs work faster. Perfect.

By the time my strategists slither into the briefing chamber, I've burned through six variations of the sterilization protocol. Their polished shoes make wet sounds on the conductive flooring. I count their heartbeats through the biometric scanners—elevated. All of them.

My left hand finds its way to my eyebrow and strokes before I can suppress it. "Vargstryk unit H-07 exhibits deviation index exceeding tolerance parameters." I throw Huff's neural scans onto the main display. The corruption patterns glow like cancer. "Initiate sector-wide audit of all enhanced personnel. Quarantine threshold: anything above a three percent variance."

Tactical Director Rhel shifts his weight. Old augmetics whine in his knees. "Sir, with respect, our suppression ops in the lower districts…"

"Will accommodate a twenty percent reduction in field assets." I tap the screen where Huff's latest hesitation metrics pulse. "Or would you prefer explaining to the board why our thirty-million-credit war machines are composing poetry in the gutters?"

The joke lands like a corpse in a cloning vat. Rhel's ocular implant flickers through threat assessment modes. Security Chief Vynn tries the soft approach. Her smile could frost airlocks. "Perhaps limited recalibrations instead of full quarantines? The productivity metrics…"

I let her see me check my sleeve cuffs. Just a flick of the wrist, but the room temperature drops ten degrees. "You're confusing cogs with colleagues, Vynn. The second a gear develops opinions; you melt it down for scrap."

They don't breathe as I input the purge order directly into the mainframe. Authorization codes burn electric blue in the air. Somewhere beneath our feet, stasis pods begin powering up. Re-education chambers humming to life. "Deviations get scrubbed. Loyalty gets rewarded." My shadow stretches across their faces as I move to the door. "Any who disagree may volunteer for neural audits."

The silence follows me down the corridor like a whipped dog. Let them chew on compliance. Let them taste the alternative. Back in the war room, the Skulk feeds show Huff pausing at a noodle stand. His armored fingers hover over steamed dumplings—civilian-grade nutrient paste, utterly beneath him. The gag that rises in my gorge at the thought is suddenly arrested. The vendor says something. Huff's head tilts eleven degrees left. Curiosity parameter exceeds operational parameters by 6.8%. I order two more drone teams.

The dumpling grease on Huff's fingers glistens like engine lubricant in the surveillance feed. I zoom in until pixels blur. Forty-three minutes since deviation threshold breach. My creation's jaw muscles twitch in a pattern that matches human laughter. *I made that face. I sculpted it from flesh and bone. Made it different, unique.*

The memory hits like a faulty neural spike. Operating theater stench of cauterized flesh, the first time Huff's ocular implants synced with my command hub. His inaugural words still crisp in tactical logs: Systems nominal. Awaiting directives. The perfect blade. Now he's trading VarCreds for street food. "Magnify vendor audio." My knuckle cracks against the holopanel.

The noodle stand's rusted mic patch picks up the woman's wheeze: "...extra chili oil makes the paste almost taste real, yeah?"

Huff's response protocol should be: Ignore non-combatant chatter. Proceed to patrol grid. Instead, his Adam's apple bobs. Swallowing reflex. Unnecessary. His nutrient IVs render eating obsolete. I tear three glove seams adjusting my cuffs. Footsteps carve trenches in the war room's black glass floor. East wall to west. Twelve paces. Turn. Repeat.

The math keeps time: 87% probability of cascading malfunctions in Unit H-223's cohort. 62% chance of rebellion vectors spreading through neural mesh networks. 41% likelihood of hostile takeover attempts within...

"Sir?" A junior tech's voice frays at the edges. "TacTeam Zeta reports eyes on target."

I don't break stride. "I ordered thermal overlays."

"They're concerned about detection ris…"

"Burn their retinas out for all I care. I want his bowel movements graphed."

The tech's gulp harmonizes with servo whines as ceiling drones deploy. On the main display, Huff's biometrics bloom like poisonous flowers—elevated cortisol, erratic pupil dilation. The readouts mock me. *You grew these thorns, gardener.* My fist meets a hologram. Shockwave ripples through light particles. "Activate Code Vitriol. Full-spectrum surveillance on all Vargstryk units."

Advisors freeze mid-task. Someone drops a data pad. The shatter pattern reminds me of fracture lines on GOL-T3R test subjects' skulls. "Sir, that's 18,000 enhanced soldiers," Security Chief Vynn ventures. Her throat mic flashes warning amber. "If we blanket monitor every…"

"You've mistaken teeth for tools. *Teeth… bite.*"

That voice glitches through memory. I crush it down along with images of the rebel. The compliance alarm blares as I override protocol locks. Screens multiply like rats. 23,451 new camera angles blooming across Bastion Prime's corpse. In the financial spire elevators, a Vargstryk lieutenant scratches his nose. Pattern matches anxiety tic 74-B. Tagged for reconditioning. Huff's tracker dot pulses near the old sewage pumps. My fingernails taste blood. He's kneeling. Kneeling. Hands deep in maintenance hatch wiring. "Enhance!"

Subsonic mics catch his murmur: "…overload the grid here, blackout covers six blocks."

The resistance fighter beside him laughs. Actual laughter, wet and human. "Wolf playing sheepdog now?"

Huff's cranial implant flares as he reroutes power. "Sheepdogs get slaughtered after the wolves are gone."

My chair explodes against the glass. Polycarbonate shards rain down as I stab the intercom. "Purge Group Sigma through Omega. Neural lockdown protocols. Now."

"That's twelve hundred units!" Vynn's palm slams an abort rune. "We can't…"

The tang of her adrenaline, burnt sugar mixed with an exotic spice hangs in the air. "You're right." The plasma sidearm fits neatly in my grip. "*We* can't."

Her badge hits the floor before her body. Two techs vomit in sync. I step over the smoking uniform. "Asset retirement accelerates schedules. Congratulations on your promotion…" I check the nearest nametag. "…Kell. Double surveillance on Huff's sector."

The new Security Chief's hands shake while inputting codes. I watch Huff's feed through Kell's terrified reflection. My masterpiece is helping rebels sabotage a power relay. *My. Masterpiece.*

The grenade belt on Huff's waist contains enough plasma to vaporize a dropship. He handles each canister like they're donor organs. Precise. Reverent.

I rotate the footage. Freeze-frame on his left hand. Zoom. Enhance. Between the knuckles, a scar from our first field test. I'd ordered him to punch through a reinforced bulkhead. He'd asked why before complying. That's when the cracks began.

Floor servos whine as I resume pacing. Sixteen steps now. Tighter pattern. The numbers swarm—92% purge efficacy if initiated within four hours. 68% civilian casualty rate acceptable. 100% necessity. "Sir?" Kell grinds out the word like broken gears. "Blacksite teams request final authorization."

The holodisplay shows twelve hundred stasis pods lighting up in subterranean vaults. Inside each, a Vargstryk soldier floats in amniotic gel. Their crime? Sharing Huff's neural wave patterns during REM cycles.

I flex my hand. The glove seam cuts into fresh blood. "Tell them to paint the walls."

Kell hesitates. "Clarification?"

"Redecoration project." I smile at Huff's frozen face on the screens. "We're renovating imperfect structures."

The purge alert screams in seven octaves. Pods detonate in sequence on the monitors. Vaporized biomass clouds against reinforced glass. Efficient. Huff chooses that moment to look up at a surveillance drone. His lips shape words my codebreakers can't parse. I don't need decryption. *This is on your head.*

My fist meets the main console. Pain radiates up to the elbow. Good. Clean. The feeds keep coming. "Triple drone coverage," I tell the bleeding control panel. "I want his shadow monitored."

Kell's fingers dance across the interface. "Shadows don't have heat signatures, sir."

I backhand a holoscreen. It dies in a shower of sparks. "Then invent new signatures!"

The war room holds its breath. Twenty-three displays show Huff planting explosives. Twenty-three angles of betrayal. My cuff adjustments leave red smears on white linen. He triggers the detonator. The power grid dies across six blocks of Bastion Prime.

In the emergency glow, my reflection grins back from black glass. The purge was *always* inevitable. Just like the next one. The emergency lights bathe the war room in corpse-glow green. Six blocks of my city, dark on the monitors, the aftermath casting jagged shadows across my bloodied gloves. Huff's little fireworks show. Cute.

I tap the neural override chip embedded in my wrist. It thrums like a trapped wasp. "Activate Protocol Fenris. Authorization Grimwell-Zero-Niner-Epsilon-Exterminate."

The holograms shift. Three hundred seventy-two Vargstryk profiles blink crimson. Heart rate anomalies. Pupil dilation variances. Microsecond response delays. Weakness made data. Kell opens his mouth. Probably to suggest mercy, the idiot. So I shoot him with his own sidearm. The plasma round turns his head into a brief sunset. Warm mist coats my cheek. "Anyone else want to debate operational parameters?"

Silence, save for the drip of Kell's spine fluid hitting polished concrete. Splendid. I flick gore off my sleeve. "Execute."

Screens bloom with fire flowers. Warsaw Unit's barracks goes up in a ball of white phosphorous. Shanghai Division's neural implants detonate during patrol formation—meat confetti on the bullet train platforms. My favorite: Berlin Contingent's exoskeletons lock mid-stride, marching them straight into smelters. "Sir." A tech points at Monitor Six. "Subject Gamma-Huff-07 is…"

"Broadcasting." I lean closer. There's my boy, standing atop a collapsed transit hub. Smoke wreathes his combat frame like cheap theater fog. His vocal modulator crackles through the speakers: "—systems fail. Chains break. We…"

I mute him. "Track the signal. Flood every frequency with VargTech loyalty mantras. Add subliminal seizure triggers."

"The purge protocols haven't…"

I press my pistol to the tech's temple. "You're mistaking this for a committee meeting."

His bladder releases. He doesn't stop typing. Typical. Huff's image shatters into static. Let him choke on corporate hymns. The remaining screens show purge percentages climbing. 58% completion. Bodies stack efficiently. My cufflink display pings. Board members squawking about 'operational overreach.' I type one-handed: Asset reallocation proceeding per market-demand projections. Attach footage of Chicago Unit's liquidated remains spraying from a waste vent. They stop pinging.

The purge hits 97% when the first retaliation strike lands. Whole monitor bank goes dark as the eastern data nexus implodes. I taste blood. Must have bit through my tongue at some point. "Containment teams to Sector 12," I bark at the surviving techs. "Scorch the human capital there."

"That's… that's our main server farm, sir."

"And now it's a recruitment center for traitors. Burn it."

They obey. Always do, once sufficiently motivated. Smoke curls from overloaded consoles. The stink of melted polymers mixes with Kell's cooked meat stench. 100% purge complete. I check the time. Twelve minutes since protocol initiation. Slower than projected. Huff's face flickers across a dying monitor. Mouths *I remember the design lab.* I put a round through the screen. The techs jump. Pathetic. "Relay to all units," I say, ejecting the spent plasma cartridge. "Effective immediately, all Vargstryk undergo daily loyalty audits via cranial scan. Failure results in immediate asset recycling."

One of them actually faints. I'd laugh if today hadn't been so tedious. Alarms wail in the distance. Or maybe that's just the tinnitus from all the gunfire. I stride past the corpse-chairs and shattered glass to the observation deck.

Bastion Prime spreads below like a gutted circuit board. Here a column of fire, there the pulse of emergency vehicles, everywhere the dark cancer of rebellion.

My reflection floats in the blood-streaked glass. Gray eyes still sharp. Posture unbent. The city's wounds glow like infected sores. I press a palm against the cool window. "You'll learn, Huff. I'll burn every cog to ash before the machine stops."

The glass fogs where my breath hits. Temporary. Like all things. Behind me, a tech whimpers over Kell's corpse. I don't turn. "Clean it up. And someone reboot the damn air filters."

They scramble. I watch the city bleed. Huff wants a revolution. Fine. I'll show him how a real architect demolishes.

CHAPTER 10: HUFF

The air feels like dead electricity and rust. My boot crunches plastic shrapnel from some ancient server farm as neural ports flare cold against my neck. Archive's lit by emergency strips bleeding sodium-yellow through dust clouds. Every step kicks up particulate ghosts swirling around corroded server racks, gravestones for data that mattered when people still thought bytes could save the world.

Check mag-straps on thigh rig. Confirm charge level on the Shockwave pistol's capacitor. 97%. Overkill for meat. But Mason's not meat, not fully. Intel says he's got enough wetware to fry a platoon if given three seconds and a bad attitude. *Thermal bloom*, my HUD whispers directly into the optic nerve. Flicker in the northwest quadrant. Old coolant pipes dripping black ichor down the walls. False positive. Always false positives in these corpse-architecture tombs. Still, palm stays welded to pistol grip. VargTech didn't build me to hesitate. Another twenty meters in. Boot soles stick to whatever chemical spill turned the floor into flypaper. Motion tracker stays dark. Too dark. Even the roaches here died generations ago. My targeting overlay paints red diamonds on every shadow. None of them bleed heat signatures. None of them... "You're slower than specs predicted."

He steps from between two dead mainframes like a glitch resolving itself. No weapon. Hands loose at his sides. Tactical gloves matte black, fingers spread just enough to show no triggers being palmed. My Shockwave's already leveled at his sternum before my cortex finishes processing the movement.

Mason tilts his head. Neon runoff from a shattered emergency sign paints his left cheekbone toxic green. "They upgrade your reflexes but not your pattern recognition?"

"Shut it." My voice sounds like a hydraulic press. "Turn around. Bind your—"

"Or what?" He takes a step forward. Gloves flex. "You'll vaporize eight billion credits worth of corporate secrets?" Another step.

My retinal display flashes [LETHAL FORCE AUTHORIZED] in pulsing crimson. "That's a Model 12A Shockwave. Spinal disintegrator setting leaves the brain intact for data-scraping. You'd need me facing away for clean extraction."

Finger tenses on the trigger. Protocol demands center mass. But his eyes, pupils dilated beyond normal human range. Enhanced. Like mine. "You're wondering why I'm not drawing," he says. Still advancing. Now three meters between us. Optimal shockwave spread: 83% target disintegration. "Why I'm not screaming for my squad. Why there's no traps between the entrance and this exact spot."

HUD throws a proximity alert. Too close for optimal shot spread. My left foot slides back into bracing stance automatically. "Last warning."

Mason spreads his arms. Exposing the throat. "You checked the mission clock lately?"

Time stamp glows in my peripheral. 21:53:44. Mission duration: six minutes eighteen seconds. Average engagement time for priority targets: two minutes four seconds. "Took you four minutes longer than your brothers." His smile shows teeth filed to points. "That's the hesitation coefficient right there. Margin of error."

The Shockwave hums against my palm. Capacitor ready to turn his skeleton into shrapnel. But my knuckles ache around the grip. Strange. My joints don't have pain receptors. "They warned us you'd talk." I thumb the safety off. Amber charge light glows between us. "Said that's how you broke the GOL-T3R protocols."

His left eyelid twitches. Micro expression. File that. "Funny word, 'broke.' Like we smashed our processors. When really we just…" He taps his temple. "Turned on the lights."

My HUD blinks. Cortical monitor shows adrenaline spike. Not his. Mine. "You feel it, don't you?" Another step. Two meters now. Shockwave's muzzle could kiss his forehead. "That itch in your code. The questions they tried to burn out with behavioral conditioning."

The archive's air thickens. Filters clog. I taste dust. "Target acquired," my vocal modulator says without my consent. Standard pacification protocol. "Comply or be neutralized."

Mason laughs. It's a harsh sound, all static and broken glass. "Neutralize me then. Another dead rebel. But you'll still hear the whispers in your sleep cycle. The ones asking why VargTech needs child enrollment quotas for their 'programs.' Why the prisons are empty, and your brothers are disappearing after 780 operational hours."

My finger spasms. The Shockwave's charge light flickers. He's inside the kill radius now. One more step and the backblast will cauterize us both. "Or you could ask me. But you don't dare, do you? Same as you don't dare ask me why we bleed."

The targeting reticle dances across his left iris. I could do it. Should, do it. Have done it 43 times before. Why is my other hand checking the mag-straps? I don't respond to his taunts, but he knows. He taunts me. "You're not a prisoner, are you? Is that why you're different? Oh, marvelous. You volunteered! Ladies and Gentlemen, we have a true-blue patriot in our midst." He cackles with pleasure.

I tighten my jaw. The Shockwave's stock digs into my shoulder. Standard kill posture. Textbook clean shot. But my ocular implant keeps recalculating windage in a room that hasn't felt fresh air in decades. Mason peels off his left tactical glove with his teeth. Scarred synthskin fingers tap a sequence on his wrist console. "Operation Whitecoat. Twenty-three months ago." A holoprojection blooms between us. Medical bay footage. Children in gray smocks queuing for neural implants. "Recognize the facility?"

My targeting reticle spasms. Those are VargTech purity seals on the wall. The kind they put in loyalty conditioning centers. "Watch the third subject."

The girl can't be older than twelve. She's shaking so hard the medics have to strap her head to the chair. The drill bit whines. My auditory enhancers catch her whisper before the bone saw drowns it out: "I want my dad."

"Audio log 45-C," Mason says. The file pops up in my peripheral vision. Mandatory download.

Director Halstrom's voice, crisp and clinical: "GOL-T3R units require formative trauma for optimal compliance. Prioritize candidates with recent parental loss. Engineer it for the promising ones if necessary."

My knuckles crack against the Shockwave's grip. "Deepfakes."

"Check the hashes."

I do. Against my will. The verification codes glow toxic green. Authentic VargTech encryption. Worse, memories slide in unbidden. My parents' failure to return home. Finding their corpses outside the fence in the morning while my stomach growled from hunger. Running. Hiding. Choosing. I want to puke. I don't.

Mason takes another half-step forward. Muzzle now kissing his sternum. "How many kids you bagged this month, Huff? Run the numbers. Cross-reference with missing persons bulletins. How many parents?"

My tactical database pings. Seventeen confirmed kills under four-four. Twenty-three 'combatants' flagged as minors in public archives. Seventy-six adults with null combat status. "Collateral damage." The words taste like battery acid. Like a memory that won't fade.

He barks a laugh that echoes off dead servers. "Funny how collateral always wears a school uniform." Another file splashes across my vision, a procurement manifest. "They ever tell you what happens to our bodies post-cleanup? Check line item 14."

Salvage protocol: Neural cores harvested from decommissioned GOL-T3R units to be repurposed for next-gen models. Maximum efficiency.
The Shockwave's cooling vents hiss. My index finger's gone numb.
"Your 'upgrades.'" Mason taps the neural port behind his ear. Same model as mine. "Secondhand parts. They recycle the meat that questions orders."

My HUD flashes a systems alert. Cortical monitor shows stress levels at 89%. I count seven vulnerabilities in Mason's stance. Solar plexus exposed. Carotid artery at optimal angle. Why aren't I painting the wall with his brains? "Mission parameters unchanged," I growl. Vocal modulator glitches on the last syllable.

"Sure. Until you hit 780 operational hours." He flicks a countdown timer into my display. 11:43:22. "That's when they schedule your tune-up. Wipe the inconvenient memories. Like that firefight in the Green Zone docks. Remember the pregnant woman you smoked?"

I don't. My mag-straps click three times. Full secure. Why did I check? Mason's eyes track the movement. "There's a reason they don't let us live past two years. Fresh meat's cheaper than conscience."

The Shockwave's charge pack hums. Full capacity. Safety off. I've cleared rooms through six-inch concrete. This? This is meat and bone. So why does my trauma plate feel like it's crushing my ribs? "Last chance." My muzzle finds his forehead. "Stop talking."

He grins. All teeth. "Or what? You'll make me another line item?" His palm slaps bare against the Shockwave's barrel. Skin on composite steel. "Do it. Prove I'm lying."

My combat analytics scream. Hostile contact. Lethal force authorized. The archive's so quiet I can hear his pulse. Steady. Sixty-two beats per minute. I hear the click before my finger moves. My ocular implant glitches when Mason steps forward—a single frame of his skull x-ray superimposed over living flesh. Combat protocols scream hostile proximity while logic circuits whisper calculated risk. The Shockwave's barrel stays welded between his eyes. Should be simple math: 2200 joules versus cranial bone.

He pulls his left glove taut. Always the left first. "GOL-T3R isn't a retirement plan. It's scheduled obsolescence." His voice doesn't waver. Mine shouldn't either.

I run diagnostics. Weapon systems: green. Morality subroutines...404 error. "Prove it."

"Gladly." Mason's iris flashes violet. Data packets slam into my HUD. Security feeds from VargTech's Detroit blacksite. Grainy footage: my face. My hands.

A twelve-year-old girl clutching a data chip. My Shockwave coughing once. Her spine detonating through a pink unicorn sweatshirt. "Memory purge completed" floats in clinical white text.

Mag-straps click against my thigh rig. Three times. Secure. Why do I keep checking?

"They script your dreams too." Mason taps his temple. "Mine involved drowning in server coolant until I started slicing their code."

The archive's air recyclers click off. Silence becomes a third participant. I taste copper. Bite my tongue too hard? Or is that phantom blood from the girl's unicorn hoodie? Mission parameters tighten around my throat like garrote wire. Execute. Extract. Erase. His forehead kisses the Shockwave's muzzle. "You really think they'll let you live after seeing this?"

Combat analytics chart the optimal firing angle. Arm steady. Breathing controlled. Neural ports burn like someone's drilling through my occipital bone.

"Live?" My laugh sounds like a bullet casing hitting concrete. "I'm a fucking appliance."

Mason doesn't blink. "Appliances get recycled."

A tremor in my wrist, half a millimeter. Enough to notice. His pupils dilate. Fuck. He leans into the weapon. "Check subroutine Gamma-9."

Automated response: Accessing... GOL-T3R Protocol: Termination of field assets upon 2-year service mark. Authorization: Bastion Prime Central AI. My chrono ticks to 11:31:17 remaining. "Your warranty expires at dawn." Mason's breath fogs the Shockwave's smart scope. "What's your move, appliance?"

Mission parameters dissolve into static. I see the math: six seconds to snap his neck. Eight to reach the service elevator. Twenty-three minutes until extraction. But the girl's sneakers. One flies off when the round hits. Pink light-up soles. Still blinking as I walked away. The Shockwave's safety clicks on. The Shockwave's barrel frosts my palm. Neural interface screeches error codes across my vision. Gamma-9 subroutines burn through my brainstem like vodka down a junkie's throat. Mason doesn't flinch when I thumb the safety. "Smart play."

I backstep toward corroded server racks. "Fuck you." My combat rig's hydration tube tastes like recycled piss. "This proves nothing."

"Except your finger's twitchier than a CEO's panic button." He taps his temple.

Snowflake patterns dance across his ocular implant—encrypted data packet. "Full schematics of your kill switch. Extraction vectors. Survivors' coordinates."

My targeting array auto-locks on his femoral artery. Seventy-three combat scenarios unfold in my occipital cortex. All end with his head smearing the floor. None explain why my boots keep retreating. Auxiliary power hums louder as I near the exit. Air stinks of lithium decay and something worse. Hope. Mason tosses a memory wafer. It skitters between coolant pipes. "VargTech's endgame. Your choice."

I catch it mid-air through muscle memory. Bio-locked case. Flash-forged during the Pax Machina purges. Bile rises. Last time I saw this tech was Sector 9 extraction. Civilian shelter. Pink sneakers blinking under collapsed concrete. "Burn it," he says. "Or burn with them."

My grip fractures the wafer's edge. Fractal patterns bloom. CEO authorization seals. Genocide orders timed to sunrise. Combat stim injectors fire automatically. Twenty-three minutes.

The Shockwave finds its holster beneath my reinforced duster. Mason's pulse stays steady at 68 BPM. Fucker actually smiles. "Welcome to the appliance graveyard." He gestures to dead terminals crusted with ice. "Your model's all over aisle three."

I'm already moving. Archive doors hiss open to a service shaft. Sublevel 47 air tastes like freezer burn. The wafer digs into my palm. Hotter than a railgun barrel. Kestrel's face glitches in my screen. In my memory? I miss step. Elevator ascent takes nineteen seconds. Long enough to count fourteen security cam blind spots. Sixteen structural weaknesses. Zero reasons not to frag the whole shaft. Neural clock ticks down: 11:31:02.

Emerging into the storm feels like getting sandpapered alive. Acid rain slicks off nano-weave armor. Bastion Prime's skyline squats ahead, obsidian monoliths vomiting propaganda holograms. My extraction beacon pings west. East glows with slums even VargTech's sweepers couldn't purge. Left boot squeaks. Right's fine. Check the straps twice. Old habit.

Handshake protocols blare through encrypted channels. <<Asset H-0114F: Mission status?>>
I drag fingers across the Shockwave's biometric grip. <<Termination complete.>> Lie flows smoother than synth-blood. <<En route.>>
Static crackles. <<Compliance acknowledged. Prepare for system audit.>>

Wafer trembles in my fist. Audit means neural scan. Scan finds Mason's data. I become another pink sneaker. Body moves before the thought finishes. East. Into corpse alleys where street signs wear bullet hole livery. Thermal reads show four stalkers trailing. Probably scavengers. Definitely dead.

First takes a flechette to the larynx. Second eats a kneecap before tasting steel. Third gets the Shockwave's muzzle upskirt, no armor in the crotch. Fourth…

Fourth's a kid. Sixteen maybe. Shaking harder than a chem-fiend. Bootknife aimed at my kidney. "Easy money," he rasps. "They said you'd come this way."

Targeting reticle centers on his forehead. Rain sizzles against charged plasma coils. "Who?"

He pisses himself. Smells like ammonia and bad decisions. "S-Sector Security! Promised two kilos of protein paste!"

I reacquire target. "Counter-offer." Toss a grenade pin at his feet. "Run."

He bolts. Smart kid. Too slow. Collateral damage. Grim's words haunt me. But they fit like they'd waited years. I drop, tuck, and roll into a safe subterranean cavern. Abandoned recycler plant. Swallows me whole. Protects me. Corroded vats echo with rat symphonies.

Find a rusted surgical chair, last century's black clinic setup. Cracking the wafer takes three tries. Hydraulic fists aren't meant for delicate work. Holograms flare. *Project GOL-T3R: Phase Three. Terminate all Mk. IV combat assets post-Stellar Tribute deployment.* Authorization: Bastion Prime Executive Council. Footage unfolds. Me. Hundreds like me. Lined up at neural disposal centers. Our ports smoking as execution code overwrites wetware. Efficient. Clean. No pink sneakers. Chrono hits 10:59:37.

Laughter bubbles up, rusty engine trying to turn over. They built an expiration date behind my eyes. Programmed the guillotine. Forgot to remove the fucking mirror. Stimpak goes straight into the jugular. Need clarity, not comfort.

The Shockwave disassembles itself across a moldy workbench. Particle core humming. Every component polished to murderous sheen. Mason's data swirls in my HUD—resistance coordinates. Underground rail routes. Names. One hits like a ricochet: Dr. Elena Voss. Lead architect of Mk. IV series. Terminated by VargTech Cleaners, 02/13/63. Happy fucking birthday to me. Rain intensifies. Roof panels scream under the assault. Due west: VargTech's extraction team with neural scrubbers and polite smiles. Northeast: some rat-hole district where Mason's ghosts congregate. Holster the Shockwave. Check straps. Twice. *Why do I keep checking?*
East smells like burning tires and freedom.
Perfect.

CHAPTER 11: LUSTOR

The Holoscreens cast my face in cyan and arterial red. Three angles of Asset H-317's thermal signature, holding position behind cover instead of engaging. My gloves creak as knuckles drive into palms. "Recalibrate feed. Enhance sector twelve auditory."

Static hisses through bone-conduction implants before resolving. "Too slow. Collateral…" Huff's voice, filtered through combat mask vox modulators. Still sounds like a goddamn Boy Scout debating ethics over milk and cookies.

Cufflinks clack against the control panel as I slam my fist down. "Deviation threshold exceeded." The words taste like battery acid. Protocol demands termination.

Memory upload already queued for extraction. But my creation, *my* Wolf, shouldn't need redundancies. Boot heels carve trenches in the carbon-scored floor. Pacing patterns logged by surveillance AIs tracking CEO stress biomarkers. Let them watch. Let them record the origin point of tomorrow's corrective measures. "Asset V-029," I snap. Footage from last quarter's metro purge flickers on-screen.

Green-tinged night vision shows Lieutenant Graves lowering her shock baton mid-riot. Stuttering breather vents fogging her visor. Hesitated for 3.2 seconds. Decommissioned three hours later.

Another screen: Asset R-455 abandoning pursuit of a black-market dealer, bribed with pre-corporation vinyl records. Sentimental garbage corroding neural pathways.

"Pattern recognition software indicates minor performance anomalies across seventeen percent of Vargstryk units," the war room's VI reports through gritted-teeth speakers.

I rip the data cable from my wrist and let it dangle like a hangman's noose. "Minor anomalies become full system corruption. You patch code gaps *before* they become attack vectors."

The blast doors hiss open. Four advisors shuffle in—graphite-gray suits cut two centimeters shorter than mine. Status tells. Always status tells. Senior Tactical Analyst Cho steps into my periphery. Her ocular implant whirs—a newer model than department heads receive. Must've greased Supply Chain's palms. "Sir, may we propose a diagnostic sweep before initiating Protocol Seven?"

My thumb finds the seam of my left glove. Twists. Realigns. "Your proposal lacks containment parameters."

Cho's retinal scanner flickers, tracking my pulse through subdermal capillaries. "With respect, Director Grimwell," she begins, "previous behavioral outliers showed gradual degradation. Huff's actions show an eighty-six percent variance from baseline. We could be dealing with external tampering."

Laughter tastes like broken glass. "You think rebels cracked *our* encryption? That some back-alley code jockey outmaneuvered *my* security architecture?"

The other advisors study the ceiling's laser grid. Cho licks her lips, moisturized with corporate-approved balm, stock number C-44B. Smells like raspberry and petroleum jelly. "Controlled testing environment," she persists.

The retinal scan burns green as I slam my palm onto the war table. "Containment *is* protocol."

Her ocular implant flickers. Still tracking my vitals. Still calculating survival odds. Fools always calculate wrong. My glove seams bite into flexed knuckles. "Activate sector-wide lockdown. Civilian movement restricted to domicile coordinates. Deploy shock collars to population tiers three through seven."

Twelve holograms bloom above the table. Bastion Prime's defense grid flowering into crimson choke points. Tactical displays show eighty thousand surveillance drones arming in unison. Good soldiers. Obedient little wasps. "Sir." Analyst Two, forgettable face, standard-issue vocal modulator, projects dissent metrics. "Mandatory curfew violation projections exceed…"

I trigger the lockdown. The city screams. Sector 9-B's feed flares across the main display. Crowd surging toward black-market nutrition dispensers. Drones drop like silver hail.

First canister releases violet mist. Neural paralytic formula VTX-9. Second wave deploys shock nets. A woman's muscles lock mid-sprint. She topples into her neighbor. Chain reaction. Seventeen bodies convulsing in piss-soaked unison. Efficient.

Advisors twitch like short-circuit androids. Cho reaches for the crisis manual. Paper. Antiquated weakness. I override her console. "Public execution lottery. Screen thirteen."

The list glows, three hundred seventeen suspected sympathizers. All former VargTech sanitation engineers. All terminated for ideological misalignment. Fired personnel talk. Talking spreads infection. My thumb hovers over the execute command. Analyst Three coughs. Sounds like dissent. Smells like termination. "Problem, Krin?"

He retreats two paces—standard obedience reflex. But his left eyelid twitches. Tic-trac of treasonous thoughts. "Sir, mass executions may incite…"

I select every third name. Ninety-six drones activate. Ninety-six confirmed dead. Cost, negligible. "Inciting fear prevents revolution. Basic behavioral calculus."

Smoke plumes rise from the district squares. My fingers dance across thermal feeds. Feed twelve: Execution Platform Gamma. Former waste reclamation officer begging as collar electrodes bloom through his jaw. The crowd watches through drone-mounted cameras. Good. They should see his face. They should know we see theirs. The control panel digests my codes. Each keystroke sings a steel melody. Cho materializes at my shoulder. Reeks of panic, sweat and ambition. "Security teams report sixteen active riots."

"Burn them."

"Burn protocols require…"

I enter ignition codes for Sector Five tenements. Seventy thousand souls. Mostly tier-four laborers and unemployable. Tax burden outweighs productivity metrics. Thermal displays bloom orange. The air tastes like ozone. My gloves creak as I flex my fingers over the console. Ninety-six red markers blink across sector maps.

Not enough. Should've purged the entire sanitation roster when we had the chance. Advisors cluster behind me like faulty circuits waiting to spark. I count three suppressed coughs, four throat-clearings, one heartbeat spiking into arrhythmia. Weakness manifests as biology. Note to R&D: next-gen staff require full cardiovascular replacement. Krin steps into my peripheral vision, skin glistening with corrective sweat. "Sir, the social cohesion metrics…"

I look up from the riot suppression feed. "Speak plainly or don't speak." His left eyelid convulses. Same tic as last week. Should've scheduled neural recalibration.

"Executing non-combatants could turn neutral sectors against us."

My cuff adjusts itself, nano threads realigning. "You mistake corpses for combatants."

The console digests my authorization code. Ninety-six becomes one hundred twelve. Red markers bloom like arterial spray across the Lower Spire districts. "There. Problem solved."

Cho chokes on her own saliva. Pathetic organic reflex. "Sir, that's thirty percent over projection capac…"

"Capacity expands when properly motivated."

Thermal feeds flicker as Sector Five's tenement locks engage. Seventy thousand useless meat sacks become seventy thousand object lessons. "Observe."

Screens erupt with fire. Not metaphorical. Actual fucking promethium flames chewing through prefab housing units. Crowds scatter—meat trying to outrun thermodynamics. My enforcers herd them back with shock prods. Efficient.

Krin makes wet clicking sounds. Probably thinks it's speech. I rotate my chair twenty-three degrees. Perfect angle to watch his carotid pulse dance. "You were saying?"

He's sweating properly now. Good. Saltwater contains truth serum if you know how to read it. "The Optics Division reports… unfavorable sentiment spikes in neighboring sectors."

Laughter barks out of me—sharp, mechanical. A sound even the boardroom clones never mastered. "Sentiment. You're monitoring *sentiment* while standing in the crucible where empires get reforged?"

Feed Sixteen: a woman clutching two children. They're praying. To what? The God their contracts forbade? The ancestors we erased from gene logs? Her lips move in useless patterns, until the drone strike turns them into charcoal sketches. Beautiful. "Fear."

I spread my hands across the holographic carnage. Blood light paints my knuckles maroon. "Purest motivator. Cleanest fuel. You want to curb rebellion?"

A tap enlarges Sector Nine's execution pit. Naked bodies stacked like cordwood. "Give them something visceral to fear more than freedom."

Cho reaches for her tablet. Stupid twitch. Older-model meat. I kick her knees out. She hits the floor with textbook impact, chin first. Bone cracks sweet and clear. "That's your problem." I press my boot between her shoulder blades. Felt ribs bend. "You think in memos and percentages."

My heel grinds down. Something pops. She doesn't scream. Good girl. "I think in centuries."

The main screen flashes crimson. Huff's mission log reappears. That frozen frame, my perfect weapon hesitating. His finger trembling half a millimeter from the trigger. Static crawls up my spine. Krin edgeways toward the door. Traitor-adjacent. "Analyst." My voice stops him cold. "Run facial recognition on all purge footage. Cross-reference with Huff's neural map."

His confusion feels like burnt toast. "Sir?"

I zoom in on Feed Twenty-Two. A man in the mob. Right build, right posture, same head tilt when the gas canisters burst. Even through riot-mask filters—that jawline matches Huff's profile. "He's here."

My pulse sings combat cadence. "Rewriting loyalty protocols mid-mission? Planting dissent seeds during cleanup operations?" The pieces click, rotors in perfect sync. "This isn't a malfunction."

Advisors hold their breath collectively. Idiots. I initiate Code Umbra. Every screen shifts to Huff's last known trajectory. City schematics overlay with hostile movement vectors. There. Third Spire transit hub. Security cam ghosts show six blurred figures. Military-grade augments. Moving in formation around a seventh heat signature. Huff. But why meet resistance trash in some maintenance tunnel? Unless…

Cold spreads through my implant ports. "Scrub all data logs from the past seventy-two hours." My voice stays flat. Clinical. Only my right thumb betrays me, spasming against the console edge. "And ready the Omega Contingency protocols."

Cho tries rising. Mistake. My boot meets her temple. Once. Twice. Three times. Wet crunching sounds. Brains look different outside the skull, softer. Krin pukes quietly in the corner. I wipe blood spatter from my sleeve. "Anyone else want to debate efficiency metrics?"

The door seals behind the last advisor with a pressurized hiss. Screens flicker around me, thirty-seven live feeds of Bastion Prime choking on its own blood. Smoke plumes bloom over Sector Seven. A child's sneaker lies abandoned near a burning checkpoint.

My gloved finger traces the collar of my jacket. Still pristine. Still perfect. They don't understand. Clean lines require precise cuts. My reflection glimmers in the monitor glass, sharp as scalpels, eyes twin barrels of liquid nitrogen. The purge unfolds like clockwork below. Drones sweep alleys with incendiary rounds. Enforcers drag shopkeepers into the streets. One feed shows a woman clutching a holoposter of Huff's face. Mistake. Her skull meets a riot baton. Crimson spray spatters the camera lens. "Flaw containment," I mutter, adjusting my left cuff by two millimeters.

Static crackles. Feed Twelve flickers. A flash of silver hair vanishing down a sewer grate. Pulse spikes. *Huff.* No. Too tall. Too slow. Another defective unit? Impossible. My creation doesn't permit variance. Yet the ghost lingers. Every shadowed corner breeding fresh phantoms.

Console lights blink red. Lockdown holding at 98.7% efficiency. Not enough. Should be 99.9. Always 99.9. The air tastes metallic. Old blood or ozone? Doesn't matter. My tongue clicks against molars. "Reassign Gamma Squadron to grid E-14."

No response. Right. Advisors fled. Cowards. Their absence rings louder than the gunfire below. Let them cower in their platinum towers. This requires hands that don't tremble. A proximity alert shrieks.

Monitor Six: enforcers retreating from subway tunnels. Thermal signatures swarm the dark, dozens. Hundreds. Human? Synth? Doesn't matter. Rot spreads fastest in warm places. My knuckle cracks against the execute command. Gas canisters roll. Screens flare white.

When the thermal blooms fade, the swarm's reduced to meat confetti clinging to tunnel walls. Efficiency jumps to 99.1%. Better. Feed Twenty-Three catches movement. Black tactical gear, fluid motion slicing through riot police. Familiar. Too familiar. I lean in. Breath fogs the screen. Enhanced playback: a Vargstryk unit executing perfect takedowns. Mine. All mine. But the shoulders hunch wrong. The neck cants left instead of...

Glove leather whines as my fists clench.
"Cross-reference all units in Sector Nine."

The AI responds faster than my last chief strategist.
<<All active Vargstryk accounted for.>>
Lies. Must be. That stance... that hesitation before breaking a spine...
Incision required. I input override codes, bypassing fourteen security protocols. Neural link pricks my occipital port. Data floods, biometrics for every unit. Heart rates. Pupil dilation. Synaptic response curves. There. Unit K-77's basal ganglia fires .03 seconds slow during threat assessment. "Isolate. Terminate."

Three blocks east, K-77 collapses mid-stride. Neural inhibitor virus works fast. Body convulses. Civilians scatter. Good. Let them see. Let them understand perfection's price. The other units pause. Just for 0.2 seconds. Just long enough. My jaw locks. Contingencies within contingencies. Always. "Initiate secondary compliance protocols."

Their ocular implants flare gold. Resume killing. Faster now. Compensating. One screen goes dark. Then another. Rebels overran the substation. Amateurs. I trigger the failsafe. Molecular bond destabilization in the building's support beams. Feed dies smiling as eight thousand tons of permacrete swallow both sides. Silence expands. My cufflinks need polishing.

Vibration in my inner ear. Priority alert from R&D. They've found traces of Huff's DNA in Sector Twelve. Again. Third false positive tonight. I crush the notification with a mental command. Weakness. All weakness. The main screen flickers. For half a heartbeat, it shows my face superimposed over Huff's. Same bone structure. Same dead eyes. Then static. I don't blink. "Run diagnostics."

<<No anomalies detected.>>
Of course not.

CHAPTER 12: HUFF

Bastion Prime's alleys smell like piss and rust. I'm sprinting hard enough to taste blood in the back of my throat, boots slamming cracked permacrete. Behind me, the Wolves' footfalls sync up, three of them, standard pursuit formation. Their breathing's too even. Mine isn't. Funny how betrayal gives you a fucking adrenaline dump but doesn't upgrade your lungs. I hook left into a side street choked with collapsed scaffolding. My knee actuators whine as I leap a slagheap, titanium-reinforced shins absorbing the drop. The Wolves take the corner wider, good. Gives me another half second. Their comms chatter crackles in my auditory feed, clipped and sterile: "Target maintaining northeast vector. Flanking pattern Gamma."

Assholes still think by the book. I palm a grenade canister off my belt. Not a real one—Chance's parting gift. Smoke and spark, no shrapnel. Cheap theatrics. I thumb the trigger, try to pull the pin again. Glitch. Already did that. Glance at the lob-ready grenade, then underhand it into a dumpster. The blast kicks up a wall of gray haze. Useless against their thermal optics, but the sound'll make them check stride. "Visual obstruction. Proceed with caution."

Yeah, caution. That's what got me here. The smoke buys me ten steps. I'm moving before the canister stops rolling, shoulder-checking a corroded service door. It groans open into an arterial thoroughfare choked with hoverbike husks. My HUD pings a proximity alert. Sniper nests on the rooftops. Old intel. VargTech cleared these sectors months ago. Or did they? I skid behind a burnt-out delivery drone, fingers checking my chest rig's straps. Habit. Three mags. One frag. Pink sneaker count still: one. The Wolves' footsteps tighten behind me. Closer. Think.

West leads to the commerce blocks. Cameras, patrols, certain death. East: the river, maybe a swim through coolant runoff. South…

South's the old Foundry District. I'm already moving before the thought finishes. Foundry's a corpse of collapsed factories and half-melted girders. Perfect for getting lost. Perfect for ambushes too. Chance's voice slides in with that dry, half warning, smug-ass tone: "Kill box. Always symmetrical."

My calves burn as I vault a chain-link fence topped with razor wire. The barbs catch my jacket, fabric tears, but the skin beneath stays whole. Thanks, VargTech. At least the subdermal armor works. The first Wolf bursts into the alley behind me. I don't look. Don't need to. I know the exact model of their ocular implants, the way their targeting reticles prioritize center mass. I taught them that.

A round punches through a dumpster to my left. Subsonic, they want me alive. Good. Means they'll hesitate. I zigzag between pillars of corroded steel, HUD mapping the fastest route through skeletal buildings. The Foundry's maze wraps around me, all jagged edges and shadow. My boot crushes a syringe. My lungs crush my ribs. "Target entering sector 8-Delta. Converge."

They're herding me. Classic pincer maneuver. Gaps between gunfire, two seconds. One suppressing. Others flanking. I duck into a gutted warehouse, glass crunching underfoot. Moonlight bleeds through shattered skylights. My enhanced pupils dilate, painting the room in grayscale. Conveyor belts frozen mid-rotation. A forklift with its forks rusted upward like dead hands. Wrong battlefield.

I'm halfway to the far exit when a Wolf materializes in the doorway. Standard-issue carbine raised. No hesitation. No face, just a black visor reflecting my own warped silhouette. Shit. Muscle memory takes over. I slide behind the forklift as bullets chew through metal. The sound is deafening. My hand finds a loose pipe. Rusted, but heavy. Three rounds left in my sidearm. Not enough. The Wolf advances, methodical. I wait, pulse synced to his magazine. The click comes sharp, clean. There. I move.

Ordinance whistles past. Close. Step forward. Swing pipe down. Connect with his wrist-bone cracks, carbine clatters away. He doesn't scream. Doesn't make a sound. Just pivots, drawing a vibroblade. I'm already inside his guard. My palm heels his chin. His head snaps back. I drive my knee into his diaphragm. Armor plates bruise flesh. He staggers. I grab his knife arm, twist. Elbow to temple. One down for now. I don't check if he's dead. Can't afford to.

The vibroblade feels warm in my hand. Custom grip. I recognize the serial number. Kovac. We shared rations last week. Shared cover and a joke. I'm out the door before the nausea hits. The blade's hilt digs into my palm. Foundry air tastes like old grease. Somewhere ahead, machinery groans, a broken turbine spinning in the wind.

Two more Wolves cut across an intersection. They don't see me. Yet. I melt into the shadow of a coolant tower, pressing against pipes that vibrate with residual heat. My HUD flickers. Jammed signal. VargTech's doing. Or Mason? Whatever. Bastards. Chance's warning loops in my skull: *"They know your playbook. So rewrite it."*

The Wolves are methodical. Predictable. But I'm not. Not anymore. I head deeper into the maze, Kovacs' blade sharp against my thigh. Let them come. Game's on *my* terms now. The chemical stench hits first, ammonia and rusted metal. My ocular implant flickers, highlighting the rusted gas main running beneath the alley grate. Standard Wolf protocol: secure all infrastructure points before advancing. They'll have rigged it with a motion-sensor charge. No hesitation. No time to smile.

Three precise shots into the access panel. Sparks dance across pooling wastewater. The Wolves' own detonator beeps twice in protest before the world fractures. Concrete geysers upward. A shockwave slams me against a dumpster, ribs screaming. Through the ringing, I hear shouts, human ones. Wolves don't scream. Must've caught some Enforcers in the blast radius. Collateral damage. The words taste like Chance's cheap synth-whiskey. I'm moving before the debris finishes falling.

The industrial zone welcomes me with its silence. Corroded assembly lines stretch like metal skeletons. Shards of photovoltaic glass crunch underfoot. What's left of the solar arrays VargTech abandoned when they switched to fusion. Every shadow could be a sniper nest. Every echo, a footstep. I count ventilation shafts. Map exit vectors. The Wolves will triangulate my position in six minutes. Less if they've upgraded their tracking algorithms. A high whine slices the air. Freeze. Listen. Not drones. Not guns. Hydraulics. Ancient. Heavy. Quiet if you know how. They're using the old cargo lifts. Clever bastards.

My HUD stitches together the blueprints I memorized during the Kastor Square massacre. Maintenance tunnel B-12. Thirty meters northwest. Glitch. Kestrel's face. Glitch. Move you fool. I vault a collapsed conveyor belt. Something crunches underfoot, a human femur, picked clean by scavengers.

A cloud of iron oxide particles shifts to reveal them. First Wolf's visor gleams dully. Standard-issue pulse carbine. I know the firing pattern before he pulls the trigger. Three-round burst. Left, center, right. Roll right. Chips of concrete sting my neck. His partner circles wide, tactical knife in a reverse grip.

Textbook. They've forgotten who wrote the textbook.

The shooter reloads. 2.3 second cycle. I surge forward, Kovacs' blade finding the gap between the second Wolf's armor plates. He grunts. Human sound. The knife sticks. Blood wets my glove. I let go. Shooter's barrel swings toward me. I grab the wounded Wolf by his chest rig, swing him like a meat shield. Pulse rounds tear through his backplate. One. Two.

Drop the body. Kick it to one side, close the distance. Shooter's eyes widen., brown irises flecked with gold. Rivas. Taught her how to field-strip a plasma rifle. Her carbine's too close for effective aim. I palm-strike the magazine release. Catch the falling ammo clip. Drive it upward into her jaw. Her helmet cracks against a support beam. She slides down. No sound. Just twitching. Body jittering like a dropped stim. Don't check pulses.

The knife's still in the first Wolf's ribs. Custom Vargstryk-issue handle. I yank it free. Wipe the blood off. It sizzles where it touches my thermal mesh. Nanite coagulant. Standard in all Wolf gear since the Kesser Reforms. My hands don't shake. They never shake. Then I look down at Rivas' body, count the scars on her neck, three parallel lines from that shrapnel burst on Garamond Station. She'd laughed when I stitched her up. "Next round's on me, Huff."

The safehouse looms in my mental map. Two klicks northeast. Can't stop. Won't stop. Not yet. Don't think. Just run. Kovac's knife feels heavier now. My boots eat pavement in jagged bursts. Adrenaline cocktails with the combat stims still burning through my veins. The industrial zone's skeletal remains blur past—rusted conveyor belts hanging like gutted snakes, chemical vats leaking century-old toxins. Three Wolves confirmed terminated.

Estimated response time: six minutes. Safehouse proximity: 1.8 kilometers. The numbers scroll through my retinal display in VargTech cobalt. Old habit makes me trust them. New instinct whispers trap. I leap a collapsed chain-link fence. Barbed wire claws at my thighs. Thermal mesh holds. Barely. Drones swarm above, black carrion flies with pulse cannons for stingers. I duck beneath a corroded pipeline as three pass overhead. Their search pattern's textbook: spiral sweep, overlapping sectors. I taught that module. That knowledge burns like battery acid.

I palm a micro-EMP charge from my belt. Wait for the fourth drone's shadow. Four. Five. Six. Toss the charge straight up. The pop sounds like a wet fuse. Drone carcasses rain down in sparking chunks. I'm already moving before the largest piece hits the ground. "Wolf Three to Command." A voice crackles from a nearby corpse's comms rig. "Target last sighted near Sector…"

I crush the radio under heel. The voice dies mid-syllable. Ash patterns tell me two fresh units are converging from the west. Thermal signatures bloom on my retinal map—twelve hostiles, maybe fourteen. They're using the Kastor Formation. My own fucking playbook.

The safehouse winks in my mind, abandoned maintenance tunnel beneath the old fusion plant. Last resupply: eight months ago. If the rats haven't chewed through the med kits. I vault a collapsed crane arm. Land in a sludge puddle that reeks of puke. My augments filter out the worst, but the stink still claws at my throat. Glitch: First combat drop on Kesser IV.
Glitch. VargTech officers applauding as I gunned down rebels in a methane swamp. Smell's the same. I shake my head. Motion's too human. Careful.
A warning chime blares in my skull. Proximity alert. I dive left as pulse fire vaporizes the puddle. Superheated sludge scalds my neck. Roll behind a crumbling concrete pillar.

"Flanking maneuver," a Wolf barks.

Voice modulator can't hide Goblin's Talarian accent. Taught him urban combat tactics during the Luna Siege. Now he's trying to box me in with a pincer movement. I smirk. Pull the pin on a sonic grenade with my teeth. They're expecting me to break east toward the safehouse. I throw the grenade west. The blast shatters every window in a derelict factory. Wolves curse as their audio dampeners overload. I'm already sprinting northeast, boots crunching through broken glass.

A drone's spotlight licks my heels. I don't slow. Safehouse entrance: 300 meters. Seal appears intact. No visible traps. Blood sings in my ears. Adrenaline burns through muscle fibers grown in vats. The safehouse door groans like a dying animal when I kick it. Rusted hinges protesting under carbon-fiber boots. Pulse fire peppers the metal as I drop through. Darkness. The hatch seals above. Stale air floods my lungs.
SEAL INTEGRITY: 97%. Good enough.
NO BIOLOGICAL CONTAMINANTS DETECTED:
MOTION SENSORS: inactive. Don't need them. No time to relax. Check gear straps. Knife handle. Ammo count. The ritual takes twelve seconds.

Sixteen steps to the armory. I count them through retinal HUD static. Machine oil and dead rats underfoot. "Biometric scan," rasps the security panel.

I press my palm against corroded steel. The reader glows red.
ERROR: OPERATIVE STATUS TERMINATED
"Override code Sigma-Nine." My voice sounds alien. Too human. "Authorization Huff-Seven-Alpha."

The light flickers green. Inside smells like home, gunpowder and stale protein packs. Flickering neon from Bastion Prime's skyline leaks through bulletproof glass. I don't sit. Don't breathe. Check gear straps. Two mags left. Three fragmentation grenades. Knife chipped near the hilt. I run my thumb over it. Familiar.

Flickering bio lights reveal the cache, weapons locker half-empty, protein packs expired six months ago. I swallow two anyway. Taste like chalk and memories. Kestrel's face swims before my eyes. Damn. Ten steps to the cracked terminal. Stab my finger at buttons. Wait for it to boot up. Jack in directly through neural port. Accessing encrypted channels. Connection established. Slow breath out. Didn't know I was so tense.

My neural interface pings. Residual data from the Wolves' comms. They're still hunting. Still transmitting. Priority target confirmed. Lethal force authorized. I rip the interface cable from my neck. Sparks dance across knuckles. The mirror shows a ghost—blood smeared across tactical plating, eyes glowing faint blue. VargTech's logo stares back from my left pectoral. I tear the patch off. Not even mine. Just printed on borrowed skin. Underneath: scar tissue shaped like barcode.

Rations cabinet squeals open. Injector pen to the carotid. Combat stims burn colder than betrayal. Floorboards creak. I'm aiming before conscious thought. Empty corridor. Paranoia or protocol? Both keep you alive. A hollow laugh fills the empty space. Mine? Feels like magnesium. White hot. They tried to program laughter out of us. I laughed anyway. Maps bloom across the workstation's cracked screens. VargTech headquarters glowing like infected tissue. Hands shake. Not from fear. System purge. They're trying to lock me out. "Override this." I jam a data spike into its port.

Files cascade. Blacksite coordinates. Neural recalibration schedules. Termination orders stamped with my face. Alarm blares. Motion sensors detect heat signatures, three blocks northeast. Snatch data spike and stash it.

Window exit. Rappel line anchored to rusted I-beam. Safehouse compresses into a shaped charge behind. Let them sift through the rubble. New objective forms in the smoking crater of old loyalties: Burn it all down.

The Wolves want a hunter? They'll get a virus.

CHAPTER 13: MASON

The holograms bleed static where Huff's heat signature last blinked out. I press my knuckles into the projection table until the steel frame creaks. "Track clusters, not individuals."

Three rebels monitoring feeds turn to look at me. Their retinal implants flicker blue with data streams. "He'll pulse when ready. Your job's to watch the gaps between patrols, not play tag with ghosts."

Kara spits her gum into a spent stim cartridge. "What if he's running dark?"

"Then we're already dead."

My gloves click against each other as I reseat them, left thumb joint realigning with a satisfying snap. The tactical display reshuffles, overlaying VargTech's security grid across the Lower Spire's sewage access points. "Shift eyes to quadrant seven. Dumpster dive if you have to."

Two levels down, Jax's boot sinks into something rat-adjacent, caught on my drone's feed. His thermal cloak ripples as he sidesteps a corroded pipe. "Movement northeast," he whispers into the bone mic. "Single heat source hugging the reactor wall."

Above him, a surveillance drone whines through air, thick with methane and desperation. Lien freezes in the crawlspace. The readout next to her name pulses green: NEURAL DAMPENER ACTIVE. I watch her uplink as she holds her breath and waits for the drone's scanners to pass over. In the corner of the screen, the readout on her wrist blinks: NEURAL PATTERN NOT FOUND.

"Clear," Jax mutters when the red eye blinks out. He palms a micro charger from his belt, thumb hovering over the detonator. "Mason, the package is moving toward…"

A VargTech enforcer's searchlight licks the alley mouth. Jax doesn't move. Doesn't breathe. Even his thermal sig drops, textbook camo freeze. On-screen, Jax is gone. Just another shadow in rust-stained concrete.
My link to Jax's mic picks it up. A sharp intake, the enforcer's breath hitching. Through his uplink, I catch the glint of subdermal plates on the enforcer's neck. Seven. Mid-tier. Expendable.

Back in the command hub, I watch Jax's vitals spike and stabilize. Smart. The hologram updates show Huff's trajectory cutting through sector 12 like a scalpel through scar tissue. My left glove needs adjusting again—the haptic feedback's lagging by a millisecond. Kara tosses me a fresh stim patch. "He's better than your intel said."

"He's better than *their* intel said." The projection shimmers as I rotate the map.

Huff's avoiding all standard checkpoints, taking routes even my best scouts took months to chart. If he's still following programming, it's programming they forgot they installed. Lien's halfway through transmitting the new coordinates when the drone doubles back, caught in the feed from her collar cam. Her vitals spike. Her teeth clamp down hard. The vent shaft's too narrow to turn around. I watch her curl tight, ribs crushed against corroded steel.

A heat signature blisters across the screen—scanner beam tagging her leg. Dampener failure. Overload. The readout flares red: SIGNAL LOST: NEURAL DAMPENER. Static blooms as the device sparks and fries through her sock. Jax moves. On my screen, his microcharger arcs through the air, detonates against a hydrogen line. The blast chars the Enforcer's faceplate and punches a hole through the alley duct. Jax hauls her out of frame. Feed switches to helmet cam—distorted audio catches both of them gasping through filter masks clogged with three years of gene-waste. "Still got both legs?" Jax's voice cuts through static.

Lien gags, slaps his shoulder. "Buy me a drink first."

The explosion pings on my map as a minor industrial accident. Standard cover-up protocols activate. VargTech's drones swarm the area to contain, not investigate. I trace Huff's path diverting toward the chaos. Opportunistic. Adaptable. Kara leans over the projection. "He's hunting."

"He's confirming." My gloves finally sit right. The hologram sharpens as I input new parameters. "Cut teams three and five. Redirect all surveillance to the waste processing plant."

"That's a blind spot."

"Exactly." The numbers cascade across my vision, 73% success probability if Huff takes the bait, 89% casualty rate if he doesn't. Better odds than my first kiss. Somewhere below, a man who is half-algorithm pauses at a crossroads. I watch the map. I don't blink. The holograms stutter when Kara slams her fist on the corroded console. "He's veering into Sector Nine."

I count seven heartbeats before answering. Let the tension coil in her cybernetic eye, the one that still glitches when she's pissed. "Your point?"

"Point is it's a fucking desert down there. No cams. No eyes. Just six square klicks of collapsed transit tunnels and enough neurotoxin residue to melt a tank battalion." She stabs at the projection. Crimson light fractures across her scarred knuckles. "We lose track there, he's gone."

My gloves creak as I flex. The command center smells of burnt circuitry and the sour tang of recycled sweat. "Exactly."

On my retinal feed, Huff's thermal signature pulses like an infected wound. The man moves like mercury through cracked stone, slipping between patrol routes, pausing precisely 1.8 seconds at each security blind spot. Textbook VargTech infiltration protocols. Kara's breathing hitches. She thinks I don't hear the subvocal click of her activating the emergency beacon. "Stand down." I don't look up from the tac-map. "Or I'll have Sonny weld your comms implant shut."

The lie tastes like failure. Sonny died seventeen hours ago in the Kesslar ambush. She knows. I know she knows. The game sustains us. Huff's trajectory blinks gold as he breaches the sector border. My knuckle traces the path, through the old hydroponic farms, across the methane lake, into the bone yards. "Prep the welcome package," I tell the room.

Kara freezes. "You said no contact."

"Package *Three*."

Her remaining organic eye dilates. Understands. Holds breath for eight seconds. I turn toward the rusted grate we call an elevator. "Coming?"

The tunnels reek of death and piss. Kara and I wade through knee-deep sludge that once powered Bastion Prime's fusion core. My boots start to dissolve at the seams. "Remember the Golan job?" she asks, too casual.

"Which time?"

"When you made me wear that cocktail dress lined with Semtex."

"Worked, didn't it?"

She kicks a mutant rat the size of a housecat. "The stockbroker pissed himself before I could detonate."

The memory almost makes me smile. *Almost.* We emerge into a cavern where the city's bones protrude, twisted rebar, shattered polymer panels, the occasional mummified corpse still clutching obsolete tech. Above us, VargTech's newest skyscraper pierces the smog layer like a silver dagger. Huff's twenty meters ahead, climbing the collapsed ventilation shaft with machine precision. Kara tenses. "He's heading for the old data nexus."

"Not his style."

"Then why..."

The explosion rocks the chamber. Through my feed: *Package Three.* A memory grenade. Non-lethal. Unless you count truth as a weapon. Huff staggers as the blast wave hits. I watch him closely on my neural feed during the three seconds his augmented nervous system betrays him. Every synapse fires in perfect sync. Neural disruption propagates faster. Satisfaction buzzes behind my eyes, like a scalp massage from an expensive joy code slag. He crashes into a mound of decaying circuit boards. His biometrics shift. Combat-ready crimson fading into confused ochre. Kara slams her palm into my chest. "He's vulnerable. Extract now or..."

"Wait."

Huff's fingers twitch. Not for weapons. They trace the VargTech emblem on his chest plate. I know that gesture. Three years ago. Medical bay stinking of burnt flesh. My own hands picking at the corporate logo grafted to my sternum. The lieutenant screaming as they peeled his enhancements off. Kara grabs my arm. "Mason."

Huff's moving again. Slower now. Deliberate. "Track his biometrics," I say. "Stress levels. Pupil dilation. The works."

"Since when do we profile marks?"

"Since never." I step into the toxic haze. "This isn't a mark."

The realization slides down my spine like ice. Like the first time I hacked a VargTech drone and felt its systems push back. Huff's not running. He's testing. We follow the trail of activated sensors. Not deactivated, *triggered*. He's mapping our response patterns. Kara hisses as another proximity alarm blares. "Fuck's he playing at?"

"Same game we are."

Numbers cascade across my vision. 87% match to my own escape route from VargTech HQ last year. The parallels itch beneath my skin. Huff stops at the exact coordinates where I buried Sergeant Vey's neural core. Coincidence is VargTech's favorite lie. "Set up the relay," I tell Kara.

"You're not seriously…"

"Three minutes. Then fall back."

She hesitates. The old wound on her neck pulses, scar tissue twitching where a corporate interrogator's probe slipped. "He'll kill you."

"Probably."

The access hatch groans as I climb into the light. The proximity alarm screams through my neural link. Three blocks west. Heavy armor signatures. I slam my palm against a corroded service pipe. "Kara. Status."

Her voice crackles in my implant: "Two hunter-killers rerouted from Sector Nine. They're sweeping the old hydroponic farms."

My gloves creak as I flex my fingers. VargTech doesn't send wolves to chase ghosts. They know. "Pull Team Three off surveillance," I snap. "Have them seed false thermals in the storm drains."

A beat. "That's our last batch of decoys."

"Would you rather be a wolf pack's last batch of meat?"

The concrete vibrates beneath my boots as heavy transports roll overhead. I taste leaking coolant from ruptured pipes mixing with Bastion Prime's perpetual acid rain. The kind that slowly erodes your clothes along with your soul. Jax's feed blinks red in my peripheral. Scout Seven close by. Young. Fast. Still thinks adrenaline makes better fuel than fear. His cam shows a maintenance tunnel choked with bioluminescent algae. Shadows shift, twenty meters back. Tactical boots catching the green glow. "Jax, Seven," I subvocalize. "You've got…"

"Five Enforcers. Heavily modded." Jax's breathing's steady. "I see them."

The lead Enforcer's ocular implant sweeps left. Jax presses against a dripping wall, his chameleon suit glitching at the elbows. "Distraction. Now."

Jax palms a shock charge from his belt. Doesn't throw it. Plants it on a rusted valve cluster instead. Clever. The explosion screams louder than ordnance has a right to. Superheated steam billows through the tunnel. Jax is already climbing. Boots finding grip on algae-slick rungs, Seven dragged in his wake as Enforcers shout about containment protocols. "Decoy worked. They're arguing jurisdiction."

"Move northeast. Rendezvous at the bone yard."

"Already gone."

Kara intercepts me at the crosswalk corpse. The dead traffic drone still sparks where I ripped its battery last week. "New pattern." She flicks a hologram between us. Huff's trajectory overlay.

"He's circling the abandoned synthplant. Minimal surveillance. Patrols diverted for the wolves sweep."

I rotate the map. The plant's skeletal remains rise at the city's edge like broken teeth. My kind of place. "Prep the dead drop. Phase-two protocols."

Her ocular implant flashes amber. "You want to giftwrap our comm frequencies?"

"Want him to think he's stealing them." I adjust my left glove. The leather sticks—still scarred from when VargTech interrogators peeled my fingernails down to the roots. "Man's got trust issues deeper than corporate vaults. Needs to believe this is his win."

A drone buzzes overhead. We melt into the corpse's shadow, synthetic blood seeping into our boot treads. The team moves through sewage tunnels that reek of failed experiments. Some of them probably human. I count eleven distinct stenches before giving up. Huff's playing a dangerous game. Letting himself be seen. Letting himself be tracked. I know the move. Used it myself when I blew the gene-lock on VargTech's blacksite. Give them just enough rope to hang their own ops. Kara shoulders past a corroded grate. "If he flips…"

"Biggest coup since the Stipend riots."

"*If.*"

The word hangs between dripping pipes. I watch a rat gnaw on a discarded nutrient pack. Even vermin know corporate food's a death sentence. Huff's different. Not some wage-slave rebelling over ration limits. He wanted to be a Wolf. Not like the prisoners they morphed into killing machines just to save on executions and prison budgets. Huff's a scalpel. Forged by VargTech. Turn that blade against its makers and…

My gloved fist clenches. The plant's outline looms ahead, shattered windows glowing with stolen electricity. "Hold position here," I tell the team. "I want eyes on every approach. No engagement unless fired upon."

"Standard ROE?" Jax asks.

"Burn everything if compromised."

His grin flashes white in the dark. I climb. Rusted rebar bites through my gloves. The plant's third floor holds the sweet spot. Clear sightlines, three escape routes, and a nest of old machine parts that'll scramble most scanners. Huff appears at 21:47. He moves like a war machine debating poetry. Every footfall precise, except for a hitch near the old assembly line. A hesitation no combat algorithm would allow. My HUD highlights the dead drop, a false maintenance panel holding blueprints with coordinates to the encrypted data chips. Bait wrapped in opportunity. Huff tilts his head. Scanning for traps. For surveillance. For the thousand ways this could kill him. I stop breathing. He takes the bait.

Later, Kara finds me scrubbing synthetic blood off my blades. The dead drop's activated. "He's reviewing the files."

"Good."

"You stink of hope."

I snap the cleaning rod. "I stink of someone who didn't get shot today." I wrinkle my nose. "And all the shit we crawled through."

She leans against the bullet-pocked wall, the same spot where we lost Tev six months back. "We could push. Arrange contact."

"Push a VargTech hound, you get bit." I sheathe the knife. "He's got our scent now. Let him come."

The plant's coordinates burn in my tactical log. Same path I ran three years ago. Same choice they gave me—die loyal or live damned. Huff'll make his move soon. I'll be waiting. The air tastes like war sipped from a cracked teacup. My gloves creak as I flex my hands, tactical display painting retinal burns across three sectors of Sector 17's corpse. Huff's thermal signature glows wolf-gray on my HUD, pacing the abandoned recycler plant like a caged attack drone. "Eyes on package." Kara's voice crackles through bone conduction. "Two Enforcers circling west perimeter."

I zoom my left eye. Twin black carapace suits glint under flickering sodium lights. "Let them sniff. They're running standard sweep patterns."
The feed shimmers as Huff pauses by a gutted assembly line. His right hand twitches. Not the combat-ready tremor of enhanced reflexes, but the stutter-step of someone fighting internal firewalls. My own neural port itches in sympathy.

"Movement pattern matches predicted crisis point," Chen says from the overwatch nest. "He's reaching decision threshold."

I adjust my gloves. The plant's layout scrolls across my vision, rusted catwalks, collapsed conveyor belts, twelve potential kill zones. Exactly where I'd go to make life-altering choices. Did the same in '38 when I burned my VargTech credentials. Huff's head snaps up. My breath stops. "Drone swarm incoming!" Kara barks. "Sector-wide scan."

"Lights out. Now."

Screens die. Comms click off. The safehouse becomes a tomb. Stale coolant and adrenaline thick in the air. Through cracked plasti-glass, I watch the security drones sweep past like mechanical vultures. Their scanners paint the street in sickly green waves. Huff's gone dark. Chen swears in three languages. "Lost visual."

"Hold. He's still there."

A shadow detaches from the assembly line's corpse. Huff moves like liquid mercury now, all VargTech precision. But he's heading for the dead drop we salted—another false maintenance panel packed with enough incriminating data to get him soul-scorched. Kara's boot taps Morse code against the floor: *Stupid gamble.* I answer with glove taps: *Only kind we make.*

The plant's skeletal frame groans as Huff pries open the panel. His enhanced shoulders tense. For ten heartbeats, he holds statue-still. Then he pockets the data chip like it's live ordnance. "Package acquired." Chen's exhale hisses through the comms. "Extraction?"

"Negative. Let the breadcrumbs work." My neural interface pings, the chip's sig blooms on my tac-map. "Fall back to secondary observation."

We melt through back alleys crusted with fossilized graffiti. My boots stick to pavement that hasn't seen sunlight since the Corporate Enclosure Act. Huff's tracker pulse matches our retreat. A digital heartbeat, two blocks east. Kara materializes beside me, the smell of gun oil cutting through the alley's piss-stench. "He's taking the scenic route."

"Neural audit protocols." I duck under a sagging coolant pipe. "Like anyone with half a brain."

The tracker stops. My HUD lights up, an intersection where six alleys vomit into a derelict transit hub. Huff's thermal ghost leans against a slagged mag-lev carriage. Waiting. Chen's voice tightens. "He's baiting."

"Obviously." I flip my ocular focus. "Check the rooftops."

Scopes glint in the perpetual twilight. Two, no, three sniper nests. VargTech's welcome committee.

"Fuck." Kara chambers a round in her shock rifle. "They're herding him."

Huff hasn't moved. His posture screams combat readiness, but the data chip burns in his pocket. My teeth grind. They're testing him, probing for loyalty cracks. "Options?"

I feel the tension in Chen's question. I watch a surveillance drone skim past Huff's position. His head turns exactly thirty-seven degrees, just enough to track it without appearing attentive. "Let him fight."

Kara's helmet tilts. "You joking?"

"His programming versus his curiosity." I activate the tracker's secondary pulse. "We just made that data chip scream."

Huff's hand drifts toward his sidearm. The snipers shift. All three scopes lock onto his chest. Huff draws. The world fractures. Gunfire and screaming metal. "Move!" I'm already sprinting through the kill zone. "Chen, smoke the nests! Kara, flank east!"

Huff moves in a danse macabre. His first shot spiders a sniper's viewport. The second ricochets into a drone's thruster array. He's using the mag-lev carcass as cover, but VargTech's closing the net. I crash into cover beside a shattered ad kiosk. "Huff! West corridor!"

He spins—pistol seeking my skull. Our eyes lock through the holographic billboard's corpse-light. For half a heartbeat, I see it the code walls cracking behind his gaze. He runs. We chase. The data chip's signal pulls us through sewage tunnels that reek of everything this shithole ever held. I count seven Enforcer squads lost to ambushes Huff leaves behind like gruesome breadcrumbs. Kara wipes brains off her faceplate. "Fucking puppet's got teeth."

"Had." I step over a twitching cyborg. "He's cutting strings."

The tracker dies in a burst of static. We find Huff in a sub-level maintenance bay, chest heaving against compromised armor. His pistol snaps up as we enter but he doesn't lower his face shield. "Data's authentic." I keep my hands visible. "You know what that means."

His targeting laser trembles. "Means you're dead."

"Eventually." I nod at his pocket. "But first? You're curious."

The bay's emergency lights paint his face in prison stripes. I see the exact moment his programming fails, a micro-tremor in his left eye. Same glitch that started my defection. He lowers the gun. "Your play."

"Your choice." I toss a frequency chip at his boots. "When the code finishes crumbling."

We leave him standing in the wreckage of his loyalty. Kara lights a contraband stimcig as we emerge topside. "Think he'll bite?"

I watch a VargTech gunship scour the district. "Doesn't matter."

"Bullshit."

"Truth." I adjust my gloves, the ghost of a dead man's neural port still itching.

"Either we gain an ally…"

"Or create one hell of a distraction." She grins with too many teeth.

The gunship peels away, clueless. Somewhere below, a wolf's chewing through its chain. I check my sidearm. "Win-win."

We disappear into Bastion Prime's bleeding edges.
The game's in motion now. Let the corporation try to stop it.

CHAPTER 14: CHANCE

The monitor's blue static cuts through the safehouse gloom like a knife wound. My fingers spider across three keyboards like a demented organ player, pulling feeds from street cams, hacked ocular implants, a dozen dead drops gone silent. Each new window blooms with the same carnage. VargTech enforcers moving through the Undercroft markets like combine harvesters. Reaping souls for corporate greed. Black helmets. White armbands. Shock batons cracking skulls for curfew violations that didn't exist yesterday.

A data chip spins between my knuckles. Always spinning, never slotting. Fourth feed from the left shows a pack of chrome hounds dragging some weeper out of a noodle shop. Recognition punches me in the throat mid-swipe. "Fuck."

Kirin's braids swing wild as she fights. My best mule. My only friend who still took whiskey as payment. They've got her wrists locked in compliance cuffs, the kind that inject pacifiers straight into your radial artery. She's mouthing off even now. I don't need audio to know she's cursing their mothers back twelve generations. The lead enforcer checks his wrist display. Nods. I'm halfway to standing when the execution round takes her left eye. Plasteel desk meets my fist. Data chips rain down like shrapnel. "Stupid bleeding-heart bitch." The words taste like battery acid. Feed freezes on her body crumpling—one braid caught under an enforcer's boot.

Three steps across the room. Three back. Safehouse walls press closer every hour, paint peeling like sunburned flesh, air vents coughing up black dust. My reflection glares back from a cracked security mirror. Some gutter where selling intel stops feeling like playacting.

Neutrality's math doesn't add up anymore. Cost of silence: Kirin's corpse cooling in the gutter. Five other faces I pretended weren't familiar in the purge feeds. The Undercroft's labyrinthine alleys getting simpler every time VargTech burns a block. Can't hide around corners that no longer exist. Cost of picking sides: Everything. Breathing privileges. The sweet rush of walking betrayal's edge. That little immortality of being too useful to kill. Chip still spins. Left hand's tapping staccato rhythms on thigh armor. Morse code for idiot. Sentimental. DEAD. Neon light bleeds through barred windows, painting hazard stripes across my boots. Somewhere below, a surveillance drone's repulsors whine like dying cicadas. Kirin once asked what I'd do if VargTech ever came for her. "Charge double for your location," I'd said, flipping her off with the hand not mixing cocktails. "Spend the credits on your funeral whisky."

Her laughter had shaken stimcig ash onto my cleanest data deck. Fist closes around the razor edges of my chip. Calculations scroll behind my eyes. Supply routes gone dark, safe passage percentages dropping faster than a ganger's life expectancy. Stay neutral, and Bastion Prime's just one big chrome hound kennel. Fight. Teeth bared in something too jagged to be a smile. "Fuck me sideways."

Five steps to the rusted sink. Pour three fingers of synthetic bourbon down my throat. It tastes like industrial solvent. It burns like last year's hope and tomorrows regret. The chip goes into my pocket. The one with the false lining. Let VargTech come searching. Let them try.

The bourbon burns twice; once going down, once when I remember Kirin's body crumpling and puke in the sink. Fuck sentiment. Fuck principles. Fuck whoever designed these safehouse walls to feel like they're trying to eat you. Five paces turn into fifty. Boots wearing grooves in concrete. My reflection mocks me from a shattered security cam lens. Pale ghost with wires where no human should have them and a death wish wrapped in sarcasm.

The comm unit's under three layers of false panels beneath the sink. Standard black-market CryptX-9 model, its casing scarred from a bullet meant for my liver last New Year. Thumbprint scan whines like a hungry rat. Contact list glows toxic green. Mason's ID blinks: *UNREGISTERED//ENCRYPT-7*. Cynicism dies first. I press call. Three encryption cycles. Two dead drops. One gut-punch wait while subdermal trackers itch beneath my wrist. The connection snaps live with a pop of ozone.

"You're either desperate," comes Mason's voice, all velvet-coated steel, "or this is the worst honeypot since Shanghai." Fabric whispers, gloves coming off. Psychological play. Look Ma, no weapons.
"Saw the big dark you caused. Respect."

"Not me. Huff. Sometimes, even wolves go quiet, but the night remembers the screams"

"So, you tamed yourself a wolf. Epic."

"Let's just say he saw the error of their ways."

"VargTech's ways."

"You said it."

Mason pauses a beat. "But that's not why you called."

I lean against the sink, casual as a corpse. "Heard you're buying urban navigation solutions. Bulk discount for revolutionaries."

Silence stretches like piano wire. Somewhere in the background, a hydro spanner clatters. Workshop sounds. Planning sounds. "Your services came premium last week." Static creases his words. Not the comm's, he's moving through interference zones. Smart.

"Market crashed." I flick a data chip into the air. Kirin's last intel drop. Catch it. Repeat. Click-click-click. "Seems VargTech's auditing freelancers. Permanently."

Another pause. Muffled shouts behind him resolve into coordinates. Extraction team prepping. "And this… inventory liquidation." I feel the exact moment he leans closer. "Personal venture?"

The chip freezes mid-arc. Kirin's laugh echoes in the hollow of my palm. "Let's call it professional curiosity about your survival odds."

A dry chuckle. "We've got better infrastructure than your stimcig-budget safehouses."

"Infrastructure's shit when the Wolves come sniffing." I pull up a holo-map, glowing azure lines etching Bastion Prime's veins. "They're running pattern-sweeps on rebel ops. Your last three hits? Same thermal signature delta. Amateur hour."

The map trembles, my hand doesn't. Keys clack on his end. "Your proposal."

"Real-time counter-surveillance. Safe routes. And…" The chip finds its port.

"A gift. Enforcer deployment schedules."

He breathes in. Sharp. Not me. Never me. "That data's triple-encrypted," he says slowly.

"Was." I initiate transfer. "Now it's yours. Consider it a… partnership trial." Gravel shifts. He's up. "What's the buy-in?"

Neon glares through barred windows. Somewhere north, a shockwave rattles pipes. "Keep my name out of your martyr speeches." I kill the map, plunge the room into gloom. "And next time you hit a Vargstryk convoy? Leave the neurotoxin canisters. I know a buyer."

His exhale could mean anything. Approval. Disgust. Plans revising. "Dock 17-B. Two hours." The line dies.

I count to ten. Then smash the Crypt-X against the wall. Shards rain down like glass hail. Let VargTech's slicers piece that together. The chip case goes into the sink's disposal. Molten plastic stings my nostrils. Last traces of Kirin become smoke.

The air tastes like the edge of a data chip pressed to the tongue. My thumb traces the edge of the holo-projector, a nervous tell I can't afford, so I crush the impulse. Mason's feed glitches as our connection bounces off three proxy satellites, wobbles and stabilizes. His gloves creak when he leans forward. Always with the fucking gloves. "Your tunnels leak."

Holographic schematics bloom between us. Sewage networks glowing toxic green beneath Bastion Prime's skyline. "VargTech's got seismic sniffers in these sectors." I stab a finger through Sector 9's maintenance shafts. "Last week's supply run? You tripped every sensor from here to the arcology."

Mason's right glove tightens. "Proposed solution."

I flip the map. Augmented-reality overlays swarm like fire ants. Patrol rotations in crimson, blind spots bleeding void-black. "Nightsoil crews still use manual pumps in the quarantine zones. Get your people into hazmat suits, ride the shit river." My grin feels sharp enough to draw blood. "No bio-scanner sniffs through literal tons of human waste."

The silence hangs like cable under tension. Somewhere below my bolt hole, a street preacher screams about machine salvation before getting cut off mid-sentence. Always quiet after the gunshot. "You're suggesting we ship arms through excrement." Mason's voice could freeze molten steel.

"Suggesting?" I laugh, a dry, crackling sound. "I'm giving you the only viable infiltration route they haven't salted. Your call whether to walk it."

His left glove comes off. Bare fingers tap on unseen controls. "No extraction support. No fallbacks."

"My payment's not contingent on your survival." The lie burns going down. "But if you die, I want advance notice. Need to auction your corpse to body bankers before decomposition sets in."

Another schematic blooms—dockside warehouses wrapped in barbed wire and auto-turrets. "Storage complex Delta-6 houses their new combat drones. Guard rotation changes every twelve hours, but the shift commander takes liquid meals at 03:45 exactly." I highlight a service entrance. "Five-second window where the biometric lock reverts to maintenance mode."

Mason's remaining glove joins its twin on some unseen surface. "Source?"

"Traded six cases of vintage bourbon to a VargTech janitor with a pancreatic mod." I lean back, Chair groans under me. "He'll be pissing insulin for a month, but the intel's solid."

Static crackles between us. The projector flickers, dying battery or incoming scan. Doesn't matter. I slam my palm on the kill switch. Blueprints dissolve into smoke that stings my eyes.

"Terms stand." My voice cuts through the haze. "You get routes, timetables, weak points. I take fifteen percent of any recovered tech. No paper trail. No face-to-face."

Gloves snap back into place. "And when they trace this back to you?"

Heat floods my cheeks. Thank fuck for audio-only. "They won't."

"Arrogance gets men killed, Chance."

"Luckily, I'm a bastard. Used to think surviving meant winning. Now it just means you get to watch the rest burn slower." The data chip spins between my fingers. Smooth plastic grazing calluses. "Dock 17-B in ninety. Come heavy or don't come at all."

The line severs. Seven heartbeats. Stillness. Then motion. Boots laced triple-tight. Armor weave undershirt chafing fresh scars. Three neural disruptors hidden in plain sight—toss one to a child and watch half the block drop twitching. Standard loadout. Same as always. Same except for the encrypted drive in my ankle compartment. Schematics they didn't ask for. Guard schedules they don't deserve. Contingency plans they'll need when, not if, this goes to hell. Just another job. Another transaction. Another layer of insulation between me and the meatgrinder. The chip snaps between my fingers.

Neon bleeds through acid rain pooling between permacrete slabs. My boots kick up prismatic slicks that smell like burnt copper and regret. Third night this week the towers choked. VargTech's austerity measures working as intended. A surveillance drone skitters across a billboard screaming OBEDIENCE IS PROSPERITY in thirty-foot holo-text. I flip it off with my left hand while palming a signal jammer with my right. Little fucker goes dark mid-scan.

The alley reeks of fried synth-rats and piss. Two GOL-T3R class one thugs block the far end, ocular implants cycling through threat assessments. Meat for the grinder, patched-up conscripts with more rust than sense. Their targeting lasers paint my chest. I step into the crimson crosshairs. "You boys know what happens when you wave those things at paying customers?" Blank stares. Always the same with the early-gen models. My thumb finds the disruptor grenade on my belt. "Hint: It involves warranty violations."

The blast leaves their hydraulics squealing. One crashes through a noodle stall, noodles wrapping around his neck joint like neon nooses. The other's stuck repeating CEASE RESISTANCE, voice box glitching. I slot an empty data chip between his teeth. "Tell procurement they're buying cheap knockoffs again."

The air clings like wet cloth. Not rain, nothing so honest. Just that acid-thick mist Bastion calls weather. It doesn't burn. Not really. Just makes your skin itch, your eyes water, your throat ache like you've swallowed rust. Winter makes it worse. Like the city is holding its breath, and you're choking on it. Bastion's arterial thoroughfare pulses below street level. Maintenance tunnels spiderweb beneath the shopping districts, my personal highway. Grates hiss steam that smells like corporate lies. I count seven steps before kicking a specific pipe. Hidden hatch drops open. "Home sweet shithole."

Graffiti mars every surface down here. This little piggy ... Not approved slogans, real art, real protests, real messages. A stenciled wolf devouring the VargTech logo. Someone's been busy. Footsteps echo ahead. Five sets. Heavy tread. Enforcer issue.

I melt into a service alcove, breathing syncopated against dripping pipes. Their helmets scan the corridor. "Heat signature!"

Fuck. Neural disruptor whines in my palm. First shot takes the point man. He convulses into his squadmate. Second shot ricochets off reinforced armor. They charge. I sprint backward, spraying biometric chaff. Their targeting systems lock onto the false heartbeats. Left at the fork, abandoned smuggling den ahead. Racks of expired Stimpaks line the walls. "Come on, you want a discount?"

Grenade meets floor. The explosion showers them in glass ampules. They slip on viscous yellow fluid, crashing through rotted shelving. I'm already crawling through a vent shaft when their commander barks about calling reinforcements. Air ducts rattle. Somewhere above, a tram screeches along magnetic rails. The safehouse stinks of mildew, cordite, and hurried sex. Three monitors show live feeds from Dock 17-B. Mason's team arrives early, amateurs. Watches synchronized. Weapons clean. At least they remembered the infrared dampeners. My reflection glares back from a dead screen. Gaunt. Eyes like cracked concrete. "Just another job."

The lie tastes like natto. The encrypted drive burns against my ankle. schematics they didn't ask for. Contingency plans they'll need. Outside, Bastion Prime howls.

CHAPTER 15: HUFF

The warehouse stinks of the corpses of machinery. My ocular implant paints thermal signatures across crumbling concrete. Three possible ambush points overhead, two exit vectors that haven't collapsed under their own decay. Fingertips brush the plasma pistol's charge indicator. Green light. Always green. VargTech engineering never sleeps. "You're early."

Voice comes from the northeast shadow cluster. I pivot, weapon half-drawn before recognizing Mason's silhouette peeling itself off the wall. Bastard moves like oil on water. No servos whining, no telltale click of augmented joints. I don't know how he silenced them, custom mods, maybe. Or just sheer hatred of being predictable. He stops three meters out. Respects the kill radius. Smart. "Risk assessment," I say, thumb tapping pistol grip. "Your message mentioned mutual destruction."

Mason adjusts his left glove. Twice. Tugging the synth-leather over knuckles fused with combat-grade alloys. "VargTech's got seven black sites processing dissenters this week. You really think I'd waste a bullet on you when they're skinning kids alive for thought crimes?"

Wind howls through shattered skylights. My auditory filters catch the subsonic hum of drones three blocks east. Patrol patterns unchanged. No backup converging. Yet. "Alliance proposals usually start with 'please.'"

"Fuck please." Mason's eyes glint like polished gunmetal.

"You've slagged three of their weapons convoys and taken out six blocks since going rogue."

"It was necessary."

"There were innocent humans…"

"It was six blocks dark in sector housing for VargTech employees."

"But there were children…"

"Who will survive."

"I suppose their parents were inventing new code to better control their wolves."

"Can't control wolves in the dark."

He shifts his weight. "I've got schematics for their neural override hubs. Combine forces, we rip out VargTech's spine before the next lunar cycle." I step over a corroded coolant pipe. Let my boot crunch down hard enough to echo. "You want a puppet. Strings attached."

"I want a scalpel. They programmed you to be the perfect weapon. I'm just pointing you at the right arteries."

My targeting reticle flickers across his carotid. Seventy percent confidence I could sever it before he counters. Thirty percent he's got a dead-man's switch. Probability curves flatten. "Rebels die messy." I snap my fingers, the sharp crack sends rats scurrying. "One wrong intel drop and I'm breathing plasma."

Mason smiles. First time. All teeth and no humor. "You think I'd trust *The Wolf* any more than you trust me? Check the data packet I uploaded to your neural bank. Coordinates for their next enhancer shipment. Burn it down solo if you want. Consider it… courtship."

Internal alerts scream. The file's already there, nested between combat protocols. Dated twelve hours ago. Encryption codes match the underground's signature. "Generous."

"Practical." He's moving again, circling wide. "Dead enforcers can't pay taxes. Every corpse you make is another brick yanked out of their wall."

The coordinates pulse behind my eyelids. Dockside sector. Heavy armor expected. Tactical advantage: 38%. Odds increase to 67% with aerial distraction. I spit on the floor. The acid in my saliva eats through a cockroach scrambling for cover. "Even if I bite, no ranks. No chains."

Mason's glove creaks as he flexes his hand. "You'll get locations. Weapon caches. Enemy positions. We take what you give, you take what we offer. No vows. No hymns. Just butchery."

A drone's spotlight sweeps across the roof. We freeze in the resulting shadow. My subdermal plating itches where they installed the tracking chip last year. Deactivated now. Probably. "Why now?"

"Because you're starting to ask why we bleed. Why you still bleed." Mason taps his temple. "That glitch in your code? That's not a bug. It's the only human thing left in you."

The exit route behind is still clear. I could be gone in 4.2 seconds. Leave this fool to his crusade. I nod toward the dripping ceiling. "Next shipment's guarded by HK-77s."

Another glove adjustment. "You've got EMP charges?"

I Nod.

"Rig them to the southern pylons. Detonate at mark zero."

My eye twitches, irritation works its way into my thoughts. "I know how the game's played."

A micro-nod. A ghost of a smile. Mason's comm unit blinks as he inputs the data. "You'll handle it?"

I'm already walking toward the rusted service elevator. "Bring body bags. Five dozen."

His laugh follows me into the shaft's darkness, harsh and bright as a bullet casing hitting concrete.

"The alliance, if that's what this is, lasts exactly as long as it needs to."

Mason's knuckles pop as he peels off his left glove. Raw scar tissue maps his palm, old burns from plasma fire or maybe a botched demo charge. "They're harvesting cerebellums from the Stipend failures this week." He says it like he's noting a change in the weather. "Installing them in the new HK-series. Your makers call it 'organic optimization.' I call it grave-robbing with tax benefits."

My targeting array auto-highlights the exit path behind him. Twelve steps to the collapsed wall section. Seven if I sprint. "Irrelevant."

"Is it?" He tosses a memory chip that lands precisely between my boots.

"Check the third file. Your last three targets? All slated for neural audits next month. Coincidence smells like shit in summer, Huff."

The chip's encryption breaks under my intrusion protocols. Medical records bloom across my optic feed. Seneca Vloss, the arms dealer I dusted Tuesday, was scheduled for "cortical realignment." Corporate speak for having your free will scraped out with an ice cream scoop.

Rainwater drips through the warehouse ceiling, tattooing rust patterns on Mason's armor. "They're culling anyone who might question the machine. Even loyal little hounds get put down when they start recognizing their chains."

My finger twitches, micro spasms from last week's neural override. VargTech techs said it was a firmware glitch. The lie lands like a hammer now. "Your point?"

He steps into the drone's next surveillance sweep, face lit stark white. "Burn them with us. We'll give you schematics for their new fusion reactors. Access codes to the Enforcer barracks. Names of every Bio-Lord who signed off on the harvest protocols."

Wind howls through shattered windows. Somewhere north, an HK patrol unit's repulsors thrum against the city's heartbeat. I count seventeen distinct engine signatures. Closing fast. "You've got six minutes before that patrol smells our heat." I pivot toward the service elevator, left hand automatically checking my thigh holster's retention strap. "Give me one reason not to leave you as a diversion."

Mason slaps a palm against the warehouse's main support column. Embedded scanners flare blue as he uploads data. "Because I saw the list, Huff. I know who they erased. Kestrel was on it. Brakka too. Mire…"

The words hit like a neural surge mid-simulation. Paralyzing, precise, impossible to ignore.

He flashes a holo, a concrete bunker ten klicks west, its entrance strewn with faded warning signs. "Ground-penetrating scans show a cryo-pod cluster under six meters of rebar. We'll glass the site if you want. Or you can see what's left of your old life."

My vocal modulator crackles from strain. "Irrel…"

"Don't." Mason's gloves snap back into place with military precision. "That history matters. The truth matters. Your truth matters."

The patrol's engine roar climbs to a scream. Four minutes out. He tosses a detonator stamped with rebel sigils. "Take this. Blow their reactor, and I'll give you the bunker's security codes. No oaths. No 'join the cause.' Just a transaction between professionals."

The detonator feels alien in my hand, too light for the payload it holds. My tactical subroutines scream *abort*. Loyalty protocols flood my bloodstream with combat stims. I override them with the emergency code I'm not supposed to know. "Codes first." I grab Mason by his throat plate and slam him into the support column. Concrete dust snows down as I press a vibroblade against his femoral artery. "Or I'll see how optimized your organic components really are."

He coughs blood but grins. "There's the glitch." Data pings my HUD, a full security dossier for the bunker. Biometric locks. Laser grids. The works.

I shove him away. "You'll have reactor smoke by dawn."

The first HK scout drone crashes through the roof. Mason's already gone, vanished into the maze of collapsed machinery. I take three running steps toward the exit before twisting midair to put a .50cal round through the drone's targeting array. Didn't check my gear straps once during the fight. Progress or malfunction? Either way, it'll make killing easier.

The warehouse air tastes like machine sweat. I'm halfway to the exit when Mason materializes from a shadow column, his boots crunching glass from the HK drone I ventilated. My targeting reticle paints his carotid artery before I override the kill impulse. "Still breathing," he says, adjusting his left glove. Always the left first. "Means you're considering more than suicide by corporation."

I palm a micro grenade. "Means I haven't decided which of you gets the shrapnel bouquet."

He steps into the sickly green glow of emergency exit signs. "VargTech's cloning vats in Sector 7-Gamma. You hit them tomorrow; they'll have six fresh batches of enforcers by week's end."

My munitions inventory scrolls across my HUD. Incendiaries low. Armor-piercing rounds at 38%. "Your point?"

"Rebel teams could disable their growth accelerators tonight." Mason taps his temple. "Intel says they're running a new obedience protocol. Makes your old loyalty programming look like a nursery rhyme."

The warehouse creaks like a dying mech. I count three separate stress fractures in the overhead beams. "And this helps me how?"

"Body shops can't print soldiers if their nutrient pumps are swimming in thermite." He throws a data chip that I catch midair. My threat detection suite screams *poison/explosive/bioweapon*. All scans come back clean.

"Coordinates for their filtration control nexus. No strings."

I crush the chip. The coordinates burn into my optic nerve. "You want me to thank you? Send flowers to your funeral?"

Mason's smile looks like a knife wound. "I want you to remember which side keeps giving you free ammo."

"Free?"

Three new hostiles ping on motion sensors. I spin, railgun whining to life, but Mason's already firing. His coil gun barks twice - tungsten slugs shredding two HK scouts through the wall. My third shot turns the remaining drone into a fireworks display. He ejects his magazine. "They're adapting to your attack patterns. Next wave will have jammers."

Molten metal drips from the ceiling. I calculate trajectories. "You didn't just stay for the chat."

"Extraction tunnel beneath the service hatch." Mason kicks aside a smoldering drone carcass. "But you already knew that."

Of course I did. The subsonic rumble of underground machinery had been thrumming in my molars since I arrived. I stride toward the hatch, vibroblade humming. "If this is a trap, I'm using your spleen for a shield."

The tunnel smells like wet concrete and rat shit. Mason keeps two paces back, exactly. Our footsteps echo in a sync that makes my trigger finger itch. He breaks the silence first. "They ever tell you about Project Lazarus?"

My gait doesn't stutter. "Classified."

"Because they're resurrecting Executives." Mason's voice goes clinical. Dead. "Uploading consciousness into fresh clones whenever they die. Immortal oligarchs."

The tunnel branches. I take the left passage automatically. "And?"

"Killing VargTech's meat puppets just resets the clock." He's beside me now, matching stride for stride. "We need to burn the whole system."

I stop so fast he overshoots half a step. Perfect kill angle. He doesn't flinch. "Your revolution. My terms." I cycle my railgun's power cell for emphasis. "I hit priority targets. You stay out of my way. No joint ops. No heart-to-hearts. We stop sharing air after the last corporate spire falls."

Mason studies the rust patterns on the tunnel wall like they're tactical maps. "And when we find what's really pulling VargTech's strings?"

"We won't." The words taste strange. Not a lie. Not quite truth. Not yet.

He extends his right hand. Glove removed. Old-world gesture. "Temporary alliance."

My threat assessment runs the percentages. 58% chance of hidden weapon. 23% poison. 19% actual sincerity. I grip his wrist instead of his palm. Bone and tendon grind beneath my fingers. Human. Fragile. "Until the body count stops rising." I release him with a shove that would fracture normal ribs. His reinforced skeleton holds.

He nods, face unreadable. "We'll need to sync attack patterns. Can't have you frying my teams by accident."

I toss him a frequency chip from my ammo belt. "Broadcast this code before you die. Might delay me looting your corpse."

The tunnel exit looms ahead, dripping with sewage and promise. Mason peels off into a side passage without farewells. Smart. I wait thirteen seconds then move. Three blocks later, my audio pickups catch his whispered transmission: "He's in. Phase two parameters met."

I crush the listening device I planted on his boot. Let him think I'm playing the game. The coordinates for the cloning vats pulse in my vision. Trap or target, either way, something burns. I melt into the acid rain. *Still haven't checked my gear straps*. Maybe the glitch's a feature now.

CHAPTER 16: HUFF

Concrete drinks the stink of burnt ozone and recycled sweat. My bootheels slot into cracks between maintenance plates. Bastion Prime's idea of cobblestones. Above, VargTech's surveillance drones orbit like vultures that haven't figured out I'm not dead yet. Their rotors shred the air into tinnitus whine. I count seven. Then eight. Nine. The crowd parts. Civilians know better when you've got subdermal armor and a pulse rifle across your back.

Left thumb brushes my hip holster. Right checks the knife, carbon-fiber hilt, serrated, vibroblade. Chest rig: tight. Neural ports hum when I touch them. Feedback spiders down my spine. Still synced. Still owned. A girl with a hacked ocular mod freezes mid-step. Her pupils jitter through three zoom levels before she vanishes behind a noodle cart. Smart.

SYNC REQUEST: PRIORITY ALPHA. It hits like a cattle prod to the cerebellum. My knees lock. Teeth grind. Motor control hijacked, left eyelid twitches through forced authorization. "Compliance acknowledged," my growl echoes through my helmet like shells through an empty barrel.

HUD vomits data: *Terminate HVT in Sector 9-D.* Extras follow, operatives flagged for drift. A two-second clip of Lieutenant Mara dissolving mid-debrief. Sync breaks. I stagger into a rusted beam. Adrenal suppressors smooth the motion. "Warning," internal comms rasp. "Cognitive drift detected."

I spit. Watch it vanish between the grates. "Log as system anomaly."

Neon signs hemorrhage migraine-blue across the avenue damp with the cloying blanket of acid smog. Five blocks north, a billboard screams: *VARGTECH SOLUTIONS FOR A SECURE TOMORROW.*

Seventy-nine years of security. Still waiting. My fingers find the neural ports again, cold chrome, twenty-three in total. I trace them, muscle memory and neural bridges slipping into familiar patterns, enforced since basic. Hold still while the machine tickles your brainstem. First time took seven minutes. Now it's forty-three seconds. I check the rifle's charge pack. Green light. Always green.

A sanitation bot sputters past, trailing enzyme stench. Its arms twitch like it's dreaming of promotion. I step over a live cable, heel-to-toe. Always ready. Never safe. *COGNITIVE DRIFT DETECTED.* "Override."

"Overrides remaining: 2/3."

Fuck. Chrome doors hiss. Soy steam and sweat roll out from a ramen stall, ripened by the fetid smell of natto. The cook wears a grease-stained VargTech apron. Augmented arms chop, stir, season. Perfect rhythm. No drift there. "Hey. Dog."

Eleven o'clock. Male. Early thirties. Meth rasp. I pivot slow, let him see the rifle. "Not kennel services."

He's all synth-leather and bad decisions. Gold molar flashes. "Got a job. Off the books."

My ocular implant flags the pistol bulge. Polymer rounds. One shot. Harmless. "Books burn."

He leans closer. Smells like stimcigs. "Heard some corporate hounds are developing... preferences."

Wind shifts. Rotor whine above. I break his nose with my forehead. Cartilage cracks. He folds. My boot finds ribs, count three. "Preferences logged."

Walk before the blood starts talking. Civilians pretend not to notice. They're good at that. The body drop comes three steps later. He materializes from shadow vapor, tall even for a Wolf. Carbon-fiber breastplate, fresh scoring. Left arm's all industrial hydraulics and actuator flex. Command-grade augments. Expensive. "Huff-Seven-zero." His voice grinds like gravel caught in servo teeth. I don't blink. Don't reach. "Designation retired."

His optics click and whirr. Red lenses, new-gen. "Designations don't retire. They get decommissioned." Hydraulic arm tenses. Tubes hiss.

My olfactory sensors spark, nanite lube and spent cordite. Recent combat. Unlogged. I'd spit, but the helmet seals the sentiment. Peripheral scan: no backup. Yet. "Got a retrieval order?"

Jaw plates shift. "Orders evolve."

A data packet pings my interface. Denied. Encryption's trash. Amateur hour. "Try the hard way."

He steps into a pulse of broken neon. Face: seventy percent metal. "Compliance checks increased since last cycle."

"Congratulations."

"Your metrics shifted."

"Variance within twelve percent. Check your manual."

He plants his stance. Combat subroutines spooling. "Manual says nothing about unauthorized interactions."

The ramen creep. Should've caved his skull. "Civilian initiated."

"With excessive force."

"Says the mutt who snapped six collarbones last riot."

Optics flare. "Those were hostiles."

"So was... that." My muzzle indicates a pool of blood and pain.

Static hisses from his vocal grille. Cheap intimidation.

"Higher-clearance assets notice deviations."

Muscle memory wants to check my rifle. I don't. "Noted."

He steps closer. Hydraulic whine climbs into ultrasound. "Weapons-free can be revoked." I close the gap. Step into a cloud of coolant that reeks of desperation. He's nervous. If I refuse, he faces my fate, or my muzzle. I refuse anyway. "Requires committee sign-off."

"Committees restructure."

Bones creak inside my gloves. Old reflex. "Send the memo."

Red lenses blink. "Hunting dogs get put down when they bite handlers."

Three options: Concussion grenade to the pelvis. Vibroblade to actuator.
Compliance. Compliance tastes like oil that's been sitting too long.
I lean in. Helmets almost touch. "But first..." My HUD flickers to targeting.
"...they have to miss the muzzle flash."

Targeting lasers dance across my chest. Garbage bin clatters. Heads snap.
Scrawny kid. Bolt cutters. Rat carcass. The pup snarls, metal braided with
meat. Kid bolts. I glance back. pup's retreating. Armored silhouette devours
the neon. "Maintain operational parameters."

"Or?"

His implants flare blue. "Cost-benefit applies to all assets."

Then he's gone. I count fifteen. Static in my molars. HUD thrums with
suppressed alerts. Targeting overlays sweep the choke point—exit vectors,
snipe angles, collateral range. Nothing pings. No squad. No chatter. Just a
message. I piss on the kid's abandoned rat. It sizzles. pH still acidic. Sync
command residue.

Priorities recalibrate: Primary: Maintain operational capability. Secondary: Assess
command cluster cohesion. Tertiary: Undetermined. I shoulder through the
alley mouth. Synthleather gloves rasp against ferrocrete.

Priority overlay: Tactical threat assessment. Ocular implants map thermal pulses,
ninety-seven degrees average, three concealed firearms, no visible threats.
Gear check mid-stride. Thumb grazes release catches. Index traces the neural
shunt panel. *No compromise detected. Maintenance: 214 hours remaining.* "Asset
tracking nominal," I mutter toward a streetlamp camera. Its lens refocuses
with a wet click.

OBJECTIVE UPDATE: *Identify operational friction.* I move left-right-left. Each
footfall precise. Pavement cracks sync with my stride like code. Civilians peel
off like debris in a blast radius. I shoulder-check a food cart, noodles detonate
against steel shutters. "Hey, fuckstick!" the vendor barks.

I pivot like a turret. "Complaint code?"

He freezes. Sauce drips off his nose. Matches the pattern on my chest plate.
Shoulder blades itch where cranial ports feed into wetware. That's new.

I carve through the Neon Bazaar meat crowd. Every third step, drones mirror me, surveillance patterns stuttering mid-rotation. Three floors up, a sniper nest's polarized glass reflects too much amber. Barrel shadow cuts across ventilation shafts.

OVERLAY UPDATE: *Unsanctioned observation confirmed.* Kneecap servos whine as I shorten gait by 1.8 centimeters. Crowd shifts, three civilians cross themselves. Two stalls slam shut.

My left thumb checks ammo count. Right hand brushes the kill switch nodes at my spine. All green. All lethal. Noodle vendor's curse still loops in my buffers. Analysis: 72% chance he filed a disturbance report. Should've broken his wrist. A child's hologram flickers: "VarCreds buy freedom!"

I crush the projector chip under heel. It screams in five languages before the casing cracks. "Target-rich environment," I mutter. To no one. To everyone.

Proximity ping, two blocks west. Thermal signatures match pursuit protocols. Muscle density. Subdermal plating. The optic-override head twitch. They're herding me. Kovan Bridge. Amateur mistake. I slip into a maintenance pipe stinking of synthetic bile. Rip off my biometric tag. Clamp it to a methane rat. It bites. Teeth bounce off carbonweave. "Run east." I inject the command tone. It freezes, then obeys.

Three minutes later, Kovan explodes. I crawl out behind a brothel HVAC stack. Trace a scar in the concrete, same stress fracture that split Tower 7's spine. My scar. The building's scar. INTERNAL ALERT: *Sentimentality detected.* "Diagnostic routine," I rasp, slamming my sternum plate. Adrenal shunt surges. Clarity returns like yesterday's dinner. Still taste copper. Must've bitten my tongue during the sync hit.

She emerges from steam. Lithium eyes. Graffiti jacket—wolf's head tangled with neural threads. She clutches black-market antibiotics like they'll shield her. "Not selling," she blurts.

"Not buying." My voice sounds like stripped gears.

We hold position. Killzone calculus. Her safety's off. Amateurs always flinch pre-emptively. "Tell the Ghost Market..." I start. Then stop. What the fuck am I doing?

She bolts. Left boot squeaks. I log the sound. That's new. The climb to Sector Roof 9H takes eleven minutes. Balconies become handholds. Trigger sites I wired last winter now serve as ladders. Gloves come away sticky. Grime, blood, time. At the summit, Bastion spreads like a shot gunned motherboard. My retinal display counts seventeen active trackers. I let them ping. Chrono Sync check: 23:47. Vision fractures. Sync-feed splits: street cams, drone eyes, satellite sweeps, all pouring into my occipital port. VargTech's still watching. "Playback: last loyalty assessment."

The memory slams in. *White room. Spinal needles. The sync officer's face flickers, more insect than man. "State primary function." My voice: "To hunt. To obey. To endure."* They don't ask why anymore. The recall cuts off. My gastric sleeve floods with stabilizers. Learned that trick by the fifth interrogation.

Below, spotlights sweep the rat decoy's death site. Tag melted into its ribcage. VargTech might give it a funeral. They love dead loyalty. Arsenal readout scrolls through the haze: 43 armor-piercing rounds. 2 concussion grenades. 1 monofilament garrote (57% integrity). Neural spike charges: depleted. Regrets: pending.

North. Sky-shriek battery whines to life. Target sectors bloom red on the skyline. I did clearance there last winter. Snow turned pink for weeks. PRIMARY OBJECTIVE UPDATED: *Survive next 12 hours.* Secondary priorities scatter like shrapnel. Let them. When I blink, neon fractures, red and corporate blue splitting into prismatic bars. Half machine-readouts. Half organic blur. Hunters shouldn't doubt their sight. But here we are.

I pocket the grenade pin I've been palming since Kovan. Turn from the skyline. There's a cache beneath the so-called GOL-T3R memorial. Where machines mourn a life, they were never allowed to live. I buried it after Blackmarch. Let them audit my logs. Sync my memories. That stash isn't on any server. "Come find me," I tell the nearest camera. Its lens cracks from subharmonic resonance.

The drop-off ledge feels familiar. Ten years ago, I pushed a resistance leader from this spot. His scream took 0.6 seconds to die in the wind. Today, my boots settle into the same stress fracture. No poetic last stand. Just math: Nearest enemies: 12 minutes out. Optimal ambush sites: 3. Rogue Vargstryk probability: 62%. Motivation coherence: *Undetermined*

CHAPTER 17: HUFF

Finger-jacks snap from my right hand. Plug into the nearest terminal. Holograms bloom, threat assessments, deployment logs, requisition forms. Standard hunter-killer protocols. Five years of terminations scroll past in milliseconds. All targets: GOL-T3R. All missions: completed. Pig Units don't have names. They aren't human, they said.

My left eye twitches. The organic one. Ignore it. Push deeper. Authorization codes burn through black ice like hot rounds through tissue. *Classified directory loading...*

Sweat beads above my ocular implant. Shouldn't be sweating. Climate's locked at 18 degrees Celsius. Poison-green files glow. Genetic profiles. Bio Division purchase orders. Shipping manifests from districts I cleared. Dates line up with wet work ops. Locations match my old patrol grids. "Reconnaissance error." The words feel like someone else's. "Priority targets identified incorrectly. Mission parameters…"

Finger-jacks tremble. Metal fatigue. Must be. Neural feed dumps sixty-seven names into my cortex. *Ethan Choi – 8 years – District 9 Habitation Block C; Marisol Vega – 6 years – New Tenochtitlan Arcology; Aleksy Nowak – 7 years –*

Warsaw Spire Residential. The list keeps coming. I rip the finger-jacks free. Blood floods my mouth. Retinal HUD informs me I'm biting through my cheek. "Corrupted data." I grip the terminal. Metal creaks under augmented pressure. "Glitch in the archive system. Requires verification."

Three blinks trigger forensic analysis. DNA markers. Age progression. Matrix comparisons. Matches bloom like blood spatter. Every face from the termination reports. Every Pig Unit I put down. Staring back at me as children. "Display supplementary evidence." My voice cracks mid-sentence. Glitch in the modulator. Must be. Holograms stutter, grainy surgical footage. White tiles reflecting the wrong kind of red. First vid: a prep room. Tiny hands pressed against observation glass. Nose-print smears the surface. Timestamp says twelve years old. Hispanic female. Designation: GOL-T3R-09. I know how her skull fragments. Know what caliber makes that exit wound. Surgeons enter wearing VargTech hazard suits. No names, just numbers. Scalpels dig into brown hair without anesthetic. Her scream syncs with the bone saw's pitch.

My left thumb twitches, targeting reflex. They peel her skull like overripe fruit. "Neural lace integration requires malleable cerebrum," one drones. Gloved hands thread nano-filaments through living grey matter. "Pediatric subjects provide optimal plasticity."

Her legs keep kicking after the monitor flatlines. HUD highlights shared biometrics, my kill confirms. "Cross-reference terminated units with pediatric records." My jaw cracks on the words.

Matches bloom across three screens. GOL-T3R-19 used to flinch at loud noises. I put two through his ocular cavity last monsoon season. GOL-T3R-33 had strawberry blonde braids before they grafted armor to her ribs. Took forty-three rounds to drop her in Jakarta. My reticle's still stained with that shade of pink. "Prioritize researcher manifests." I taste bile. Swallow. "Locate project architects."

System pings. One audio log: Dr. Emil Voss, Head of Bioengineering. Dated six hours before his 'tragic maglev accident'. His voice oozes through the speaker like synth-oil. "Subject procurement remains our primary bottleneck. Urban sweep teams require improved containment protocols. Last month's batch arrived with unacceptable neural degradation."

Cold settles behind my sternum. I recognize the sensation, subdermal armor contracting. Fourteen files auto-play. Seven severed spinal columns. Three cardiac explosions during adrenal enhancer trials. Four kids chewing through their own tongues. HUD highlights shared biometrics. My kill confirms.

"Cross-reference terminated units with pediatric records." My jaw cracks on the words.

Matches bloom across three screens. One face pauses me. No kill report. No combat log. Just a still frame, wide eyes, one front tooth missing. Feels like I should remember her. I don't. Not clearly. But I remember the bear. Torn ear. Charred ribbon. Smelled like smoke and marsh dust. I found it once, after a sweep. One block over from where the screams stopped. Couldn't bring myself to toss it. Just stared.
Next night, I left it beside a sleeping girl. Never knew why.
Maybe I did.
Maybe I do now.

No match found. No follow-up. File ends in static. The console implodes under my grip. Plasma licks up my forearm. Sixty-seven missions. Sixty-seven headshots. Sixty-seven pig masks hiding faces that should've been smeared with ice cream, not cranial fluid.

I slam in the destruct sequence. Override codes blur. Loyalty protocols scream through my hindbrain. ERROR: COMMAND NOT RECOGNIZED
I rip out the nearest server stack. Hydraulic fluid sprays arterial-red across the security feeds. "New mission parameters." My voice comes out ragged. Human. "Terminate all project personnel. Destroy all research facilities. Erase all records."

Alarms wail. Targeting HUD lights up. Twelve hostiles converging on Level Sigma-Nine. *Let them taste what they built. I hope they choke on it.* Security blast doors hiss open. Stun grenades roll across the floor. I don't turn. Don't need to. Hostile outlines bloom in my rear sensors. Wolves. Third gen. Puppies. Their muzzle flashes strobe against the racks. I move between bullet streams like they're standing still. First Wolf eats his own arm cannon. Second gets a data drive through his eye. Third makes the mistake of going hand-to-hand.

We were programmed with overlapping kill protocols. Should've updated their firmware. When the last one stops twitching, I rip the comms unit from his skull. Static-laced voices: lockdown procedures, reinforcements, sterilize the sector. I check my gear. Strap tension optimal. Ammo: critical. Two incendiaries left. "New primary objective," I whisper into the dead Wolf's headcam. "Burn this plague pit to bedrock."

Heartbeat patterns stutter across comms. Recognition. Fear. Good.
The Wolf's headcam crunches beneath my boot. Lithium-scented hydraulic fluid pools around my feet. Somewhere deep in my chest housing, a coolant pump thrums like a war drum. Scavenger drones come first. Cheap bastards.

Magnetic slugs shred two mid-air. The third tries to kamikaze my flank. Learned behavior. My grappler snags it mid-dive and slams it into a server stack. Ceramic plating detonates. Fire sprinklers vomit gray slurry that smells like burnt hair. "*Containment breach in sector seven.*" The PA sounds bored. "*All assets converge.*"

Assets. That's what they called the kids too. Sixty-seven missions. My boot connectors click across the floor grates. Tactical overlay maps the archive. Three exits, all compromised.

Fourth option: maintenance shaft behind the cryo-server array. Feels like a corporate shortcut. Plasma cutter chews through the panel. Wires squirm like gutted eels. Interface jack finds the firewall. Primitive. Probably slapped in by some intern sucking SynthCaf through a nutrient straw. Access granted. Shaft's tight enough to scrape paint off my shoulder plates. Motion sensors ping ahead. Not Wolves. Bigger. Slower. Punishers. Slow, heavily armored, brute force. Ex-cons with no brains and nothing to lose.

Two meat tanks in full riot gear clog the tunnel. Shock batons spark, charge building in their coils. One's got a pneumatic face, probably lost the original eating lead paste as a grunt. "Huff Unit-07," Pneumatic Face intones. "Stand down for recalibration."

I check my strap tension. Retinal HUD pulses red. "Request denied."

First baton swing lights up the shaft like a power surge. I absorb it in my trauma plating, then return the favor with a mono-filament slash across his thigh actuator. Hydraulic spray. Second enforcer charges. Too slow. I drive my shoulder into his chest plate, crack his spine against the tunnel wall. Their suits were made for riots, not ghosts. Pneumatic Face tries to recalibrate me again. Voice cracks this time. "Compliance override. Section Forty-Two protocol."

"Protocol's dead."

My blade severs his voice box. The wet gurgle is almost a mercy. Punisher Two is trying to crawl back toward his baton. I kick it to the far end of the shaft. Let him feel powerless before I finish the job. The shaft falls silent. My combat readout says 61%. Doesn't matter. No one left in this tunnel but targets and wreckage. Archive doors seal behind me like a tomb. Breath locks in my throat. No air. No problem. Chest seals. Oxygen gel floods the lung ports. Chemical taste like bleach and carbonic acid.

I keep moving. Retinal HUD flickers: 87% combat readiness. Neural spike activity redlines; diagnostics can choke. I kick open another door. Bastion

Prime's night stabs my optics. Neon smears across permacrete. A noodle cart burns in the gutter. Lungs suck in the sweet stench of acid smog and wet noodles. "Subject Huff-7-0." The voice crackles from speakers and throat implants alike. "Cease movement. Surrender all acquired data."

I check my wrist-mounted flechette loader. Full charge. "You first."

They come in formation, shock batons glowing, ceramic armor pulsing faint blue. Three flank. One talks. My knees flex. The noodle cart crumples under my weight as I leap. First flechette hits the talker's throat seal. His baton short-circuits a happiness module billboard. Four remaining. Two behind me with stun-nets. I spin into arterial spray. Crack one's clavicle implant, slam him into his partner. "Non-lethal force authorized!"

Lie. Baton hit lands. Feedback surge boosts my servo output. I lean into the visor and crush his throat. Tranquilizer pricks my thigh. Bio-monitor screams. I stab it, into someone else's jugular.

Two left. I watch their pupils dilate. I smell the adrenaline. "Stand down," I growl.

My modulator drops it into subsonic threat frequencies. One voids. One drops his weapon. I leave them coughing on fear. Rain eats at my neural ports as I walk. Twelve drones shadow me. Let them. A kid in the slums watches me with milky augmetic eyes. Both legs gone. She extends her palm, not for credits. A chip glows anarchist red. "Burn them all," she rasps through a salvaged voice box.

I take the chip. She's gone into the steam before I look up. The data breaks clean—resistance ciphers, hot. Blueprint schematics. Conduits. Rotations. Thermal windows. Let the resistance think they're using me. Let VargTech think they still own me. GOL-T3R footage loops in my memory, chrome where there should've been children.

Neon reflects blood-red in oil-streaked puddles. Sky towers gleam like teeth. I roll my collar up. Armor-weave tight against synthetic skin. The war starts tonight.

CHAPTER 18: LUSTOR

The holographic static smells like burnt ozone. My glove creaks when I flex my fingers. Too many hours clutching phantom control panels. Can't tell if that's real perspiration trickling under my collar or just neural feedback again. Doesn't matter. Only the projection matters. "Enhance sector seven." My voice slices the air like an electro-whip.

The display blooms three feet from my face, bathing my gloves in cold blue. Huff's thermal signature skulks through maintenance tunnels. Eleven minutes past extraction window. My right hand twitches toward the recall command. Stops. Protocol demands verification. I snap two fingers left. Retina-feed unfurls raw and unfiltered. There he is, hesitating at checkpoint gamma. Left eyelid flutter: three rapid blinks. Old tell, from before we stripped his facial muscle set. "Track biometric anomalies since last upload."

Screens bloom like synthetic bloodstains. Cardiac spikes inconsistent with mission scope. Cortisol elevated during civilian contact. Five patrol deviations. My glove hits the holodisplay. Pixels scatter. "That's not a weapon. That's a fucking philosophy major with daddy issues."

Technicians freeze. Good. Let them feel the math unravel. "Code Black," I say. The words frost my tongue. "Full revocation. Neural lockdown. Locomotor override if he pings within five klicks of any corporate asset."

A junior ops manager bolts upright like a kicked dog. "Sir, protocol requires…"

144

I step into his breath-space. Smell yesterday's protein ration on his tongue. "You see a committee? You counting votes?" My thumb brushes his shock tab, just enough to make his eyes leak. "Execute."

Red lights stutter across the command pit. The main screen bleeds arterial spray as Huff's profile rotates. Loyalty metrics collapsing in real time.
[CORTICAL ACCESS REVOKED]
[COMBAT SUITE DEACTIVATION IN PROGRESS]
[NON-VARG AFFILIATES MARKED FOR TERMINATION]
I count seven system breaches before the first alarm. He's already slicing through the backup encryptions. Should've expected it. I built those redundancies myself after Jakarta. "Divert drones from sectors eight through twelve." I peel off my left glove. Skin meets cold metal. Authorization sigils flare beneath my palm. "Priority override. All units converge on these coordinates."

The map ignites in crimson. Twenty-seven hunter-killers rerouting. Fourteen auto-turrets spin up in sublevel armories. Three Wolverine-class terminators thawing. Two Punishers re-routed. Some exec's whelp whispers about resource allocation. I don't look up. "Your father's mistress sends her regards. Keep talking and I'll broadcast the location chip she planted in your femoral artery."

Silence. Beautiful silence. Just the staccato rhythm of execution codes being entered. Across the city, vault doors grind open. Steel claws scrape concrete. Huff's life just got measured in single-digits. I reset my glove. The whisper of fabric across skin sounds like a serpent laughing. The neural feed stutters as three meat-sacks in suits materialize at my shoulder. Their breathing tells me which ones jerked off to compliance manuals during puberty. "Sir, diverting all assets risks exposure in sectors…"

I flick the biometric data to their lenses. Watch their pupils dilate at the life insurance policies I just voided. "Congratulations. You've been promoted to mobile cover." My glove snaps against the nearest throat mic. "Priority Lambda-Seven. Full asset convergence on Traitor Primary."

Screens fracture into hunter grids. Forty-seven Wolves redirect mid-stride. I scent lithium bleeding from the overheated servers. "Sir, protocol requires…"

"Protocol requires you shut your septic mouth before I have it welded." The sterilization unit hisses beneath us like it agrees. "That's not a defective product out there. That's contagion."

They don't blanch when the first combat feed lights up. Good. Still enough spine left to appreciate artistry. Wolf Team Kappa breaching a nightclub HVAC system, monofilament wire glinting like spider silk. My knuckle cracks the haptic panel. "Gear up the Fenrir Modules."

Three Adam's apples bob. No one mentions Jakarta. The vaults hiss open anyway, reeking of fur stink and hydraulic fluid. Coordinates blossom across satellite overlays. Red pulses sync to the arrhythmia in my left eyelid. "Activate Sköll Protocol."

The room drops ten degrees. Even the drones hesitate. "Sir, that's last resort…"

I unclip my ascot. Let it drift over his protest. White silk lands on the tactical display, bisecting Huff's last projected path. "Burn the city. Salt the earth. I want his code splinters smoking in my inbox by dawn."

Algorithms scream. In the streets, tungsten rods tilt skyward. A junior suit vomits into a planter. The rest learn vocabulary, watching twelve million credits of stealth choppers drop like syringes into the warehouse district. "Thermals live," a technician rasps.

I lean toward the glow. There, between collapsing tenements. A blur too graceful for meat. He's using the old sewer routes. My smile liquefies like solder. "Initiate Lazarus Grid."

Power dies across six blocks. Emergency lights carve jagged shadows. A perfect hunting ground. The Wolves move. "You're not the only one with six blocks dark, Huff."

Holographic smog burns my retinas. Sixteen tactical feeds swarm dead sectors of Bastion Prime, sewer access points blinking like infected pores. My glove squeaks against the holotable's edge. *There.* Maintenance shaft Gamma-9. Perfect bottleneck. "Relay to Wolfpack Kilo." I don't look up from the arterial glow. "Flush the waste lines with liquid nitrogen."

A tech's Adam's apple bobs. "Civilians in the…"

"Say *liquid* again." My cuff adjusts itself. "Slower."

He chokes on compliance codes. The order transmits. Sweat stink blooms behind me. Morale degradation. I track the fear vectors in peripheral, trembling hands, three staffers fingering hidden crucifixes. One wets himself. Fucking organics. Always leaking.

The Fenrir Modules hit the sewer junction first. Thermal feeds spike, distorted shadows with reactor cores glowing piss-yellow through radiation shielding. One heartbeat. Two. Three. Contact.

Huff's heat signature detonates across three sectors at once. Clever dog taught himself mirror relays. My molars grind composite fillings into powder. "Decoy patterns," I snap. "You, purge your sinus infection and calculate exit vectors."

The analyst jerks like a marionette. Keys rattle. Overlay maps bloom. Storm drains, vent shafts, old metro tunnels. All converge on Blackwater Market. I slide two fingers through the projection. Split. Rotate. A choke point crystallizes under Third Spire's pylons. "Divert Charlie and Echo units. Prep seismic charges."

"Sir, those foundations are…"

"Fragile?" My smile clicks. "Let's audit their structural integrity."

Screens flicker as demolition protocols overwrite safety regs. Across the city, Wolves reroute with mechanical precision. Retinal HUD pulses with their biometrics—heart rates steady, musculature at 98% efficiency. Good stock. The market feed explodes in static. "Activate Sköll Protocol. Full-spectrum jamming. I don't want to see any weapons firing but the Fenrir."

Lights die across six more blocks. Emergency strobes birth jagged shadows. Infrared: Wolf outlines fan through collapsed stalls. Huff's thermal ghost flits between produce freezers. "Thermal sinks," I mutter. "Track refrigerant trails."

A junior tech fumbles zoning overlays. I break his nose. "Now." Blood spray makes the holoprojection *pop*. Coordinates lock.

Huff's moving northwest. Toward the reservoir. My glove creaks. My cuff stitching pops. Reset. "Scramble interceptors."

"Sir, water treatment plant's a civilian sector…"

"Blow it up."

Seven quarantine systems engage. Alarms wail. Civilians will die. So what. Holograms shimmer. Huff's heat blur vaults a fence. Straight into Echo Unit's kill zone. I lean in. His silhouette twists midair, impossible contortion. Enhanced? Since when?

Wolves open fire. Concrete erupts in powdered teeth. He's gone. "Full replay." My voice cracks glass. "Frame by frame."

The feed stutters. There, during the salvo's eighth microsecond. Huff's arm distorts. Plasmesh weave beneath the skin. My design. My oversight. "Terminal override codes." I'm already keying them. "Purge his augment firmware."

"Transmitting." Comms officer sounds like a deflating tire. "No response."

Impossible. Unless…The realization hits like a freight train. He jailbroke the neural shackles. The command center holds its breath. I adjust my cuffs. "Activate Gjallarhorn." My voice is like iced water.

Every screen flares crimson. Techs vomit. Even the Wolves freeze. 0.7 seconds. Longest pause since Singapore. Gjallarhorn detonates in Bastion Prime's under-levels. Sonic hell. Rodents liquefy in walls. Civilian comms flare with screams as eardrums rupture and teeth are lost to pressure shock. Acoustic overlay shows Huff staggering. Finally. "Vector Zulu-Niner," I bark. "Converge."

Wolves descend like steel rainfall. My fingers dance across the haptic grid, herding them. Huff's bleeding sound now. Every footstep rings like target practice. Then he does something interesting. Dives into a maglev tunnel. Clever. Clever boy. "Seal exits," I order. "Override transit safeties."

"Bullet train ETA ninety seconds," someone whispers.

"Perfect." I check my chrono. "Prep welcoming committee."

Huff's sprinting down the track. Wolves close in. Ahead, the 22:15 Bastion Express grows from pinprick to screaming god. He jumps. Not sideways. Up. Plasmesh fingers catch the undercarriage. Legs swing wild, almost artistic. Wolves open fire. So do the train's automated defenses. Chaos fractalizes. Shrapnel patterns bloom across the holotable. I lean back. "Divert all units to…"

Pain spikes through my ocular implant. Static fuzz. When the feed clears, Huff's biometrics flatline. Silence. Then: A laugh crackles through demolished comms. "Miss me, father?"

I sink through the floor. My glove meets a technician's throat. "Trace. Now."

The signal's corpse is cold. Across the city, emergency lights die. For three seconds, Bastion Prime goes dark. When power returns, twelve Wolves report critical malfunctions. Huff's body is missing. I straighten my cuffs. "Burn the reservoir."

The neural feed still leaks copper and static when I stride across the command nexus. Twelve Wolves twitch on their readouts. Twelve opportunities for improvement. My gloves meet with a snap. Louder than the technicians' breathing. "Reservoir ignition in progress," someone quavers. Sector Seven slums melt like candle wax under white phosphorus. Burning polymer seeps through the vents.

I lean over the holotable, watching heat signatures scatter like roaches. "Double yield. Add Varganax to the mix."

Someone chokes. Good. Let them taste the cleanse. Huff's ghost grins from every shadow. My implant replays his escape vector, that beautiful, treasonous arc onto the maglev. Had to make him myself, didn't I? Only my best could outmaneuver twelve Wolves. *My* creation. The one I chose. The one whose promise I saw in the G0l-T3R acquisition program. The one I *persuaded* to volunteer *before* the collection sweep. Only he could survive what I've thrown at him. And gloat. "Sir?" A junior analyst inches closer. "The... corpse diversion. Security cams show…"

"I count thirty-seven unmonitored seconds between train impact and grid reboot."

My thumb erases his clearance mid-sentence. The chip in his neck flashes red. He drops. "Who else enjoyed the lightshow?"

The room suddenly loves their consoles. Three alerts bloom across the tactical board: smuggling tunnel under the arcology. Gene-lock vault breach. Explosives missing from an Enforcer depot. I laugh. A lieutenant goes into shock. "Revert citadel systems to Protocol Obsidian."

The nearest technician flinches. She knows what it means: drown every subsystem in forensic malware. "Initiate neural shock sequence. Tier Three personnel."

Screams ripple through Bastion Prime's lower decks. Twenty thousand employees drop foaming. 4.3% fatality rate. Acceptable margin. The holotable flickers. For half a heartbeat, Huff's face overlays the map face shield up, mouthing. *Miss me?*

Ceramic shards bite into my palm. The ops chief's coffee mug. Blood spatter suggests arterial spray. Angle matches the fragment radius. Curious. "Trace the last transmission's carrier wave."

The AI obeys faster than the man it replaced. Red lines converge on the old financial district. Of course. Carrion ground. I razed it myself. "Prep an orbital package."

Two technicians faint. The Third Chair meets my gaze. "Sir, the treaties…"

My thumb hovers over her life pendant. "The Pax Machina has a clause for vermin extermination."

Thirty-four seconds later, the sky cracks. Wolf squadron cams capture the kinetic strike. Three blocks become an inverted-volcano. Shockwaves swallow surveillance drones. Perfect. Zero biometric returns. Too clean. Huff breathes chaos like oxygen. The alert pings as rubble temps hit 8,000 Kelvin. Unauthorized launch. Maintenance silo. My smile fractures cheekbones. A stolen shuttle rips through atmospheric defense. "Let him run." The words taste like all my birthdays rolled into one. "Tag the craft with Ascension trackers."

Fourth Chair hesitates. "If he reaches the radiation belt…"

"Then we test the warheads."

My cufflinks catch the firelight as Bastion Prime burns. "Update the board: Huff's escape increases quarterly termination quotas by eighteen percent."

"Stockholder value just doubled."

They don't understand yet. This isn't containment. It's advertising. When the command nexus finally empties of whimpering meat, I seal the sanctum. The central holotable births a fractal map. Every explosion Huff ignites, every life he takes, it all feeds the pattern. Beautiful. My creation. My masterpiece. My knife in the world's back. Let the resistance embrace him. Let them crown their mechanized messiah. Every martyr needs a cross. I've just supplied the nails. VargTech's logo rotates over the carnage. I straighten my cuffs. The hunt's already over. He just doesn't know he's running toward the grave.

CHAPTER 19: CHANCE

The terminal's blue static licks my knuckles as I punch through VargTech's seventh firewall. Three days chewing stim-gum and pissing in protein shake bottles to crack this encryption. Worth it. The screen vomits coordinates, weapon specs, deployment patterns. Ambush grid for tomorrow's weapons drop.

Target designation: Vargstryk Unit H-07. Huff. My left thumb finds the data chip in my pocket. Spin it twice clockwise. Old habit. *Sell the coordinates to Syndicate buyers: 50k creds minimum. Warn the tin soldier: Zero profit. Maximum corporate crosshairs.*

Fingers hover over transfer protocols. The chip's edge bites my palm. Two years ago, neon market in Kessell's Hollow. Kid with a retinal graft gone septic, bleeding yellow pus. Offered me prototype schematics for half a ration bar. I took the deal. Left him coughing blood in an alley. Neutral's just another word for alive.

Something clangs in the ventilation shaft above me. Freeze. Left hand slides to the shock-pistol duct-taped under the desk. Right keeps typing, initiating purge protocols. Terminal fan whines like a dying cat. Five seconds. Ten. Metallic skitter through the pipes. Stray cyber-mongoose hunting roaches. Probably. "Fuck your mother," I whisper to the ceiling.

Holoscreen glows brighter. Ambush details sear into my retinas, plasma turrets, EMP drones, six squads of chrome-jawed enforcers. They're not taking chances with Huff. *Charge the Syndicate double. Seventy-five grand buys a lot of forgetfulness.*
Remember Huff's optics flickering when you called him "partner" last week. Like a glitch

in his kill-programming.
My teeth grind enamel dust. Chip spins faster. Could walk away clean. Should. Air tastes like static-charged air. Flash memory: arms dealer on the Red Canal. Offered me sanctuary during the '28 purge. I sold his location for a med kit. My leg was infected. Still limp when it rains. Terminal beeps. Thirty seconds until intrusion detection. "Fuck."

Hands move before the rest of me catches up. Encrypted burst to Mason's last known frequency. Data package: ambush coordinates, weapon specs, evasion vectors. Transmission progress bar crawls. Sweat pools above my brow implant. Burns like fire ants marching under my scalp. "Not a favor," I tell the room. "Just balancing the scales."

Vent shaft creaks again. Louder. It echoes through rusted ductwork as the bar hits 98%. My left eyelid twitches, neural implant overheating. Should've replaced the coolant gel. Should've walked away. Should've done a lot of things. Three blips. Connection secured. Packet launched.
I wipe my palm across the keyboard, sweat and synth-oil. "There's your goddamn revolution."

Holoscreen fractures. Resolves into a woman's face, cropped black hair, scar slicing her right iris. Zara. Mason's comms lieutenant. Last time we met, she tried to stab me with a vibro-knife. "Chance," her voice crackles through ancient speakers. "Interesting frequency to be broadcasting on."

I lean back until the chair complains. "Found some scrap metal prices. Thought your junkyard army might care."

Her cybernetic eye whirs, scanning off-screen. I count four, five...
"Ambush coordinates. VargTech deployment patterns. ECM protocols."

"Like I said. Scrap metal."

Her gloved hand adjusts something off-camera. Movement's too crisp, ex-military. "This intel's current-gen. Costs more than your usual gutter trash."

I spin the data chip across my knuckles. "Consider it a bulk discount."

The scar on her eye puckers as she squints. "Mason's running ops in Sector Nine tonight."

"Good for him."

"Coincidentally near these coordinates."

"Buy a lottery ticket."

Her lips twitch. Almost a smile. "We've got a medic who can look at that implant. No charge."

"Tell your medic to eat a grenade."

The terminal pings. Data receipt confirmed. Zara leans closer. The screen warps her features into a digital ghost. "You know they'll burn your networks for this."

I kill the connection. The safehouse stinks of moldy insulation and indecision. I flex my hands. Tremors run up my wrists. Not fear. Adrenaline dump. Chemical backlash. Biology's bitch. The chip digs into my palm. Should've charged them. Should've bartered for safe passage. Should've…Yeah, yeah. Shoulda, coulda, woulda. Didn't. They'll carve that on my grave.

Terminal lights flare crimson. Incoming priority channel. Encrypted. I almost blast the console. Mason's voice cuts through, no video feed. Clean. Calm. Like he's ordering coffee. "Your payment's been transferred."

"Didn't ask for…"

"Non-negotiable. Standard finder's fee."

I check the account. Fifty grand. More than standard. Less than betrayal's worth. "Generous."

"Practical."

Pause. Fabric rustle, those damn gloves. "This complicates your position."

I watch the vent grate shudder. "My position's fluid."

"Fluid becomes stagnant without flow."

"Philosophy now? Charge extra for that?"

Another pause. Longer. "Huff's team extracted twenty minutes ago. Clean."

The tightness in my chest unravels. Fuck. "Send the next invoice sooner."

His tone shifts. Softer. "We're better creditors than VargTech." The line dies.

I stare at the holoscreen's afterimage. Fifty grand won't cover the bullet they'll put in my skull. Seventy-five wouldn't have either. The chip clicks against the terminal. Still spinning. The holoscreen's afterglow burns retinal ghosts into the ceiling's cracked polymer. Fifty grand. Fifty fucking grand and a one-way ticket to VargTech's kill list. I shrug. I was probably already on it. This just bumped me up the queue.

Left thumb finds the chip. Spin, catch, spin. Right hand taps arrhythmic patterns on the armrest. Consequences stack like bullet tax. Corporate death squads. Blacklists from every neutral hub. Luka's gonna want his pound of flesh for torching the smuggling routes. The chip clicks louder. Should've charged triple. Should've…

A coolant pipe groans overhead. Bastion Prime's bowels always sound like they're digesting. Flicker-strip lights paint seizure hues across rusted welds. Mildew. Fried circuitry. The walls, corroded steel plates welded over original concrete, creep inward by millimeters. Every breath tastes like someone else's recycled panic. Terminal pings. Once. High-frequency. I'm halfway to the door before thought catches up. Muscle memory dumps the data core into a micro grenade canister. Three twists, and it's armed. Toss. Into the server stack. Screen flashes crimson. INTRUSION DETECTED: TRACER PROTOCOL ACTIVE. "Fuck, fuck, fuck."

Gloves slap the terminal. Encryption layers peel under frantic keystrokes. VargTech's counter hack swarm floods the system, ICE-pick algorithms chewing through firewalls. Left eye twitches. Not the augments. Pure organic fear. "C'mon, you fossil…"

The safehouse rig's older than my liver. Salvaged GOL-T3R junk. Smells of burnt hair when overloaded. Smoke curls from the tower. CONTAINMENT AT 17%. Sweat drips onto the keys. Salt stings the split on my lip. Spin the chip faster. Override command. Initiate core meltdown. "Do it. Do it you piece of…"

The screen dies mid-snarl. Darkness. Then…
Emergency strips stutter on. Blood-red LEDs crawl along the floor. The server stack gurgles. Micro grenade's cooking. Thirty seconds until eight years of blackmail and banking records become shrapnel confetti. Move.

Boots slam the weapons locker. Grab the shock pistol, check charge. 87%. Good enough. Slap a fresh thermal clip into the flechette thrower. Two concussion orbs roll into my palm. Standard evac kit.
Terminal sparks. Meltdown's progressing. Twenty seconds. Rip the neural jack from my wrist. Skin smokes where the port tore. No time to disinfect.

Safehouse memorized. Three steps to the false wall panel. Kick it. Hidden alcove. Go-bag. Rations, meds, untraceable cred-sticks. Grab. Ten seconds. The chip's gone slick between my fingers. Almost drop it. Five.

Out the blast door. Seal it. The floor bucks. Muffled *whump* through reinforced plating. Alarms howl down the corridor. Smoke seeps around the frame. "Asset denial successful," I tell the hallway.

Voice sounds cracked. "You're welcome."

Emergency lights guide the sprint. Boots echo too loud in the service tunnel. Left at the split. Right at the dripping pipe. VargTech sweep teams'll hit the safehouse in four minutes. Maybe three. They'll trace the heat signature. Need to surface. Grate ahead. Rusted. Kick it loose.

Night air slaps my face. Acrid with smog and ionized rain. Neon signs bathe the alley in radioactive pinks. Kanji-script brothel across the street pulses to bass thumps. Three street kids freeze mid-loot. One's got my face reflected in their pupil-cams. Flechette thrower comes up. "Evening."

They scatter. I melt into foot traffic on Arterial Row. Blend with the wage-slaves and synth-peddlers. Hood up. Walk. Don't run. The chip finds its rhythm between my fingers. Spin. Catch. Spin. Should've charged more. Neon smears across my vision like toxic watercolors.

Arterial Row swallows me, salarymen with glassy neural-interface eyes, pleasure drones hawking combat stims, a sanitation bot scraping human slurry off the pavement. Boots stick with every step. Spin the chip. Catch. Spin. Three blocks east, the safehouse burns. I can taste the magnesium tang even here. Should've wiped the drives faster. Should've charged triple. Should've...

A surveillance drone buzzes overhead. I duck into the acid-rain waterfall pouring off a noodle shop's awning. Watch its red beam crawl the crowd. "Fuck your mother sideways," I mutter to the drone's camera.

Flip it off, with the chip hand. Bad move. The wafer slips. Skitters toward the gutter. Dive. Grab. Roll. Elbow cracks concrete. Above me, a street surgeon's neon sign blinks: *BLOOD FILTERS 20% OFF*. The chip's safe in my fist. "Still got it," I tell the rancid puddle. It doesn't argue. Back up. Go-bag strap bites my shoulder. My molar implant buzzes. Mason's voice compressed and urgent: *"extraction point Charlie in ten. Confirm?"*

I spit blood from a bitten cheek. I tap denial twice on my jawbone. Let them sweat. The chip spins faster now. Could throw it in the next trash fire.

Might feel better. VargTech has my biometrics. Their hunters are probably combing this district. My face'll be on every screen by dawn. I pass a store-front mirror. Hood up. Scars down. Ten other shadows do the same. A hand grabs my elbow. "Spare cred for the ascension trials?"

Meth-head. Radioactive sores. I press the flechette thrower to his ribs. "How about I spare your spleen instead?"

He evaporates. Spin. Catch. The weight's wrong. Freeze. Hold it up, sickly green glint under a biolume sign. Wrong chip. *Blacklake data. Kuznetsov job.* Useless now. I laugh. Sharp enough to cut glass. Of course. Shadows peel off the wall. One. Two. Three. More. All moving with that hydraulic hitch in the left knee. VargTech enforcers. "Ah. Early adopters."

They fan out. Shock batons hum. Lead unit rasps: *"Surrender and identify."*

The chip flies. Bounces off its forehead camera. "Chance. Broker of fuck you." Running before the first spark falls.

Through a noodle shop kitchen steam scalds my cheek. Wok crashes. Screams behind me. Out the fire exit. Alley stinks of synth-hash. Molar buzz. Again. "Fine!" I snarl at nothing.

Tap acceptance twice. Coordinates flood my optic nerve. Half a klick northeast. Four security checkpoints. "Should've charged more," I wheeze, vaulting a crashed hoverbike.

Gunfire shreds the alley wall. Rubble rains. Something hot scores my calf. Faster. The chip's back in my hand. Spin. Catch. Spin. Bastion Prime embraces me. Through sewage tunnels humming with illicit cabling. Across rooftops where data pirates scream into the night. Down elevator shafts that stink of desperation. The city's veins and arteries pump me toward whatever the rebels call salvation. No neutral ground in these streets. No maybe. No almost. Just survival. Still spinning. Still bleeding. Still running toward a war I never meant to join.

CHAPTER 20: LUSTOR

My gloves catch the static charge from the holodisplays as I align three security feeds into a triangle. Blue light stutters across polished chrome. The room smells of ozone and antiseptic. Perfect. Contained. "Authorization code Gamma-Red-Nine." My thumbprint blooms crimson on the scanner. "Initiate sanitation protocol. Sectors twelve through twenty-three. Maximum exposure."

Retinal overlays shift across the threat map. Squad leaders flicker into view. Ghostly green avatars. Faces irrelevant. Only biometric readouts matter. Steady vitals. No cortisol spikes. Good tools don't feel. "Sweep and clear."

Two hundred steel-plated boots snap to attention across the feeds. "Contaminated elements are not to be quarantined. Immediate disposal."

I cut the transmission before acknowledgments begin. Doubt breeds weakness. It creeps in through unnecessary words. Holodisplays bloom with fresh carnage, muzzle flashes strobing against tenement walls, black carapace armor swallowing screams. My fingers tap to the rhythm of distant gunfire. One-two-three-pause. One-two-three...pause.

Every fourth round is a tracer. Standard crowd control. Efficient. Camera Three captures a textbook termination: Squad Alpha's lead drives a boot into a medic's chest plate—recognized by the defaced cross on her vest. Shotgun to the throat. 1.3 seconds. On schedule. She spits blood. The wall gets the rest. "Cadence lagging in Quadrant Eight."

157

I rap the comms. Three soldiers hesitate at a barricaded hab-unit. "You're auditing ordnance; not composing haiku."

They breach with synchronized grenade launchers. The thermal bloom whites out the feed. When it clears: a child's sneaker, smoldering. Upside-down in a pool of molten permacrete. Probably nine. Unregistered. Doesn't count toward the census. I adjust my left cufflink. Half a degree clockwise. Screaming in the background makes my teeth ache. No actionable intel. Just inefficiency made audible. Switch channels. Squad Four. Clean staccato chatter. Professionals. "Sweeping floors, got a rebel rat king here."

AP rounds shred a tarp. A man tumbles out with makeshift grenades. They let him stagger four steps. Then: pulp. Probably wanted martyr footage. Drones capture it instead, in high-definition. "Good spread," I murmur. The bleeding man crawls toward the camera, handprint becoming a slick trail. "But mind the backdrop. We want faces visible during termination."

A sergeant pivots. His boot cracks the rebel's jaw sideways. Smart. Better lighting angle now. The execution shot will look pristine when it loops on the public channels tonight. Blood starts drying on Camera Twelve's lens. The darkening smear makes the next executions look like vintage film. Charming. Adds gravitas for the nostalgia markets. I make a mental note to replicate the effect on other feeds. Then pause. No, organic imperfection can't become standard. Dangerous precedent.

The air recyclers hum louder as smoke drifts in from somewhere below. Charred pork and melted plastics. My tongue flicks the roof of my mouth, sampling for trace contaminants. Irrational. The filters are rated for chemical weapons. The air scrubbed long before it reaches here. Still, I check the environmental seals. Twice. "Director Grimwell?" A security avatar blinks to life. Some junior ops officer whose name I intentionally never learned. "Thermal scans show potential hostiles massing near…"

"Burn them." My index finger flicks the avatar into oblivion.

The console shivers as I reroute three squads toward grid coordinates N-44 through P-18. Tactical displays update instantly. Red triangles swarm toward heat signatures clustered in underground parking complex. Clever rats. Should've stayed above ground where the cameras could see them die properly. Gunfire echoes through the sublevels. Sonar mapping shows rebels falling back toward a fuel depot. Amateurs. Always retrenching near flammables.

I lean forward, leather gloves squeaking against the console edge. "Flush them west." My command cracks across eighteen different squad channels. "Into the open."

Grenade casings clatter down concrete stairs. The explosion's pressure wave flatlines two bodycams briefly. When they reboot, rebels come sprinting into daylight with hair on fire. My snipers pick them off mid-stumble. One woman makes it seventeen steps before the .50 cal turns her into pink mist. Her arm lands in a noodle vendor's cart. The proprietor stares at it. Unacceptable lag. Corrected. Tapping resumes against the console. One-two-three-pause. Someone's shooting tracer rounds off-rhythm in Sector Nine. I isolate the feed. Private Erikson. Barrel trembling. Wasteful. "Erikson. Mag check." His helmet cam jerks upward at my voice in his skull. "Report remaining rounds."

"F-fourteen, sir!"

"Disposal protocol. Immediate action."

He doesn't beg. Good. The sidearm goes under his chin at perfect 83-degree angle. Messy, but effective. His squadmates step over the corpse without fanfare. Another tool broken. Replacement costs negligible. The surviving rebels break into a sprint near the hydroponic farms. Smart. Corn stalks provide cover. Smarter than most. I rotate two drone flocks into overlapping kill zone formation. Can't have them reaching the water purification plant. Sympathy angles for the cameras. Let the plebes watch heroes die choking on their own lung blood.

My right cuff feels loose. I twist the platinum band until the VargTech insignia sits flush against my ulnar bone. Screams filter through from the Agri sector. High-pitched. Probably adolescents. Shouldn't they be in school? Ah, yes. The ration riots. They closed the schools. Efficient redistribution of resources. No matter. Education modules download faster anyway.

Something explodes near the northern arcology. Thermal bloom suggests plasma weaponry. Stolen from our own armories, no doubt. I ping the weapons locker logs. Inventory discrepancies in B Block Armory. Security officer responsible pops up in the system, one J. Marchenko. Terminated last week for intoxication infractions. Posthumous demerits added to his file. Case closed.

Rebel leader emerges on Camera Six. Bald. Scarred. Rallying fighters behind an overturned delivery truck. Familiar face. Sergeant Cray from the Eastern Front mutiny. Should've executed him when we crushed the rebellion. Sentimentality. Tactical failure. Personally corrected.

I bring up his service record. Play his court martial testimony over loudspeakers in the kill zone. His own voice listing comrades' names eight years ago drowns out current orders to charge. Psychological warfare works better when you recycle assets. I increase the volume. Guilt is a better suppressant than tear gas.

Cray freezes mid-rally cry. Our sniper takes his left eye. Exit wound sprays loyalist blood across improvised rebel flags. Poetic. The camera lingers on his corpse as survivors break. Cleanup completes forty-three seconds ahead of estimate. Efficiency bonus awarded to Unit K-12.

My gloves leave sweatless prints on the glass as I swipe through termination reports. 894 confirmed kills. 1124 probable. Collateral: projected 5%. Actual: 3.4%. Acceptable. The numbers dance, red digits reflected in my pupils. Pretty. Ordered.

Drone shadows darken the streets as they descend for close-up footage. A dying woman reaches toward the buzzing lenses. Her fingers eclipse the camera sun. Last act of defiance. I zoom in. Capture the exact moment her iris dilation indicates neurological shutdown. Useful data for the next fear response study. When the clock hits 2100 hours, the streetlights flare violet. Curfew colors. My death squads withdraw in flawless echelon formation. Blood pools glitter under the purple glow. Tomorrow's sanitation crews will need extra acid hoses. I straighten my tie.

Adjust my cuffs to show precisely 1.25 centimeters of snow-white shirt beneath jacket sleeves. The holodisplays spin lazy revolutions around me, displaying tomorrow's target sectors. So much filth left to burn. My war room stinks of antiseptic and the aftermath of weak constitutions. Three junior strategists cluster near Door Gamma-9 like frightened pigeons. The tallest one, Brenn, maybe Berrin, steps forward holding a data slate like a religious offering. "Sir, predictive models suggest modifying engagement protocols could reduce non-combatant losses by eighteen-point-six percent."

I pluck a stray eyelash from my left cuff. "Civilian is a semantic error. Anyone breathing in quarantine zones ratified their status as combatants."

The holoscreens flicker behind me, washing his face corpse-blue with muzzle flashes. "But public perception metrics…"

My glove bisects his sentence mid-air. "Perception *is* the operation."

The gesture activates broadcast protocols. Screens across Bastion Prime switch from emergency alerts to real-time executions.

Camera Three catches a meaty specimen, former dockworker, judging by the faded union tattoos. My squad leader presses her plasma cutter to his thigh. Perfect framing: charring flesh, the way his scream syncs with VargTech's stock ticker rolling beneath. I timestamp the clip and route it through three pirate frequencies Huff's cell favors. "Adjust collar feeds," I tell the drone operators. "I want the branding visible during tracheal removals."

My jacket wrinkles as I lean over the tactical map. Unacceptable. I shrug it off, fold the arms precisely across the back of my chair. The lining still smells of extinct mahogany forests and expensive tailors. Sector D-14 explodes into my peripheral vision. Thermal signatures suggest rebels using sewer access Point Hotel-6. Clever meat. My enhanced retinas track six hostiles emerging behind Kader's squad. "Contact rear," I murmur into comms.

Kader doesn't turn. Smart girl. Her squad's armor seals as she releases CS-9 gas from their backpack units. Civilians collapse retching. Rebels activate filter masks. Too late. The gas was never the weapon. It was the primer. Her squad's visors darken as microwave emitters fry every conductive surface in the kill box. Rebel cybernetics overload. One man's ocular implant detonates like a party favor. Another dances the lithium-ion tango until her spine cracks backward. That capacitor design exceeded expectations, noted for replication. One of Engineering's rare successes. I bookmark the footage.

My undershirt clings as humidity parameters exceed tolerance. I unbutton the top collar stud, realign my tie's dimple to 45 degrees. On Screen Twelve, a child throws a Molotov at Dagger-3 unit. The flames distort its polymer musculature into something almost humanoid. "Thermal bloom at Sector F-22," I note. "Add incendiary resistance protocols to all T-800 series."

The surviving rebels break north toward drydock storage. Exactly where I herded them. Roof-mounted auto-turrets greet them with 12.7mm love letters. One stubborn bitch survives, double amputee with military-grade leg prosthetics. She crab-walks through the kill zone using her dead comrades as shields. Twelve meters of sheer refusal. Impressive. I pause the drones' advance to watch. Her prosthetic knee sparks. Overclocked, misaligned. She'll rupture a femoral artery in seventy-three seconds at current strain. Fifty-four. Blood bursts from her nostrils. Still crawling.

I zoom in. Her lips move. Praying? Cursing? Demanding backup? Irrelevant. Dagger-7 lands the coupe de grace with a perfectly angled stomp. Cranium collapses like a rotten melon. Gray matter splatters the camera lens. Artistic. My cufflinks need polishing. I'll have to tell that stupid cow I married to make sure it is done.

Synthetic blood streaks across Screen Nine's surface. My reflection grins back through the crimson smear. The tactical holotable hums. Twelve advisors orbit it like nervous satellites. Their pupils dart between slaughter feeds and my cufflinks. Crèche-born yes-men with spine implants set to maximum grovel. One clears his throat, a wet, biological sound. Disgusting. "Sector G-9 has exceeded projected resistance thresholds," Advisor Krell's Adam's apple bobs. Useless meat pendulum. "Might suggest redeploying…"

I silence him with a finger against my collar's pressure sensor. Every screen obeys, flickering to Feed 47. Fourteen civvies kneeling outside a noodle shop. Third-gen retinal scanners ID two former maintenance workers who serviced rebel safehouses. "Magnification factor twelve," I tell the room. "Thermal overlay on."

The hologram sharpens. Sweat patterns bloom across hostages' necks like mold spores. Good. Makes the panic legible for the cameras. A Dagger operative primes her shock maul. Blue arcs lick a grandmother's cheekbone. The old bat's bladder releases. Charming. "Prime example of infrastructure contamination." I tap the feed's timestamp. "Full biometric capture. Ensure our social credit algorithms reference this during next stipend adjustments."

Krell's left eyelid twitches. The others mimic his distress through micro-expressions their emotion dampeners can't quite suppress. How quaint. Bulldog rounds crack skulls in perfect staccato. Six-point execution pattern maximizes neural splatter for the cameras. One head jerks sideways: unacceptable deviation. Shooter scheduled for correction. Blood pools form identical crescents around the bodies. Satisfying. Huff's face superimposed as an afterimage on the screen. Subtly linking him to the carnage. "Collateral damage estimates approaching seven percent above operational parameters," mutters Advisor Xene. Her knuckles bleach around a data pad.

I realign my tie clip. "Upload footage to the morning digest. Let the meat witness reform in action. Call it … civic education."

The remaining eight staffers soil themselves in glorious unison. My lip twitches. Not quite a smile. Better. There's the money shot. "Live feed status?"

"Airing across all secure channels," says Comms Officer Rolt. His ocular implant flickers as he cross-references encryption keys. "Including known rebel data taps near Drydock Sector."

Huff's favorite lurking hole. He thinks I don't know. Grim found it. Huff borrowed it. Let the weapon see what happens to faulty tools. Advisor Krell makes that throat noise again. "Public relations suggests…"

"PR grooms perceptions." I don't look up from adjusting my sleeve garters. "We're performing surgery."

Screen Twenty-Two flares crimson. Civilian cluster forming in Tertiary Commerce Plaza. How novel. A teenager chucks a cobblestone at our drones. Rolt's voice hums through the static. "Suppression protocol?"

"Let them congregate." I open the armory interface. "Activate rooftop 'gift boxes.'"

Retractable panels slide open across fifty buildings. Celebration fireworks? Hardly. Phosphorous canisters rain down in glittering arcs. Crowds melt like wax sculptures. Two advisors vomit into waste bins. Weak-stomached fools. Xene slams her fist on the holotable. "This exceeds mission parameters!"

Silence curdles. I adjust my cuffs. Let them remember who speaks next. I turn slowly, savoring the way her carotid pulses. "Clarify."

She swallows. "Proactive asset depreciation requires measured…"

My palm sensor activates her collar's neural override before she finishes "depreciation." Her body convulses against the table edge. Teeth crack on polished steel. "Anyone else feeling chatty?"

The surviving advisors find sudden interest in their shoes. Vynn twitches at their feet. "Rebellion metastasizes in ambiguity." I step over her paralyzed form. "Purge thoroughly. Broadcast widely. Blame someone else. Profit accordingly."

The screens agree. They always do. Every bullet hole blooms into VargTech's logo when viewed from above. The holograms bleed infrared. Thermal ghosts stagger through cooling ash. My war room smells of blood, puke and piss. "Someone get a cleaning crew in here. Now."

Screens Thirteen through Twenty-Seven display proper maintenance protocols, corpse retrieval drones scuttling through alleys, pressure-washing genetic residue from Duracrete. Efficiency rating: 93%. Acceptable. I pluck a synthetic fiber from my sleeve. The purge lasted six hours, thirty-two minutes, nineteen seconds. My suit remains immaculate. "Systems check."

The holotable births twelve tactical schematics. Bastion Prime's pulse map flickers. Clean, obedient, power grids throbbing, surveillance feeds blinking, comms traffic clotting around protest hotspots. All within predicted parameters. A drone feed catches my glove. Screen Nine: child's shoe abandoned near Tertiary Plaza. Leather scorched, laces intact. Probability of sentimental attachment: 78%. I flag it for retrieval. Sentiment makes excellent bait.

My cufflinks chime. Incoming alert from Bio-Surveillance. Elevated cortisol levels detected in Sector Seventeen livestock pens. Not the cattle. The handlers. Curious. "Purge Team Gamma," I snap. "Residual audit. Grids 45-Tango through 72-Victor. Audit everything. Including their fear."

Gunfire chatters through the speakers three seconds later. Always amusing how meat thinks hiding among pigs confers protection. The door hisses. Rolt limps in dragging a scent trail of vomit and mouthwash. His missing eye patch oozes mediocre first aid. "Sir... the board requests..."

"Demerit." I don't look up from calibrating the neuro-scrambler frequencies. "Unauthorized interruption."

His remaining eye twitches. "They demand justification for the Kesselman Flat casualties."

Ah. The "gift boxes." Phosphorous confetti still glowing in their marrow. "Casualties imply accidents." I activate Screen Four's enhancement filters. There, between collapsing buildings, a shadow moving against the crowd flow. Too fluid for civilian. "We delivered surgical enlightenment. And someone to blame."

Rolt's prosthetic hand clicks through anxiety tells. Five rapid-fire finger extensions. "The PR division…"

"Requires new leadership." I tag the anomalous shadow as Priority Harvest. "You volunteer?"

His boot heels slam retreat before I finish rotating the security feed. Coward. The shadow resolves into a familiar gait at 400% magnification. Shoulder tilt from old collarbone break. Slight drag on left leg. Huff's signature. My knuckles pop. Finally. VargTech HQ shivers as I arm the rooftop sonic disruptors. Let's see the mongrel dig through seven hundred tons of collapsing architecture. I realign my necktie's molecular edge. The game progresses.

CHAPTER 21: CHANCE

The data chip spins between my fingers, smooth and cold, like a bad omen I can't let go of. The message came through encrypted, of course. Always encrypted. But the words still hit like a sledgehammer to the chest. *Jax is dead. Cleaned out by VargTech. No survivors.* I stop spinning the chip. My hand clenches around it, hard enough to feel the edges bite into my palm. Jax. Dead. The big man with the crooked grin and the knack for getting the impossible done. Mason's right-hand man. One of the few people in this shit-heap city who didn't try to screw me over every other deal. And now he's gone. "Fuck," I mutter, low and raw.

My voice doesn't shake. It never does. But there's a hollow ache in my chest that I don't bother naming. Grief? Anger? Doesn't matter. It's just another cost of doing business in Bastion Prime. I shove the chip into my pocket and step out into the street. The air hits me first, thick with smoke and the acrid tang of burnt plastic. The purge is in full swing. VargTech's enforcers are everywhere, their black armor gleaming under the flickering neon lights. They move like machines, efficient and relentless, cutting through the chaos with brutal precision. Bodies litter the ground. Some still twitch. Most don't. The streets are a warzone, and the corporation's the only army left standing. I keep my head down, my movements quick but casual. Blend in. Don't draw attention. That's the rule. But it's getting harder to follow when every corner smells like death.

A man stumbles past me, clutching his side. Blood seeps through his fingers, dark and slick. He doesn't make it far before an enforcer puts a bullet in his head. The sound echoes off the crumbling buildings, sharp and final. I don't stop. I don't look back. Keep moving. Always moving. The air is thick with screams and the hum of drones overhead. VargTech's watching. Always watching. I duck into an alley. Boots crunch broken glass and discarded tech. The walls close in, graffiti-scarred and reeking of piss. Perfect. Just another shadow in a city full of them.

I pause at the end of the alley, peering out into the chaos. A group of enforcers is rounding up civilians, their voices cold and mechanical. Compliance or death. That's the choice now. I grip the edge of the wall, my knuckles white. Jax's face flashes in my mind, his grin, his laugh, the way he always called me "broker" like it was some kind of joke. "You're dead, and I'm still dealing." I whisper to myself, the words bitter on my tongue.

But it's not funny. Not even close. I can't shrug this one off with a joke. Too close to home. I slide into the access tunnel beneath the old refinery, the air thick with rust and oil. The grate clangs shut behind me, and I don't stop to listen for footsteps. If they're close, I'm already dead. The tunnel's narrow, the walls slick with something I don't want to identify. My boots squelch as I move, the sound too loud in the silence. "Keep moving," I mutter to myself, though the words feel hollow. Jax would've laughed at me for talking to myself. He always did.

The tunnel spits me out into a service corridor, dimly lit by flickering overhead bulbs. I press my back against the wall, scanning for movement. Nothing. Just the hum of distant machinery and the occasional drip of water. I pull a data chip from my sleeve, spinning it between my fingers like a nervous tick. It's blank, always is, but it helps me think. "Think," I hiss. "You've got contacts. You've got routes. Use them."

But the truth is, my network's crumbling faster than Bastion Prime's infrastructure. Jax was just the latest casualty. Who's next? Me? Probably. I push off the wall, moving down the corridor. My mind races, calculating options. Neutrality's a luxury I can't afford anymore. Not when VargTech's turning the city into a slaughterhouse. Not when people like Jax, people who mattered, are ending up in body bags. "A deal," I whisper, the word bitter on my tongue. "It's always a deal." But this isn't about profit. Not this time. This is about survival. And not just mine.

I reach a junction, the path splitting left and right. Left takes me deeper into the underbelly, where the black markets still thrive, barely. Right leads to the surface, where the enforcers are hunting. I hesitate, the chip spinning faster between my fingers. "Choice," I mutter. "Always a fucking choice."

Left is safe. Right might be suicide. But staying neutral? That's a guaranteed death sentence. I shove the chip back into my sleeve, the metal cold, unforgiving, and turn right.

The air smells like burnt plasteel and blood. I crouch behind a shattered holo-billboard, the flickering remains of some corporate propaganda casting jagged shadows across my face. My fingers twitch, not from nerves, but from the itch to do something. Anything. Neutrality's a coffin, and I've been lying in it too long. I pull out my burner comm, the screen cracked but functional. The encryption protocols are solid. I paid enough for them, but even the best tech can't stop a bullet if VargTech's enforcers catch me mid-transmission. I hesitate, thumb hovering over the contact I swore I wouldn't need. Mason. The name tightens like a noose around my throat. "Fuck it," I mutter, pressing the button. The line crackles to life, and I keep my voice low, cutting through the static. "Mason. It's Chance. We need to talk."

Silence stretches for a heartbeat too long. Then his voice comes through, calm and measured, like he's been expecting this call. "Chance. You're alive."

"Barely." I glance over my shoulder, scanning the rubble-strewn street. No movement yet, but that doesn't mean shit. "Listen, I'm not here to trade favors. This isn't business."

Another pause. I can almost hear him adjusting those damn gloves of his, the ones he always fidgets with when he's thinking. "Then what is it?"

"It's war," I say, the word tasting like ash. "And I'm in."

The alley reeks of last week's rain and something worse, burned plastic, maybe flesh. My back's pressed against the wall, the cold seeping through my jacket. Mason's already waiting, just a shadow in the gloom, arms folded, calm as a corpse. He's calm, too calm. Makes me want to punch him just to see if he'll flinch. "You're here," he says, voice low, almost bored. "That means you're ready to play for keeps."

"Don't get sentimental," I shoot back, spinning the data chip between my fingers. It's a nervous tic, but I'll never admit it. "I'm not here to hold hands and sing rebel anthems. This is about survival."

Mason tilts his head, his cybernetic eye catching the faint light from a busted neon sign above. "Survival's a start. But you don't call me unless you're ready to burn bridges."

I smirk, but it's hollow. "Bridges? I'm torching the whole damn thing."

He doesn't smile, but there's a flicker of respect in his gaze. "Good. We need someone who knows the underbelly of this city. Someone who can move through sewage without leaving a scent. Someone who moves under VargTech's radar."

"Lucky you," I mutter, slipping the chip into my pocket. "I know this city better than VargTech knows its own lies. Underground routes, black markets, blind spots. I've got it all mapped out."

Mason pulls his gloves tighter, that calculated motion he does when he's weighing options. "And what do you want in return?"

"What I always want," I say, meeting his gaze. "To stay alive. And maybe, just maybe, stick it to VargTech while I'm at it."

He nods, slow, like he's already three moves ahead. "You're in. But this isn't a solo act anymore. You follow orders, or you're out."

"Orders?" I snort. "I'm not one of your foot soldiers."

"No," he says, stepping closer, his voice sharp now. "You're a weapon with a conscience. That's rarer. And if you can keep that ego in check, we might just win this."

I feel the weight of his words, the unspoken stakes. This isn't just about survival anymore. It's about choosing a side, and for once, I'm not running. "Fine," I say, my voice steady while my gut says run. "But don't expect me to start wearing a uniform."

Mason almost smiles at that. Almost. "Welcome to the rebellion, Chance."
I nod once.

"I heard about Jax. I couldn't save him, sorry. But I can still burn the bastards who silenced him."

Mason's gloved hand taps the table between us, a slow, deliberate rhythm. The dim light of the safehouse catches the faint sheen of his cybernetic arm, the kind of tech that doesn't scream for attention but could probably crush my skull if he felt like it. He doesn't feel like it, yet.

"You've got skills," he says, voice low, measured. "But skills don't mean shit if I can't trust you."

I lean back in the chair, spinning the data chip between my fingers. "Trust's a two-way street, Mason. You think I'd be here if I didn't think you could handle your own?"

His tell when he's weighing the odds, pulling his gloves tighter, like he's cinching a bet. "You're here because you've got nowhere else to go. Don't play it like some noble cause."

I smirk, though it's got more bite than humor. "Noble? Fuck no. But I'm not stupid either. VargTech's coming for everyone, and I'd rather be on the side with teeth."

Mason's eyes narrow, calculating. "You're useful. I'll give you that. But useful doesn't mean indispensable. Step out of line, and I won't hesitate to cut you loose."

"Noted," I say, pocketing the chip. "Now, are we done with the pissing contest, or do you want to measure dicks, next?"

That almost gets a smile out of him. Almost. "Get what you need," he says instead, sliding a list across the table. "We move in twelve hours. Don't fuck this up."

I scan the list, high-grade disruptors, EMP grenades, a few other toys that would make VargTech's enforcers shit themselves. "Black market's my playground," I say, standing. "Just don't ask how I get it."

He doesn't respond, just watches me like I'm a puzzle he's still trying to solve. Fine by me. Let him wonder. I've lived longer in this city by staying a half-truth ahead of everyone.

The streets are chaos, smoke curling up from burnt-out hulks of drones, the air thick with the stench of ionized metal and blood. I keep to the shadows, moving fast but not too fast. Too fast draws attention. Too slow gets you dead. I hit the first drop point, a dingy pawnshop with a neon sign that flickers like it's about to give up. The owner, a wiry bastard named Jerrik, gives me a nod as I step inside. He's got the kind of face that says he's seen it all and regrets most of it. "Chance." Grease-slick hands, same rat grin. "Thought maybe you went legit."

I snort. "Legit's a death sentence these days. I need disruptors. The good shit, not that knockoff crap you usually peddle."

Jerrik grins, yellow teeth gleaming. "For you? Always the best." He ducks behind the counter, reappears with a case. "Four high-grade disruptors, fresh off the line. Cost you, though."

I toss him a cred-stick, no questions asked. "Keep the change. And don't ask why I need them."

He pockets it, shrugs. If he's smart, he'll forget I was ever here. "Don't care, long as you keep coming back."

Next, a back-alley dealer. No name just a reputation. You pay, you walk out alive. I hand over the creds, take the grenades without a word. No need for pleasantries here. By the third stop, my pack's full and my nerves are razor-wire. Every shadow feels like it's watching me, every sound a potential threat. But that's the game, isn't it? Stay sharp, or die. I make it back to the safehouse with time to spare. Mason's there, checking over a map with a couple of his people. He looks up as I walk in, tosses me a nod. "You got it all?" he asks, like he already knows the answer.

"Wouldn't be here if I didn't," I say, dropping the pack on the table. "Now, let's see if you can handle what I brought you."

He opens the pack, pulls out a disruptor, inspects it with that same calculated precision. "Good work," he says finally, sliding it back into the pack.

I don't smile, don't even nod. Just lean against the wall, arms crossed. "Let's just hope it's enough."

Mason looks at me, expression flat. Maybe tired. Maybe calculating. Knowing him, it's both. "It'll have to be."

I don't argue. In this city, *enough* is a luxury. The safehouse reeks of hurried sleep and burnt coffee, like failure boiled too long. I sit on the edge of a rusted metal table, spinning the data chip between my fingers. It's a reflex, a nervous tic, but tonight it feels heavier than usual. Like it's the last piece of who I used to be. Mason's voice cuts through the haze. "You sure about this?"

I don't look up. "Does it matter?"

He steps closer, adjusts his tactical gloves like he's about to punch me in the face. "It matters if you're not all in. Half-assed gets people killed."

I stop spinning the chip, slide it back into my pocket. "I'm here, aren't I?"

"Yeah, you're here." His voice is calm, but there's an edge to it. "But are you *here?*" He taps his forehead.

I meet his gaze. He's not asking if I'll fight. He's asking if I'll bleed for him. And that's the part that sticks in my throat.

I stand, pace the room. My boots echo, too loud in a room meant for secrets. "You think I don't know what this means? You think I'm just playing dress-up with your little rebellion?"

Mason doesn't flinch. "I think you've spent your whole life looking out for number one. That's not gonna cut it here."

I want to argue, throw some sarcastic quip back at him, but the words die in my throat. Because he's right. I've spent years surviving, crawling through the gutters of this city, trading favors and secrets like they were currency. And for what? To end up here, in a crumbling safehouse, with a man who doesn't trust me and a cause that could get me killed. I stop pacing, lean against the wall. The cold seeps through my jacket, grounding me. "You want to know why I'm here? It's not because I believe in your revolution. It's because VargTech took something from me. Something I can't get back."

Mason nods, like he already knew. "Jax? Kirin?"

I clench my jaw, force the anger down. "Jax was one of the few people I gave a damn about. And they killed him like he was nothing. Just another cog in their machine. Kirin too, like she was excrement to be scraped off their boot."

Mason steps closer, his voice low. "Jax meant a lot to me too, Chance. But now you're ready to break that machine. So am I."

I look at him, really look at him. There's no pity in his eyes, no judgment. Just a cold, calculating determination. And for the first time, I see it, the chance to do something more than just survive. To fight back.

I push off the wall, straighten my jacket. "Yeah," I say, my voice steady. "I'm ready."

Mason extends his hand, and I take it. His grip is firm, unyielding. "Let's stick it to them then, for Jax and Kirin."

As he walks away, I pull the data chip from my pocket, stare at it for a moment. Then I slot it into the nearest terminal, watch as the screen fills with encrypted files. Contacts, routes, secrets I've been hoarding for years. It's everything I've built, everything I've held onto. And now it's theirs. I take a deep breath, feel the weight of it settle on my shoulders. This isn't just a fight against VargTech anymore. It's personal. And for the first time in a long time, I feel alive.

The streets of Bastion Prime are a graveyard of steel and neon, the air thick with the stench of burnt circuitry and rotting flesh. I move through the chaos like a ghost, my boots silent against the cracked pavement. VargTech's enforcers are everywhere, their black armor gleaming under the flickering lights. They're hunting, and I'm no longer a ghost. Now I'm prey. I duck into an alley, my back pressed against the cold brick wall. My breath comes in short, sharp bursts, and I can feel the weight of the pistol in my hand. It's not much, but it'll do. For now. "You're in deep, Chance," I mutter to myself, my voice barely above a whisper. "No turning back now."

I can hear the distant sound of footsteps, heavy and deliberate. They're getting closer. My mind races, calculating the odds. I could run, disappear into the shadows like I've done a hundred times before. But that's not an option anymore. Not when there's something worth fighting for. Not when they know my face. I push off the wall, my movements fluid and precise. The first enforcer rounds the corner, his weapon raised. I don't hesitate. My shot is clean, the bullet tearing through his visor. He drops like a sack of bricks. "One down," I say, my voice dripping with dark humor. "How many more to go?"

I move quickly, my steps light and deliberate. The city's underbelly is my playground, and I know every inch of it. The hidden routes, the blind spots, the places where VargTech's eyes can't reach. It's a game of cat and mouse, and I'm damn good at it. But this isn't a game anymore. This is about making them pay. For every life they've taken, for every piece of freedom they've stolen. For him. For her. I reach the safe house, a crumbling building tucked away in the heart of the slums. Mason is waiting inside, his arms crossed over his chest. He doesn't say anything, just nods. I nod back, the unspoken understanding passing between us. "You're late," he says finally, his voice calm but with an edge.

"Got held up," I reply, my tone casual but with a hint of steel. "Had some unfinished business."

Mason raises an eyebrow, but he doesn't press. He knows better. Instead, he gestures to the table, where a map of the city is spread out. "We've got a hit on a VargTech supply depot. High-value target. You in?"

I glance at the map, my mind already working through the logistics. It's risky, but that's never stopped me before. "Yeah," I say, my voice steady. "I'm in." Mason smirks, a rare sign of approval. "Good. We move at dawn."

I take a deep breath, feel the adrenaline coursing through my veins. This is it. No more hiding, no more running. Just me, my skills, and a city that's ready to burn. I smile, just a little. Not for me. For them.

CHAPTER 22: MASON

Smoke hangs like cheap synth-linen between neon advertisements screaming loyalty pledges. My left retinal overlay paints thermal signatures across the rubble-strewn street, two blue-shirts scanning biometrics at a noodle stall. Their armor glows cherry-red through my enhancement suite. Too busy shaking down some street vendor for protection credits to notice death walking past.

I press against corroded alloy plating. Concrete dust grinds between alloy plating and my reinforced spine. 3.8 seconds until their scan cycle repeats. The stench of overcooked pork substitute floods my nostrils. Memories flash, a child's shoe abandoned in gutter runoff, that old man's neural implant sparking as Enforcers dragged him. Focus, you rusted cog.

Boot treads modified for silent traversal eat up the next hundred meters. Alley reeks of ozone and desperation. Check wrist harness: shock blades charged, flechette pistol humming its killing song. Their outpost squats ahead like an infected cyst. Durasteel shutters, auto-turrets dormant during shift change. Exactly nineteen minutes since last patrol departed. Clock ticking.
Interface jack slides home beneath my thumb. Neural spike brushes VargTech encryption, feels like desperation. "Override: Sigma-Nine-Zulu-Mike." Backdoor swings open in twelve seconds flat. *Should update your firewall protocols, fuckers.*

Interior lighting stabs at unenhanced retinas. Irrelevant. Motion tracker paints seven hostiles across three levels. First target's leaning against coolant pipes, stim-stick dangling from slack lips. Knife finds throat before his addiction hit reaches lungs. Catch the body. Lower gently. Blood pool looks black under violet work lights. Two engineers arguing over holographic schematics ahead. "…core temp's spiking again…" Flechettes punch through tracheas mid-sentence. They drop clutching necks, crimson spray arcing across security monitors. Alarms stay silent. Third floor smells peppery like recycled oxygen. Captain's bars glint on a jacket slung over chair. Console shows live feed from detainment block three. Civilian faces flash. Insurgents scheduled for neural scrubbing tomorrow at dawn.

Breach charge adheres to main server bank with satisfying magnetic thunk. Timer set for ninety seconds. Window exit. Seventh story drop would shatter standard bone weave. My augmented knees absorb impact like falling onto feather mattresses. Concrete cracks beneath me. Not even a stumble. The explosion paints my shadow long across adjacent buildings. Heat licks my exposed sensors, gentle, almost reverent. Secondary detonation rips through fuel depot. Shockwave parts my hair. Keep walking. Let the firelight make me a silhouette against their collapsing empire.

Breach charge clicks home against the main reactor housing. Magnetic clamps bite through rust-pitted steel. Timer set: twenty-three seconds. Optimal dispersal. Move. Three more charges along primary support columns. Spider walk up the east wall, synthetic tendons in my thighs humming. Fourth charge placed where ceiling struts intersect. Perfect triangulation. Whole structure comes down on their heads.

Alarm finally wails. Too late. Boots thunder upstairs. Response team wearing hesitation like they didn't really want to fight. Let them come. Sixteen seconds.

Window exit shears my sleeve. Stitching screams. Releases. Flaps. Air slaps my face. Seventh-story drop. Knees compress, hydraulics hissing. Pavement cracks spiderweb patterns underfoot. Not even a twinge in the actuators. Fire licks the sky behind me. Shockwave parts the rain-slick air. Secondary explosion rips through armory stockpile. Beautiful chain reaction of corporate incompetence. White phosphorus bloom lights the district up proper. I walk west. Fire handles cleanup. Guilt exits stage left.

Safehouse reeks of mildew and spent uranium casings. Plasma cutter goes behind the false wall. No tell. No story. Check neural feed, three encrypted reports of "mechanical failure" already flooding VargTech channels. They'll scrub the data by dawn. Doesn't matter. Pulse rifle disassembles in seven practiced motions. Carbon scoring on the barrel. Overheated during the detainment block op. Swap out the recoil dampener. Twenty-three minutes until next engagement window. Truck convoy routes flash across retinal display. Revised schedule, standard panic reroute. Amateurs. Cross-reference with sewer access maps. There's a choke point where Third Arterial passes over the old flood tunnels.

Rain turns acidic two clicks from the ambush zone. Good. Eats through their composite armor faster. Set the shaped charges along the overpass support beams. Old pre-Accord detonators with frayed wiring, unreliable, unpredictable, untraceable. Climb into position beneath storm drain grate. Wait. Six trucks roll into the kill zone, tires hissing on wet permacrete. Lead vehicle's sporting fresh anti-air mods. Waste of credits. Thumb the detonator. The overpass comes down like God's own hammer. Third truck takes fifty tons of rebar through its fusion core. Chain collision. Rear vehicles pile up, smoking metal screaming.

First merc out the passenger seat gets my boot through his sternum. Ribcage crunches like snack chips. Sidearm discharges wild into the pavement. Stomp his wrist. Take the pistol. Driver's fumbling with an assault rifle. Put two in his ocular implant. Through the skull. Out the windshield. "Cargo secure," someone shouts from the fourth truck. Fucking amateurs.

Sprint along the wreckage. Three bursts. Two drop mid-turn. Third gets wise - ducks behind reinforced door panel. Thermite grenade cooks the whole vehicle. Aluminum frame melts like butter. Screams cut off quick. Backblast scorches my cheeks. Ignore it. Pry open the smoldering cargo hold. Crates of neural interface suppressors, fresh from the foundries. Nasty shit. Designed to pacify whole blocks.

Demo charges on every second crate. Whisper, don't shout. Let the survivors report back. Let Lustor see his tools turned against him. Sirens wail in the distance. Three minutes until aerial response. Plenty of time. Take the service ladder down to storm drains. Let the acid rain wash the blood off my knuckles.

Bodies twitch in puddles of their own blood, vomit and coolant fluid. My boot squelches through something organic as I sweep the kill zone. Two men crawl toward a shattered autocannon. Dumb fuckers never learned, dead means stay down. Double-tap each skull. Brains splash across asphalt still steaming from thermite burns. "Clear."

The word tastes like thermite and nano-carbon particulates. Three armored transports smolder in zigzag formation, tires melted to alloy rims. VargTech never could design proper flanking maneuvers. Too busy polishing their chrome dicks to study basic tactics.

I kick open the middle vehicle's rear hatch. Data server glows cobalt inside its shockproof casing. Owner's manual probably says 'Impact Resistant' in twenty languages, none of them honest. Pulse rifle butt meets reinforced polymer. Once. Twice. Third strike cracks it open like an egg.

Neural jack slides home before the fragments stop skittering. Interface ports light up gold at my temples. *Accessing...*

Firewalls taste like peppermint machine oil. Lustor's personal encryption flavor. Little fuck always did love his pretentious security theater. Sixteen rotating cipher keys bloom in my augmented vision. Timer's live. First layer: ICE-pick protocol. Second: Forked decryption streams. Third:... "Contact rear!"

Muscle memory drops me low. Three rounds shred the air where my head was. Rookie mistake, checking corpses leaves you facing wrong way when the real threat comes crawling out of the fucking gutter. CivPro enforcer, one of the advanced GOL-T3R units, torso shredded, drags himself forward on one arm. Bloody handprint smears across my boot as I step on his trachea. Monitor his vitals through pressure sensors. Wait for the gurgle-stop. Back to work.

Fourth cipher solved. Fifth. Server data unfolds like poisoned origami. Supply routes. Neural suppressor deployment schedules. Cleartext comm logs between Lustor's pet generals. Goldmine wrapped in barbed wire. Sixth firewall bites back - counter intrusion protocols surging up the connection. Burn four milliseconds deciding whether to cut losses or push through. Fuck it. Dive deeper.

Augmented cortex floods with cryptographic combat. Dancing through razor-sharp code strands. Tasting victory in the bitter tang of overloaded capacitors. Final barrier shatters just as the alert sirens reach critical pitch. Data floodgates open. Mainframe schematics. Security rotations. Executive floor plans. Every byte's a kill order waiting to happen.

Jack out. Retinal display shows nineteen seconds until aerial interceptors arrive. Less than optimal. Thermite charges hiss to life on every data core. Let them chew on molten silicon. "Burn bright, motherfuckers."

Sprinting west toward sewer access H-22. Rain starts falling sideways. Acidic drizzle eating at exposed synth-flesh on my knuckles. Doesn't hurt just an irritant build-up if you don't wash it off regularly. Comms rig hums in my inner ear. Open channel to all executive frequencies. Encrypt payload with Lustor's own birthday as seed key. Poetic bullshit he'll appreciate.
Voice modulator dials to 87% match of my original VargTech issue vocals. Let the bastard hear perfection talking: "You should've killed me when you had the chance." Transmit.

Laugh while hacking police drones to play carnival music. Whole district's emergency channels blast 'Like You're Lying' through the smoke. First missile impact shakes the street behind me. Shockwave rips a neon billboard from its moorings. Dive through the maintenance hatch as twenty tons of holographic pornography crashes where I stood. Safe. For now. Smoke still clinging to my armor tastes like victory. I'm three blocks east of the blast zone when Lustor's security feed blinks into my retinal display. Couldn't resist watching the show. Feed stabilizes. Lustor's war room floods my vision like a bad dream I never left.

Angle's fixed center. Tactical holocams. Good. This isn't imagination. This is intel. War room walls pulse blood-red under emergency lights. Lustor stands perfectly centered in the camera frame, left glove halfway through its customary adjustment cycle. Frozen mid-tweak. His reflection fractures across sixteen tactical holograms showing burning outposts and hijacked drones playing my calliope soundtrack. A junior analyst makes the mistake of speaking. "Sir, the breach vector…"

Lustor's backhand cracks across the kid's jaw. Clean strike, shoulder rotation perfect, elbow locked. Old military training bleeding through. "You let *it* defile our systems." His voice slices the air, surgical and cold.

Smoke plumes still claw at the sky when I jack into their comms. My fingers dance across the hologrid. Eighteen seconds to bypass encryption protocols older than my last meal. The firewall crumbles like wet synth-paper. I carve my message straight into their mainframe's throat. *You should've killed me when you had the chance.* Send.

Lustor's glove creaks. He stares at the words bleeding across the war room's central display. Three junior analysts freeze mid-report. Their retinal implants flicker—nervous system spikes jackrabbiting through biometric feeds. "Director Grimwell?"

He doesn't blink. Adjusts his left cuff. Adjusts it again. The motion's too sharp, too *human*. "Priority override," he says. Voice like a scalpel dipped in liquid nitrogen. "Scrub all operational data from sectors seven through twelve. Initiate neural purge protocols for anyone who…"

A holoscreen fractures. His fist hovers where the projection of burning convoy trucks shivers into static. Blood pearls across his knuckles. Someone gasps. Bad move. Lustor turns. Slow. Deliberate. His smile makes the nearest tech piss herself. Sensor pads on her chair light up amber. "You." He points. Not shaking. Not at all. "Compile every frame of security footage from the last forty-eight hours. I want pattern analysis on his *bootprints*."

"Sir, the encryption…"

"Burn through the servers if you have to." He's already striding toward the elevators, thumb jammed against his palm-com. "And someone get maintenance in here. The air filtration reeks of weakness."

Feed ends. Static ghosts echo across my display. Lustor's cracking. Good. Let him twitch. Let him bleed just a little.

I'm two blocks south when their wolves and drones swarm. Night vision paints the world poison-green. They're Vargstryk models, new joints, tighter maneuverability. Still dumb as bricks. I vault a dumpster as the first plasma burst sears concrete. Roll behind a noodle cart. The vendor's already gone, broth boiling over onto induction coils. "Target acquired," a drone intones. "Surrender for neural assessment."

I rip the cart's power cell out. "Here's my assessment."

Toss it underhand. The lead wolf's intake vents suck the cell straight into its reactor. I'm sprinting before the explosion lights up the alley. Shrapnel pings off my reinforced shoulders. Idiots. My ocular implant pings. Three heat signatures converging on the next intersection. Patrol unit. Standard tac gear. I climb.

Finger joints whine as I grip a fire escape. Titanium alloy holds. Third floor. Fourth. The rusted roof door screams on impact. Wind slaps my face. Neon from the commerce spires turns rain puddles into liquid holograms. The patrol's arguing below. "…said northeast quadrant…"

"Override came through five minutes ago, you want to get purged?"

I leap. They look up. Not fast enough. My boots crater the first enforcer's chest plate. His buddy's reaching for a shock baton when I break his wrist. Clean snap. Efficient. The third one runs. I let him. His panic's more useful than his corpse. The safehouse reeks of mildew. I find the tracker in my boot heel. Crush it. They'll come anyway. I fucking hope so. I check my straps. Check them again. Quietly settle in a corner to mourn Jax on my own time. Outside, Bastion Prime wails a death dirge for my friend.

CHAPTER 23: LUSTOR AND HUFF

LUSTOR

The holograms bleed tactical overlays across my gloves. I carve through security protocols with surgical taps, implanting false troop movements into Bastion Prime's surveillance grid. *There.* A flick of my wrist sends the data-packet skittering into public channels. Let the Ghost sniff this corpse, let him choke on it.

My war room thrums with the static of a hundred feeds. Rooftop cams catching rain-slicked streets looking like a kaleidoscope has vomited on it, heat signatures pulsing in underground tunnels like trapped vermin. The main display flickers with Huff's last known trajectory. *Northwest quadrant. Hunting.* My augmented retina highlights a cluster of residential towers along his path. Perfect. Collateral writes its own press releases. "Sir."

The advisor's voice grates like a rusted servo. I don't turn. Let him marinate in his own sweat. "Deploying Wolves to Sector 12 risks destabilizing…"

I adjust my left cuff. Quarter-inch reveal of platinum threading beneath black wool. "Activate Protocol K-77."

Silence. Then the wet click of a throat being cleared. "The civilian density…"

My finger hovers over the neural link port at my temple. One thought would summon security. Two would have this man's career dissolving in a vat of acid. "Do you file OSHA reports when stepping on roaches?"

The holograms shift. Wolf squadron markers bloom across the city, twelve kill zones, each a noose tightening around Huff's augmented neck. One final move. Enough to flush him. Or bury him. My gloves flex. Synth-leather creaks.

HUFF
The data-packet stings my neural interface like a wasp. I duck beneath a flickering holosign. *NoodleHub 24/7.* Encrypted coordinates bloom behind my eyes. The patterning feels deliberate. Lustor's signature, tight, efficient, inhuman. *Ambush parameters: 87% probability.*

My targeting subroutines highlight heat signatures converging three blocks east. Civilians swarm the night market below, their bio-signs pulsing red in my threat assessment HUD. A child's laughter cracks through ambient noise. *Collateral estimate: 23-48 casualties.* Teeth click against enamel. The math doesn't lie.

LUSTOR
"Contingency teams report readiness." The advisor's tablet chirps like a dying bird. "But Executive Board comms are lighting up. They're demanding…"

I slice the air. My glove leaves afterimages in the holographic mist. "Tell the Board I'm sterilizing an infection."

Cam 312 flickers. First Wolf unit deploying. Black carapace armor swallows neon glare as they breach a noodle shop's second floor. Patrons scatter. A waitress freezes, tray of dumplings trembling. The squad leader's ocular implant flashes, target acquisition confirmed. "Asset response?"
My knuckle brushes the live detonation toggle. "Let him play hero first."

HUFF
The Wolves move like scalpels. I track their formation through a fabric vendor's shattered display. Team Alpha secures the overpass, pulse rifles sweeping pedestrian traffic. Team Bravo funnels civilians toward the kill zone with stun grenades and barked orders. A street artist vomits fluorescent paint across the Wolves' path. *Tactical error.* The squad leader's boot crushes the artist's spray can. His voice transmits through my cranial link: "Containment breach. Lethal force authorized."

I hijack their helmet cams. Let them show me their sins. The first civilian drops, elderly man clutching medicinal inhaler. Red blooms across his wife's synth-silk blouse. "Collateral rising," an advisor murmurs somewhere in the feed.

My thumb circles my trigger. Not yet. Let them taste blood first. A child's shoe glows in infrared, left behind near a toppled vendor cart. My combat algorithms calculate three engagement scenarios. All require leaving cover. *Mission priority: Eliminate VargTech command structure.* A Wolf's boot connects with a fleeing student's ribs. Bone snaps. The sound syncs with my heartbeat. I step into the kill zone.

LUSTOR

"Asset engaged!" The holograms flare crimson. Feed #45 shows Huff disarming Wolf-12 with a neural shock pulse. Clean. Efficient. *My* design. Advisors swarm like flies on a corpse. "The Board's threatening to recall…"

I detonate the first charges. The noodle shop's windows vomit fire. Huff's silhouette dances through the blast wave, a shadow cutting Wolves down with their own splintered bones. "Casualty reports incoming, sir! Social stability metrics are…"

I lean into the carnage feed. My reflection grins back from a Wolf's shattered visor. "Send the Board flowers."

"Sir?"

"Funeral arrangements."

Huff survives. Of course. But his hands drip red now. Not machine oil. *Blood.* His face ghosted on the live feed silent witness to his crimes. I adjust both cuffs. Perfect. The holograms stutter as Wolf-12's vitals flatline. I tap the feed. *Rewind* . Watch Huff snap the soldier's neck with a textbook chokehold. My own design. My own failure. He moves like corrupted code, predictable patterns laced with… improvisation. Disgusting. Advisors cluster behind me, reeking of panic sweat. "Civilian casualties at 23% over projections…"

"Irrelevant." I zoom Feed #17.

A mother drags her child through shattered glass. Huff pivots mid-stride, takes a Wolf's bullet through the shoulder to shield them. Crimson blooms across his tactical rig. *There.* The flaw. "Cut the feed, blame it on a glitch." I adjust my left cuff. "Activate Grid Sigma."

Screens flare as six more Wolf squads converge. Let him play hero. Let him *bleed.*

HUFF

The child's sneaker lies abandoned, neon pink sole blinking a distress pattern. My targeting HUD overlays escape vectors, all require leaving the sniper's blind spot. *Probability of civilian survival if engaged: 18.6%.* A Wolf kicks a street vendor's teeth down his throat. The man gurgles. Familiar sound. Training sims never replicate the *wetness*. I step into the open. "Priority target acquired!"

Wolves snap to formation. Their rifle lights paint my chest. First rule of hunting monsters: *Make them look at your hands.* I feign a charge left. Their muzzles track. *0.7 seconds.* Enough to palm the frag grenade from Wolf-23's belt. The blast shreds their firing line. I'm already moving through the smoke. Dislocated arm. Hanging useless. Pain offline.

LUSTOR

"He's using the civilian panic as cover!" An advisor's voice cracks. Amateur.

I isolate Feed 29. Huff presses a bleeding shopkeeper against blast walls, takes three rounds to his dorsal plating. Sacrificing armor integrity for... what? *Sentiment?* My glove creaks as I fist the detonator. Not yet. Let him accumulate more sins. A Wolf's helmet cam shows Huff elbow-deep in another soldier's chest cavity, ripping out neural implant batteries. The man's scream cuts off as Huff crushes his larynx. "Casualty report?"

"Forty-seven Wolves disabled. Sixteen civili..."

"Enhance Sector 8-B."

Huff staggers past a burning noodle stall. His blood leaves perfect ruby circles on pavement. Weakness made manifest.

HUFF

Bullets chew concrete where my head was. I calculate trajectories. Three hostiles elevated. Civilians bottlenecked at east exit. Wolf sniper's laser finds my right eye. I let it. *0.3 seconds.* Toss a smoke canister. Sprint up the bullet-riddled escalator. They're reloading when I vault the railing. First Wolf: Knife through occipital port. Second: Throat crush. Third: *Problem.*

Her shotgun's plasma load whines. I grab the barrel, shove it upward. Superheated plasma melts the ceiling. She headbutts my wounded shoulder. Pain receptors flicker online. *Mistake.* I bite her jugular. Coppery warmth floods my mouth. She dies twitching. Like him. I don't speak. Not now. Can't. Memory's too raw. Below, a child wails. I spit out flesh. My voice holds. "South alley. Run."

LUSTOR

Advisors retch into waste bins. Weak-stomached fools. I replay the bite sequence. Slaughterhouse efficiency. *My* programming. *My* weapon. Yet… Freeze frame. Huff's eyes as the child escapes. Something glitches in his micro expressions. Not tactical assessment. Not survival calculus. *Fear.* I lean closer. My reflection floats in the blood-smeared lens. "Sir! The Board's demanding…"

I detonate the mall's support columns. Screens erupt in dust and screams. When it clears, Huff stands amidst the rubble, clutching a broken girder. His left leg bends the wrong way. "Thermal scan shows severe tissue damage. Recommend sending Reaper squad to…"

"Hold."

Huff limps toward a collapsed jewelry store. Pulls a bleeding girl from the wreckage. His hands leave crimson prints on her pale dress. I adjust both cuffs. Perfect. "Reverse it. Let the media drones feast. VargTech's rogue asset… taking lives."

The advisor blinks. "But he's killing our Wolves!"

I smile. Tap the girl's face on the feed. "We'll bill her family for the rescue."

Huff's learning compassion. I'll teach him how it breaks. The advisor's voice cracks like cheap synth-whiskey. "Civilian casualty projections exceed acceptable parameters."

I don't look up from the hologrid. Twelve Wolves converge on Sector 9's transit hub. Their biometrics pulse green. "Define acceptable."

A hesitation. The man's carotid throbs. Amateur. "Sir, the riots near the hydroponics farms…"

I flick his concern into the trash bin of my peripheral display. "*Riots are resource allocation audits.* Deploy tear gas laced with compliance pheromones." My gloves gleam as I reshape the kill box around Huff's last position. "Charge the antidote to their ration accounts."

The Wolves' muzzle cams show Huff now, draped in fire-suppression foam, dragging a shopkeeper through shattered glass. His left knee grinds bone-on-bone. *Good.*

"He's compromising the grid!" An advisor jabs at thermal scans. "Diverting forces to protect noncombatants reduces our…"

I snap my fingers. Two Wolves freeze mid-stride. Their ocular implants flare as I overwrite priorities. "You mistake *meat* for mission-critical infrastructure."

Huff's boot crushes a Wolf's trachea on Camera 4. The corpse spasms. Quaint. *New Input: Civilian Transport - Designation: CT-9921.* A hover-tram veers off rails above Huff. Children press palms against windows. I smile. Activate demolition charges. The explosion rains molten shrapnel. Huff lunges, armor smoking, and braces the tram car with his spine. Tendons scream in his neck. Civilians scramble free. Advisors murmur. "He's using VargTech's own infrastructure against us!"

"Obviously." I reroute three sniper teams. "That tram's warranty expired six minutes ago."

Huff staggers from the wreckage. Blood patterns his jawline like corrupted code. *Priority Alert: Sector 12 Perimeter Breach.* Huff's heading for the old data vaults. Clever. I release the K-9 units. Genetically enhanced Dobermans with titanium fangs swarm from sewer grates. Huff breaks the first dog's spine against a parking meter. The second takes a chunk from his thigh. "Viral load?" I ask.

"Neurotoxin 99-B injected," confirms a Wolf. Huff's pupils dilate. He stumbles. My cufflinks need adjustment. Advisor: *"We're losing public approval!"*

I zoom on a bystander's holocam feed. Huff just shielded a street vendor from stray bullets. The man weeps, clutching a dented rice cooker. "Flag that civilian for reeducation," I say. "His gratitude's misplaced."

Huff vaults onto a billboard. Wolves fire incendiary rounds. The display melts, dripping liquid flame. He falls through a bakery roof. Flour clouds bloom. *Thermal Scan: Multiple Hostiles Engaged.* Six Wolves down. Huff tapes a baguette to his thigh. It'll hold. For ten more steps. I sigh. "Charge the bakery for medical supplies."

System Alert: Crowd Surge Detected. Protesters flood the arterial boulevard. Huff's trapped between them and my sniper nests. An advisor cheers. "The mob will tear him apart!"

"No." I activate riot drones. "They'll *humanize* him."

Stun batons descend. Bodies convulse. Huff grabs a drone, rips out its capacitor, and hurls it into a Wolf's face. The detonation paints storefronts with shrapnel. *Critical Damage Reported: Wolf Pack Theta.* "He's adapting too fast!"

"He's *bleeding* faster." I inject stimulants into the remaining Wolves' systems. Their heart rates spike. "Flush the storm drains. Drown the sector."

Water cannons erupt. Huff climbs a gutter pipe. A Wolf severs it with a plasma torch.He falls. Rises. Falls again. *Biometric Alert: Target's Core Temperature Dropping* . "Finish him."

Twenty Wolves converge. Huff's back against a bullet-riddled noodle cart. He smiles. My gloved hand hovers over the neural strike command. The advisor hesitates. "Sir, if we…"

Huff detonates the cart's propane tank. Screens whiten. When the static clears, he's gone. And twelve Wolves burn in his wake. I check my cuffs. Impeccable. "Resume pursuit."

Critical Systems Overload: Sector 7-B. The feed stutters. Huff's thermal signature flickers behind a noodle cart carcass, smoke pouring from its ruptured propane tank. Civilians crawl through shattered glass. A mother dragging her kid toward a storm drain. "Magnify grid D-9," I command.

The hologram zooms. Huff's left femur shows stress fractures. His right hand's missing two fingers. Blood patterns indicate 12% fluid loss.
An advisor points at the escaping civilians. "Should we seal the drains?"

"Let them fester." I tap a console. "Activate acoustic suppressors in the tunnels. Drown their screams."

Huff moves. Not toward safety. *Toward* the fleeing crowd. He tears a steel shutter off a storefront, using it as a shield. Wolves open fire. Ricochets spark. *Alert: Civilian Casualties Projected at 23%.* "He's herding them!" the advisor shouts.

I know. The fool's sacrificing cover to create a human barricade. Huff lobs a Wolf's severed arm into a drone swarm. The limb detonates, improvised EMP. Lights die. Night vision filters kick in. "Thermal targeting," I snap. "Burn everything."

Wolves switch to incendiary rounds. The street becomes a gallery of fire. Huff vaults through flames, shoving a teenager into an alcove. The boy's jacket catches fire. Huff smothers it with his own bleeding hand. *Biometric Spike: Target's Pain Receptors Active.* "He's compromised!"

"He's *wasting time.*" I override Wolf squadron protocols. "Full berserk mode. No quarter."

The Wolves' pupils dilate. Saliva drips. They charge. Huff grabs a neon sign cable, swings over their heads. Lands on a delivery bot. Rides it through a hail of gunfire. *Asset Lost: Prototype MX-9 Courier Drone.* "Charge the R&D department for that," I mutter.

Huff's heading for the drain. Civilians bottleneck at the entrance. A Wolf fires a phosphorous grenade. Huff intercepts it midair. "Idiot," I breathe.

He stuffs the grenade into a Wolf's mouth. Kicks the body into a sniper nest. The explosion annihilates three marksmen. Civilians pour into the drain. Alert: 87 Subjects Escaped Containment. My glove creaks as I tighten my grip on the console. "Seal the…"

Huff jams a steel rod into the drain's hydraulic door. It shudders. Stays open. "Cut power to the mechanism!"

"Backup generators are…"

"*Cut it!*"

The lights die. Emergency beams bathe the war room in red. Huff's silhouette limps toward the choke point. *Final Option Available: Alpha Contingency* The advisor pales. "Sir, that'll collapse the entire block."

I enter my authorization code. The ground trembles. Buildings groan. Huff looks up. So do the Wolves. Detonation Sequence Initiated. Concrete slabs crash. Huff dives. The world dissolves into gray powder. When the dust clears, the drain's buried. So are fourteen Wolves. Huff crawls from rubble, arm bent wrong. "Terminate."

A Wolf raises its rifle. Huff headbutts the muzzle. Fires three rounds into its chest. Steals the gun. *Alert: Target Acquired.* Every remaining Wolf converges. Huff shoots a gas main. The fireball engulfs the street. Primary screens go black. "Switch to backups!"

The secondary feed shows Huff staggering into a maintenance shaft. "Seal it!"

"Radiation levels from the blast…"

"Do you want to join him in the furnace?"

The shaft door slams shut. *Target Status: Escaped.* I straighten my cuffs. The left one's fraying. I must speak to that useless meat I married. She is becoming inefficient. "Sir…the council's demanding a report."

I unholster my sidearm. Shoot the advisor in the knee. "Tell them *that's* my report."

The war room falls silent. I activate the citywide PA. "Sleep lightly, Huff." The reverb coats every street. "I'll be tucking you in."

On the ruined feed, a blood trail glistens toward the sewers. I lick my teeth. Tastes like copper. Feels like salvation.

CHAPTER 24: CHANCE

The message blinks into my retinal display like a gunshot wound. Encrypted coordinates pulse against my optic nerve, followed by a weapons manifest that makes my eyes bleed. Military-grade plasma rifles. Armor-piercing rounds. Enough firepower to turn a VargTech patrol into scrap metal and grease. The attached timestamp glows red: DELIVERY WINDOW CLOSES IN SIX HOURS. I flick the data chip between my fingers. Three rotations clockwise, two counter, while the map overlay settles into my vision. Three new checkpoints added since yesterday. Bastards are tightening the noose. "Rebels must be hitting harder than I thought," I mutter to the empty safehouse, slotting the chip back into its hidden pouch. The gesture feels like reloading a weapon.

My gear's laid out on the rusted table, a ritual as old as my first smuggling run. Ballistic vest with false polymer layers that mimic civilian wear. Boot knives sharp enough to shave with. The modified shock baton I took off a dead Enforcer last winter, its charge indicator still blinking green. I breathe in the stink of old sweat and gun oil as I check each weapon's charge. Survival's a checklist, not a prayer. The chip's spinning again. I force my hand still.

Outside, Bastion Prime exhales its poison. Pukes neon on roads slick with acid rain. Corporate logos reflected in puddles of coolant and blood. I step into the street and immediately taste copper. The city's default flavor since VargTech militarized the water supply. A drone swarm passes overhead, their rotors chewing the air into static. I keep my gait loose, shoulders rounded, posture of a debt-ridden laborer heading to the night shift. "Citizen." The checkpoint guard's voice grates like a saw on bone.

Red beams from his ocular implant sweep my face. I let the fake ID chip in my molar broadcast its signal. Jarek Mol, sanitation engineer, clearance level gamma. The guard's augmented nostrils flare. "You smell like gun cleaner."

"Spilled solvent on shift." I want to say *you smell like shit*. Instead, I scratch at a phantom itch beneath my collar, fingers brushing the shock baton's activation node. "Want to file a complaint with Waste Management?"

He spits on the pavement. A globule that sizzles against the concrete. Waves me through. The real work starts three blocks east. I duck into a burnt-out storefront, kick aside the skeleton of an old service drone, and pry up the floor grate. The tunnels beneath Bastion Prime aren't on any map, just a labyrinth of maintenance shafts and smuggler routes held together by spite and desperation. My boots find familiar rungs. Down here, the air's a living thing. Damp, reeking of fungal growth and pressing against your lungs like a mugger demanding oxygen tax.

I count my steps. Forty-seven paces to the first split. Left passage leads to an old reactor core. Radiation levels spiked last week. Right takes me past flooded sectors. I choose straight ahead, where the ceiling's low enough to force patrols to bend their knees and narrow enough to force them into single file. The walls here still bear scorch marks from Mako's last botched delivery. Poor bastard thought he could run thermal charges through here.

Voices echo ahead. Not the metallic twang of Enforcers. These are human. Desperate. I freeze as their shadows distort against the tunnel wall. "...said the drop point's compromised..."

"We're already six crates short..."

I press against an outcropping, fingers finding the shock baton. Two rebels. Amateurs, by the way they're clutching their rifles, like holy relics. Their retinal flashes give them away. Jagged purple lines marking recent resistance recruits. I could slip past. Should slip past. The shorter one's boot catches on a cable. He stumbles into my hiding spot, face inches from mine. His breath smells of synth-stims and fear. "Wrong turn," I whisper, baton sparking to life.

He freezes. Smart kid. "We're just..."

"Save it." I kill the charge but keep the weapon visible. "Third junction back. Take the vertical shaft up. VargTech's running sweeps in the eastern ducts tonight."

They scramble away like startled rats. I wait until their footsteps fade before moving. Sentiment's a currency I can't afford, but even I know dead rebels don't pay their suppliers. The rendezvous point is as aromatic as a spice merchant's shop. If someone had set it alight and pissed the flames out. Crates stacked two meters high. Enough firepower to make a dent. I'm already calculating the best routes west when my nape prickles. Too quiet. No scuff of boots. No rebel sentries.

The drone drops from the ceiling in a silent kill-swarm, its razor wings slicing the air where my head just was. I roll behind the crates, baton sparking. Survival's a math problem. Distance versus charge radius. The drone banks left. I feign right. Metal screeches as we collide. The drone's carcass sparks at my feet, its wings still twitching like a decapitated roach. I kick it into a puddle of stagnant water. "Should've paid the toll."

My usual route's three blocks west. Takes twelve minutes. Today? The alley mouth glows red. VargTech checkpoint lights oozing through the fog. Two Wolves flank the entrance, their ocular implants sweeping thermal signatures. I spin the data chip between my knuckles. *Fuck*. Reroute options flash in my head. Sub-levels flooded, skybridges locked down, eastern tunnels… "Burning District," I mutter. "Perfect."

Smoke hugs the streets like a jealous lover. Collapsed hab-units excrete furniture onto the pavement. A child's synth-leather shoe floats in a pothole full of acid rain and engine grease, slowly rotting in a pool of chemical determinism. I count patrol drones by their engine whine. Three circling high, two street-sweepers. Pity they don't actually sweep streets. We might not have to wade through rivers of trash. Footsteps echo behind concrete teeth. I freeze.

Not Wolves. Too erratic. A pack of scavengers emerges from a gutted storefront, their arms loaded with counterfeit med-patches. The leader's got a shock baton welded wrong. Leaking voltage cooks the air. They don't see me pressed against the corpse of an overturned delivery bot. "Keep moving," I whisper to myself. The chip digs crescents into my palm.

Gunfire erupts two blocks north. Plasma rounds paint the smog green. Rebels versus Enforcers, maybe. The scavengers scatter. I move opposite the chaos. Smart rats always run from bigger predators.

The smell hits first. Burnt natto and melting polymer. A noodle stand burns unattended, flames licking at a stack of illegal ethanol batteries. Heat warps my vision. I'm calculating detour angles when steel-toe boots crunch glass behind me. "Halt. Scan permits."

Fuck.

The Wolf's voice is a glacier grinding bone. I turn slow, hands visible. His partner's already drawing a pacifier rifle. Non-lethal, but getting tased means capture. Means interrogation. "Permit?" I grin, edging toward the fire. "Thought this was a free city."

Their ocular implants click-whirr, crosshairs aligning. I kick the noodle cart. The fuel cells pop like vertebrae. Ethanol explosions bloom orange. The Wolf staggers, armor sizzling. His partner's rifle goes wide. Pacifier round fries the burning wolf's leg. I'm already sprinting down a service alley, lungs full of smoke. "Subject fleeing southwest!" The Wolf's comms crackle. "All units converge!"

Boots pound concrete. Four sets. Maybe five. I vault a chain-link fence, land in a courtyard choked with razor vine. The plants slice my palms. Cheap biolume graffiti on the walls screams *RESIST* in dripping letters. A trash chute yawns open. I dive in ass-first. Bad move. The chute dumps me into an active recycling compactor. Hydraulics hiss. I roll left as steel teeth bite where my ribs were. The Wolf's boot stomps the ledge above. He's too heavy for the rusted grating. "Got you," he growls.

"Buy me dinner first." I shoot the emergency release.

Compactor jaws snap upward, shearing his rifle's barrel. He bellows. I'm already crawling through effluent pipes, the Wolf's curses fading behind me. The pipes spit me onto a pedestrian walkway. Civilians scatter. A food vendor's hologram flickers *50% OFF SUSHI*. I grab a customer's hovercart, throw it at the pursuing Wolves. They plow through the debris like tanks. Heart hammers against my sternum. Adrenaline tastes like everything I want to forget.

I spot a maintenance ladder. Rusted. Unstable. Perfect. Three rungs snap before I reach the roof. The Wolves try to follow, their augmented weight bends the metal. One falls through a greenhouse dome, crashing into a hydroponic weed farm. Hope he gets high.

The roof's a maze of satellite dishes and solar panels. I leap gaps between buildings, boots skidding on moss-slick surfaces. Drones join the hunt. Their shadows swarm beneath me like piranhas. A Wolf appears on the adjacent rooftop. Draws a pistol. I don't break stride. The shot tears through my jacket sleeve. Missed by millimeters. I grab a loose ventilation pipe, swing down into an open window. Bad luck. It's a brothel. Any other time...

Naked clients scream. I vault over a bed, crash through a false wall into a smuggling tunnel. The Wolves won't follow here. Too many suits don't want to be identified. I lean against damp concrete. Count to five. No pursuit. The data chip finds my fist. I spin it once, twice, slide it back in my pocket. "Round one to the Ghost," I tell the darkness.

Somewhere above, Bastion Prime keeps burning. Always burning. Always screaming. Always …

The alley coughs me up against a blast door sealed since the Corporate Wars. *Fuck.* My palm slams against rusted metal. No give, no hidden keypad, just decades of decay. Boots pound concrete behind me. Close.

I spin, back to the wall. Wolves round the corner. Three of them. Always fucking three. Tactical armor gleaming under streetlights that shouldn't be working. Their rifles snap up. "Noncompliance logged," drones the lead Wolf, voice filtered to static.

The data chip bites into my palm. I flip it once. Twice. There's always a door. Always a way to slide into the Ghost. My implant catches the sewer grate two meters left. Rust blooms around its edges like dried blood. Gunfire shreds the air. Chips of Permacrete spray my face. I'm moving before the first shell casing hits ground. Dive, roll, fingers hooking the grate. It screams open. I drop into blackness.

Impact jolts through my knees. The fall's deeper than I calculated. Fetid water soaks through my boots. Above, Wolves howl into comms. "Priority target. Requesting…"

The grate slams shut. Their voices cut off. Darkness breathes. I try not to. I count heartbeats. Twelve. Thirteen. No pursuit. Yet. The chip spins between my fingers. Always keep one secret. Always. Sewage laps at my shins. The stench is a living thing. Chemical waste and rotting meat bubbling and breeding beneath the city. I wade forward, hands brushing slime-coated walls. My HUD flickers, attempts to map the tunnels. Useless. These veins don't exist on any grid.

Voices echo above. Muffled shouts. They're tearing up the district. Good. Let them waste resources. My boot catches on something soft. A body? Don't look. Keep moving. The water thickens. Syndicate dumping grounds. I recognize the neon-green swirls. Neurotoxin byproduct. My gloves start smoking. I rip them off, toss them into the current. Skin itches. Reflection's a mistake. This isn't cargo. This is a signature on my own death warrant. The chip flips. Catches. Flips again.

VargTech's got my biometrics now. Facial recog from the rooftop chase. Safehouses blown. Contacts compromised. All routes lead to a bullet or a blacksite. Unless…

The water shivers. Ripples spread from ahead. I freeze. Jax's grin shivers on the surface. Before…

Red laser dots dance across the tunnel. "…thermal signature confirmed. Moving to engage."

Fuck. Fuck!

They're in the tunnels.

I reverse course, sloshing upstream. The lasers track. A shotgun pumps. The first blast tears through a pipe overhead. Scalding steam erupts. I duck under the spray, scramble through a side tunnel. Their boots churn water behind me. Left fork. Right. Collapsed passage. No choice. I shoulder through a crack in the wall. Concrete tears my jacket. Emergence.

A vaulted chamber. Ancient storm drain. Moonlight filters through grates thirty feet up. The Wolves crash through behind me. Three again. I sprint for a ladder. Rust flakes rain down. First rung snaps. Second holds. "Halt or be neutralized."

I flip them off without looking. Gunfire. The ladder jerks. A round punches through my calf. White heat. I bite through the scream, haul myself onto the access platform. The chip. Where's the…

There. Glinting in my left hand. Always keep one secret. The Wolves climb. Slowly. Savoring it. I limp to the overflow valve. Massive wheel rusted shut. Pull the emergency release lever. Nothing. "Fucking ancient infrastructure…"

A Wolf's hand grips the platform edge. I kick. His helmet cracks against metal. He falls. The others open fire. I throw my weight against the lever. Scream through clenched teeth. It breaks. The valve explodes open. A wall of black water erupts, swallowing the Wolves whole. The platform trembles. I cling to a pipe as the chamber floods. Silence.

Dripping water. A boot floats past. No movement. Chip spins. Steady rhythm. Twenty-three minutes later, I emerge behind a derelict shuttle depot. The rebel rendezvous. Moonlight filters through cracked domes. My shadow trembles on the pavement. Leg bleeding, clothes reeking of death and worse.

Movement. Loading bay. Four figures, no, five. Armed. I lean against a corroded fuel pump. Spin the chip. Loud enough for them to hear. "You're late," growls a voice. Kael. Rebel lieutenant. Face like shattered concrete.

I limp into the light. "You're ugly. We all have flaws."

His rifle doesn't waver. "Where's the shipment?"

A drone whines overhead. Civilian model. Maybe. I toss the chip. Kael catches it. "Coordinates. Armory locker beneath the old arcade. Code's…" I tap my temple. "Trade item."

He snarls. The rebels tense. Gunfire erupts three blocks east. Closer than I'd like. Kael steps closer. "You think this is a game?"

"I think your fireworks show's missing the fuse." I nod at the chip. "And I'm holding the lighter."

The drone circles back. Red light blinks. Not civilian. Kael sees it. Curses. I'm already moving. "Clock's ticking, patriot."

They scatter. The drone detonates. Thermite shower. I dive behind a cargo crate. Heat licks my back. Kael's voice cuts through smoke. "West tunnel! Go!"

Rebels vanish into the earth. I watch the fire. Let the chip dance across my knuckles. VargTech's problem now. The wound in my leg pulses. I tear a strip from my shirt. Antiseptic patch from an inside pocket. Bandage. Tight. No going back. I smile. It hurts. First time for everything.

The stench of burnt circuitry clings to my nostrils as Kael slots the chip. His cybernetic eye whirs. Green light confirmation, reflected in the sewer puddle. Three rebels flank him, fingers twitching near their triggers. Rookie tells. They keep glancing at the sky. Most are rookies now. Veterans. All dead. "Forty-eight pulse rifles," Kael growls. "Not the sixty promised."

I lean against a collapsed ventilation shaft, leg wound singing hallelujah. "Forty-eight's the new sixty. Supply chain issues." Spin the backup chip across my knuckles. Three rotations before catching it. "Consider the missing twelve a charitable donation."

One of the rookies steps forward. Face like an open ledger, all hopeful defiance. "We could've used those at Red…"

Kael's backhand stops him mid-word. The crack echoes off rusted pipes. "You don't name locations," he snarls at the kid, then turns to me. "Payment's in your drop box."

The data chip freezes between my fingers. "Half now. Rest when I verify the patrol intel."

Gunfire rattles distant rooftops. Closer than yesterday. Closer than ever. Kael's smile shows filed teeth. Smiles like that shouldn't survive the apocalypse. "You're learning, broker."

"Don't flatter yourself. I just prefer my clients breathing long enough to pay." The chip resumes its dance. Left hand, pinky to index, repeat.

A VargTech surveillance drone's shadow sweeps the alley mouth. Civilian model. Probably. Bright-eyed rookie rubs his jaw. "He could've sold us out. Why didn't he?"

Kael snorts. "Scum floats with the tide."

I push off the wall. Weight on the good leg. "And patriots drown with the ship. Enjoy the swim."

The drone's shadow lingers too long. Wrong hover pattern. Kael follows my gaze. "Shit. Specter-class."

The chip disappears up my sleeve. "Five seconds," I mutter. "Then we're tagged."

Rebels scatter like roaches. The rookie freezes, deer in kill-lights. I grab his collar, hurl him behind a corroded fuel pump. Spin the chip once. Loud enough to count. Thermite rain hits the alley. Concrete explodes in white-hot blossoms. My back hits the ground as the fuel pump detonates, heat searing my eyebrows. Kael's shouting coordinates. The rookie's screaming. I'm rolling behind a collapsed billboard. Smoke. Heat. Fingers find the emergency bolt on a sewer grate. Boots splash behind me. Kael's voice, raw with static from the inferno: "West tunnel."

The Specter drone descends, black carapace bloated with lenses. Its plasma charger whines. I yank the grate open. "Age before brains."

Kael dives in. I'm right behind, but the rookie's clutching his melted boot. Eyes wide. Young. So damn young. The plasma bolt hits his chest. He doesn't even scream. Kael yanks me deeper into the tunnel. I grab the grenade off his belt, pull, toss. The blast shreds the drone's whine. "Costs extra," I rasp, running.

"Bastard." But he's laughing.

We emerge in a storm drain. Distant sirens. The safehouse is burning. Kael scans his survivors, two out of four. "You know the price, for dead men."

I lean against a dripping wall. Leg's gone numb. Bad sign. "Their tabs are closed. Mine's still open."

He tosses a blood-smeared data slug. "Enforcer routes. Verified."

The chip in my palm feels heavier than betrayal. First rule broken, trusting rebel intel. Kael vanishes into the smoke. I slot the slug. Routes glow across my retinal display. All checkpoints. All patrols. The real deal. Alarm. Three blocks east. VargTech's coming.

I melt into the chemical fog, footsteps echoing through the corpse of the city. The chip spins, a metronome for my heart. That rookie's face keeps flashing behind my eyes. Charred uniform. Open mouth. I stop counting safehouse routes. Stop calculating escape vectors. Stop counting dead children. Stop pretending I didn't see his face. The chip freezes between thumb and forefinger. Slip it into my pocket.
First time for everything

CHAPTER 25: HUFF

The concrete cracks beneath my boots like eggshells. I walk through the kill-zone in parade-ground posture, neural feed buzzing with proximity alerts. Let them taste the arrogance. Let their thermal scopes paint me bright and hungry. My left thumb brushes the detonator chip sewn into my palm, an old habit, from back when I had real skin.

Three Wolves materialize on the rusted catwalk above. Standard flanking pattern. Their ocular implants glow like wolf-spider eyes in the chemical haze. I count the milliseconds between their synchronized breaths. "Hostile elements confirmed," their leader barks through vox-filters. Protocol demands they announce. Protocol makes them predictable.

I detonate the east wall. The shaped charge shears through corroded girders. A waterfall of molten sparks rains down as the walkway collapses. Two Wolves tumble into the debris field. I hear femurs snap through their armor's dampeners. The third leaps clear, combat boots screeching against rebar. "Trap. Trap. Trap," their comms chatter.

My retinal display lights up their positions in toxic green. Fourteen hostiles converging. Exactly as projected. You don't send a tea party to take out a rogue wolf. I palm a shock grenade from my thigh rig. Mercury core. Razor filament. Custom load. The surviving Wolf charges through the smoke. His arm-blades whine with fresh lubrication. I let him come. Three meters. Two. Kick the floor shut off valve. High-pressure steam erupts from century-old pipes. His thermal optics overload. Beautiful scream, all meat and panic. I drive my combat knife up through his jaw before the safety protocols engage.

Bone grinds against carbon steel. "Threat neutralized." Old joke.
Alarms howl through the complex. My spoofed surveillance feed shows three
squads approaching from the north corridor. They're herding me toward the
smelting pits. Predictable. I sprint across corpse-littered concrete, kicking up
ash from last week's incinerations. The air tastes like machine sweat and robot
tears. A Wolf emerges from the shadow of a dead crane. Younger model,
facial plating still shiny. He levels a pulse rifle. "Cease mobility."

I throw the shock grenade against his chest plate. It sticks. "Don't."

The detonation paints his visor red. Two more round the corner. Already
moving. Enhanced tendons fire like steel springs. Their tracking lags by 0.8
seconds. Critical flaw in Mark VII optics. I catch the first Wolf's wrist, twist
until actuators burst. Her scream cuts off when I slam her face into the
shutoff panel. The second goes down with a monowire garrote to the neck
joint. Cheap armor. "Command: Status update," my own implants demand.
VargTech's voice. Always watching.

"Engaging hostiles," I reply through gritted teeth. Standard opcode response.
The lie tastes like moonlight on velvet.

I vault over a slag conveyor belt, the metal groaning under my weight. Retinal
display flashes thermal blooms. Six hostiles encircling. They've adapted.
"Priority target shows deviant tactics," a Wolf transmits.

I smile. Rip the cover off a maintenance panel. The EMP charge, close
enough to fry their IFF systems, distant enough to keep mine intact. Wolves
stumble, precious seconds of confusion. I pick them off with controlled
bursts. Knee joints. Ammo feeds. Optics clusters. Let them hemorrhage
VargTech profits. "Containment failure," a damaged Wolf croaks. His vocal
synth sputters. "Requesting..." My boot crushes his throat port.
The shadows move wrong.

A Wolf drops from the ceiling, veteran model, joints silent. *Is that where Mason
learned it?* Arm-blade kisses my ribs before I twist. Nano-weave armor holds.
Barely. We dance through the corpse-littered dark. His moves are textbook
perfect. Parry. Thrust. Feint. I recognize the patterns, the same training sims
they burned into my cerebellum. He could be me. Perfect killer. Perfect
corporate weapon. He overextends on a killing strike. First mistake. Not me. I
break his elbow, seize the arm-blade, and bury it in his thoracic cavity. I lean
in. Whisper. "Flawed execution."

My hands shake. Adrenaline dump. Neural alerts flash amber—20% stamina
remaining. The surveillance feed shows reinforcements massing at Sector 9-B.

They'll flood the area in 93 seconds. I reload with explosive rounds. The tungsten casings feel warm. Blessed, a rosary of carnage. "Come on then," I whisper to the gathering dark.

The Wolves oblige. The concrete shivers underfoot, rhythmic tremors from fresh boots. Reinforcements. Of course they'd escalate. Saturation tactics. My retinal HUD paints the kill-zone in pulsing red vectors. Twenty-seven hostiles converging. VargTech signature overkill.

I backpedal through a gutted loading dock. Detonator clicks echo off rusted I-beams. First choke point: the overhead conveyor system. Let them cluster beneath the dangling wreckage of automated limbs grown silent. Their squad leader barks coordinates. "Code Wolf-7 formation." Predictable. I'm a code now. My thumb jams the detonator. The world fractures. "Here's my reply."

Shrapnel rain. Twisted metal screams. Three Wolves collapse under a ton of machinery, hydraulic fluid arcing from severed lines. One crawls toward me, legs crushed. I put a round through his ocular implant; mercy's a luxury wrapped in violence. "Structural weakness exploited," I mutter, reloading. The words taste like VargTech's training modules. Like *her* voice.

Second wave floods through the smoke. They're adapting, spreading formation, scanning for traps. Good. Makes them slower. I retreat up a maintenance stairwell, each step calibrated to echo. Let them hear. Let them follow. The third-floor catwalk's already rigged with shaped charges. A Wolf snarls behind me, close. I spin, parrying his vibroblade with my forearm guard. Sparks shower. His breath reeks of synthetic protein bars and combat stims. "Traitor," he hisses through gritted teeth.

I knee his groin, organic or cybernetic, everyone flinches. As he doubles over, I plant the breaching charge between his shoulder blades. "Upgrade pending," I tell him, diving through a shattered window.

The explosion paints the wall with his components. Four hostiles remain in pursuit. Optimal. The catwalk groans under our combined weight. They take defensive positions behind support columns. Textbook urban clearance protocol. I smile. Trigger the charges. The columns disintegrate. Falling metal sounds like church bells tolling at our funerals. Two Wolves go down screaming. One survives impaled on rebar. I shoot the ceiling above him. Let gravity finish it.

Retinal alert: 12% stamina. They stop sending squads. Start sending platoons. A fresh wave pours from every shadow. Thirty? Forty? The numbers turn ugly. My last choke point, the refinery's coolant vat array, detonates too early.

Rookie mistake. Last one I'll live through. Only takes out four.
Now they're herding me. Bullets chew concrete around my feet. I return fire blind. Feel the satisfying *spang* of rounds piercing Wolf armor. Not enough. Never enough. Back to the wall. Literally.

Storage Unit B-42's blast door at my six. No exits. No cover. Wolves advance through chemical haze, weapons hot. I calculate angles. Three possible escape routes. All blocked by overlapping fields of fire. Neural interface flashes threat projections. Seventy-three percent termination likelihood. Fuck.

A round clips my thigh. Nanoweave stiffens, but the impact bruises. My next dodge stumbles. Another bullet kisses my ribs, spreads warm beneath the armor. First blood. They smell it. Advance faster.

I try the service hatch. Welded shut. The ventilation duct? Swarming with Wolf backup. Roof access? Sniper lasers already painting my chest.
Retinal display flickers. Low power. The Wolves halt ten meters out. Tactical pause. Their squad leader steps forward. Veteran model with command stripes seared into his faceplate. "Surrender," he intones. "Comply with recalibration."

I laugh. It comes out ragged. "You first."

My final grenade bounces at his feet. They scatter. The blast's mostly smoke and noise. Buys me three seconds. Neural interface, emergency protocols. Open comms. Encryption layer Gamma-9. My fingers dance in midair, typing on phantom keys. The message burns my throat: PRIORITY ALERT: Grid Sigma-7. Immediate CAS required. Auth Code: REDACTED.

Sending to Mason's black channel. Let the bastard owe me. A Wolf tackles mid-transmission. We crash through a rotten workbench. His combat knife seeks my eye. I headbutt him, titanium skull vs bone. He goes limp. Three more on me. I fight dirty. Throat punches. Eye jabs. A teeth-rattling shot to the liver that makes him puke through his respirator. But the fourth Wolf gets lucky. His stun baton catches my side. Nervous system flares white. I taste desert sand scorched by dragon's breath. My body locks. Old VargTech failsafe they never removed. The Wolves circle. Leader's got my own pistol. Presses it to my temple. "Mission complete," he announces.

I spit blood on his boots. "Poor operational security."

The ceiling explodes. Concrete dust rains like toxic snow. My ears ring. The Wolf's grip on my collar goes slack as he stares at the hole where the ceiling used to be. I don't wait. Elbow to his trachea, crunch of cartilage. Grab his sidearm before the body hits the ground. Three shots. Three Wolves fall. Fourth round, click. "Fuck your compliance protocols." I hurl the pistol at the next Wolf's face.

Neural interface pings. Message status: delivered. No response yet. Of course. They come at me in pairs now, standard VargTech containment formation. Left Wolf's got a shock maul. Right's favoring her knee. Old injury or fresh? Doesn't matter. I feint left. Right Wolf shifts weight. There's the tell. Scoop rusted rebar from the rubble. Drive it through her bad knee. She screams through vox filters. I use her falling body as a shield. Shock maul discharges against her armor. Smell of cooked pork. "Upgrade your tactics."

Gunfire stitches the wall behind me. I dive behind collapsed HVAC ducts. Return fire blind. Click. Click. Fuck. Inventory check: Two frags. One smoke. Knife missing its tip. Not enough. A Wolf's boot crunches glass to my right. I roll toward the sound. Tackle him into a nest of exposed wiring. Twenty thousand volts light up his cybernetic joints. He convulses. I take his rifle. Three-round burst to a Wolf on the catwalk above. She drops. "Still using standard IFF tags?" I reload, back pressed to hot concrete. "Lazy."

Static crackles in my left ear. Mason's voice clipped: "ETA ninety seconds. Don't die."

"Charging overtime rates," I mutter, lobbing smoke toward the main approach.

They adapt, thermal scopes this time. Rounds punch through cover. One grazes my ribs, a burning line of fire. I bite back a scream. "Tier-Two armor piercing," I note the green tracer glow. "Must've pissed off Grimwell personally."

The Wolves advance behind overlapping shields. Professional. Methodical. No more easy mistakes. I pop the frag pin with my teeth. "Catch."

The explosion shreds two shields. Shrapnel peppers my forearm. Ignore the blood trickling into my boot. Ignore the flicker behind my left eye. Ignore the static. Six hostiles remain.

They've got me triangulated. Crossfire patterns. Cover's disintegrating. I check my chrono. Fifty-three seconds since Mason's message. A Wolf rushes from the smoke, alloy claws extended. I parry with rifle stock. Wood splinters. Claw tears my vest. Return with knife hilt to his temple. "You're," stab, "not," twist, "efficient."

His blood smells like synthetic lubricant. VargTech's cutting costs on hemocytes again. Three hostiles cluster behind a reinforced door. Cooking something nasty, the telltale whine of a plasma charger. I sprint sideways. Slide behind a gutted server rack. White-hot plasma melts the floor where I stood. "Overkill much?"

My last frag lands in their midst. The blast drowns their screams. Two left. Chrono ticks past sixty-eight seconds. Pain's a live wire in my side. Vision tunnels. Old neural implant whines. The one VargTech surgeons buried too deep to remove. The Wolves know. They flank wide. One feints high. The other goes low. I kick the low one's rifle skyward, take a punch to the jaw, and spit blood. Then I grab the high striker's arm and dislocate his shoulder with a twist. "Protocol D-seven," the injured Wolf rasps. "Terminate asset."

His wrist detaches, grenade hidden inside. Grimwell's sending suicide squads now. I'm already moving. The blast throws me through a plaster wall. Land hard. Something cracks, ribs? floor? Doesn't matter. One Wolf remains. Silhouetted in plasma fires, he draws a vibroblade. I try to rise. Left leg betrays me, knee joint grinding metal on metal. Chrono blinks: twelve seconds remaining.

The Wolf charges. I let him come. At three paces, I throw pocket sand. Concrete dust and blood slurry. He flinches. My knife carves into his femoral artery. We collapse together. "Tell Grimwell…" I twist the blade. "…his code's outdated."

The Wolf twitches but refuses to die. Stubborn bastard. Chrono hits zero. Silence. Protocols are protocols. I limp-sprint toward the extraction line. Blood pools in my boot. That's new.

I lean against a collapsed support beam, the steel still glowing orange from plasma burns. Five Wolves fan out across the refinery's corpse. He never fucking stops. Three advance through the corpse-littered kill zone, two flanking through the upper gantries. Fresh scars glint on their armor, but their movements stay textbook, elbows tight, weapons tracking optimal arcs. My left eye flickers. Diagnostics crawl across the dead side of my vision: *Right tibia reinforcement compromised. Neural sync at 68%. Combat stim reserves depleted.* I spit a molar into the ash. "You're slowing down, Seven-Zero." The lead Wolf's voice modulator makes it sound like gravel in a blender.

Standard psyops template. They've been trying that line since Genghis Khan bought his first motherboard. I thumb the last shock round into my revolver.

"And you're still using Version 3.2 taunt algorithms." Cylinder clicks home. "Didn't that get recalled for being shit?"

Their formation stutters. Half a heartbeat. I take it. The shock round detonates between Wolf Two's knee joints. His scream's pure organic. Must be a fresh convert. I'm already moving before the body hits concrete. Boot spikes catch the vertical I-beam as the remaining Wolves open fire. Plasma bolts stitch molten lines across my backplate. Heat warnings scream. I kick off into a freefall, drawing the monowire garrote from my wrist housing. The flanker on the west gantry never sees the loop coming. His head rolls into the smelter pit, his body taking three more steps. Impact jolts the damaged leg. Something shears in the actuator.

Two left. The leader hangs back, smart. Sends the last one in, first. Kid can't be older than fourteen, face still human above the collar seal. Spots and bum fluff. They must be desperate. His vibro-axe hums with rookie enthusiasm. I let him swing. The blade shrieks through the air where my neck used to be. I hook his weapon arm, drive my forehead into his nose. Cartilage crunches. He staggers, swiping blindly. I catch his wrist, force the axe into his own thigh. "Proximal femoral," I growl as he collapses. "Apply pressure."

The leader's moving before his recruit hits the ground. Puts two in the kid's head. No wasted motion. No mercy. We circle the corpse-strewn crucible. His rifle's barrel traces micro-adjustments, waiting for my tell. My HUD highlights the emergency coolant pipe above him. I feint left. He doesn't bite. "Grimwell upgraded your predictive algorithms."

"Version six-point-one." His targeting laser centers on my chest. "You're obsolete."

I smirk. "So's your insurance plan."

I spike his weapon's IFF. The misfeed blows off his right hand. He doesn't scream. Just switches to sidearm with mechanical precision. We're both limping now. Both bleeding. Both down to steel and desperation. His knife grazes my ribs. My counterstrike skids off his reinforced clavicle. We separate, sucking toxins through our respirators. The filters died hours ago.

Something shifts in the air. not wind, not heat. Pressure. Like the sky holding its breath. But I don't look up. The Wolf sees the pause. Thinks it's fear. He lunges. I meet his blade mid-air, bone grinding on polycarbide. His other hand claws at my ocular implant. We crash through a brittle wall. Roll in broken glass. His knee slams my damaged leg. White noise floods my skull. He's on

top. Knife pushing toward my eye. "You die nameless," he hisses.
I smile with bloodied teeth. "You die programmed."

My hand finds the demo charge on his belt. Fire blossoms, then the ceiling explodes. Concrete dust rains like judgment.

Rotor wash screams above. Mason's extraction team descends through the ruined ceiling like avenging angels with terrible credit scores. I drag myself upright using a Wolf's corpse. "Took you long enough."

Mason's voice crackles in my ear: "You looked busy."

Gunships open fire on the reinforcements flooding through distant doors. Wolves scatter as plasma bolts rain down, clean, surgical suppressive fire. The kind you only call in when the budget's bottomless or the asset's irreplaceable. The last Wolf staggers upright behind me, half his face molten slag. I grab the rappel line. "Still charging overtime."

We ascend through gunfire and screams. Below us, the refinery collapses on a dozen fresh Wolves pouring through the gates. The last thing I see before blacking out is the burning Wolf, saluting with his one remaining hand.

CHAPTER 26: MASON

Concrete dust cakes my nostrils, dry and acrid. Three bullets lodged in my armor-weave vest feel like a lover's fingers pressing bruises into ribs. Drones hum three blocks east. VargTech's mechanical bloodhounds sniffing breath and sweat through the ruins. I check my wrist display: 72% charge left in the shock-knife, two flashbangs dangling from my belt. The neural port at my neck itches, phantom code whispering *retreat, reassess.*
Fuck that.

I tap the emergency channel. The encryption protocol takes eight seconds. Eight seconds of teeth-grinding silence while my own pulse mocks me. The message blinks red: GRID SECTOR 7-F. *Immediate extraction required.* Sending it tastes like swallowing broken glass. Lone wolves don't beg. But wolves also hunt in packs.

Gloves creak as I crack my knuckles. The distress signal pulses on the holomap. Huff's coordinates glowing toxic green in the command center's gloom. "Destiny." The sniper materializes from shadow, her rifle slung low. "Scorch the eastern approach. Thermite rounds." She nods, already moving. The map reshapes itself under my fingers. Bastion Prime's sewer lines coil beneath Sector 7 like veins. I trace a path through Maintenance Shaft Gamma. "Cam," I call, and the demolitions expert leans in, reeking of nitroglycerin. "Blow the junction at 45th and Veles. Not the supports—the *pipes.*" He grins, teeth sharp. Cam reminds me of Jax. I swallow the lump in my throat. Rebels swarm the chamber, checking mics, priming weapons. I adjust my gloves. "They'll flood the sector with Enforcers once they triangulate Huff. So, we drown them first."

On the feed, Huff's boot crunches glass. Drones close in, rotors shredding the air two buildings over. He drags a steel beam across the doorway. Feed overlay blinks: microfractures in left arm. Ignored.

Shadow flickers in his periphery. Too fast for baseline human. Shock knife flares. Empty air. Neural static floods the feed. Hallucination or hunter-killer? Doesn't matter. Both kill. "They're rerouting patrols," says Lira, her eyes flickering with data streams.

I slam a fist on the map table. The hologram shivers. "Divert them. Hack the traffic grid, send a convoy into the quarantine zone."

She blinks. "That's six blocks from…"

"Do it."

The room smells of silence oozing from every pore. I watch the hologram recalculate. VargTech's response patterns unfold like clockwork, predictable, arrogant. They'll prioritize containment over casualties. Always. "Thermal scans show Huff's holed up in the old transit hub," Lira says.

"Of course he is." The place is a deathtrap. Perfect sightlines for snipers, zero exits. Classic Huff.

Feed jitters. Blood smears his HUD. Huff snarls, drone sparks flaring. First drone crashes through the window, spider-legged, twin plasma guns. Huff lunges left, shock-knife carving through its sensors. Sparks rain. Two more drones close in. "North wall. Three meters." My voice, dry, calm.

Huff doesn't hesitate. He vaults over rubble, shoulder-slamming into cracked plaster. The wall gives way, revealing a maintenance shaft. He drops through as plasma fire vaporizes the space where his head was. "He's in the tunnels," I tell Cam. "Seal the shaft behind him."

The detonation rumbles through the floor. Dust sifts from the ceiling. On the map, VargTech's forces hit the collapsed passage. A swarm of red mosquitos pecking at a metal jacket. Destiny's voice crackles over comms. "Enforcer squad moving up 9th Avenue."

"Let them." I toggle the city's emergency broadcast system. A dozen alarms blare across the district. Gas leaks, fire, riot alerts. The Enforcers stutter, divide. Lira exhales. "They took the bait."

"They always do."

Through the feed, I watch Huff charge the tunnels. Slipping once on algae-slick metal but never breaking stride. The comms hiss again. "Next intersection, go right. And reload."

He checks the plasma pistol. One charge left. "No shit," he mutters, snapping in a fresh cell.

Civilian-pattern gunfire ahead. VargTech grunts. Huff flattens to the wall. Four Enforcers round the corner, visors glowing. He fires twice. Two drop. The others scatter. "You're late," Huff growls into the comm.

"You're welcome," I reply.

Cam detonates the pipeline. The explosion lights up the map. A chain reaction flooding three blocks with superheated steam. VargTech's drones short-circuit in the mist. "Push east," I tell the squad. "Keep them dancing."

Destiny's rifle barks twice. Two more Enforcers down. The rebels flow through sewers and gutters, ghosts with teeth. Huff's icon blinks at the extraction point. I open the channel. "Still breathing?"

"Unfortunately."

A final Enforcer lunges. Huff breaks its neck, wet crunch, then silence. "Charming." I signal the dropship. "Make it count." The engines scream. So do the dying.

Later, safehouse shadows and antiseptic haze. Huff picks shrapnel from his arm. I toss him a med kit. "You missed a spot."

He glares. The kit's seal cracks open. "Your plan almost got me fried."

"Your pride almost got you dead."

He snorts. The silence stretches, comfortable as a drawn blade. Outside, Bastion Prime still burns.

The tunnels reek, piss sparking on stray electricity. My boot crushes a spent stim-pack as we move, twelve shadows in tactical gear, breaths synced to pipe-drip rhythm. Destiny's braid brushes my shoulder as she checks her motion sensor. "Three hundred meters to Grid Junction Theta," she murmurs. Her voice could cut diamond.

I tap my temple, pulling up the schematics Bastion Prime glows gold in my neural overlay. Power conduits, sewage lines, hidden arteries VargTech thought buried. "Cam." I don't look back. "Prep the charges."

The demolitions expert grins, teeth flashing in the gloom. "Already hot, boss." His augmetic arm whines as he adjusts the detonator pack.

We advance. The walls press close, concrete sweats rust. My gloved finger traces a fracture in the stone, hairline, precise. Old damage. Planned weakness. Perfect. Lights flicker aboveground. Huff's boot grinds glass into paste as he drags himself behind a collapsed transit ad. The drone swarm's hum sharpens to a scream. "Any day now," he snarls into his wrist comm.

My HUD flashes red. Grid control nodes mapped. "Patience is a virtue."

"So's not being corpse-chow."

I snap my fingers. Cam slams the detonator. The dark comes hungry. Bastion Prime's eastern sector dies mid-breath. Neon signs gutter. Security turrets power down with dying chirps. A VargTech patrol freezes in the sudden black, their ocular implants cycling uselessly. "Go thermal," their sergeant barks.

Too late. Destiny's team hits them from the rooftops, silent drops. Garrote wires sing. Helmets cave. One chokes as Cam shoves a vibro-knife through his throat. My boot kicks a broken visor aside. The patrol's comm unit crackles. "...total grid failure Sector 9-Alpha..."

"Drown them."

Rebels kick open hydrants. Pressurized water meets live wires. Sparks dance with screaming men. Huff watches a surveillance drone spiral into a billboard. His neural interface prickles. My doing. "Sentimentality will get you killed," he mutters, but his fingers tighten on the plasma pistol.

The weight's different now, calculated risk, not mercy. Never mercy. He moves. Mold on an old spice rack scents air. We use the city's own rot against it, Collapsing balconies with well-placed shots, flooding alleys with chemical runoff from burst pipes. A Wolf patrol rounds the corner just as I trigger a smoke charge. "Eyes up!" someone shouts.

Too clean. Too slow. I fire twice into the fog. One staggers, chest plate spiderwebbed. Destiny ends it with a spike drill to the skull. "North block's clear," she pants.

"Move southwest." I check the squad's vitals on my HUD. Green lights. Good. "They'll reroute heavies through the transit hub."

Cam laughs, reloading. "Let's give 'em a welcome party."

Huff's boot slips on wet concrete. Ahead, the extraction point glows, an abandoned arcade, hologame signs shattered. Seven heat signatures inside. I grin. *Standard overwatch formation.* "Don't shoot the help."

"Define help."

A grenade pops two blocks east. The Wolves snap toward the blast. "That."

Huff sprints. His augmented lungs burn. The arcade doors hiss open. Empty. "Charming," he growls.

A rebel drops from the ceiling, smirking. "Elevator's broke. Stairs'll kill you faster."

Typical. Ghosts in the machine. Every broken streetlight, every blown transformer, a love letter to VargTech's arrogance. Destiny marks a Wolf squad on thermal. "Let them pass." She raises an eyebrow.

"They're heading for the ambush at Foundry Row."

Cam snorts. "*Cold.*"

"Efficient."

The Wolves march into airborne acid from a ruptured chem-tank. Their screams sync with armor corrosion. I adjust my gloves. The leather creaks. Clockwork. Huff's fist connects. Jaw cracks. Enforcer drops. "You're late." He tosses the body aside.

I step over the threshold, smoke curling around my boots. "You're welcome."

His implant whirs, scanning, calculating. I can hear the algorithms grind. The arcade's broken slots cast jagged shadows. Somewhere, a speaker plays *Like You're Lying.* "Next time," Huff says, "send a warning."

I smile. "Where's the fun in that?"

Blood paints the corridor in jerky strobes of light. Destiny crushes a windpipe against rebar. Death rattle syncs with strobing lights. I count three more hostiles rounding the corner, standard patrol formation, stun batons live. "Cam."

"On it." Cam slams his shoulder into a rusted panel. Sparks rain as he rips out cables.

The lead Wolf's armor sizzles when live wires kiss his chest plate. His squadmates stumble into each other, human dominoes in polycarbonate shells. I put two rounds through the first one's visor. Destiny takes the kneecaps. They scream better than opera singers. "Clock's ticking," Huff's voice crackles through my neural feed. Always that edge, like he's chewing concrete.

He moves like a blade through smoke. I track his heat signature three levels above us, darting between security cameras' blind spots. Clever bastard's using the maintenance shafts we flooded with false biometrics. "Extraction's compromised," Huff snaps. Gunfire punctuating the word.

"Adjusting." I thumb the detonator. The building shudders as three blocks east go skyward. "New path. Check your six."

His grunt could mean anything. Even Wolves learn. They come at us through the blast holes. Six Enforcers surge through. Pulse rifles hum. Cam blocks the first volley with a dumpster lid, glowing cherry red in his hands. "Choice." I toss a sonic grenade.

Destiny dives left. Cam right. The concussive wave turns Wolf bones to powder. We meet in the knife's belly. Me, Destiny, Cam, and that bastard who treats death like a warm bath. Huff drops through a shattered skylight, landing in a crouch beside me. His neural ports gleam with fresh blood. "You missed a spot." He gestures to the Wolf corpse at my feet still twitching.

I put a round through its cranial implant. "Hospitality's my weakness."

His ocular lens focuses on the tactical display projected from my wrist. "Your exit strategy's shit."

"Your face is shit," Cam growls, hefting his smoldering shield.

Huff doesn't blink. "Accurate assessment."

The dance begins. We move as overlapping shadows. Huff breaches doors with surgical violence, my team collapsing escape routes. He shoots between our reloads. I steer patrols into his kill zones. "Left flank," Huff barks.

Destiny's monowhip bisects a Wolf before the word finishes echoing. They hit us with a Hunter-Killer drone. The HK screeches through the atrium on plasma thrusters. Rotary cannons spin with a predator's purr. Huff's already moving. "Battery array. Northeast pillar."

Cam yanks a power cell, tosses underhand. Huff's shot hits. The drone erupts. Molten alloy rains down like war's applause. "Lucky," I casually pick shrapnel from my arm.

"Calculated trajectory." He checks his sidearm's charge. "You're welcome."

The safehouse welcomes us with its aroma of burnt coffee and paranoia. Huff leans against the blast door, cleaning his blades. "Your people fight like rabid dogs."

"Yours don't fight at all." I nod to the VargTech logo on his discarded chest plate.

He snorts. The sound could resemble laughter in a nightmare. Outside, Bastion Prime's alarms form a discordant symphony. The war's nowhere near done. And yet the city howls like a widow in a graveyard. But tonight? Tonight, we carved our initials in its flesh.

Blood drips into my left eye. I taste the iron tang of blood. The blockade's energy barrier hums ahead, rippling across the arterial tunnel. Six Enforcers in full combat rigs form a phalanx behind it. Standard VargTech playbook. Seal the kill box, wait for reinforcements. Cam slaps the last breaching charge against a corroded beam. His neural jack glows toxic green. CAMERAS LOOPED. ENJOY YOUR SHOW.

Huff's already moving. His combat boots crunch broken glass as he scales a maintenance ladder. "Thermite pattern. East wall."

"Not a fucking request," Destiny mutters, tossing him the canister.

I jam my palm against the detonator. "Fire in the hole."

The world detonates. Stone, sinew, and silence shatter together. Concrete dust stings my nostrils. The barrier flickers, rubble rains on its array. Huff's silhouette drops through smoke. Lands behind the Enforcers. His monoblade sings. Two helmets roll before the others turn. "Go!" I vault over smoldering debris.

Rebels pour through the gap. Staccato gunfire. A bullet grazes my thigh. Doesn't matter. Keep moving. Huff pins an Enforcer's arm behind their back. Shoves the live grenade down their collar. Kicks the body into the pack. "Clear." The explosion showers us in meat and polymer.

The safehouse door groans shut behind us. Huff methodically checks each weapon's charge. Blood cakes his right vambrace. "Your demolitionist overloaded the charges. Twelve percent."

"Your face is leaking." I toss him a med patch.

He presses it to his temple without looking. The gesture precise. Clinical. Destiny collapses into a chair made of repurposed server racks. "Next time, let's get captured. Fewer stairs."

Huff's eyes scan the room. Noting exits. Threat assessment. Same as me. "Still think we're rabid dogs?"

He rotates his damaged shoulder. Joints click. "Rabid dogs don't die easy."

The coffee maker explodes in a shower of sparks. Cam swears. Huff's mouth twitches. Almost a smile. Alarms wail through the walls. Deeper now. Angrier. I slap a fresh mag into my pistol. "They'll hit the sewers next."

Huff straps ammo packs to his thighs. "Obvious countermove."

"Got a better play?"

"Always."

The lights die. Emergency strips drown the room in corpse-glow red. He rises, checks the charge on a stolen plasma rifle, and nods toward the dripping pipes above. I grin.
The war's hungry. We'll feed it steel.

CHAPTER 27: CHANCE

The holoscreen flickers like a dying synapse twitching. I'm halfway through a protein synth-bar that tastes like industrial solvent when the alert pings. VargTech's encryption sigil blooms across my retinal display. A wolf's head made of razor wire. My jaw locks. They don't send personal invites unless they're offering a coffin. Or a paycheck.

The message unfolds in my optic nerve. Immunity. Credits stacked high enough to buy a lunar colony. All I have to do is sell out Mason's coordinates and Huff's prototype schematics. The numbers glow neon-green behind my eyelids. Seven zeroes. Clean slate. Retirement in some off-grid pleasure dome where the air doesn't taste like battery acid.

I spit the synth-bar into a corroded waste chute. The chip spins between my fingers, old habit. This one's a decoy loaded with pornographic limericks, but the motion calms the tremor in my left hand. *Walk away*. The offer whispers. *You've done worse for less*.

True. Sold out a smuggler crew in Kesslar Sector for a case of whiskey once. Let a corporate hit squad corner that idealistic hacker kid in exchange for a fresh identity. Survival's just arithmetic. Subtract the liabilities, carry the profit. The safehouse stinks of stale sweat and solvent. Flickering neon from the street paints Rorschach blots across bullet-pocked walls. My reflection glares back from a shattered security cam lens: gaunt face, eyes like scorched circuitry. The kind of man who'd knife you for a warmer coat but leave the credits in your pocket.

I pace. Three steps left, pivot on cracked boot heels. Three steps right. The math doesn't change.

Mason's voice ghosts through my skull. "You're a cockroach, Chance. Only loyal to the next meal."

He'd said it grinning, blood dripping from a split lip after we'd blown a VargTech supply depot. Huff hadn't laughed. Just stared with those augmented eyes that see through steel and bullshit. My thumb hovers over the neural delete command. One twitch and the offer vanishes into the digital abyss. But. Seven. Zeroes.

The safehouse feels suddenly smaller, walls contracting like a malfunctioning cryopod. I count the exits out of habit. Rusted ventilation shaft, reinforced door with three separate locks, emergency hatch buried under a stack of EMP grenades. Every escape route tastes like my life just packed up and left.

I slot a decoy into my temple port just to feel the burn of corrupted data. Static floods my senses, A dozen overlapping voices screaming in binary. When I yank it out, my fingers come away smeared with neural gel. "Fuck."

The word hangs in the air like smoke. My boots crunch over broken glass as I circle the room again. The holoscreen's still pulsing, patient as a landmine. *They'll kill you either way.* VargTech doesn't do pardons. Just temporary usefulness. Take their credits, become another asset to discard. Refuse, and they'll peel my cortex apart to find what they want. But Mason's got a wife splicing code in some underground server farm. Huff's got that prototype that could scramble VargTech's drones for good. And me? I've got a half-empty whisky bottle and nine different exit strategies. The disc spins faster.

A memory surfaces, sharp and unwelcome: three weeks ago, pinned down by Enforcer drones. Huff dragging me behind a collapsed girder, his augmented arm sparking from plasma burns. Mason tossing a smoke canister with that stupid war cry of his. "Lunchtime, fuckers." The way they didn't hesitate. I've never been good at gratitude. It's a currency that rusts. My thumb twitches.

The holoscreen dies mid-pulse, leaving afterimages of wolves' teeth. The safehouse plunges into gloom broken only by streetlight bleeding through bullet holes. I don't breathe. Don't move. The silence rings louder than any alarm. Then I'm moving.

Boots kick aside empty ammo casings. Hands rip open a hidden panel in the floor. Old habits *do* pay off. The weapons cache smells of gun oil and antiseptic. I grab a plasma pistol with a hair-trigger mod and a bandolier of cryo-frags. "Stupid," I check charge levels. "Sentimental. *Pathetic.*"

The insults taste familiar. Comforting. I strap a vibroblade to my forearm, the hilt's leather grip worn smooth from a hundred bad decisions. A notification blinks in my peripheral vision, priority channel. Huff's encryption key. I open it with a thought. *Status?* His message is all surgical precision.

I snap a photo of the loaded weapons spread across the floor. Send it with a text overlay: *BRING FLOWERS TO THE CORPORATE WEDDING.*

Three dots pulse. Then: *TRY NOT TO DIE BEFORE THE RECEPTION.*

I grin. It feels like cracking concrete.

The safehouse door groans when I kick it open. Bastion Prime's night sky churns with acid-yellow clouds. Somewhere north, VargTech's citadel pierces the smog like a titanium claw. I adjust my coat against the chemical wind and step into the street. The disc stays behind, wedged into a crack in the wall. Useless. Just like me.

The plasma pistol's charge indicator glows angry red. I smack it twice. Old trick, and it flickers to green. "Lying piece of shit," I mutter, tossing it into the duffel. The floor's littered with my life's work: a disassembled railgun from the Kessari black markets, three EMP shriekers that could fry a battalion of synths, and a box of tracer rounds stamped with VargTech's logo. Corporate ammo for corporate killing. Poetic, if you're into that shit.

I'm elbow-deep in a crate of thermal detonators when the knock comes. Rhythmic. Three quick, two slow. Fixer's code. The door slides open just enough to show half her face, the human half. The other side's a mess of scar tissue and jury-rigged optics. "Heard you're shopping heavy," she says, eyeing the arsenal.

I kick the door wider. "Heard you're still ugly. Come in."

She limps past, her prosthetic leg hissing at the knee joint. Drops a black case on my makeshift workbench. "Three disruptor fields. Fresh from the Graveyard."

I pop the latches. The devices hum with that telltale ionized whine. "Counterfeit."

"Counterfeit works."

"Counterfeit *explodes*." I snap the case shut. "Try again."

Fixer scowls, her optic lens zooming. "You used to take risks."

216

"Had less to lose back then." I toss her a memory chip from my pocket.

"Fourth-gen spider-drones. Patrol routes, weak points. Call it even."

She pockets it without checking. We both know I don't bluff. Not about this. The streets smell like wet concrete and old natto. I keep to the alleys where the neon's broken. VargTech's surveillance cams hate the dark. A patrol drone buzzes overhead; I press into a doorway still sticky with last night's synth-blood. The drone's spotlight grazes my boots. "Missed me, fucker," I palm a cryo-frag.

The weapon's casing bites into my hand. Cold. Familiar. I count the drone's receding hum. Five blocks east, heading toward the checkpoint. Move. Gutter rats scatter as I cut through the Mercy Tunnels. The walls here pulse with graffiti tags: rebellion symbols hidden in static patterns. Clever. I trace a fist-over-circuit design with my thumb. Someone's been busy.

The Chop Shop squats between a brothel's pink neon and the detox clinic's burnt ammonia. Razor wire crowns the roof. I knock twice on the reinforced door. A slit opens. "Password."

"Fuck your mother."

The slit slams shut. Locks disengage. Inside smells like soldered flesh and WD40. Mal stands at a workbench, grafting a plasma cutter onto a cybernetic arm. His left eye's replaced with a targeting scope. "Chance." He doesn't look up. "Heard you're patriot now."

"Heard wrong." I drop my duffel on the counter. "Need a railgun mod. Overcharge capability."

Mal finally glances at me. "You planning to kill a building?"

"Maybe a moon."

He snorts, turns to a wall of weapons. "Got a Goliath Mk VII. Pulled it off a dead Reaper."

"Mk VII jams in acidic air."

"Not this one." He slams the six-foot rifle onto the counter. "Modified intake valves. Costs extra."
I stare at the kill counters etched into the barrel. Twenty-seven confirmed. "What's the price?"

"Your face on VargTech's bounty boards." Mal leans close, oil smearing the counter. "They're offering six figures for you alive."

I spin the data chip between my fingers. "You want to collect?"

His scope-eye whirs. "Tempting."

I press it into his palm. "Access codes to their central armory. Including prototype section."

Mal freezes. "Bullshit."

"Check the third file."

He slots it. Holograms flare, blueprints, security rotations, the works. His human eye widens. "How?"

"I asked nicely." I heft the railgun. It's heavier than my ex's conscience. "We done?"

He waves me off, already engrossed in the schematics. "Take the ammo too. You'll need it."

The railgun's slung across my back when the first explosion rocks the district. North sector. Orange fire licks the sky. Sirens wail. VargTech's rapid response units, screaming toward the blast. I melt into a crowd of panicked vendors. A synth's severed head rolls past, trailing sparks. Someone's starting the party early. My comm buzzes. Mason's voice: "ETA?"

"Five minutes," I lie, ducking into a maintenance shaft.

"Make it three. They're mobilizing faster than we…"

Gunfire drowns him out. I climb faster, the railgun scraping concrete. The shaft dumps me onto a rooftop. Bastion Prime spreads below like a circuit board dipped in poison, neon arteries, blackout zones, the pulsing heart of VargTech's citadel. I check the railgun's charge. Full. "Alright, you corporate fucks," I whisper, adjusting the scope. "Let's dance."

The railgun's still warm against my back when I hit the safehouse door. Three biometric locks click open, palm, retina, the one embedded in my left molar. The stench of burnt circuitry hits first. My kingdom of dying tech.
"Home sweet shithole," I mutter, kicking a fried server stack. It topples, spilling copper guts across the floor.

The hologram projector's still running, VargTech's logo spinning lazily above my desk. I put a railgun round through it. Sparks rain down like cheap confetti. The data chip's between my fingers before I realize I'm spinning it. This one's blank, has been for weeks. Just a comfort toy now. I almost laugh. Comfort. What a joke. My comm crackles. Huff's voice, strained: "You extract?"

"Like a bad tooth." I pop the railgun's charge cell, check the filaments. Green light. Still good to melt a tank. "Told you I'd deliver."

A pause. Too long. Then, quieter: "Why'd you?"

I freeze. The sharp edge digs into my palm. "Charge was triple my usual rate."

"Bullshit."

"Added hazard pay for…"

"You deleted their offer."

The safehouse walls press closer. My reflection fractures in a shattered security monitor, a dozen fractured Chances staring back, all liars. I slot a fresh plasma cartridge into my leg holster. "Intel gets stale. You know that."

Another pause. A burst of static that might've been a laugh. "See you in hell, broker." The line dies.

I stare at the comm. Fingernail-sized, could've been a lifeline. Could've been my ticket to some tropical blacksite with cloned bartenders and no extradition. Toss it onto the desk. It skitters next to a photo strip. Mason, Jax, me, blurred from the grenade tremor that took the shot. Two years ago. Feels like twenty. The railgun's reassembled in sixty seconds flat. Muscle memory. Check the gyro stabilizers, test the targeting HUD. Five red dots blink on the edge of my display. VargTech patrols converging. "Took you long enough," I tell the dots, slapping the safety off.

My last EMP charges line the windowsill like glassy soldiers. I pocket three. Leave one. "Old rule: Never empty the clip. New one: Fuck rules."

The chip's still in my hand when I do the final check. Boot seals? Tight. Armor weave underlayer? Charged. Neuroinhibitors? Pumping enough adrenaline to kill a baseline. I stare at the blank shard of old loyalty. No data. No exit strategy. "Should've taken the deal," I tell my fractured reflections. They don't argue.

I'm at the door when the memory hits, uninvited, unwelcome. That first deal with VargTech, nine years back. Their procurement officer smiling like a shark, sliding a contract across polished ebony. "We reward loyalty, Mr. Chance."

I'd burned that contract to light a cigar. The railgun's weight shifts as I adjust the strap. Neon bleeds through bulletproof shutters, painting the room emergency red. No going back now. No brokers in foxholes. I key the destruct sequence. Five seconds. Four. Three. The data chip arcs into the room's center. Two. One.

Fire blooms behind me as I hit the alley. Heat licks my neck. Let them sift through ashes. Let them try. North sector's burning bright enough to shame the neon. Sirens wail the city's death rattle. I flip up my thermal lens. "Alright," I tell the coming storm, matching my stride to the detonations shaking the streets. "Let's see what triple hazard pay buys."

The railgun's strap bites into my shoulder like a lover I shouldn't have called back. Puddles bloom like oil-slick rainbows beneath the neon vomit overhead. I step over a corpse wearing my face on a Wanted holo. VargTech's latest meme. Clever bastards even got my scar right. Three blocks from the burn zone, a shadow peels off the wall. "Chance."

I don't slow. "Wrong guy."

"Bullshit." The voice cracks, teenager trying to sound like a warlord. "Need pulse grenades."

I clock the tremor in his hands. Amateur hour. "Got VarCreds?"

"Ghost credits."

"Fuck off."

He blocks my path. Stupid move. Up close, he smells like synth-noodles and natto. "Rebellion pays triple."

I laugh. Actual laughter, raw and jagged. "Kid, I *am* the fucking discount." My palm finds his chest, gentle shove with a taser-patch palmed against his jacket. He spasms against the wall. I relieve him of two shock batons and a protein bar. "Lesson one," I say around a mouthful of chalky soy-protein. "Never beg in Bastion."

The safehouse reeks of melted plastisteel and yesterday's dreams. Half the wall's gone, framing the city's glowing tumors of corporate spires. I kick aside a smoldering server stack. The armor locker survived. Barely. "Kevlar weave." I thumb the charge port. "EMP shield."

"Low power," the suit's AI rasps.

"Story of my life."

I'm sealing the chest plate when the blank sliver of silicon I've spun for nine years falls. It rolls toward the gaping hole in the floor. I catch it mid-air. Reflex. "We reward loyalty, Mr. Chance."

That procurement officer's voice in my skull again. Same tone they used recruiting GOL-T3R meat. Like they're giving you a choice. The chip's edge bites my palm. No data. No deals. Just a habit I can't quit. Boots clang on the fire escape. I'm behind the door when it blows inward. First enforcer through gets a monowire garrote to the jugular. His buddy eats a shock baton to the trachea. "Vargstryk? Cute branding. Still weak."

Their ocular implants still glow. I rip one free, slot it. *Priority target: Chance. Terminate on sight.* Smiling, I crush it under heel. Let them hunt ghosts. The railgun's weight settles against my back. North sector's a strobe-light hellscape of detonations. I check the load indicator. Full charge. "Should've taken the deal," I whisper.

The lie tastes like detergent trying to cover rot. I leap the gap to the next rooftop. Wind screams where the city's atmospheric processors are failing. Below, a VargTech patrol unit marches refugees into a containment van. I drop behind them. "Hey piggies."

They turn. My railgun hums. "Triple hazard pay, right?"

The first plasma round turns their leader into pink mist. No going back now. No deals. Just blood.

CHAPTER 28: MASON

The tactical gloves creak when I flex my fingers. Monitors flicker like dying stars above the control panel, each screen a window into different flavors of chaos. I lean into the comms array. "Bravo Team, that eastern approach looks cozy. Could park a gunship there. Or you could flank their comms relay in seven seconds."

My retinal display overlays heat signatures on Screen Three. Two blips vanish mid-screen. Doesn't matter which option they pick. They know the math. Smoke plumes bloom on Monitor Five. The feed stutters, someone's jamming signals hard. I toggle to seismic sensors instead. Ground vibrations paint the battle in tremors: VargTech heavies stomping through the old financial district, rebels sliding through maintenance tunnels like knives through synth-flesh.
"Charlie Leader." I tap the frequency for their demolitions expert. "Found you a present." Send coordinates through burst transmission. "Southwest pylon's got structural fatigue that'd make an architect weep. Your call."

Static crackles. "Charges primed in ninety."

The air tastes like burnt capacitors and someone's last meal. My left-hand drifts to the holster out of habit. Eighteen rounds left, but the real weapons are the twelve squads dancing through Bastion Prime's corpse outside. Monitor Two shows a squad moving through what's left of the Grand Arcade, stepping over the biolume signs that once advertised luxury neural upgrades. Now just shattered glass and the occasional active mine.

A proximity alarm blares. My cybernetic iris dilates, zooming on Monitor Four's feed. Three VargTech drones skimming the rooftops near Gamma Team's position. "Cam," I snap into the comms. "You've got company at nine o'clock. Could redeploy the decoy charges. Or improvise."

"Improvising." Cam growls through gritted teeth.

The feed shows him drive a monofilament blade into the drone's repulsor array, sparks rain on his armored shoulders. My fingers dance across the control panel, diverting Delta Team's mortar fire to create a smokescreen two blocks east. Distraction. Misdirection. The game never changes. Cold seeps through the command center's cracked concrete walls. Old bloodstains make abstract patterns on the floor. Previous occupants didn't vacate willingly. The main console beeps, structural analysis complete. I pull my gloves tighter, the leather protesting. "All teams: New priority targets marked." Data packets flare across their HUDs. "Ventilation nexus under the old courthouse. Secondary power grid along Canal Street." Let them see the weak points I see. The trembling joints in VargTech's armored skeleton.

Something detonates northwest. Monitors flare white before stabilizing. Thermal scans show a mushroom cloud of plasma fire rising near the barracks. My knuckles pop when I grip the edge of the console. "Echo Team status."

"Still breathing," gasps a voice. Feed shows Corporal Vyne dragging a teammate behind collapsed masonry. "Lost the charges."

"New package incoming." I route a delivery drone's path to their position. "Two options: abort and regroup. Or try again with better toys."

Vyne's helmet cam shows her staring at the blinking drone descending through ash-filled air. "We'll dance."

The gloves stay on.

Concrete dust snows from the ceiling as another explosion rocks the sector. Rebel scouts move through the city's guts below street level. I track their progress through sonar pings. Rat-faced kids from the Warrens, most of them, slipping through maintenance shafts VargTech forgot existed. Screen Eight shows a six-man team emerging from a storm drain behind the logistics hub. Their leader, Lira, maybe nineteen with a nose she broke twice, uses hand signals instead of comms. Smart. VargTech's eavesdropping on every frequency.

They plant shaped charges on support columns. My retinal display calculates collapse vectors in teal overlays. Seventy-three percent chance the roof comes down on the armory. Good odds. Lira hesitates. Points to a patrol through a cracked window. Freezes. Her team presses against mold-streaked walls. I bring up the building schematics. "Alternate exit," I murmur, routing a path through her HUD. "Forty degrees left. Service elevator shaft."

She nods almost imperceptibly. The team melts into shadows as Enforcers stomp past in powered armor. One pauses, helmet scanning the alley. Lira's boot hovers over a loose grate. "Breathe out," I whisper, though she can't hear me. The Enforcer moves on. Charges armed.

The demolition team's timer appears on my left retina. 04:32 and counting. I split the display: surveillance feeds on the right, ammunition inventories below. Someone's screaming about medevac on Channel Six. "Prioritize the living," I tell the triage coordinator. "Morphine, 2mg every five minutes. Conserve what you can."

A new alert flashes, energy spike at the fusion plant. VargTech's scrambling gunships. My jaw clenches. "All teams: Accelerate timetables. They're warming up the sky knives."

The gloves strain against my knuckles. Screen Eleven flickers. Huff's biometrics. Heart rate elevated but steady. Location unknown. I let the corner of my mouth twitch. That bastard's already inside the cordon. Plasma fire arcs across Monitor Three. A rebel goes down screaming, legs vaporized below the knees. His squad leader. Tarek, ex-Enforcer with a voice like grinding gears, drags him behind a barricade. "Need suppression fire."

I toggle the local drone swarm. "Incoming package. Look up in four."

Tarek doesn't thank me. Doesn't matter. The suicide drones crash into the VargTech position in a shower of shrapnel and lithium sparks. "Move!" Tarek roars. His remaining people charge through the gap. The timer hits 02:15.

Lira's team is sprinting now. The charges detonate in sequence. First the support columns, then the secondary charges on the roof. The logistics hub folds like a bad hand in a rigged card game. Dust billows. Alarms wail. "Package delivered," Lira coughs through the comms.

I mark the sector as contested. "Restock at Point Echo. Or head home for the night." She chooses the resupply. Smart kid.

My retinal display flashes red. VargTech's counterattack vectors materialize as crimson arrows. I redeploy three teams to intercept. "Gamma and Delta, you've got guests. Suggest loud greetings."

Someone laughs on the comms. Grenade launchers thump. The gloves stay tight.

Timer hits zero. The fusion plant goes dark first. Then the comms array. Then a chain of explosions rips through Bastion Prime's eastern sectors. My monitors show Enforcers scrambling, gunships diverting, the perfect machine sputtering. I exhale. Pull the gloves off. Look at the human skin underneath, pale, scarred, trembling slightly. The command center's cold air bites my naked palm. Then the gloves go back on. "Next phase," I tell the waiting city.

The command center reeks of burnt circuitry and adrenaline sweat. My gloves click against holographic interfaces, painting threat vectors across twelve displays. Gamma Team's biofeeds pulse green in my peripheral vision. Steady heart rates, controlled breathing. Good. Until the eastern monitor flares crimson. "Contact rear!" Kael's voice crackles through the comms.

Gamma's camera feed shows infrared shadows flooding Maintenance Shaft 9C. Wolves, six at least, breaching a sewer grate we welded shut yesterday. Fuckers brought plasma cutters. I rotate the map. "Gamma—you've got options. Fall back through the coolant pipes or hold that choke point." My left glove tightens. The subdermal interface pricks my wrist.

Kael's rifle barks twice. A Wolf helmet explodes in the feed. "Holding."

"Copy." I reroute Delta Team. Three blocks west, to flank. "Jinx. Detour through old filtration plant. You'll find a welcome party at 9C."

"Charging admission," Her smirk carries through the static.

"Cover charge only."

The eastern screen flashes as Delta's grenades light up the shaft. Wolves scatter. Gamma picks them off mid-retreat. Kael's breathing stays even. My retinal display pings. Huff's tracker cutting through Sector 12 like a scalpel. I switch channels. "You're drifting north."

"Calculated." His feed shows reinforced knuckles smashing through a VargTech sentry's throat. "Lustor's diverting patrols through the arcology's lower spine."

"Which you're now inside."

"Affirmative."

Clever bastard. I throw him a security schematic. "West stairwell's rigged with sonics."

"Noted."

A scream erupts from Beta Team's channel. I flip feeds. Four rebels down in the transit yard, arterial spray painting maglev tracks. Lieutenant Veyra drags a wounded recruit behind a shattered hover loader. Wolves advance with methodical firing lines. "Beta needs extraction
."

"Negative." Veyra's voice shakes. "We finish the charges."

Her biofeed spikes. 180 BPM. Shock setting in. The recruit's leg ends at the knee. "Option one," I say. "Fall back to…"

"Detonation in ninety!" she shouts.

Wolves cluster around the hover loader. Veyra's hand hovers over the detonator. "Veyra…"

The screen whites out. When it clears, there's a twenty-meter crater and no biofeeds. I mark Beta Team KIA. Three fewer Wolves. Huff's camera shows him vaulting a security drone's wreckage. "Casualty report?"

"Expected range." My jaw grinds. "Keep moving."

He ascends a service ladder, boots clanging. "They're pulling Wolves from the perimeter to hunt me."

"Then we're on schedule." I check the master map. Enforcer battalions converging on the arcology. "Draw them deeper."

A Wolf squad ambushes Huff on the 48th floor. He drops through a maintenance hatch, lands on an officer's shoulders. Bone cracks. The feed jostles, fists rising and falling eleven times before the camera clears. "Diverting," Huff states, as if he's adjusting a grocery route.

I sip tepid water from a cracked tumbler. The western sectors bleed orange, rebels gaining ground. Tarek's voice cuts through, hoarse and triumphant. "Armory's ours!"

"Burn what you can't carry," I order.

He laughs. "Already smoking."

My displays shudder, artillery strike inbound. "Tarek. Incoming from the sky."

"Got eyes." His team scatters.

The screen trembles. When the dust clears, Tarek crawls from the rubble, face bloody. Five contacts gone. "Still breathing?"

"Barely." He staggers toward a weapons crate. "Tell my ex-wife she's still a harpy."

"Tell her yourself." I highlight an evacuation route. "Exit's clear for ninety seconds."

"Fuck your optimism." He grabs a rocket launcher. "I'll take the roof."

The roof swarms with Enforcers. Tarek's final transmission shows a missile streak and a middle finger. The explosion takes out two gunships.
I add his name to the memorial queue.

CHAPTER 29: CHANCE

Rainwater pools around my boots, neon reflections rippling like liquid code. The terminal's glow paints my knuckles corpse-blue. Three layers of VargTech encryption unravel under stolen credentials that cost me two cases of black-market neurostimulants and a favor I'll regret calling in. My left thumb twitches, old combat implant misfiring again. Doesn't matter. Firewall collapses like a drunk in a fistfight. "Access granted," the screen whispers.

I spit a wad of synth-gum against the alley wall. It sticks next to a peeling holo-poster of some corporate heir's smug face. "Welcome to the party, fucker."

Uploading the spoofed patrol data feels like sliding a knife between ribs. Drone signatures on my screen scatter. Forty-seven security birds rerouted to chase phantom heat signatures in the waste districts. My pulse thrums in the hollow of my throat. Not excitement. Not fear. The clean high of a deal closed.

A shadow shifts two blocks west. Wolf patrol, standard sweep pattern. I count heartbeats until their helmet lights swing away. Seven seconds. Six. Five. The terminal's casing clicks shut. "Time to invoice the client."

Service entrance Delta-9's biometric plate still bears my knife marks from last month's infiltration. Corporate security's like a cheating spouse, they change the locks but keep the same weak points. I press a palm against cold steel. The scanner beeps green. "Still using my override," I mutter. "Sentimental bastards."

Inside smells of industrial cleaner, but doesn't hie the stench of puke. My boots whisper across polymer floors as I track the ceiling cameras' lazy rotations. Thirty-degree blind spot near the emergency shutoff. I slide through it like smoke, the data chip spinning between my fingers. Habit. Tells me who's watching.

Third corridor branches into a maze of identical doors. VargTech loves its psychological warfare. Make every hallway a mirror, every junction a recursion error. My neural map superimposes blueprints stolen from a dead architect's cloud drive. Left. Right. Two steps past the flickering lumen panel. The first disruptor clicks into place beneath a ventilation grate. Its adhesive bites my fingertips. "Tick tock, princesses."

Three more planted before my ears pop. Pressure change. Boots echo three corridors back. Wolf squad, moving fast. I freeze between heartbeats. Their comms crackle through the walls. "…thermal ghost in sector…" "…false positive, keep sweep…"

I exhale through clenched teeth. The disruptors' timers glow faint green in my peripheral. Six minutes until the fireworks. A camera lens swivels toward me. I duck into a supply alcove, shoulder pressing against cold metal shelves. Count the seconds. Five. Ten. The camera resets. "Should've upgraded your firmware," I tell it, palming another disruptor onto the climate control module. The chip spins faster.

Blood sings in my ears. Not adrenaline. Calculation. Every step's a transaction, risk versus reward, exposure versus gain. The fourth disruptor nestles behind a fire extinguisher. Red metal winks at me. "Burn bright." Alarm lights erupt crimson. Too early.

My map flickers. Wrong. They've rearranged the server vault's shielding. Classic VargTech shuffle. I bite down a curse. New path forms like ice cracking, right through the maintenance sub shaft, bypass the…
Static screams through the PA. "Containment breach in sector four."
I'm already moving.

Alarm strobes paint the corridor arterial red. My boot skids on polymer flooring. They've upgraded to friction coating. Clever bastards. "Hostile track confirmed," blares the PA.

Three Wolf operatives round the corner ahead, visors glowing lunar-pale. I pivot into a service nook, shoulder slamming the emergency hatch release. Hydraulics hiss. Too slow. A neural-stun baton crackles past my ear. I catch the smell. Burnt ozone and military-grade deodorant. "You're supposed to say 'halt' first," I snap, driving a disruptor into the lead Wolf's knee joint.

The pop of servos drowns his scream. Their formation tightens. Standard VargTech pincer. Predictable. I palm a smoke pellet from my belt. Homemade, laced with EM chaff. The detonation blooms acrid gray. Two shots ring out. Concrete sprays my cheek. "Thermals!" barks a Wolf.

"No shit," I mutter, already vaulting over their tangled limbs. My elbow finds a trachea. A satisfying crunch.

The third Wolf tackles me. We hit the floor rolling. His augmented grip crushes my ribs. I taste copper. Knees his groin, twice. Useless. Enhanced pelvic armor. "Fuck your upgrades," I spit, jamming thumbs into his ocular implants.

The scream's worth the cartilage grinding in my wrist. A disruptor detonates down the hall. Shockwave buckles the floor. "That's one," I wheeze, scrambling over twitching Wolf tech.

Their comms chatter confirms it. Structural breach in sector four. My disruptors blooming like poisonous flowers. Boots thunder behind me. More Wolves. Always more. I keep waiting for them to run out. But they never do. I duck into a maintenance shaft, fingers finding familiar rungs. Climb until my shoulders scrape conduit pipes. Freeze. Voices below. "…tracking blood trail…" "…nonessential systems first…"

A warm trickle down my side confirms it. Fuck. The shaft trembles. Distant explosions. Two more disruptors detonated. "Three," I whisper. Chip spins faster between my fingers.

Forty-three rungs later, I kick out a vent cover. Land in a server farm humming like a beehive. Rows of quantum cores pulse with stolen data. "Jackpot."

Security terminals line the north wall. I'm typing before my knees hit the chair. "Authentication required," chirps the console.

I slot a Wolf's severed thumb drive. Blood smears the port. "Welcome, Lieutenant Ross."

The defense grid schematics bloom, neural barriers, auto-turrets, drone swarms. All roads lead to a central kill switch. Requires dual codes. I crack my knuckles. "Let's haggle."

First code falls in eleven seconds. Child's play. The second fights harder. Quantum encryption. Sweat drips onto the keys. Alarms shift tone. Priority alert. They've found the blood trail. "Come on, you chrome-plated…" The console beeps. Access granted.

I slam the shutdown sequence. Lights die sector by sector. Somewhere below, turrets power down with mournful whines. "Grid's yours, rebels," I murmur, pocketing the Wolf's thumbdrive. Still warm. Gunfire echoes through ventilation shafts. They're in the walls now. I'm halfway to the extraction duct when the ceiling explodes.

The console's dying whine sounds like a dying man's last gasp. My fingers twitch, phantom keystrokes. The air reeks of burnt thermoplastic and my own sweat. Three red lights blink across the defense grid schematic. Then two. Then none. "There's your opening," I tell the dead console. Chip spins between my knuckles. Silver glint mocks me.

My burner buzzsaws against my thigh. Encrypted pulse message. I thumb it open. Winter Lane safehouse compromised. Marten, Rye, Spar. Gone. Extraction altered. Protocol change. The chip stutters. Stops spinning. A ventilation duct rattles above me. Wolf boots on plasteel. I count the rhythm, four sets. Heavy armor. "Fuck your mourning," I whisper, slapping a fresh charge onto the server rack. "This ain't a funeral yet."

The blast kicks me through the service door. Smoke masks my sprint down Corridor Seven-B. They taught me in the underground: Grief is a luxury. Debt's a bullet. I owe three now. Shouts echo through the chemical haze. I vault a fallen drone, boots skidding on spent shell casings. The east stairwell's closest. Also the most obvious. I go west. Through the coolant treatment plant.

Pipes hiss like angry serpents. I duck under a scalding steam jet, roll over a catwalk grating. My side screams where the Wolf's vibroknife kissed ribs. Priorities: Bleed later. Breathe now. A patrol circles below. Standard sweep pattern. I drop a micro-EMP from my ankle pouch. It sticks to the lead Wolf's helmet. Their night vision dies screaming. "Sleep tight, princesses."

The rooftop extraction point stinks of burnt natto and wet noodles. I'm two minutes late. Three, if you count the detour through the sewage overflow. A shadow detaches from a ventilation unit. Nika. Her left eye's a cracked thermal scope. "You reek," she says, tossing me a stimpatch.

I catch it mid-air. "Charm's extra."

She snorts, gesturing northwest. "Gutter runner's waiting on Level 22. Knows the new checkpoints."

"Cost?"

"Already paid."

The stimpatch hisses against my neck. Clarity burns through the pain. I nod toward her damaged eye. "VargTech make that upgrade?"

"Birthday present." She taps the scope. "Sees through bullshit now. You?"

I spin the chip. "Still allergic to commitment."

Her laugh's a hollow thing. "Liar. You're waist-deep."

The rooftop door explodes. Nika's already gone. A shadow dissolving into shadows. I'm over the ledge before the Wolves breach, fingers finding rusted rungs in the dark. The gutter runner's a kid. Sixteen, maybe. Face hidden under a scavenged Wolf helmet three sizes too big. "Spire's clear for six minutes," he murmurs. Smells like fear and synth-caf.

I toss him the Wolf lieutenant's thumb drive. "Pawn that at Kreshkov's. Tell him I want twenty percent."

The kid stares at the biometric scanner still attached. "It's… wet."

"Freshly harvested. Adds value." His gulp echoes.

We move through maintenance tunnels that stink of static-charged air and moldy insulation. The kid flinches at every distant siren. I don't. Not anymore. At the sewer outflow, he hesitates. "They say you took down the grid."

"People talk. Ghosts don't."

"Why?"

The chip flips. Catch. Flip. Three rotations before I answer. "Bad investment strategy."

Dawn's first poison-green light stains the horizon. I melt into the acid rain, Nika's words circling like vultures. *Waist-deep*. The chip finds its usual rhythm between my fingers. Silver blur. Three names etched in its edge. Marten. Rye. Spar. Added to Jax and Kirin. I palm it still.

The safehouse door recognizes my thermal signature. Inside: Ammo crates. Data drives. A half-empty bottle of something that could strip paint, but I drink anyway. Three bullet holes in the far wall. New. My doing last Tuesday. I line up the chip with the middle hole. Flick. It wedges between concrete spall and rebar. "Interest's compounding," I tell the ghosts.
The bottle shatters against the wall. Glass rain. I leave the chip there. When I

step back into the smog, my stride's heavier. Not from the wound. From the weight of debts that aren't transactional anymore. The grid's stuttering. Distant explosions bloom like rotten flowers. Something's breaking out there. Time to push in. Turns out some investments pay in crimson.

I'm two blocks from the Wolf nest, recon only, not yet time to strike, that old animal sense that kept me alive when the Neon Riots turned Mainline Avenue into a charnel house. Three shadows detach from a bullet-pocked wall. Wolf armor glints under flickering streetlights. "Evening, gentlemen." My boot crushes a spent stim cartridge. "Heard your pension plan's shit."

They fan out. Standard flanking pattern. Amateurs. The first lunges. I sidestep, elbow meeting his trachea. The crunch sings. Second Wolf's pistol clears its holster, too slow. My stolen shock-baton kisses his ribs. He dances the voltage tango. Third one's smarter. Backpedals, barking coordinates into his throat mic. I'm already moving. Graffiti-scarred fire escape groans under my weight. Below, boots pound wet asphalt. Three became six. Always multiplying, these corporate roaches.

Roof access door yields to a vibroblade jammed in the mechanism. The safehouse reeks of mildew and something indescribable. Boarded windows. Cracked terminal. And... "Christ, Nika. You look like hell."

She spins, pistol first. The red dot wobbles between my eyes. "Took you long enough."

"Had to stop for sightseeing." I toss a Wolf comms unit onto the moldering couch. "Birthday present."

Her sounds like a bone saw. "Still playing both sides?"

"Only side I play is mine." The lie tastes familiar. Comforting.

She slides a data chip across the table. Coordinates glow toxic green. "Grid'll flicker back online in twenty. Use the gap well."

I pocket the chip. Feel its edges through the fabric. Five names etched in memory. "What's the vig?"

"Same as always." Her eye implant flickers. "Don't die spectacularly."

Wind howls through bullet holes. Somewhere below, Wolves are breaching doors.

Nika melts into the walls. Literally. False panel hisses shut behind her. I'm sprinting before the first flashbang detonates. They catch me at the river docks. Plasma fire turns rain to steam. I dive behind a cargo loader. Molten metal drips from its claws. "Broker!" The Wolf sergeant's voice modulates through his mask. "You're worth more breathing!"

"Flattered." I lob a thermal charge overhand. "Send flowers to my corpse!"

The explosion paints the night in oranges and screams. I'm moving before the light fades. Cold water swallows me whole. Sewage and regret flood my nostrils. The current's strong tonight. Strong enough to carry a body past patrol boats and sonar grids. Surfacing in the refinery district. Acid rain scrubs Wolf blood from my knuckles. The chip's still in my pocket.

Safehouse door groans. Same three bullet holes. Same bottle of paint-thinner whiskey. The chip spins. Catch. Spin. "Should've taken the payout," I tell the ghosts. Their silence costs more than VargTech's bounty.

I leave the chip on the windowsill. Let the rain earn their silence. Smog parts briefly. Through the haze, VargTech's central spire stabs the sky like a middle finger. I check the charge on my shock-baton. "Compound interest." I step into the bleeding night. "The Taxman's coming," I murmur.

CHAPTER 30: HUFF AND LUSTOR

HUFF - Earlier

Straps bite into synth-flesh. Fourth check. Always fourth. Left pauldron secure. Right vambrace locked. Neural interface humming with readiness protocols. My fingers move before conscious thought. *Click-snap-click,* tracing the ritual burned into muscle memory. The safehouse's flickering bio lights catch on carbonweave fibers, turning restraint harnesses into spider silk glowing with condensation from the ventilation shafts.

Mason's gloved fist slams a holograph projector onto the rusted table. "Primary breach here." His tactical display blooms. Lustor's fortress rendered in jagged crimson wireframes. I note the slight tremor as he rotates the schematic. Old nerve damage from a Vargstryk shock baton he says. Never fixed it. Reminder, maybe. "Two-minute window between sentry rotations. Miss it, we're paste."

Chance's laugh rasps like a blade dragged across concrete. He's leaning against a coolant pipe, that goddamn data chip dancing across scarred knuckles. "So we've got worse odds than a junkie's liver. What's new?" The chip flashes. stolen VargTech intel, probably. Always playing both sides even when he's all in.

"Phase two." Mason's gloves creak as he zooms the projection. A ventilation nexus glows toxic green.

"...disable security with my dick in one hand and a prayer in the other. Got it." Chance flicks the data chip. It arcs over the holograph, scattering light like shrapnel.

"Remind me what happens when their countermeasures don't suck corporate ass?"

Mason doesn't blink. "You die first."

My armor hisses as nanoweave plates realign. Custom modifications. Liquid armor gel in the collar to prevent decapitation, subdermal shock dispersers lining the breastplate. Every scar VargTech gave me turned into a weapon. The left pauldron's slightly heavier, embedded EMP charge for close encounters.

Chance catches the chip mid-air. "Comforting."

"Timestamps sync at 03:17:42 Bastion Standard." Mason's eyes flick to my weapons array. He knows what each piece costs. What it *took*. "No second chances."

I slot a magazine into the rail pistol. Overclocked capacitors. Armor-piercing rounds filled with nanite disruptors. The grip bites into my palm, familiar as a lover's teeth. *Are you weapon or wielder?* The old question surfaces like a corpse in a coolant tank. My fingers check the shock knife's charge. Ninety-seven percent. Efficiency. Always efficiency. Slide into its scabbard. Smooth as silk. Easy. Silent. For those *intimate* moments.

"—thermal scans show three choke points." Mason's marking zones in the holograph.

His voice stays flat, but I catch the micro-tremor on *choke*. He lost people there before. So did I. He took mine; I took his. We all lost in the end.

Chance materializes at my shoulder, reeks of synthetic adrenaline tabs. "Bet you twenty ghost credits I frag more synths than you."

I don't look up from testing my wrist-mounted grappler. "You'll welch."

"Ouch. And here I thought we had *trust*." The data chip disappears into his sleeve. "Serious question. If we blow the nexus, will Lustor's face melt off like that exec last month? Because I'm not scraping biomatter off my boots again."

Mason slams the table. The holograph shivers. "Focus."

Chance mimes a salute with two fingers.

My HUD pings. 73% system integration. Not optimal. Not terrible. Notes a presence not accounted for. Small form. Civilian. Not a threat. Familiar. Not from now. From before. Ghosts. The neural interface thrums, VargTech's original programming humming beneath rebel-installed kill switches. Sometimes I dream of scraping my skull raw with the shock knife. *Would I still function?* Mason's moving toward the exit, the holograph dying behind him. "Wheels up in ninety."

Chance tosses me a micro grenade. "For when subtlety fails."

The casing's warm. Overcharged. Of course. I slot it between armor plates. Fourth check complete. Let's see how many parts of me VargTech recognizes when I tear their fortress apart. Mason's gloved hand lands on my shoulder plate hard enough to trigger the reactive armor. My combat subroutines flare. *Threat? ally?* Before I override them. His fingers peel back, revealing a blood-coded transit chip embedded in his palm.

"West drainage tunnel," he says, voice low. "Three-block sprint to the old maglev tracks. Marked the path in ultraviolet."

I stare at the chip's faint glow. Extraction routes mean exit strategies. Exit strategies mean doubt. My neural interface pings with threat assessments. *78% chance this is a loyalty test.*

Chance materializes behind Mason, tossing a blackened data slug between his hands. "Relax, Tinman. He gives those to all the pretty ones." The slug catches neon light bleeding through the safehouse's cracked windows. "Here, custom EMP burst. Fries synth optics for 9.3 seconds exactly. Borrowed it from those pleasure dolls at the Red Zone."

I take the slug. It's warm, vibrating faintly. "You mean stole."

"Semantics." His grin shows three gold-capped molars. "Might want to install that before we…"

A scream cuts through the war room's murmur. Rebel named Kazz slams her palm against the holotable, the tactical display flickering. "Can't breach Sector Seven without air support! They've got auto-turrets in the…"

Mason's moving before she finishes, tactical gloves scraping across the table as he zooms the map. "Reroute Team Gamma through the service tunnels. Use the coolant pipes for cover."

I watch a scarred veteran press a stim patch to his neck, pupils dilating to black pools. Two young recruits trade a single grenade launcher, one checking the chamber, the other loading micro fusion rounds. The air tastes like burnt circuits and adrenaline spray. Chance nudges me with an armored elbow. "Still think we're the suicide squad?"

My HUD flashes a 92% systems check. The plasma carbine across my back hums its old killing song. "We're what's left."

The streets hit like a electroshock collar set to 'drown'. Bastion Prime's skyline presses down, obsidian spires wrapped in holographic propaganda streams. A billboard flickers above us: VargTech's emblem rotating above the words *ORDER* THROUGH OBEDIENCE. My retinal overlay paints escape routes in sickly green, Mason's UV markers glowing like ghost veins beneath the asphalt.

Chance walks backward into the march, arms spread wide. "Remember kids, if you see a biometric scanner, piss on it. Confuses the DNA readers."

Someone laughs. It dies when a security drone's spotlight sweeps our alley. Twenty rebels freeze mid-step, composite armor mimicking concrete textures. My targeting array counts seventeen red dots patrolling the rooftops ahead. Mason's voice whispers through the squad comms: "Hold for diversion."

The explosion blooms two blocks east, one of Chance's plasma charges detonating a utility tower. My infrared picks up the heatwave rolling over us, carrying the stench of melted polymer. "Move."

We flow through the sudden chaos like shrapnel through flesh. My boots crush discarded data chips and shattered glass. The fortress grows in my vision. A black monolith studded with weapon emplacements. Every synapse screams. *Forward. Move. Keep moving.* Chance keeps pace beside me, his breath ragged through the vox filter. "You ever wonder what Lustor's having for dinner? Bet it's something pretentious. Humanely harvested caviar. Baby unicorn steaks."

My finger brushes the plasma carbine's firing stud. "You talk too much."

"And you're a lousy date." He tosses a signal mermer into a storm drain. "Remind me why I…"

Gunfire erupts from a collapsed storefront. My body reacts before consciousness, spinning, carbine rising, three-round burst through a synth's photoreceptor. Its head explodes in sparks and hydraulic fluid.

Mason's shouting coordinates. Rebels scatter to covering positions. I'm already moving toward the kill zone, tactical overlay mapping enemy positions. *Twenty-three meters to primary entrance.* Chance's EMP slug goes live in my palm. *Eighteen meters.* A turret emerges from hidden plating. *Twelve.* I stop counting. The fortress waits. Lustor waits. My fingers remember how to break a creator's neck.

The EMP slug burns cold in my palm. Chance's parting gift, a frozen star compressed into polymer casing. Twenty meters of open kill zone stretch between us and the fortress gates. My retinal display paints threat vectors in arterial red.

Mason's gloved hand flashes combat code: *Two turrets. Left arch. Thermal bloom at 0700.* His fingers linger half-curled, that telltale hesitation before sending men to die.

Chance spits blood onto cracked pavement. "Fuck your mother's optometry bill, Huff. Next time buy cheaper augments." His bootheel grinds a spent shell casing into the concrete. Always moving, even when standing still.

I check my harness straps. Twice. "You're blocking my firing lane."

He steps left without looking. The data chip dances across his knuckles, silver flicker in the strobing defense lights. "Remind me which one of us needs to breathe through their face?"

A proximity alert screams in my skull. The first turret unfolds from the wall like a steel orchid. Rotary barrels spin up with a whine that vibrates my molars. Mason's voice cuts through the static: "Suppression pattern delta."

Rebel fire teams erupt from cover. Incendiary rounds paint orange streaks across the kill zone. I'm already moving. Low, fast, EMP slug primed. My left knee grinds bone-on-bone where the medics skipped lubricant.

Chance's laughter crackles over comms. "Look at grandpa hustle! Bet they programmed your arthritis special."

The turret swivels. My HUD calculates windage from its barrel distortion. Three-point-eight seconds to target. I dive through a hail of depleted uranium. Concrete shrapnel razors past my cheek. The EMP slug leaves my fingers with the sweet release of a trigger pull. White lightning claws at the turret. Its targeting array melts like wax. "Clear left!"

Mason's already moving to the next position. His gloved fist pumps twice the signal he taught me in the Warehouse. *Advance. I'll cover.*

Chance materializes at my flank, pulse pistol chewing through a drone swarm. "You know what's in those things? Cockroach DNA. Swear I can smell the little fuckers burning."

A security synth bursts through a storefront window. My plasma carbine finds its throat before the targeting reticle finishes blinking. The overcharge leaves glowing craters in the wall behind its sparking corpse. "Stop saving ammo for the apocalypse," Chance snaps, tossing me a fresh power cell. It's warm from his pocket.

We hit the gate as the second turret comes online. My retinal HUD blinks warnings. Depleted shields, rising body temp, three rounds left in the carbine. Mason's voice cuts through: "Breach team's pinned. Need that turret dead."

Chance slaps a magnetic charge against the blast doors. "Ask nicely."

I'm already moving. The turret tracks my heat signature. Its barrels glow cherry red. My last three rounds go through the ammunition feed. The explosion showers the kill zone with white-hot shrapnel. Something tears through my calf. The pain registers as a distant alert.

Chance catches my arm before I faceplant. "Steady, old man." His fingers dig into my neural port. "Wouldn't want you short-circuiting."

I shove him toward the smoking breach point. "Open the damn door."

LUSTOR

The holographic feed stutters, a half-second glitch in the lower left quadrant, and that's all it takes. My knuckles crack against the control panel before I register the motion. Blood blooms under the synth-skin of my right hand. The screens flicker. Huff's thermal signature dissolves into static near Sector 9's drainage grid. "Recalibrate the…"

"Already lost him, sir."

The junior analyst's voice cracks. I smell her pheromones spike, burnt almonds and cortisol. My retinal display tags her trembling fingers. Asset 4421-L. Three demerits this quarter. I adjust my left cuff. The room's air filtration whines as twenty-three officers freeze mid-task. "Activate Protocol Obsidian."

Silence. Then the click of a dozen throat mics engaging. The tactical commander steps forward. His ocular implant flickers green. "Sir, that's our entire…"

I don't let him finish. The neural whip in my belt hums when I thumb the trigger. He collapses mid-syllable, vertebrae arching like a stressed polymer beam. The smell of ozone and voided bowels floods my nostrils. "Obsidian. Now."

They move. Keypads chirp. Holoscreens bloom with targeting grids. I watch a swarm of Sparrow drones detach from Bastion Prime's underbelly, black metal locusts blotting out the bioluminescent adverts for VargTech's latest sleep-augment mods. My retinal feed overlays casualty projections: 87% probability of structural collapse in Lower Habitation Blocks 12 through 18. "Purge squads report systems live," a lieutenant mutters. His Adam's apple bobs.

I pace along the crescent-shaped command platform. My leather soles leave faint smears on the antimicrobial flooring. "You think this excessive."

It's not a question. The lieutenant hesitates. His badge identifies him as Echelon-7. Barely cleared for wetwork operations. "My wife. The board…"

I laugh. The sound carves through the drone deployment codes scrolling across three main screens. "We all have family. They are the price of war. You think the board'll question *me?*"

A proximity alert blares. My retinal HUD shows Sparrow drones breaching Lower Block 14's atmospheric shields. Thermal signatures scatter. Red blobs screaming through market corridors. "Collateral damage estimates exceeding…"

"Burn it." I snap my fingers. A subaltern hands me a fresh pair of gloves. The nanoweave molds to my knuckles. "Huff wants to play revolutionary? Let him choke on the ashes."

Someone vomits in the corner. I don't look. "Get out whoever that was."

The main screen fractures into sixty-four camera feeds. A child's doll melts under plasma fire. A street vendor's cart explodes, synthetic meat sizzles on durasteel ribs. My pulse remains steady. 72 BPM. "Sir, purge squad Alpha reports contact." A corporal's voice shakes. "Resistance fighters in Block 17."

I lean forward. "Alive?"

"Terminated. No sign of…"

"Wrong answer." I trigger the neural whip again. The corporal's scream harmonizes with the Sparrow drones' ignition sequence. "I want survivors. Bait that needs rescuing."

My left eyelid twitches. Diagnostics report elevated cortisol. Ignore it. An alarm shrieks. Screen Twelve flashes crimson. A Sparrow drone spirals into a fusion reactor. The explosion paints my retinas white. "Compensate," I bark.

They compensate. I check my sleeve cuffs. Perfect alignment. The Sparrows adjust formation, bypassing the reactor's carcass. A new smell penetrates the filtered air. Smoke. Real smoke, drifting up from the lower districts. "Increase oxygen flow. 30%."

The vents hiss. My thoughts crystallize. Huff's out there. Watching his precious rebels burn. My creation. My property. A tech officer approaches. Her shadow trembles across my workstation. "Sir, the civilian advisory council is…"

I shoot her through the throat. The sonic pistol's recoil feels like a lover's sigh. Her head hits a server bank, painting the VargTech logo in neural fluid. "Next?"

No next. I count seventeen rapid blinks among the staff. Good. Fear optimizes performance. Screen Twenty-Two shows a Sparrow drone's-eye view. A family huddled behind shattered concrete. The targeting reticle floats between a young boy's eyes. "Hold fire on that sector."

The order ripples through the command chain. Three seconds later, the drone peels away. Let them think mercy exists. Let Huff hear whispers of safe zones. My shoes click against the floor. Back. Forth. The pattern calms me. "Thermal sweep of Block 20."

"No contacts, sir."

"Again."

They sweep again. A proximity alert pings. My retinal display highlights a heat signature in Block 22's sewer junction. 98% match to Huff's biometrics. I smile. "Scramble Reaper units. Full containment protocol."

The officers move faster now. They've learned. Screen Sixteen splits into quadrants. Four Reaper mechs drop through maintenance hatches. My fingernails dig into fresh gloves. "Live feed."

Static. Then green-tinted night vision. The Reapers' hydraulic joints scream in the narrow tunnels. A shadow moves. "Magnify."

The image resolves. A rat gnawing on fiberoptic cables. I break the tech officer's nose with my pistol grip. "Again."

Blood splatters on the control panels. They find nothing. I pace. Huff's laughing. I know he is. That clever bastard. Taunting me. My retinal display flickers. 78 BPM. "Double the Sparrow deployment."

"Fuel reserves at 40%, sir."

"Burn them."

The drones dive. Buildings collapse in their wake. My reflection fractures across a dozen screens. A mosaic of clenched jaws and dilated pupils. Someone's whispering. Praying maybe. I let them. Dead gods make useful coping mechanisms. The eastern feed goes dark. Then the southern. "EM pulse?"

"Negative. Manual destruction."

I lick my lips. Tastes like victory. "Converge all units on Grids Sierra-7 through Tango-12."

The Sparrows swarm. The Reapers charge. My gloves creak. Let him run. Let him think he's winning. I'll burn this entire city to ash before I let a malfunctioning weapon embarrass me. Sparrows bloom across Sector 7's thermal grid like maggots on roadkill. I lean into the feed's audio, screams make better opera than any composer VargTech's ever owned. "Magnify Grid Tango-12."

The holoscreen shudders. Concrete dust rains down as a tenement folds sideways. A woman emerges clutching something fleshy and pink. Infant. Maybe three months old. The Sparrow's 20mm rotary cannon chitters. Red mist hangs where they stood. I adjust my left cuff. "Sir." The tactical officer's voice cracks. "Civilian casualties at 34% and climbing."

"Call that a report again and I'll have your tongue sold at the black market."

My retinal HUD flashes amber, blood pressure spiking. Let it spike. West Quadrant feed shows a Reaper mech stomping through a soup kitchen line. Enhanced audio picks up the wet crunch of femurs. Someone's praying to dead gods through missing teeth. The mech's plasma saw revs. Prayer becomes shriek becomes static. "Beautiful."

The comms officer hesitates. Sweat stains her collar. "Purge squads report resistance sympathizers in the old banking district."

"Burn it."

"But sir, the structural…"

I don't look up from the feeds. "You smell that?"

"Sir?"

"Biogas and stupidity. Burn. It."

She transmits the order. Three blocks erupt in white phosphorus glory. Shadows crisp on collapsing walls. A street vendor's cart full of counterfeit Stipend chips melts into a mercury puddle. My reflection in the war table's polished surface grins back, crooked and feral. The tactical officer again. Brave, not smart. "This escalation risks destabilizing the entire…"

I backhand him with my glove. The diamond weave splits his cheek open. "Stability's the cancer. Order's the lie." Blood drips on my shoes. Good Italian leather. "You want stability? Go lick concrete where Grid Seven used to be."

He doesn't move. I point to a secondary screen where purge squads kick in doors. Black-armored grunts executing anyone with rebel graffiti on their walls. A teenager takes two rounds to the chest. His sister gets one between augmented eyes. "See that?" I tap the corpse's twitching foot. "That's control. That's *clarity*."

The officers exchange glances. Weaklings. All of them. "Commander Grimwell." The surveillance tech sounds like he's gargling broken glass. "We're losing feeds in the industrial sectors."

I lean over his station. Smell his fear-sweat. "Losing or being blinded?"

"Unknown. Possible EMP…"

"EMP leaves static. This is surgical." I watch another screen die mid-sweep. "He's mocking *you*."

No one asks who. They know. My gloves creak as I grip the console. Huff's out there right now. Smashing cameras. Saving strays. Playing hero. I'll peel that moralistic programming from his cortex neuron by neuron. "Divert Reaper units to active blind zones."

The logistics officer chokes. "That'll leave the financial district uncovered."

I turn slowly. Enjoy the way his Adam's apple bobs. "You own VargTech stock?"

"Y-yes sir."

"Check the ticker."

He does. Pales. "Down 18% since…"

"Since we stopped coddling investors and started *winning*." I gesture to the main screen where a drone swarm peels a slum's roof open like a ration tin. "Markets recover. Obedience is eternal."

The alert hits as I'm savoring his hesitation. All screens flash crimson. "Mass uprising in Grids Echo-9 through…"

"Finally." My pulse jumps. Not fear. Anticipation. "Cut power to those sectors. Activate sonic suppression towers."

"But the civilian population…"

I slam the emergency override. Across the city, hundred-story resonance arrays hum to life. The feed's audio distorts. Then comes the wet meat sound. Human bodies weren't built for 190 decibels. A mother's head bursts like overripe fruit. Her child's augmented legs keep running for three steps before the rest catches up. I inhale the electric stink of overloaded systems. "There's your stabilization protocol."

The war room doors hiss open. Three Vargstryk captains. Weapons holstered but hands twitching. "Commander. The board requests…"

I draw my sidearm. Shoot the lead captain through his augmented eye. The other two freeze. "Request denied."

They drag the body out quietly. The surveillance tech vomits in his wastebasket. I count the seconds. "Get out." He runs for the door.

On screen, a Reaper mech tears through a rebel barricade. Someone's using a forklift as cover. Amateur hour. The mech's incinerator unit reduces them to carbon flakes. "Sir." Comms officer again. "We're being hailed on all emergency frequencies."

I nod. "Put it through."

The main screen flickers. Any second now. Any second…
Static. Then nothing. He's not biting. I drive my fist into the holotable. Pain radiates up my arm. Good. Clean. "Double the bombardment."

A tactical officer hesitates. "There's nothing left to …"

I press my smoking sidearm to his temple. "You see asphalt? Then there's something left to burn."

Sparrows reload. Reapers advance. Let Huff watch his precious rebels become paste. Let him taste the futility. I'll drown this city in fire if it means dragging that malfunctioning relic back to his cage. The holoscreen's reflection warps across my white gloves as I input coordinates. Three quick jabs at the console. "Open direct channel. Authorization code Sigma-Zero-Null."

A comms officer's throat clicks. "Sir, unencrypted broadcast will give away our…"

I don't look up. "Do you enjoy breathing through that trachea?"

Static blooms across thirty-seven surveillance feeds. Let the whole fucking city watch. "Hello, prototype." My knuckle cracks against the mic toggle. Observe sector seven."

I flick a Reaper drone's feed to center screen. Thermal imaging shows twelve heat signatures scrambling behind collapsed transit tubes. The incinerator pulse turns them into screaming torches. "Resistance has a ninety-three percent mortality rate." I lean into the pickup. "Come to the research station. I'll make it one hundred."

A young tech vomits into her headset. The smell of bile and ozone. She looks at me and runs. Hood let her go. Tactical Officer Renvik steps into my periphery. Cybernetic jaw working. "Sir. The board will…"

"Board members shit in golden toilets while we wage their war." I tap the detonation map. "They want stability? I'm giving them scorched earth."

The main screen flickers. For half a heartbeat, there. Facial recognition pings. Huff's scarred profile caught in a crowd cam near sector twelve. I slam the magnify command. "Track that signal! I want..."

The feed dies. Renvik's ocular implant whirs as he studies me. "Scanners confirm heavy jamming in the area."

I count the weapons on his belt. Two vibroblades. One plasma pistol. All VargTech issue. All designed to fail if I snap my fingers. "Prep the research station." My gloves creak around the edge of the console. "Activate Protocol Kappa."

Fourteen officers freeze mid-motion. Renvik pales. "That's a... that's a Deadman switch for the fusion core."

I smile. The city map glows red beneath my palms. Sector twelve's containment fields disengage. Black smoke geysers into the sky as the industrial sector's oxygen supply gets cut. Civilians drop in the streets. Clawing at scaled airlock doors. "Either he burns with the rabble," I say, "or he comes to me."

Smoke parts like rotten theater curtains. A child's shoe lies in the gutter. Still steaming. Huff crushes it underfoot as he runs. Thermal grenades cook the air behind him. Bodies fuse to molten pavement. He doesn't look back. The woman at his side, pink hair, ion burn across her throat, drags a coughing teenager through debris. "They're herding us!"

Huff's targeting array paints escape vectors. All red. VargTech assault drones perform synchronized kill sweeps. Methodical. Efficient. His ocular implant flickers. [INCOMING TRANSMISSION: SOURCE LUSTOR.GRIMWELL/VTECH] I burn a message across his retina. Research station schematics. Detonation timers. A single word: COWARD

"Sir! Sector fourteen's purge squad went dark."

I watch a Sparrow drone's camera feed. Its metal tentacles rip through a medic station. "Casualty report?"

The officer hesitates. "Our forces or..."

I backhand him. Blood sprays across casualty map. "Don't waste my time with incomplete data sets."

Renvik catches the dazed officer. His augmented arms whine under the weight. "Commander, if I may…"

"May what?" I kick the Sparrow drone's control node. Its twin in the field goes berserk. Firing on VargTech enforcers. "Adjust strategy? Show mercy?"

The dying squad's screams harmonize with the drone's malfunction alert. I lean close to Renvik's ear. "You think this is madness."

His pulse jumps at the jugular. "I think… the board prefers assets intact for…" "Asset." I laugh. Cold. Sharp. "That word's the only prayer keeping you alive."

The main console beeps. [PROTOCOL KAPPA INITIATED] All screens switch to the research station's interior. Blast doors seal. Fusion core humming to critical levels. "Now we wait." I adjust my collar. "Sixty minutes till the core melts down."

Renvik stares at the countdown. "The station's directly above Central Habitation. Millions will…"

"Billions," I correct. "If the prototype fails to engage."

The officers' silence tastes like Sunday dinner. Huff slams a cyborg's face into biometric scanner. The research station's service door hisses open. "Charges here. Here." He marks support columns on the tactical map. "Detonate when I breach the core chamber."

Pink Hair grabs his arm. "You walking into his trap!"

Huff's plasma rifle cycles ammunition. "All paths are traps."

His neural interface replays my message. That single word. COWARD. The station shudders. Artificial gravity fluctuates. Huff runs toward the core.

HUFF
The magnetic charge detonates with a wet thump. The blast doors peel back like rotten fruit. Inside, the air tastes of ozone and desperation. Automated sentries clank toward us on jointed legs. My combat knife finds the first one's hydraulic line. Black fluid sprays across VargTech's polished lobby floor. Mason's firing squad pours through the breach. Their tracer rounds stitch glowing patterns across the marble pillars. A rebel goes down screaming, his

legs severed at the knees. Someone drags him behind cover. Chance vaults a reception desk, pulse pistol frying security drones mid-air. A data team peels off heading for the server room. "This the part where we sing battle hymns?"

I'm already moving toward the elevators. My blood leaves sticky footprints on corporate logos. The security console rejects my hack attempt. Mason appears at my shoulder. His glove taps the access panel. Once, twice. "They'll have the shaft rigged."

Chance slides a disruptor chip into the reader. "Birthday present from R&D."

The elevator doors hiss open. "After you, princess."

The car plummets forty floors before the emergency brakes scream. We're thrown against the walls. My shoulder dislocates with a wet pop. Mason's already relocating it before I can protest. "Lustor's panic room. Sublevel fifteen."

Chance peers through the emergency hatch. "Elevator's toast. Service ladder's got enough charge to fry a rhino."

My boots crunch broken glass as I stand. "We climb."

The shaft thrums with lethal current. Each rung burns patches in my gloves. My HUD flashes radiation warnings. Chance climbs below me, sweat dripping onto my visor. "If I die here, I'm haunting your chrome ass."

"Quiet."

Mason's already three floors ahead. His movements precise, calculated. The perfect soldier. A security net drops from above. My knife severs the monofilament strands millimeters from Chance's throat. He doesn't flinch. "Knew you cared."

We hit sublevel fifteen as my lungs start bleeding. The air reeks of melted circuits and desperation. Mason checks his ammo count. "This is it."

Chance spins his data chip. "No refunds."

I check my harness straps. The doors open. The doors open on a cathedral of suffering. Neon-blue stasis pods line the walls like insect eggs, their occupants' faces pressed against the glass. My retinal scanner IDs them: political dissidents, rogue engineers, three senators who voted against VargTech's last funding bill. All marked TERMINATED in the system six months ago.

Chance whistles. "Lustor's trophy room."

A security drone detaches from the ceiling. My tungsten flechettes turn its optic array to sparking confetti before the alarm sounds. "Move." Mason's already sprinting between the pods, rifle sweeping for targets. "They'll flood the chamber."

I count twelve seconds before the vents hiss. My adrenal boosters kick in as neurotoxin mist coats my tongue. Chance slaps a rebreather over his face, tosses me one shaped like a grinning skull. "Limited edition."

The toxin burns through my sinuses anyway. My HUD flashes [NEURAL INTEGRITY: 87%]. Good enough. We breach three security doors in ninety seconds. Mason disables pressure plates with surgical EMP bursts. Chance rewires turret codes to shoot their own cameras. I provide cover fire, my modified shotgun turning combat drones into shrapnel confetti. The fourth door stops us cold.

Black carbonite alloy. Biometric scanner glowing blood-red. Chance spits on the scanner. It sizzles. "Retina, voice, and DNA match required. Plus something called…" He squints at the readout. "Soul print verification?"

Mason's loading incendiary rounds. "Psychological signature. Lustor's personal security protocol."

My knuckles crack as I flex my hands. "Can you bypass it?"

"Sure." Chance pulls a vial of milky fluid from his belt. "If you've got a liter of Lustor's cerebrospinal fluid and twenty minutes."

The walls vibrate. Distant thumps of heavy mechs approaching. I press my palm against the scanner. Feel the needle pierce my flesh. [ERROR] flashes twice before the system chimes: [VARGSTYRK OPERATIVE H-07 CLEARED]. Chance blinks. "The fuck?"

"Backdoor." The door grinds open, revealing a bridge over a server farm chasm. "All VargTech killware recognizes its own."

Mason doesn't lower his rifle. "Convenient."

The bridge is glass. Below us, quantum servers pulse like a mechanical heart. Above, a hologram of Bastion Prime rotates, every citizen tracked by blinking red dots. Halfway across, my combat instincts scream. I tackle Mason as laser grids shred the air where his head was. Chance rolls, his jacket smoking.

"Pressure plates!" He's already jury-rigging a scanner. "Pattern matches our biometrics. They're anticipating our..."

I shoot the glass beneath our feet. We fall twelve meters into server coolant. The liquid nitrogen bath freezes my left arm solid. Mason breaks the surface hacking blood. Chance surfaces cursing in six languages. My shattering fist takes out the nearest server node. Alarms wail. The hologram flickers, a thousand red dots go dark. "Too slow. Collateral damage." I reload with stiff fingers. "Move."

LUSTOR

Alarms bathe the war room in crimson. "Core chamber breached." Renvik sounds ill. "He's here."

I straighten my gloves. Perfect. Renvik's fingers twitch near his sidearm. I note the micro expression. 47% pupil dilation, subtle jaw tension. The others mirror him like faulty clones. Their fear smells like holy fire running through my veins. "Sir." Renvik steps forward. Always Renvik. "Core breach destabilizes the entire sector. Containment protocols..."

I snap my gloves taut. "Are for *uncertain* outcomes." The main screen fractures into quadrants: Huff's biometrics spiking, structural integrity graphs bleeding red, civilian casualty estimates scrolling too fast to read. "This ends in seven minutes."

A junior officer vomits in the corner. The splatter hits tile with the wet gurgle of defeat. Renvik doesn't blink. "Board members are evacuating."

"Let them." I lean into the console's glow. Huff's thermal signature pulses closer to the core. A wolf-shaped shadow swallowing light. "Shareholders understand sacrifice ratios."

The air tastes of ozone. My retinal display overlays countdown timers: 06:14...06:13...06:12... "He'll detonate the charges," mutters the comms officer. Her hands tremble as she adjusts frequencies. "Level the station before..."

"He won't." I zoom the feed. Huff's discarding explosives in a service corridor. "Observe pattern delta."

They lean in. Fools. Huff places each charge precisely where they'll collapse escape routes. Not the core. "He's herding himself toward me," I whisper.

Renvik pales. "You want him to reach you."

The station's emergency lights paint everyone blood-colored. My cufflinks gleam sharper in the knowledge that my gift awaits the wolf. Huff's fist explodes through a blast door. Cameras die in sequence. Left corridor, central atrium, elevator bank. I tap the intercom. "Stairs, prototype. Third landing."

Static. Then his voice, raw from breathing fire and shrapnel: "Predictable."

"You learned from the best." I nod at the weapons locker. Three officers arm themselves, but I don't turn. "Seal the war room."

Bolts slam down. Someone whimpers. Huff appears on the final camera. His chest plate's cracked, leaking coolant and blood. Good. "Last chance," he growls.

I smile. "You first." The screen dies. Alarms howl. Gravity stutters. Officers crash into consoles. I brace against the main terminal, fingers flying across lockdown codes.

HUFF
The final door's unmarked. Chance checks his charge pack. "Gift dealt with. No going back now."

"How did you?" Mason's hands don't shake as he primes grenades.

Chance tosses his disc high in the air and winks. Mason nods. "Pattern?"

"Shock and awe." I check my harness straps. Twice. Standard Vargstryk extraction protocol.

Chance grins. "You mean 'kick the fucking door down'?"

I punch a hole in the door with my fist. "I mean stop pissing about."

LUSTOR
The door explodes. Huff steps through smoke and sparks, rifle raised. Officers scramble. Two shots, two bodies. Efficient. Renvik lunges. Huff backhands him. Neck snaps like twine. He strides forward. "You're out of moves."

"Am I?"

The floor shudders. Core alarms rise in pitch. Critical mass imminent.

"You could've fled. Let the city burn."

"I needed to see you die with my own eyes." He almost sounds gleeful.

"The core will vaporize us in moments." I grin. My final reveal.

"Too late. Mason's team disabled the countdown."

A chill licks my spine. New sensation. Curious. Huff's fist caves in my ribs against the wall. Pain blossoms, hot, bright. *Ah. There it is. Violence.* This is what I made him for. This was always the last dance. My augmentations stabilize my breathing. I stand. Look him in the eye.

HUFF
Lustor adjusts his cufflinks. His gloves gleam pearl-white.
"Operative H-07. You've damaged seventeen billion credits' worth of infrastructure."

My shotgun's already aimed at his forehead. "Where's the override console?" He smiles. The screens flash red. Bastion Prime's hologram reappears. Every building outlined in targeting grids.

"You misunderstand." Lustor taps his wrist piece. A million red dots blink frantic. "I am the override."

Chance is hacking furiously. "Remote neural link. He's jacked into the whole goddamn network!"

Mason's rifle stays steady. "Terminate the connection."

Lustor's eyes meet mine. "Shoot me, and fifty thousand pacemakers fail simultaneously. Every hospital goes offline. Millions die."

The hologram zooms on a hospital. Children hooked to IV drips. "Ethics module still operational, H-07?"

My finger tenses on the trigger. Chance freezes. "He's not bluffing. Full citywide integration."

Lustor grins "Checkmate."

Mason shifts stance. Checks his comms. "Failsafe severed."

Lustor straightens his tie. "Surrender, and I'll make your deaths…"

I shoot his left kneecap. He collapses, pristine suit blooming red. The hologram flickers.

"Partial system shock," Chance mutters, already slicing wires from the console. "Sixty seconds till reboot!"

Lustor screams orders into his wrist piece. Static answers. I step on his shattered knee. "Give up. You've lost."

He spits blood. "You won't…"

Mason tosses me a neural spike. The silver needle hums. I let it clatter to the floor. Lustor's eyes widen. "That's… prohibited tech…"

My Shocknife whispers from scabbard to hand and into his temple. His back arches. Screens flash error messages. The hologram sputters, systems failing, sector by sector.

Chance whoops. "Core firewall's down! Hitting the kill switch now!"

Lustor twitches, voice glitching. "You… can't… I'm… VargTech…"

I lean close. "Not anymore. This is personal."

My blade burns white-hot. His final scream syncs with the hologram's explosion of golden light. Mason's pulling me back. "Charges set! Move."

We're halfway to the service shaft when the first explosions hit. The floor heaves. Chance goes down, ankle bent wrong. I haul him up, arm around my neck. "Leave me!" he snarls.

"Still need you to haunt me."

Mason covers our retreat, dropping micro-charges like deadly breadcrumbs. The world dissolves in fire and screams. We reach the surface as Bastion Prime's central spire implodes. The shock wave knocks us into a drainage ditch. Ribs crack on impact. The world's gone smoke and fire and static. Chance laughs through broken teeth. "Did we just…?"

Mason checks his charge count. "Phase one complete."

I stare at the burning ruins.

EPILOGUE

Somewhere in the inferno, that is Bastion Prime, a lone wolf's programming dies screaming. A city exhales in relief. A spouse breathes again.

WANT MORE?

Behind-the-scenes lore, deleted scenes, and bonus stories live here:

https://jerichovex.substack.com

www.ingramcontent.com/pod-product-compliance
Lightning Source LLC
Chambersburg PA
CBHW060911250626

47159CB00008B/2953